BREAKING SHADOWS

MELISSA SINCLAIR

DARKNESS FALLS

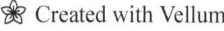

ACKNOWLEDGEMENTS

I will always thank my family first—my husband for his never-ending support, even when I don't realize it, I find out later when someone approaches and says, "You're the author!" I love you, thank you! To my children for their unending patience and excitement about my books; they are my everything, even when they are fighting relentlessly.

On to my amazing crew of people who make this book better, Mitzi Carroll, Copy and Line Editor, https://www.facebook.com/MitziCarrollEditor/ and Marisa Nichols, Proofreader, https://www.facebook.com/alatedbibliophile/. I cannot tell you thank you enough, for all the kind words and the hilarious comments in the margin.

This cover! What can I say about this cover other than that it is gorgeous, and I loved it immediately? Lucy Rhodes of Render Compose is immensely talented. I count her as a friend as well as my graphic queen. You can see her other work on www.rendercompose.com.

To my police expert, Sergeant Wilson, thank you for being so accommodating when I was asking about human trafficking. The report that you sent me with all the statistics, while unsettling, was invaluable.

To my Alpha, Sue Lopp, for reading the unedited version and for brainstorming with me. Just messaging with you opens up all kinds of ideas and steers the story in new directions. To my Betas, Joy Schabow and Jody Reynolds, I hope that I did this one justice for you ladies. Joy, one of my worries is that it isn't as good as the first one, and you loved *In the Night*. I hope you'll love this one too! Jody, your kind words and constructive criticism were taken to heart when writing book two. It was wonderful to talk to a fan about what I could do to make it better. I hope this one did just that for you!

To my author mentors, there are too many to really name you all, but I feel I need to thank a couple of you by name. I would like to thank PJ Fiala for all of your help and for suggesting Mitzi Carroll to me. I would also like to thank Abbie Roads. Your support by merely putting my book in your newsletter meant so much to me. I cannot thank you enough. The greatest compliment I can give is to share both your names. I would also like to thank the Indie Group that helps me with all my questions.

To any and all family members who supported me with my first book, thank you, thank you! Without you, it wouldn't have succeeded. To my mom, dad, and their significant others, my siblings, and my in-laws, I love you all so much. This one isn't as twisted, so you might not have to explain as much. Finally, to Pastor Lori, I love to tell people how embarrassed I was when you told me you read my book. I still laugh about how you told me you didn't mind all the swear words because other words just wouldn't have fit in those sentences.

All mistakes are my own.

To DNAR you are my everything.

1

Darkness. Pure and absolute, as if someone had spilled black paint over the world. This was all Becky could see—this was her world. Terrible, all-consuming darkness, for minutes, hours, days on end. It had been so long since Becky had seen anything but inky black darkness, and she would give her left arm to see light once again. How long ago had the mistress of the house thrown her down in this dank hole as punishment? What was she even being punished for? It had been so long that she had to search the deep recesses of her mind to remember. Then she remembered: she hadn't folded the towels the right way. She trembled with fear, remembering all too well the way the mistress had looked when she opened the linen closet. Becky knew it was all just an excuse, though. There was nothing wrong with the towels. What had bothered her was the way the master had looked at Becky. As the mistress beat her with the belt, she told her she had seen her looking at the master with impure thoughts.

What had Becky done to deserve this life? Surely, she had been a good enough child that she didn't deserve the daily beatings, the starvation, or the ridicule. It had been so long since the mistress had given her anything to eat that her stomach cramped from the mere thought of food. She no longer had any water left in the bucket that'd been left. The water had been dirty, but she hadn't cared. In the end, she didn't have much choice—drink it or die from dehydration, and Becky wasn't ready to die.

A scraping sound alerted her that she had a visitor coming. Would it be the mistress or the master? She didn't like the way the mistress treated her, but surely it was better than the sex she was made to have with the master? How he could stand to be near her rank body was a wonder to her, but she had stopped caring a long time ago. It'd been months since she had first been taken and sold to this wicked couple to do their bidding. The mistress didn't want the master to touch her, and Becky felt she was secretly thankful that the master with his cruel ways took Becky to his bed, but then the mistress would beat her mercilessly after. In her heart, she knew her parents thought she was dead, never to be seen again. Hope, a twisted thing, was all that she had. The hope that her parents were still searching was all that kept her from curling into a ball and letting herself succumb to the darkness.

Given the opportunity, even the slightest chance, she would attempt to escape. Perhaps this was that chance; no matter who came through the door, she would fight and try to leave, but she would need the key. The worse that could happen was they would kill her, though Becky doubted they would; they enjoyed torturing her too much to let her die. The door scraped open, not the metal slot that they slid the food through, but the actual door. Fear and hope coursed through her body, the conflicting emotions almost too much to handle. Fear that whoever was entering the room was merely there to torture her; hope that she was being taken out of the cell she had been held in. She jerked when a hand touched her, and a blindfold was placed over her eyes. This was new; they had never blindfolded her before. There had been no need. She was always chained and never allowed off their sprawling property.

"Shh, don't say a word, don't scream, be absolutely quiet," said a voice she'd never heard before.

"Who-who are you?" she whispered, her voice raspy from lack of use. She tried to lick her lips, but there was no saliva left. How long had it been since she had a drink? Twenty-four hours? Forty-eight? She thought somewhere in between.

"That doesn't matter. What matters is that I'm going to get you out of this hellhole."

Becky would have cried if she had enough moisture in her body to manage the simple act of creating a tear. But she was desperately close to succumbing to dehydration. Could this be true? Was he really here to help her? Hope spread through her body. Her attempt to tamp it down was unsuccessful because she wanted to believe he was here to help her and that this wasn't a cruel joke.

"Can you stand on your own?"

Could she? She didn't think so, but she would try. After a feeble attempt at sitting up, she slumped back to the ground. Gentle hands tried to help her, but as if realizing it was useless, stopped their attempt to help her gain her feet. The little hope that had dared to build started to dwindle when she remembered the chains and the lack of a key to get them off her. As if he read her mind, he began to fidget with the chains and then they fell from her raw wrists and ankles.

"I-I don't think I can stand. I'm so weak. I can't help you." When she felt him stand, she started to panic. "Please, please don't leave me here."

"I'm not leaving you. I just wanted to stand up, so I can gain leverage to pick you up. I fear that this is going to hurt, and I apologize for that. Your body is in a state of starvation. You need immediate nutrients before your organs shut down. Moving you may cause you pain. But we have to get you out of here; time is of the essence. Try to remain as still as possible and let me do the work." He paused before speaking again. "I'm going to pick you up on the count of three. One, two, three."

As gently as possible, he lifted her to his chest. She stifled the scream that wanted desperately to be released, even if it would have been a pathetic scream. There really was no worry she would cry out; she was far too weak to do more than merely whisper. She had not realized how close she was to the brink of death.

"Why did you blindfold me?" she asked weakly.

"While it might be night outside, my best guess is you've been in this dungeon for several weeks, possibly even a couple months. With no light for that long, your eyes are going to be exceptionally sensitive to any light."

"Months?"

"Most likely you have been down here almost two months from what intel I was able to obtain. Those bastards have been in Jamaica for a week and left you without nourishment. They deserve to rot in hell."

"Who are you?"

"A friend. I can't tell you my identity. Just know that I'm here to help and bring those animals to justice. I only apologize it took me so long to find you. I knew they had you hidden away, but I wasn't able to locate you until tonight."

"I-I know I smell terrible." She knew it sounded inane to worry about that.

"Shhh, don't worry about that. We can get you cleaned up at the hospital. Unfortunately, I can't bring you there, or they'll know it was me. I have a friend waiting, and she will get you to the hospital."

Her body tensed at the thought of this man handing her over to yet another person she didn't know.

"Don't worry; she works with the police. She'll help you, no questions asked. You can trust her. I trust her with my life."

He moved quickly and without noise as he carried her out of the damp room. She could sense him carrying her up stairs. With all her heart, she wanted to trust him, because he was the only option she had —it was him or nothing. If she had to choose between that gross hole in the ground or him, she chose him. The fact that she was still surrounded by darkness made her skin crawl. If she got out of this alive, she would sleep with the lights on until her dying day. He stopped suddenly, and she braced herself for an attack.

"At the top of the stairs, I want to set you down, so I can scope it out, but I don't think I should. So just hold on as tight as you can. It won't be much longer until we get to our rendezvous point." When she stayed silent, he gently prodded. "Okay, honey?"

"I've trusted you this far; I trust you to get me someplace safe." She could feel his lungs expand with the deep breath he inhaled and then she sensed as much as felt his head nod up and down.

The noise of the door creaking open was a thousand times louder in her head than it was in reality. Becky knew as soon as they had walked through the doorway, the fresh air was almost too exquisite to breathe. At first, he continued their journey as carefully as he had when they were climbing the stairs, but then he tensed, and she began to panic.

"What is it?"

"I hear someone coming. We're almost to the tree line; our ride is on the other side of those trees. Brace yourself, I'm going to make a run for it." And before she had time to fully process his words, he took off in a dead sprint with her body locked tightly in his arms that bulged with muscles. He wasn't even breathing hard with the exertion of carrying her to safety. All of her senses, except her sight, appeared to be heightened. Whether it was because she had to rely on them when she wasn't able to see for the last weeks, she didn't know, but she did know that she could hear things much better than she used to and she could hear the moment they had crossed into the trees. She heard leaves crunching under his feet as he moved swiftly. He stopped running as suddenly as he had begun their mad sprint.

"We're here," he whispered. "I don't see her. Wait, I see headlights coming this way." They were moving again, and Becky could only assume they were retreating into the tree line, just in case it wasn't his friend. Finally, he expelled a sigh, and she felt hope begin to blossom once again, and this time it sunk its hooks into her. "There she is. I'm going to wait until she gets a little closer before I leave the cover of the trees."

For what seemed like hours, they waited. She began to shiver despite the heat. She knew that wasn't a good sign, and her hope started to wither—those hooks slipping a little. Surely fate wouldn't be so cruel to let her die after she was finally free of the house of horrors she had been forced to live in for the last however many months of her life.

"What month is it?" she asked, terrified to hear the answer.

"August."

A whimper escaped her mouth as she realized that she had been taken and sold to the despicable couple who used her as their slave almost a year ago. She had heard of human trafficking but had never thought she would be a victim of it. Yet, here she was barely able to lift an arm to hold on to the man carrying her, and then she finally heard someone approaching.

"Over here," her savior whispered.

"It's clear out here for the moment; let's get her in the car."

"You need to get her to the hospital as quickly as possible. Judging by the way her teeth are chattering, she's going into shock. I have to get back. I heard someone coming."

"Then you better get going. I need to go. I have a friend in the hospital ready and waiting for her."

"Kara Vanderbilt?"

"Yeah, I didn't realize you know her. But we can discuss that another time. Right now, we need to move."

And move, he did. The man felt like a brick wall, yet he was incredibly graceful as, once again, he moved like a panther. She could hear the woman running ahead of them. Before she knew it, he had stopped, and she could hear a car door being opened, and then he was gently setting her down on the seat of the car.

"Stay lying down; we don't want anyone to see you," he whispered.

"Couldn't sit up if I wanted to," she whispered back.

"I have to get back before they miss me. Thank you, Quinn."

"Anytime, and I mean that. Any. Time."

"Let's hope I don't have to take you up on that offer."

"Wait," she whispered.

"What do you need, honey?" he asked.

"I'm Becky Plummer. Can you tell me your name before you go? Please. I won't tell a soul." The benevolent stranger that had rescued her paused for a second before he leaned forward, kissed her gently on the head, and whispered in her ear.

"Harrison. Harrison Black." Before she could thank him, he was gone.

2

_____

Once Quinn had Becky secured, she ran to the other side of the car. Harrison had disappeared as quickly as he had appeared. He never told her how he had come to find the missing sixteen-year-old girl, and she hadn't asked. All she cared about was the fact that the young lady that had been missing over a year had been found. She was definitely in trouble medically speaking, and she needed to hurry because time was of the essence right now. They weren't in the clear. Not only did Becky need a doctor fast, but they also needed to get as far away from where she was held as quickly as possible.

The car flew down the road, and she grimaced when she drove over a bump in the road, jarring Becky in the backseat. The moan was so faint that Quinn was terrified she wouldn't get to the hospital in time. Bullshit! She wasn't going to lose her when she had just gotten free of that nightmare. Using her Bluetooth in the car, she called Kara's cell phone. Kara picked up on the first ring, worry evident in her voice.

"What's wrong? Why aren't you here yet? What's your ETA?" She fired the questions at her without letting Quinn say a word.

"It took him longer to get her out than we had thought it would, and I got delayed by a freaking train. We're about five minutes out. Be ready, I'm coming in fast." Quinn didn't say more than that because she didn't want to alarm Becky—if Becky could even hear her. She was worried the girl had lost consciousness. But Kara was extremely intelligent and read between the lines in a split second.

"She's that bad?"

"And then some. Just be ready."

"Understood."

They disconnected, and Quinn began praying silently to herself that they make it in time. It would be too cruel to lose her when they were so close to getting her medical help. Quinn wanted to kill the bastards that had kept her all these months. She wanted to rip their throats out and feed them to wild dogs. Becky had been treated as if she were a dog they had picked up and decided they didn't like. The monsters had actually left her and gone on a freaking vacation. No doubt they wanted her to die while they were gone so they could feel like they weren't actually responsible.

Well, they were going to crap themselves when they came home to a police presence. Black was confident they could take down this one family and still maintain the case they were building against the actual mastermind. That mastermind was another one Quinn wanted to turn into mincemeat. If they found him or her. No, *when* they found him or her. They had to find the mastermind. Too many young kids, especially teenagers that would be considered runaways, had been going missing. The sooner they took the pervert down, the better.

Realistically, she knew that there would just be one more piece of scum to pick up where this one left off, but she didn't care. It was one less piece of scum. She had been told once, a long time ago, that sex sold. But at what cost? There were plenty of legitimate ways to get laid in Quinn's mind than buying a person, but while some of these people bought these young children for their own use, many bought them to become entrepreneurs in the sex trade. Then there were those people that bought one of these missing persons just so they wouldn't have to clean their own damn house; well, they deserved a beating as well. And why did they buy a human versus go out and actually hire one? The answer was because they were so full of greed that they would rather buy a human being to do their bidding than hire one so they could save a dime.

These people were so filthy rich they could afford a legitimate house-keeper. But did they go that route? Nope. As long as the victim stayed in their service long enough to recoup the costs, they considered it a win.

Her knuckles were white as she gripped the steering wheel. Quinn hated that people were so inherently evil. There was no way to eradicate that evil. One might say it would never be eradicated because humans had been given free will. While she knew it never would be, and even though Quinn considered herself a Christian, she didn't agree with that reasoning. It was just a way to try to explain away the disgusting things some people would do for their own pleasure and to wash their hands of the situation. Well, Quinn wasn't willing to wash her hands any longer, sitting by and helping those traumatized wasn't enough. Some of the most powerful people on the planet hid behind their carefully constructed personas, and she was tired of them getting away with it.

Her good friend, Kara, was proof that evil could be vanquished. And while Quinn's own personal tormentor still remained free, unable to be prosecuted for his crimes against her, she would damn well do her best to help anyone she could. Whether she was skirting the laws to do so wasn't a concern to her.

"We're almost there, Becky; another block. You still with me?"

Terror consumed Quinn when the girl didn't respond to her question. Was she merely unconscious, or had Becky died while Quinn was transporting the emaciated girl? Quinn didn't have that much medical training; certainly, her first aid training was not enough to help Becky, but she knew enough to know that they didn't have much time before Becky couldn't be saved and that the only chance the girl had was to get her to a hospital and fast.

Thank God, she thought to herself as she saw the lights of the hospital up ahead. It was amazing that she hadn't been pulled over at the speed she'd been going to get there. She pulled in by the Emergency Room entrance and stopped as fast as she could without sending Becky flying. She wasn't even out of her car before Kara came flying out with several hospital personnel and a stretcher.

"She didn't respond about a block ago when I called back to her." Quinn knew her voice sounded strained and close to a breaking point. She was so intent on the young woman they were carefully placing on the stretcher that she didn't hear the squeal of tires or notice the flashing lights of the unmarked car that came flying up behind her sedan.

Kara caught her eye and nodded once, indicating that she was still alive. Quinn began to slump in relief as the hospital personnel rushed Becky through the doors and would have hit the pavement if strong arms hadn't pulled her against a rock-hard body. Initially, Quinn panicked until she smelled the cologne of the one man that kept her up at night with naughty thoughts.

They rushed the stretcher into the ER, Kara running next to it barking orders.

"I need body temp, find a vein and get an IV going. I need that IV in yesterday. If her temp is low, warm blankets and IV fluids. I need bloodwork done ASAP. What's her blood pressure?"

"Pulse is a thread; blood pressure is eighty-five over forty-five."

"Start a drip of saline and then move to the lactated ringers." If they didn't get the right fluids in her right away, they would lose her; her body was already shutting down. There was no telling at this point the damage that had been done. "You got that vein yet?"

"She's so dehydrated, I'm having a hard time."

"I need that IV in place." Kara's voice was short and maybe a little bit panicky. If they didn't hurry, they were going to lose her. "Try a femoral or subclavian line. She's too dehydrated for the normal places."

He hesitated a moment too long, and Kara took control, placing a subclavian line in a matter of a few moments. She just shook her head at the rookie nurse, letting him know that it was a difficult IV placement and they would go over it later.

"Start that saline drip stat." The IV bag was up before she had finished the order.

"How's her temp?"

"Ninety-seven." The answer was clipped as the nurse grabbed the warm blankets given to him and started placing them over the small girl's body. "She's so frail."

"Not in here. Not now." Kara sounded terse. They would have to go over her preference to not discuss the status of a patient that is touch and go in front of the patient later, as well. Looking embarrassed, he nodded at her and began to check Becky's vitals again.

Kara hated that she had snapped at the new ER nurse, but she had a good reason. She didn't want Becky hearing them talk about her appearance. Kara knew what it was like to be talked about like that—people whispering about her own injuries all those years ago, and she wouldn't allow it, not when the girl needed to fight for her life. She knew that Becky could hear them—she may not be lucid, but she most certainly could hear them. The girl's lashes were fluttering as she fought to gain consciousness.

"Blood pressure has stabilized, and her pulse is less erratic," he said.

"All right, good job everyone. Let's give those fluids a chance to work. She's far from being out of the woods. Did you get that blood draw?"

"Yes, doctor."

"Good, get that to the lab immediately. It's priority. We need to know if there is anything else we're fighting other than dehydration and severe malnutrition. Let's get her a room in the ICU. Once we get her stabilized enough, we can move her up there."

"Ethan? What are you doing here?" Quinn asked without turning around.

"I could ask you the same question. Caleb, why don't you go inside and get whatever information they're willing and able to give us so we can relay it to her parents when they get here."

"They're on their way? How did they find out, and how did *you* find out?"

"Kara called us a few minutes ago; it must have been after you called her to tell her you were bringing her here. We called her parents; they're on their way."

Quinn only hoped that she was still alive when they got here and that they would get to take her home soon. Even if Becky was able to heal physically, the road was going to be a long and arduous one to begin to heal mentally. She let herself lean for another second and then forced herself to stand tall. Slowly, she extricated herself out of his arms, too, one step forward and she turned around to look at the most attractive and kindest man she had ever had the pleasure of knowing. If he only knew what he did to her just being this close, she would blush a thousand shades of red.

"Good. That's good. Any chance we can keep my name out of it, though?"

He looked at her long and hard, the blue of his eyes fixed squarely on her hazel eyes.

"That depends."

"On?"

"On how the hell you found her in the first place."

"Oh, that."

"Yeah, that. Try not to be coy with me. We have known each other a long time, and before they get here, I want to know if I'm backing the right team by not telling them you brought her in."

"You have to trust me on this. I had nothing to do with her disappearance." Even she could hear the worry in her own voice.

Ethan took a step back when Quinn said she had nothing to do with the disappearance of Becky Plummer. The idea had never crossed his mind that Quinn would have been involved in the disappearance of the young girl. Quinn was one of the most selfless people he had ever been honored to know—and that said a lot, because his sister, Kara, was pretty damn selfless herself. Maybe it was the fact that they both were just geared to help those who needed it. But Ethan knew there was more to it. He knew that Quinn had a similar backstory as Kara. She had never told him as much, but he had stared into the haunted eyes of his sister and Caleb's sister long enough to notice when someone had been a victim of a crime.

He would never say that word to Kara, though. She hated the word victim. And since she had married Caleb, the haunted look in her eyes had been replaced by a happy spark—for the most part. There were still moments when he could see her traveling back to those nights. However, Caleb always sensed it and managed to shake her out of the moment. In fact, he was getting pretty good at it. If only they could find a way to help Taylor and Quinn the way that Caleb had helped Kara.

"Ethan, I'm not a suspect, am I?"

Ethan shook himself mentally, realizing he hadn't answered her.

"Of course not. But I need to know how you found her."

"Off the record?"

"Off the record." Though it sent his hackles up that she even had to ask. Ethan trusted her, and he knew that if she was involved, it was aboveboard. That was a good thing since he didn't travel outside the lines when it came to the law. His knowing that she would do anything and everything to protect a victim and to make sure the law would prevail was all it took to trust her. Actually, she was very meticulous when it came to victim's rights and evidence retrieval at the center she worked for. She always made sure that the people that came in received medical attention and that all evidence was processed correctly. "For now, we will consider you a CI."

"CI?" She asked.

"Confidential Informant."

Right, she should have known that. She nodded her head once as if to say that it was good enough for now.

"I got a call at the center that there was a young girl being held captive."

"Who was the caller?" He would have cracked a smile at the huge roll of her eyes she sent his way if the situation wasn't so serious.

"I can't tell you."

"You have to give me more."

"He's one of ours," she said ambiguously.

"One of ours? As in, an officer? Why wouldn't he go through the proper channels? Why call in a civilian?" He was on full alert now and had dropped his voice so only she could hear him.

"He's undercover. Deep undercover."

"Enough said." Ethan knew the department had someone deeply ensconced into the human trafficking circle, but he didn't let on that he knew that. Everyone was exceptionally tight lipped about it all, no one wanted to mess the case up. Sex crimes chewed up and spit out cops on a regular basis, especially when it came to crimes against children. The people that sat in those dark rooms viewing the filth that was taken off pedophiles' computers burned out exceptionally fast.

"I want him to trust me in the future if he needs help again."

"Understood. The parents are going to want to know who helped bring their daughter home."

"I tell you what, if she makes it, you can get their number, and I will talk to them, but it has to be kept confidential."

"Deal." He looked at his watch. "They should be here soon; you need to get out of here."

"Thank you, Ethan."

"No, thank you for getting her here safely."

"It was nothing."

"No, it was something. You put your life at risk to help her."

"You would have done the same thing."

"It's my job."

"You know that it wasn't safe to allow the police to bring her in—not this time, and I'm tired of them winning, Ethan. I want—no, I need—to do more. I need to do something to try to balance the scales. Counseling them after the fact isn't good enough."

"I understand. Just…" He trailed off.

"Just what?"

"Be careful. I don't want anything to happen to you."

"Trust me, I will be; I have a lot to do on this earth yet."

With that, she climbed into her car and left. Ethan stood watching her taillights while thinking to himself, *I bet you do, no doubt in my mind that you have a lot left to do*. No sooner had her taillights faded away than another car pulled up to the curb. It parked haphazardly in front of his and instinct told him that these were the parents of Becky Plummer.

Ethan wasn't sure he liked that Quinn was involved in this. But he was grateful that she helped get the young teenager out of whatever predicament she was in. Too often that wasn't the case. That didn't mean he was going to let this slide. As a matter of fact, his brilliant sister better be willing to tell him how she became involved. Who was he kidding? There was no chance she was going to tell him anything. For now, he would have to push the mysterious Quinn Sanders to the back of his head. Even though he was a homicide detective, Caleb and he had been called in to tackle this case. Captain wanted all hands on deck on this one, and he didn't have time to think about the woman that he couldn't get out of his head. He had a case to solve.

3

Quinn took a deep breath. The farther away from the hospital she got, the more the trembles subsided. She had been worried that Ethan would pick up on how rattled she was. After all, Quinn was not a police officer. Sure, she helped them, but she was a victim advocate. Her job was to help people who had been abused mentally, physically, or sexually. Initially, the center that Kara had helped come to fruition was going to be a rape crisis center. But in the months since it had opened, it had become so much more. It'd become a home for everyone who walked through the door, herself included.

However, in recent weeks, she'd become alarmed by the chatter from the teens coming in to the center. Chatter that centered around two terrifying words. Sex trade. More and more teens were coming in saying they know someone being groomed to be sold for sex. Quinn had decided to start researching and had discovered that the average age of these children, who were overwhelmingly female, was thirteen. It still made her stomach turn.

One thing that she had accomplished in her years working with victims of abuse was gaining the trust of the police. They came to her more frequently to help with counseling someone. Even though she was a clinical therapist and had years of experience under her belt, it didn't prepare her for the depravity that people put other people through. Many nights she woke up in a cold sweat, not just from her own past, but from stories people had told her, the pictures she had seen, the beaten women, men, and children she had met.

When a young boy told her that he had heard whispers where the police might find Becky Plummer, she was no longer willing to sit back and just listen, so she sprang into action. Though her network was extensive, she was unable to find out any further information. In the end, the answer found her, and she didn't have to look any further, she was contacted by an anonymous person who'd heard she was looking for Becky Plummer. He asked to meet up with her. At the time, she didn't know who she was meeting, and while she knew it was danger-ous, she was willing to risk it to get Becky back because she was just fed up. However, she also knew that it would help no one if she walked into a trap. Making a split-second decision, she told the only person she could trust to have her back. Ethan insisted on coming with but wasn't thrilled about staying in the car. It was the make it or break it part of the deal, though. She allowed him to come with, but only if he stayed in the car. He was instructed if she didn't come out in five minutes to come in after her. It turned out it wasn't necessary. As soon as she saw Black, she knew that she had made the right decision in coming to the meeting.

While Quinn didn't know Black, she recognized him from her many trips to the precinct. Quinn was usually a great judge of charac-ter, and she knew that he could be trusted. During their brief meeting, he told her he had heard she'd been asking around about Becky, so he did some digging and found her. He explained how he was undercover and was breaking protocol by contacting her, but he felt he couldn't involve the police directly without blowing the whole operation. Knowing the officer's life was on the line if they didn't proceed cautiously was almost enough to make her turn back. Almost, but not quite, because he knew the risk and was completely on board with taking a chance to get her back.

When Black found out the homeowners were gone, he was able to come up with a quick plan to get Becky out of the hellhole she was in.

The trick was getting her out unnoticed. They lived in a gated community that had regular patrols from a security company, but in the end, it proved to be easier than anticipated. The monsters who *owned* Becky and who left her locked in a cell to die from dehydration were vacationing. Freaking vacationing, while Becky lay in her own urine and feces, clinging to life. If Quinn was given even one minute alone in a room with those two bastards... Well, Quinn would be the one going to prison. Not them.

Only at this point, since they got Becky out in an unsanctioned operation, under cover of night, there very well might not be charges brought forward. Unless Becky talked. Not just talked but knew specifics. Where she was held, who held her, who took her, who sold her. All of that could blow the case wide open. But if she didn't know more than who had her, then she wouldn't be able to bring down the trafficking ring that had sunk its claws into Darkness Falls, Wisconsin.

Quinn had begun researching human trafficking and was disturbed at what she had found out in relatively little time and with just a few clicks of her mouse. Human trafficking had become a serious epidemic, not just in major cities like Milwaukee. While nearly eighty percent did happen in the large city, there were cases documented in all seventy-two counties. The website unluckythirteen.org had so much unsettling information. She wasn't surprised. Her own history showed that even the most ordinary and upstanding citizens could be wolves in sheep's clothing.

While Darkness Falls was not as populated as Milwaukee, Madison, or even Green Bay, there was still a problem developing. One only needed to pick up the newspaper and read about the sadistic twins that had kidnapped her friend Kara not once, but twice. And the stepmother who had facilitated that abduction. Even though months had passed, and the articles had started to become far less frequent, it was still a fact that a serial killer had lived and preyed on their town. Not just their town, but towns all over the state had been their playground.

But in recent weeks, the upcoming anniversary of the disappearance of Becky Plummer had been taking up all the headlines. A lot of people had thought she was a victim of the Roman Numeral Killers.

Quinn wasn't one of them. After all, almost all the victims had been identified, and Becky hadn't fit the MO. It was frustrating that not all children received the same coverage when they went missing.

It made Quinn angry when she thought about how there wasn't an alert issued every time a child went missing. If the child is thought to be a runaway, they might make the news, but it might take days for any real coverage to happen if any coverage was given to the missing child at all. The Amber Alert that was issued for missing children was only done if the child was thought to be abducted. This was a flaw, in Quinn's opinion. The Amber Alert was an extremely important instrument to help find missing children. With smartphones, people can instantaneously know when a child has been taken and what car they were seen in.

However, unlike other states, there was no system in place in Wisconsin for missing children who weren't abducted. A child who might be a runaway. A child who might have gotten lost on their way home had no such mechanism to reach anyone with a smartphone. She had lost track of how many times a missing child notice showed up on her social media feed weeks after the child went missing. Often when she opened the article to read about the circumstances surrounding the missing child, there was an update saying the child had been found. Thankfully. Unfortunately, it sometimes took weeks to see those posts.

In the day and age where there are Silver Alerts and Amber Alerts, there should be an alert for children or even adults who have gone missing that do not fit into the former two categories. Sighing, Quinn reached for the volume on the radio. Her head often would spin in circles and tie her in knots. Right now, she needed to not think. Right now, she needed to block out what she had seen.

The emaciated and filthy body of the teenage girl was something that would give her nightmares for weeks to come. Becky didn't deserve what had happened to her, and Quinn was going to make sure that the bastards who bought her were taken down. If for no other reason, then she couldn't take down the ones who sold Becky to them. Because of that, she would see them rot in prison or she'd die trying. They didn't deserve to see the light of day.

She was pulling into her driveway when her phone rang. Taking a deep breath, she answered the phone before getting out of her car. She had a feeling she wasn't going to get to go home and pretend to sleep after all.

"Hello?" Her voice sounded tired even to her own ears.

"Quinn, it's Ethan." His voice was like velvet across her skin. It did more to soothe her than anything else could.

"What's wrong?" she asked while rubbing the sandy feeling out of her eyes. Dread filled her as she realized that he might be calling to tell her Becky didn't make it. It wouldn't have surprised her; she was barely breathing when she had been rushed to the emergency room, but it would have crushed Quinn if that was why he was calling.

"Nothing." A pause. "Well, that isn't really true."

"Just tell me." Quinn knew she sounded like a class one bitch, but she couldn't help herself. She was exhausted, and sometimes when she was tired she got cranky. "If she didn't make it, just spit it out." Damn it, but her eyes burned with tears.

"No, no, it isn't that. She's fine. I mean, she's holding her own. It's just... Well, she isn't strong enough to really talk right now, but was conscious and told us she will only talk to you, and I know that we didn't want to involve you..."

"I understand. It's fine. Of course, I'll come talk to her."

"It doesn't have to be tonight. Kara is being a hard-ass and told us to leave her alone. No more questions for the night. It isn't like Becky would be able to talk for very long anyway. She was only awake for a little bit, and we wanted to give her time to be with her parents."

"You know Kara isn't wrong to stop you from talking to her tonight. Becky is her patient first."

"I know. It's just..." She could actually visualize him raking his fingers through his messy, blond hair. Could envision the pain in his crystal clear, blue eyes.

"I know. I want to hang these bastards by their toes in the middle of Darkness Falls and let every parent have a go at them, too."

"Remind me never to get on your bad side," he said with a soft chuckle.

"My bark is worse than my bite." She leaned her head back against the headrest in her car. "I'll come to the hospital first thing in the morning. Good-night, Ethan."

"Quinn?"

"Yeah?" Quinn whispered, letting the healing powers of his voice float over and through her.

"Watch your six. I'm going to do everything in my power to keep your name out of things, but if somehow it gets leaked…whoever took her is going to be gunning for you."

She swallowed hard. He was right. There was no doubt in her mind that her life was in jeopardy if anyone found out she was involved. And they would find out. Of course, they would find out, it really wouldn't be that hard to bribe someone into talking.

"Yeah. Watch yours, too. Okay? I guess I have come to like you. Not sure why, though."

She smiled when she achieved the desired effect she was hoping for, and he laughed. It seemed to slide around her and caress her through the phone.

"Yeah, you aren't so bad yourself. Night, Quinn." And with that, he disconnected and the smile that had been on her face only seconds ago cracked and fell away.

Ethan hoped that Quinn heeded the warning that she watch her back. He was terrified something would happen to her. Terrified he would lose someone that he had grown quite fond of. Hell, who was he kidding? He was more than fond of the lady; he was head over heels for her. The timing was never right to broach the subject. He was busy chasing down criminal after criminal, and she was busy helping the people they left in their wake. Both of their jobs had them immersed in darkness all day long.

Theoretically, they understood the demands of each other's jobs. But he wasn't a fool; he knew the demands of their jobs would be hard to overcome. And neither one was willing to give up what they did.

Not that he would ever ask her to do that. Quinn was damn good at her job. He hadn't met a victim advocate better than her in all his years on the force.

When this case was over, he was going to finally make a move. He just had to get them both through it alive and well. Ethan still needed to repay her for all her help when he was recovering from the injuries he had suffered during the Roman Numeral Killer investigation. What a lame name that was. Of course, the press had to rethink the name when they found out it wasn't just one person, but three, that was responsible for all the death and destruction. His own mother being the mastermind. It still disgusted him to even think about it. He had to shake himself from his reverie when he saw Caleb and Kara making their way toward him.

"What did she say?" Caleb asked.

"What do you think?" He looked at Kara long and hard. She looked tired. It had been a while since he'd seen her look tired—Caleb had helped those dark rings and shadows disappear from her eyes. It wasn't like she had an easy job. It stood to reason that she would look exhausted. It was late, and she probably had been working for over twelve hours in a busy emergency room, but he couldn't stop himself from worrying about her. Old habits die hard.

"Knowing Quinn, she offered to come right away, danger be damned," Kara said while glancing at a chart in her hand.

"Hm, sounds familiar. I mean, they do say it takes one to know one, right?" Caleb said cheekily.

"Anyway, I convinced her to get some sleep if she can and come in the morning." He looked at his watch and sighed while raking his fingers through his hair. "Which, apparently, isn't that many hours from now."

"You should really go home and get some sleep, too," Kara said, finally looking up from her chart and studying him with those all-knowing eyes. His sister wasn't just a bona fide genius; she was very adept at reading other people. Another thing she had in common with Quinn. Her gaze unnerved him as if she could see deep inside him and see how his mind was consumed by thoughts of Quinn.

"What about you, Kara? How many hours have you been here?" He hadn't intended for his voice to sound snappy, but it did.

"I was just going to check on Becky one more time and then head home. Caleb is going to come home with me and get some sleep, right?" she asked, smiling at her husband.

And there it was—the light that had shown up the moment she met Caleb; it was almost too hard to look at. As if he could be blinded by the sheer brilliance of that light, the shine in her smile. But he couldn't begrudge her happiness. Kara had worked too hard for far too long to get beyond the demons of her past. Now that the monsters that haunted her were all well and truly dead, it was easier for her to move on. But it wasn't until Kara met Caleb, and Ethan had seen what commitment and love could be—not the tainted version their parents had shown them, but real love—that he realized what he was missing out on. And it hadn't taken long for him to figure out who he was missing out on that feeling with.

4

After a few hours of sleep interrupted by dream after dream of Becky Plummer's emaciated body, Quinn gave up and got out of bed. She never slept well, anyway. It was something Kara and she shared. Insomnia induced by trauma in their past. But Kara had told her with Caleb in her bed, the nightmares were few and far between, and she had started to sleep for longer stretches of time. If only.

Maybe someday Quinn would give herself a chance at love and maybe that love could heal her the way it had done for Kara. But Caleb wasn't a normal guy. Caleb was a superhero. He was in tune with her emotions, as if he anticipated Kara's mindset. But it wasn't just that; he knew her, inside and out. The love they shared was almost painful to see. If Quinn were a bitter person, she would hate them for finding such a special connection, but that was something Quinn was not. Scared of intimacy, slow to trust, but not bitter. Never bitter. Never jealous. She had too much to be grateful for, and Kara had become her best friend. Along with Taylor Montgomery, Caleb's sister. The three of them had spent many nights laughing and crying and sharing their stories—their fears.

After a fast shower, she made her way into the kitchen and threw her favorite hot drink in her Keurig. Hot chocolate. Kara and Taylor gave her a hard time for owning a Keurig, but not actually using it to make coffee. Quinn abhorred coffee. She loved the smell, but no matter how many times she tried to drink it, it repulsed her taste buds. Kara laughed hysterically and said that Quinn and Ethan would be perfect together, because he, too, hated coffee.

Ethan. The name was like a Band-Aid over the wounds from the previous night. As if the mere thought of him could make everything all right. At least for a little while. Sighing, she took her mug and went and sat on the stool by the island in her kitchen. She knew she should eat something, but it was hard to crave food when thinking about what Becky had been through. She turned on her laptop and checked her emails. As she deleted the junk mail, one email stood out. With trembling fingers, she opened the email and stared at the words that were on her computer screen.

You're going to regret not keeping your nose out of our business.

"Son of a bitch." She rubbed her temples. What was the purpose of the email? Was it to scare her? Blackmail her? What would the person behind the email want to accomplish? And the bigger question, did she share this with alpha male and hot detective Ethan Vanderbilt, or should she keep it to herself? The sensible side of her was shouting to tell him immediately; the side that didn't want to rely on anyone— especially a man—shouted at the sensible side to shut the hell up.

Standing, she wearily made her way to the front door and grabbed her keys and purse while putting her shoes on. It was going to be a long day. She hated to admit how rattled she was by the email, but she was, and her sensible side won out. Turning and going back into the kitchen she scooped up her laptop, deciding it was best to show Ethan than to keep it quiet. Whoever sent that email was most definitely not a friend, and Quinn was a smart girl. She had survival instincts and then some. Nonetheless, it was unnerving that someone had already found out that she had been involved in Becky's retrieval.

The question was: who had leaked the information? The police? She didn't think that was the case; Ethan and Caleb were the only ones who saw her, and she trusted them both. Was it someone at the hospital? The center? She had been asking about Becky, and it wouldn't be that hard to figure it out when the girl went missing that Quinn had something to do with her being removed from that cellar. Hadn't Harrison said that he heard someone coming? Someone must have been aware she was there. The assholes that had left her in that hole had either left her there to die or had left someone in charge of feeding and getting her water. The fact that someone was there and almost caught them led Quinn to believe that they had left someone in charge of Becky's well-being—someone who'd done a shitty job since she was barely fed and had run out of water.

She used her key fob to unlock her car, but she didn't get in until she glanced behind the driver seat to make sure no one was lurking in the backseat. Paranoid? Hardly. People were ambushed every day, and those people hadn't gotten an email that could only be described as a threat. It was a quick drive to Mercy Hospital; Quinn's apartment was chosen because of its proximity to the hospital. It was best if she got to the hospital fast if she was called in to counsel a victim and A Place to Hope was close by, as well. Oftentimes victims decided not to press charges or even get examined. In those cases, they might go directly to the center, and Quinn would do her best to convince them to be seen. She had a fairly good track record of calming a victim and encouraging them to seek the help they so needed. If they did go to the hospital, every second they waited in a sterile emergency room cubicle waiting to be examined and questioned was a second closer to them bailing from the hospital without getting the resources they needed to heal.

She parked her car in the visitor lot and sat for a moment, steadying her hands—that were still shaking—before she got out to meet with Becky. She couldn't be rattled in front of her; the girl was looking to her for strength. It was very important to not only show compassion but fortitude when she spoke with the young girl. She was just reaching for her car handle when someone rapped on her window, causing her to jump so high that she nearly smacked her head on the roof of her car. Hand to her chest, she looked out the window to see Ethan standing on the other side with an apologetic look on his face. He mouthed the word sorry, and she forced a smile on her face as she got out of the car.

"I didn't mean to startle you. I just saw you sitting there, and I thought we could walk in together. Caleb isn't here yet. He said something came up, and he would be a little late." He paused from his fast talking to look at her. She shifted uncomfortably under his scrutiny. "Tough night?"

She grimaced. It wasn't like she could hide it, and she wasn't a particularly vain person. Although, Ethan did tend to make her feel self-conscious. Anyway, she wasn't one to lie about stupid things.

"Yes. I had a hard time getting sleep. How about you?" She couldn't help but notice the dark circles around his eyes.

"I've had better. I ended up going back to the station to look over the case file with the information gathered after Becky's disappearance."

"Find anything useful? I mean, we know who had her, but we don't know who took her."

"Nothing, but I knew it wasn't going to get me anything. Since I wasn't tired and knew I couldn't sleep, I decided to give it a try."

"They haunt you, too," she whispered, knowing the shadows in his eyes all too well. When he just stared at her, she sighed. "The victims —they haunt you like they haunt me. Like they haunt Kara and Caleb. I get it. Trust me. If you ever need to talk about it—I mean, I'm not the police shrink, but I'm a good listener, and sometimes you need to talk these things out. Or it festers."

Still, he just stood there. Staring. Not blinking, and then as if he came back to himself, he closed and opened his eyes in one long blink. Then with an almost imperceptible shake of his head, he smiled his flirtatious, I don't give a damn smile. A defense mechanism. She knew one when she saw one—she had many herself.

"Nah, I'm pretty good at compartmentalizing things. Have to be in this line of work, right?"

"Whatever you say, Ethan."

"What's that supposed to mean?"

"You know what I mean. It's just that you don't have to hide it from me. You can hide it from Kara. Heck, you can hide it from Caleb, though I don't think either is oblivious to the charade, but don't hide it from me. Reach out when help is offered." Before he could say anything else, she spun on her heel and marched toward the door to go meet with Becky Plummer.

She made a conscious effort to appear that she didn't care about his response, but she had. It was as if she had put her heart out for him to see, and he spat on it and handed it back. If he only knew how hard it was to actually have voiced any of what she had said, she knew he would feel like a complete jerk. Because Ethan was nothing if not a stand-up guy, and not only was he a great guy, but she had heard more than one woman describe him as movie star hot. Platinum blond hair, blue eyes, muscular build from putting in hours at the police gym. Ethan was the epitome of every woman's naughty dreams, and he was the kind of guy you could take home to meet your parents. If you had parents to take him home to. Or parents that deserved to meet him. Which she did not. And that alone was one of the very reasons she didn't allow herself to daydream about Ethan Vanderbilt. He deserved more than her and her screwed up past. He had enough in his own past; he didn't need to shoulder hers too.

Without glancing back at him, she walked inside to the elevator bank and waited for the doors to open. Once she was inside, she pushed the button, not caring if he had followed her or not, until she realized that she had no idea what room or even what floor Becky was on. She assumed she was in the ICU, but she didn't really know for sure. Begrudgingly, she held the elevator door for the obstinate detective that was a step behind her. At least she could smile inwardly at his brooding glare. So, she had bothered him by walking away. Good.

"What floor?" she asked, trying, and failing, not to smirk.

"Four."

Without looking at him directly, she pushed the button to the fourth floor and breathed deeply. The cologne he wore always made her belly do flip-flops. He smelled so good. With his stupid Hollywood looks and his stupid swagger, and now she was sighing inwardly at her unfair assessment. Yes, he was abnormally attractive. But he wasn't cocky about it. Not even a little bit. And that just added to his appeal. Damn it. Someday. Maybe someday she would have enough courage to ask him out.

The silence was awkward, and Quinn found herself staring at anything but Ethan. Finally, he cleared his throat and turned to look at her.

"Listen, about before—" She cut him off before he could say another word.

"Don't worry about it. I overstepped, and I shouldn't have. Let's just pretend I didn't say anything. Okay?" She looked at him long and hard. His eyes looked so sad. She wondered if he knew that—if he knew that his eyes betrayed him.

"I was just going to say I was sorry for being short with you. But, yeah, we can definitely just forget about it."

The elevator stopped on the third floor, but the doctor that was about to get on was stopped by a nurse. It felt like they were stuck in the elevator forever before they finally reached the fourth floor.

"Should we wait for Caleb?"

"I'll send him a text and see if he's going to be much longer. If he is, we'll get started without him."

"Works for me."

There was no fear in Quinn. Whatever her background, she had come out fearless. Or at least that was the appearance she wanted people to believe. Ethan thought that it was a pretty accurate portrayal, though. She might have some residual fear for the victims she counseled, but more often than not, he thought she just had anger that, in this day and age, people were still being abused. In his mind, the human race hadn't quite gotten it right yet and really had barely evolved from caveman status. But he had hope. Hope that somehow, they would stop the sex trafficking business. Even if it probably was hopeless, it was all he had left. He had to focus on the good that people like Kara and Quinn had accomplished. It was the only thing that kept him centered, kept him going when everything else threatened to swallow him up.

The abduction of his sister had gutted him. His life, her life, could have gone off the tracks. Indeed, it had steered him in another direction. Instead of prosecuting criminals, which was what he wanted to do —not corporate law, that had been his parents plan for him—he decided to take down the bad guys and hand them off to be prosecuted. It was much more satisfying putting bracelets on them and locking them up. Some part of him knew that if he had gone on to become a DA, he would have been lost. Because eventually, he would lose a case. And he would be gutted all over again to know that it was his fault the criminal was back on the street. At least being a detective, he knew he could hand the case to the DA with every shred of evidence needed to put them away, and if the DA didn't do their job and the jury got it wrong, then it wasn't his fault. Naïve? Maybe. But it was the only way he could function.

They had stopped outside Becky's room. He took a moment to mentally put up the walls that helped protect him. What they had done to this girl made him so angry he wanted to go vigilante on their asses. The people that had *purchased* Becky deserved to burn in hell. But before they went in the room, he paused to text Caleb.

Where are you at? About to go in room.

Five minutes. Just getting out of car. Came the lightning fast response.

"He's in the parking lot. We can just hang tight for a bit until he gets up here?"

"Sure." She breathed deeply—once, twice. Ethan had noticed her do the same thing in the elevator. When she did, her face seemed, younger. "It will give me a moment to prepare myself. Which, I'm not embarrassed to say, I need."

"Excuse me. Can I help you?"

Ethan turned to see a young nurse standing in the hallway.

"We're just waiting for my partner so we can talk to the patient in this room." He knew the staff would know why he was there. He had wanted to have a police officer at her door, but because of budget cuts and the fact that they didn't feel her life was in eminent danger from an outside source, he wasn't able to get her one. Her parents had money and had asked Ethan for suggestions for security. He knew a reputable company owned by a college friend and had suggested them. He didn't know if the parents had done anything about it, though.

"Oh, well, I'm sorry you came all this way. That won't be possible."

5

"What do you mean 'that won't be possible'?" Quinn demanded. "Didn't she make it?"

Ethan had only seen her ruffled one other time when Kara had been taken all those months ago. Only Kara and the guard outside his door knew how Quinn had come to the hospital and sat with him while the police had been preparing to storm the abandoned warehouse she was being held in. That night, they held each other's hand, waiting. Waiting for word, for confirmation that she was okay. When Kara had finally come up to his room, Quinn simply squeezed his hand, smiled warmly, and left the room and the hospital. Kara never talked about seeing her there that night, and he had assumed Quinn had never told anyone else she was there. He assumed she didn't want people to know—she didn't want anyone to know she'd shown a moment of weakness.

"Oh no, I'm sorry, but I can't really divulge, or I would be violating HIPAA laws. I'm not even allowed to say that the patient is at this hospital."

Ethan pulled out his badge and showed it to the young woman.

"I'm the detective assigned to her case." He heard the elevator doors open and looked up to see Caleb and Kara coming their way. "And that is my partner, Detective Montgomery and his wife, Dr.

Vanderbilt. She was the one who admitted her last night. I believe she will be able to clear up any confusion, but I assure you, we have full permission from her parents to be kept abreast of her status."

"Good morning, Nurse Schabow. I overheard Detective Vanderbilt, and I can confirm that we did obtain permission from her parents to disclose her status. They would like us to cooperate in any way possible if it means we can put away the people who had her."

"I didn't know."

"No worries; you wouldn't have known. And I'm in no way reprimanding you—just letting you know. I imagine you just got on shift and you didn't know any of the details from when the patient was brought in," Kara said, her voice soothing. Ethan was mesmerized by his sister and her calming demeanor. Even though it wasn't so long ago that she had been so angry, she had never treated her patients with anything but compassion.

"I can confirm she was brought for some testing. They wanted to do a CAT scan to make sure she doesn't have any internal injuries now that she's stable enough. Her sodium and potassium levels have improved. But you're right, I did just come on shift, so I wasn't able to fully review her chart."

"Thank you. I appreciate the update. Since I just got in myself, I wasn't sure where her levels were." At his confused look, Kara continued. "It's going to be a long process since she was deprived of nourishment for so long."

"I was just reviewing her chart when the detective and his companion showed up. I wasn't able to do much more than glance at it. Admittedly, I wasn't able to look very closely."

"Once again, thank you for your diligence. It's important to be the gatekeepers for our patients."

And with that statement, the young nurse walked away beaming. This was the sister that Ethan had always known, the best of them, a diamond in the rough. And they knew how rough it had been. Very few people could have walked through that fire and come out alive. He knew he was looking at her adoringly when she shot him a goofy look.

"Would you stop looking at me like that?" she huffed.

"Like what?" he asked.

"Like I walk on water."

"If you only knew," he said and slung an arm over her shoulder. "Whether or not you realize this, I love you like crazy, kiddo."

"Kiddo," she said, giggling, and then shoved him in the ribs with her elbow.

He noticed Caleb and Quinn staring at them. Caleb with the ever-present look of a man smitten and Quinn with a soft expression, but something else, as well? Was it wistfulness? Maybe he wouldn't have to wait so long to make his move, after all. And then an imperceptible shake of her head, and she had shuttered her eyes again. He wasn't deterred. Instead, for the first time, he was encouraged.

"How long do you think the tests will take?" Caleb asked.

"I can find out." Kara walked away and came back a few minutes later. "They figure another half hour."

"Good, plenty of time to go eat breakfast in the cafeteria," Caleb said, eyeing his wife. And if Ethan wasn't mistaken, Kara grimaced at the statement.

"You know how I am about eating right away in the morning," she said. Lie. That was a lie. Sure, she had some issues if she had nightmares, he knew that much was true. But since she had married Caleb, the nightmares were reportedly few and far between. Unless they had made a resurgence.

"You okay?"

"Yep. Fantastic. Well, I had some bad dreams last night. So, just not hungry yet." She smiled, but the smile didn't reach her eyes.

"I didn't eat yet. Will it bother you to sit and watch us eat?" he asked her.

"Maybe. But I'm willing to suffer through that for three of my favorite people."

"Aw, shucks, you're making me blush," he said while rubbing her head.

"You are so immature sometimes." But once again, she was laughing, and the appreciative look on Caleb's face to hear his wife laugh made everything a little better for Ethan. Whatever the dream had been, it must have been a doozy.

"Sometimes?" He shoved her playfully.

"All right, all the time."

Watching Ethan interact with Kara so playfully was almost more than she could handle. There were times where she just wanted to throw her arms around him and thank him for being him. She was certain that he realized he was a balm to the open wounds that were still healing on his sister, but to see him do what he did best to make her smile and laugh did a lot for her, as well. If she was able to let him in, she could easily fall in love with him. Which would be the only man she had ever loved and likely would be the last.

For now, she needed to focus on the task at hand and not fixate on the man walking a couple steps in front of her with his sister. Caleb had fallen into step with Quinn and had a huge grin on his face when he glanced at her.

"What's so funny?" she asked him, genuinely curious.

"Just enjoying the interaction between the two of you." He spoke the words quietly so only she heard them.

"What interaction?"

"Don't play that game with me. I see the chemistry. I only have one question."

"And what is that?" she asked with what she hoped was a mocking tone but feared had fallen flat.

"Why do neither of you have enough gumption to do something about it." And with that final statement, he was quiet. He kept walking next to her with that huge grin on his face, but he didn't say another word. Jerk. But, she didn't really mean it. She couldn't fault him for noticing the way she had been staring at Ethan like she wanted to eat him up. However, he was off the mark if he thought that the feeling was reciprocated.

"Who uses the word gumption?" she blurted out.

"I'm trying to clean up my language a bit." He grimaced. "It isn't going that well."

"Wife got you over hot coals? No sex if you don't comply?" she asked sarcastically.

"Something like that." He winced a little.

Interesting. She shrugged it off. It really was none of her concern if he was trying to clean up his language. It wouldn't offend her if he continued to let one slip here and there or if he let it drop all the time. They were just words to her, not physical blows. Therefore, they didn't bother her. Though being that she worked with impressionable minors, she did her best to curb any language that might be deemed unacceptable. Although many of the kids that came to the center could teach her a word or two, and in the right situation, she was known to slip up.

When they got to the cafeteria, she was shocked at how hungry she was. Her stomach actually growled loud enough that Caleb laughed. She could never figure out why it embarrassed someone when their stomach growled. It wasn't like it could be controlled, and it was a simple bodily function, but she found herself embarrassed anyway and hoped that no one else had heard it. Too late; she realized that Ethan was grinning and looking at her.

"How about we get you some food there? Sounds like you might be hungry."

Gah. Her face felt like it was burning up. Blushing? Was she really blushing? Did thirty-year-old, well-adjusted women, who normally didn't care what people thought of them, blush? Not this one. Sweet Lord Almighty, what was going on?

"I was in a rush to get here, so I skipped a real breakfast."

"Well, let's get you a real one, then. They actually have really good food here," Caleb said, overhearing the conversation.

After she loaded a plate with far more food than she needed, but definitely planned on eating, she found a table with the other three, noting that Kara looked distant somehow. Obviously, the nightmare she had was still bothering her. Suddenly, she remembered the email she had gotten that morning. Grabbing her laptop, she set it next to her tray and powered it up.

"Since I have both of you here, and Kara is involved in this, and because I trust you all with sensitive information as well as to tell me if I'm overreacting, I thought I would show you this." As she talked, she accessed her email and opened the message that had been emailed to her, then indicated that they move around to look at what was on the screen. "I would prefer to be discreet about this. I mean it's probably nothing, but—" Ethan cut her off mid-sentence.

"What the hell? When did you get this?"

"I saw it this morning, but it's time stamped not long after I dropped Becky off here."

"Son of a..." Caleb stopped short, grimaced, and finished with "...bucket."

She let out a hysterical laugh. For some reason, she couldn't help herself.

"Come on, really? Son of a bucket? What in the world is going on with you?" Quinn knew she was rolling her eyes and couldn't stop herself.

"Oh, shut up. I was told that I need to be better with my language around my brother's kids." Quinn felt like her sides were going to split from laughing so hard.

"To be fair, Caleb, the word choices that your brother was offended over were not appropriate in front of the kids." Kara was smiling while she scolded him.

"Back to the matter at hand. Sorry, guys, but I couldn't give a shit about Caleb's reason for not swearing."

Quinn sobered immediately. The laughter had been welcome, but Ethan was right. This wasn't a laughing matter.

"Sorry, Ethan. I just, well, I needed something to laugh about. I'm a fairly honest person. So, believe me when I say that this email kind of freaked me out."

"It should. It means that no matter how hard we tried to keep your identity confidential, it's already too late. Someone knows you were involved, and they found out really fast. How did they get your personal email?"

"This isn't my personal email; it's my work one. I don't give my personal email to very many people. But I'm more concerned if they know who I was helping."

"He can take care of himself. Don't worry about him. He got you into this mess," Caleb said with a slight edge in his voice.

"How do you know who I was helping?" she asked with slitted eyes.

"I only know what Ethan told me." She had told Ethan he was an undercover cop. "He shouldn't have involved you."

"Caleb, he was actually helping me. I got him into this mess. He was safely ensconced until I started nosing around looking for Becky. I was just trying to do something, help someone for a change."

"Honey, you really need to get over that mistake. He didn't know the mistake he had made until it was too late. You know as well as I do that he went undercover in this case because of what happened to me."

Ethan looked startled.

"Um, how do you know who we're talking about?"

"I know my husband. He gave it away with his expression alone. He's a little slower than I am to forgive. And we will leave it at that."

Quinn smiled a sad smile. Officer Black had inadvertently let Kara go home with who he thought was an officer but ended up being part of the duo who had terrorized her all those years ago. Kara had forgiven him; she had told Quinn that all's well that ends well. She considered Kara her best friend and confidante, along with Taylor and Vanessa Brenner, the four women had become very close. It was the first time Quinn had really made friends, and because of what Kara had gone through, not once, but twice, Quinn was beyond proud of her ability to forgive and forget. Harrison had worked hard to make up for the error, even though he honestly had no way of knowing that the officer he sent her with was the sadistic killer they had been looking for.

"I'll get there. I'm working on it. It's just…"

"Get there faster. I know what you went through. I was there. But certain people deserve a second chance; it could have easily been you that made a mistake." Even though the conversation was serious, Kara laughed at the expression of outrage on Caleb's face. "Yes, love, even the amazing Caleb Montgomery can make mistakes. As a matter of fact, you are making a colossal one by not forgiving him, and you know what? I still love you." He smiled that dopey smile he wore more often than not around his wife.

"I love it when you're assertive and then give me a compliment, even if it is sarcastic."

"There was nothing sarcastic in that statement. Nothing." Kara rolled her eyes at him.

Ethan had been extremely still and silent during the exchange. Quinn glanced at him and did a double take. He was looking at her with an odd expression on his face. If she wasn't mistaken, she would think it was longing and fear. What a weird combination of emotions to cover a person's face. It made for a strange feeling to flutter around in her stomach. She didn't know why he made her so nervous. Was she ready to allow herself to be interested in a man? More importantly, why did he look so scared for that brief instant? Slowly, he blinked, and in that blink, she watched him compartmentalize whatever had been bothering him and transform back into the sexy detective role he played.

The role that he used to get people to trust and underestimate him. It was especially useful as a detective. According to Kara, he could charm just about anyone into confessing, and she believed that whole-heartedly, but that look also had women willing to take off their panties and throw them at him. He smoldered. But she saw through it all. Saw it for what it was. A defense mechanism. A fairly foolproof and effective one, but still just a mechanism to hide behind. She understood that need to barricade yourself away. The need to not let anyone too close, to not really trust anyone. After all, had she ever been completely honest with any of her friends? No. Hell, she hadn't really allowed herself friends until recently, but she knew if the threat was gone, she would tell them, explain to them where she came from. She owed that much to Kara for trusting her so completely and to Ethan for no other reason than she didn't feel they had a shot if he didn't know her history.

But not today; another day, if the threat was ever gone. *When* the threat was gone. When. She had to remind herself that it would be some day. Some. Day. She just hoped to see it before she was an old lady in a rocking chair by herself on her porch. When she realized she was still staring at Ethan and his cocky grin had faded, she looked away. Had he seen through her? Had he seen her like she had seen him? It terrified her. And yet, it enthralled her. To know that he was as intrigued by her as she was by him.

"Earth to Ethan," Kara said.

He shook his head, breaking eye contact with her to look at his sister.

"Yeah?"

Did his voice sound hoarse? Or was it her imagination? She wanted him to be affected by her like she was by him, but maybe she was imagining things. In the end, it didn't really matter; she wasn't really free to explore things, anyway. At least, that was what she kept telling herself. Would it be so bad to figuratively let her hair down and have a one-night stand with him? How many other women had he diddled and still remained friends with after he walked away from them? Couldn't they do the same thing? No. Quinn wasn't that kind of girl. She suspected when she fell, it would be hard and forever. Not to mention she couldn't betray Kara in that way, and it would be a betrayal to have sex with her best friend's brother just because she had a scratch that seemed to need to be itched recently.

"I was just saying that they sent me a text that Becky is back in her room. We can go up and talk to her, if you would like."

For a brief moment, a look crossed his face that led Quinn to believe he would prefer to do anything but go up there to speak to the emaciated girl and hear her horror story.

6

The ride in the elevator to see Becky was quiet. The silence was heavy —not awkward, but apprehensive. All of the people standing shoulder to shoulder with him had seen more than they should have, and the two women had endured more than any woman should have. Granted, he had never been told this about Quinn, but Ethan knew. He knew that something had happened to her. He'd been around enough people who had been abused—men, women, and children—to recognize an abuse victim. Her eyes were almost always shuttered, but for a moment, one small moment in the cafeteria, he had been able to see more in those beautiful hazel eyes. She had let the shutters open, and that was when Kara had called out to him. Had she realized what he'd seen?

It wouldn't surprise him. After all, Kara was fiercely protective of Quinn and Taylor. And they were equally protective of her. All three girls were linked by histories that no one should have. He was confident that at some point Quinn would tell him. That was what he saw when she had dropped her defenses for that brief moment. She wanted what she saw when she looked at Caleb and Kara. It was obvious for that one moment, and it had bolstered him. She just needed to trust him. Trust was one of the things that she coveted the most. She didn't give it out to just anyone, and it took a long time to build that relationship with her, but she did allow people in. She trusted Kara, Taylor, and Vanessa. Quinn even trusted Caleb and himself. She just didn't want to admit it out loud, and for her to trust them was a big deal, because he suspected that it was particularly hard for her to trust men. The wall she had built around her was built with pretty impressive bricks and mortar, and to crack the veneer was not an easy task.

All Ethan knew for sure was that he would never make her doubt him. He just had to prove that to her. When the timing was right. Soon. He wasn't willing to wait much longer. If she needed a little shove to see what she had in front of her, then he would do so. Of course, then he would hold out a hand to help hold her up.

They had made it to the door of Becky's room, and he sensed Quinn tense. He turned to look at her and saw that she had paled. It was a powerful and scary sight to see Quinn—fierce, proud, and tough Quinn—with her blonde pixie hair and hazel eyes scared, but that was what she was. She was terrified to go into that room and see that girl. The woman who had risked her life to get Becky to safety was now scared to see Becky. Without consciously realizing what he was about to do, he grabbed her hand and laced his fingers with hers. She flinched, and then, unbelievably, she squeezed his hand as if to thank him for realizing she needed something to anchor herself to.

After that brief squeeze, she held his hand only a moment longer. Once Kara walked through the door, Quinn let go and went in after her, with Ethan and Caleb taking up the rear. Becky appeared to be sleeping in the hospital bed that seemed to swallow her up. And Ethan found himself feeling that familiar mixture of nausea and anger. Hospitals always made him think of those scary days after Kara had been rescued. She had looked so tiny in the hospital bed. Her body had been covered in multi-color bruises, cuts, scrapes, and bug bites. He had prayed to God over and over to help them find her, and then when she was found, he prayed for her to survive the night. When she'd survived the night, he'd prayed for her to wake up, and he prayed until she had. But when she opened her eyes, the Kara he'd always known wasn't there. Her eyes had been vacant. Only recently had those eyes lit up.

Becky's parents, Frederick and Cynthia, were sitting in chairs beside the hospital bed. When they entered, her parents stood to greet them, introducing themselves to Quinn, but Ethan was looking at Becky in that bed. It sent him back to those terrifying days. When he got closer, Becky opened her eyes because she wasn't sleeping at all. He saw the same vacant expression in her eyes as Kara's held all those years ago. Lost, alone, frightened, and simply empty. He glanced at Kara and saw her tense. Ethan knew she saw it, too. Quinn had regained her composure, seemingly bolstered by the girl being awake and didn't hesitate as she strode over to the bed and sat in the chair next to it.

"Hi, Becky, do you remember me?" Her voice was soft, soothing. As if she were talking to a frightened animal, and perhaps, on some level, she was. Becky was certainly a frightened girl. Quinn reached to pick up the young girl's hand and stopped when she saw the look of fear in her eyes. Slowly, she put her hand back down. "It's okay. I won't harm you. I brought you here. Do you remember?"

There was a long pause before the slightest nod of the head to confirm that she did indeed remember Quinn.

"This nice detective, I believe you met him last night, Detective Vanderbilt is his name; he would like any information you can give us. Anything that would help us put away the people that had you, so they can't ever do it to anyone else again. Do you think you could help us?"

Another pause. While she looked at each woman to each man, panic was still etched on her face. Ethan glanced at Quinn. He knew the magic she could work, but he wasn't sure how she was going to pull this one off. The girl was clearly too traumatized right now to speak. Her mother began to protest when Quinn quietly lifted a hand to silence the woman.

"Is it okay if I call you Becky?" Quinn inquired and waited for the small nod from her, then she continued, "I think it's a bit crowded in here, don't you? I think maybe we could ask Detective Montgomery and Dr. Montgomery to step into the hallway. But my friend, Detective Vanderbilt, would like to stay to take notes. What do you think?"

If Ethan hadn't been watching closely, he wouldn't have seen the nod of her head, so slight, yet more confident than the other times she had answered Quinn's questions. Both parents seemed to relax slightly when Becky responded. Ethan glanced at Caleb and inclined his head to the door. Kara and Caleb walked out, and he followed them.

"I'll hang out just outside the door," Caleb said as soon as they were in the hallway. "Not offended in the least to be kicked out. Quinn was right, too many people in the room."

"I have to get down to the ER, anyway," Kara said and kissed Caleb quickly on the lips. "See you later. Can you remind Quinn that we have lunch plans today? She might have forgotten, and I didn't mention it at breakfast. I was preoccupied with the email she got."

"Absolutely. I'm going to head back in." Ethan grabbed her quick and squeezed her tight. "Whatever is really going on and got you looking so dazed—and don't even try to tell me it was a nightmare or the email—I just hope you will eventually confide in me." The words were quiet, meant for only the three of them. After a quick kiss on her forehead, he looked her deep in the eye. "I love you, no matter what."

Kara chuckled a melodious sound that was music to his ears.

"It's nothing for you to worry about. Really, it isn't. I just have my head in the clouds this morning, but there's nothing you should stress about. Go do what you're good at, and I'm going to do what I'm good at." *Subtle*, he thought. In not so many words, she had politely told him to get out of her personal life and focus on his job. As she turned to walk away, she squeezed his forearm. Another way to show that he shouldn't take offense to her shutting him out.

"I suppose you won't tell me what's going on either?" he asked Caleb.

"Like she said, it isn't anything for you to worry about. Better get back in there."

Ethan let him sidestep it this time. But he knew something was up, and he planned on finding out what it was. Caleb was like a brother to him, but Kara was his sister first. He wouldn't meddle, but he wanted to know what was going on. All couples fight, and he figured that Caleb and Kara were no different, so perhaps it was just a squabble that had them both jumpy. There was nothing he could do about it now.

They would tell him when and if they wanted to. For now, he needed to get back to work.

"Is that better? A little less claustrophobic in here, right?" Quinn was asking in a voice filled with empathy.

"Th-thank you," Becky responded. Her voice was raspy and weak, but she had spoken. Ethan struggled not to cry. Geez, he needed a vacation; he was feeling like a wuss. No, he needed to make who was responsible pay.

"You don't have to thank me. I just want to help you. If you need the room to be a little less full, then I make that happen."

"No. I meant, thank you for risking your life to save me."

"Like I said, no need to thank me. I would do it again."

"But why? I'm no one."

"I was no one once, too. Sometimes you can help yourself, and sometimes you need someone to help you."

"D-did someone help you?" the girl asked. She was able to pick up on the meaning behind the words that Quinn had spoken.

"Not at first. At first, I had to help myself, but then someone helped me. So, you see, that's why I would risk my life again and again to help you. Because when I was ready to give up, someone helped me."

And with that statement, Ethan was stuck between wanting to scoop her into his arms and say he was there now, when no one else had been or giving her a standing ovation for coming out of whatever hell she had endured, stronger and ready to give anything to help someone else. Much like Kara had. It was at that moment that he realized he was in serious trouble of losing his heart, because another little piece of him fell head over heels for Quinn Sanders, and it wasn't that scary after all.

Quinn had to swallow twice before she could speak, and even then, her throat was thick with unshed tears. This young girl didn't need to thank her. Quinn would gladly risk her life for her all over again if it meant that she wouldn't suffer another second. Even if Quinn had to lose her life to protect Becky, she would do it all again. Something had clicked in her when she heard about the possible location of the teenager. She meant it with every fiber of her being that she was there for Becky because when she was at her lowest, someone had been there for her. The only problem with her confession to Becky was the fact that Quinn hadn't realized Ethan had come back in the room until she heard a small intake of breath. When she turned, she saw him standing completely still, looking at her the same way he had in the cafeteria, as if scared she would disappear if he moved. And she felt like disappearing. Her story was not something she wanted to share with him, not yet anyway, maybe not ever.

Quinn was thankful that the parents hadn't stopped the interview, but they seemed as eager for answers as everyone else was, and they had moved to the other side of the room to allow Quinn to sit next to Becky while she spoke to her. She knew from the news stories that Mr. Plummer was CEO of a local bank and that Mrs. Plummer was actually a well-respected doctor. While they lived in Darkness Falls, neither worked there. Both were being very patient and respectful by allowing Quinn to conduct the interview without interrupting.

"Were you taken, too? Like me?" The whispered question was almost lost in the large room.

"Not exactly the same as you, but our stories are pretty similar. Someday I will share with you, but today I need you to share with me before you get too tired. Is that okay?" Quinn worried that the girl would clam up because she was pushing her, but she was more worried that the girl would fall asleep, and time was of the essence. They needed to find out what they could to pinpoint the leader of this sex ring before more kids fell victim to it.

"Yeah. I mean, I can tell you everything I know. But it isn't much."

"Why don't you just start at the beginning? I'm sure whatever you can share will be helpful." Hopefully. Otherwise, she was making her relive everything so soon without any real purpose, and they were back at ground zero.

"Should I start from the day I was taken?"

"However you want to tell us what happened works for us. If that's where you're comfortable starting, then start there. If there were other things that happened leading up to you being taken, then start there."

"Other things?"

"Anything important. Anything at all." Quinn couldn't lead the girl in any way, or she might start to recall things that might not have happened, but she needed to know if Becky had been groomed at all or if she had been taken off the street with no prior contact with the people who took her. Kidnapping a girl from a higher-income family in broad daylight was risky business. Much riskier than grooming a child and convincing them to come with you of their own accord. Which would turn them into a runaway in the eyes of the authorities.

If she was groomed, they might have a starting point. If she wasn't, then whatever she had to say probably wouldn't net any results. Unless she had a very detailed description of the person or persons who'd taken her.

"I guess I don't know what you mean? There wasn't anything suspicious leading up to my being taken. At least, I don't think so."

Quinn had to tread lightly, but she could still ask questions. She just needed to formulate them a certain way; the main objective was how to do it without leading the young girl. Even with this many years under her belt, it was still hard to come up with the right questions. The ones that would trigger a memory.

"Did you make any new friends in the days leading up to the kidnapping?" That was a fairly ambiguous question.

Becky scrunched her face up, clearly trying hard to think back that long ago.

"No...no, I don't think so. My parents are on the strict side. I go—I mean, I went to a private school. I had a core group of friends. I have always been a very routine person."

"Meaning?"

"You know, same routine day after day. No variance. I have a lot of extracurricular activities that I'm involved in. To find time for my current friends is difficult. To make a new friend would be even harder because they aren't as understanding about my demanding schedule."

Which meant what? She didn't have contact with the person who took her in the days, weeks, or months leading up to her kidnapping? That appeared to be the case, or at the very least, Becky didn't seem to know if she had been in contact with the main players in her abduction. There was a while where they had thought the girl was abducted for money, but when no ransom request came, it was apparent that something else was going on. Quinn didn't think the girl would lie about anything leading up to that day. Not even out of fear. Did that mean it was one hundred percent random? Quinn didn't think so. If she had to guess, she would guess that Becky had been worked on for some time and had no idea that it had been happening. The problem was finding out by whom. If that was even possible.

"So, until that day, nothing stands out. Nothing out of your normal routine?"

"No. Nothing. Except…" Again, she scrunched her face while she was thinking something through.

"Except what?" When the silence became too long, Quinn couldn't help but ask the question.

"Well, the day I was taken, I was in a neighborhood I never would have gone. Or I never had gone to before."

"What made you go there?" she asked carefully.

"It's kind of foggy; that was a long time ago." She hedged.

Quinn instantly saw red flags pop up all over the place from that one statement. There was definitely something that the girl didn't want to share. Was it because her parents were in the room? Whatever it was, it might be something that could help point them in the right direction, but for some reason, the girl didn't want to fess up. Surely, she knew that there was nothing that she could confide that would get her in trouble. Didn't she? There was no doubt in Quinn's mind that Becky was a smart girl. In fact, she knew she was. From the news articles Quinn read, she had discerned that Becky was a high honor student. Which didn't mean she couldn't get herself in trouble. Quinn suspected that she was protecting someone other than herself.

"Becky, I think that we need to set something straight here. I'm your advocate. Not the people that took you. Not the media. Not the police. Not even your parents. I'm here for you and only you. I'm a licensed clinical therapist. Anything personal that you tell me won't leave this room without your permission. If there is something you need to tell me that you need Detective Vanderbilt to not hear, I can ask him to leave, and it stays strictly between us. Even if it's something that is pertinent to the case." Becky's eyes darted to Ethan and back to Quinn. "Detective Vanderbilt is here now because you allow him to be. You can ask him to leave at any point. He knows this and is on board with everything I just said. We are your advocates. However, I implore you, if there's anything you know that can help this case, help us to stop these criminals from hurting another child. Please, please help us."

"It's not that…it's just, well, I promised her I wouldn't tell anyone."

Now they were getting somewhere.

"Promised who that you wouldn't say anything?"

"My friend, Haley Matthews." She paused, her frail fingers gripped the blanket that was tucked around her.

"I don't remember the name. And I reviewed your file last night." Ethan quietly spoke from the foot of the bed.

"Well, she isn't a friend my mom and dad would necessarily approve of my spending time with." She looked at her parents guiltily, and then as if she suddenly realized something, she glanced at Ethan, "You mean she didn't come forward when I went missing?" Becky's lower lip began to tremble, and for the first time since Quinn had seen her in Black's arms, she saw the girl on the verge of a meltdown.

"All I can say is that she wasn't interviewed," Ethan said soothingly. "That doesn't mean she didn't come forward. It might just mean the officer interviewing might not have found anything she said important." That was a lie because even if it wasn't important, if the officer did their job right, there would be notes regarding speaking with Haley Matthews. But Ethan was smooth, and Becky didn't notice it for what it was.

"What are you protecting her from?"

"Nothing really. I mean, nothing she can get in trouble for. It's just, well, she has or had, I don't know if they are still together, but back then she had an older boyfriend. One who lived in that neighborhood, and she was scared to go to his place alone. So, I would walk with her there to meet him. It wasn't a big deal, and I was just being a good friend."

"Did you ever meet the boy that she was seeing?" Quinn asked carefully.

"Yes. I always talked to him when I went there with her. They would go in another room for a while, and then Haley would come out, and we would walk home."

"Where does Haley live?"

"Um, well, I don't know." Becky began to fidget and looked distraught. Her pulse started to increase on the monitors, and her blood pressure was slightly elevated. It really was cheating to have the machines there to indicate her agitation. It was like they were betraying her to Ethan and Quinn.

"You never went to her home?"

"No. Um, I got the impression she was embarrassed by where she lived. She always walked until a block before my house and then we parted ways. I didn't want my parents to see her. Like I said, they wouldn't necessarily approve." She glanced over at the two of them apologetically.

"Why?"

"She is a scholarship student, and she dresses as wild as she can get away with. She kind of gets in trouble a lot because she skips classes."

"Did you ever ask to go to her house?"

"Once."

"What did she say?"

"She just said that her mom didn't like her having people over and that she was always drunk."

Something was still not being shared. Quinn's instincts were telling her to push the girl a little more. The worst that could happen would be that she would lose the trust of the girl or that the parents would decide to stop the conversation. Quinn hoped that she could get the girl to talk without breaking the bond she had established with her.

"But?"

"There is no but. I never asked again."

"Becky. I need you to cut the bull." Quinn paused for a second when she heard the small intake of breath from Ethan. She hoped he trusted her because even if it was risky, she thought that the little push would pay off.

"What do you mean? I'm not lying."

"I know that you aren't lying. But you are omitting something. Something that might be very important. It would really mean a lot if you could trust me to be that advocate you need."

"It's nothing, really. It's just…I waited one day and watched which direction she went. She went back the way we had come, and I thought that it was kind of strange at first." Becky paused, swallowed, and then continued. "The closer we got back to her boyfriend's neighborhood, the more I was confused. At first, I thought she lived in the same neighborhood and didn't want me to know. I mean, it's a pretty bad part of town, but it didn't make sense. I mean, she asked me to walk her there because she was scared. And then she went right back to his house and went inside. I waited for a while, and she didn't come back out at first. Then when she did, she was dressed differently."

"She changed out of her school uniform?" Why would she have a change of clothes at his house? Unless it was more than a place she visited on occasion.

"Yeah."

"How was she dressed?"

"Um, she was kind of dressed like a hooker."

Bingo! There was the connection she was hoping to find; they had just found a missing piece of the puzzle. Haley had befriended Becky and introduced her to her boyfriend. The two were clearly a team and trying to groom Becky. Only it had been taking too long, and they must have gotten impatient.

7

After the revelation that Haley was most likely trying to groom Becky, coupled with the fact that both Quinn and Ethan knew that she had no idea what had been going on and that she had gotten extremely tired, they decided that was enough for now. They managed to get an address from her just as Nurse Schabow came in and told them they had to leave—that her patient needed to get some rest. While they agreed, part of Ethan wanted—no, needed—to stay. To get more answers that might help blow the roof off this case. But he knew that they needed to have a coherent witness, not one exhausted and unable to hold their own eyelids up. He also knew that she didn't know anything else. So, grudgingly, they left the room, promising to return later.

"She has no idea she was being worked on by that girl, does she?" Quinn asked as soon as they were out of the room.

"I doubt it. Though she might suspect it now. And I doubt that the girl's real name is Haley Matthews."

"But she would have had to be enrolled in the school."

"I'm sure she was, but I think that we'll discover that the name is phony. Most likely this girl was groomed a while ago herself, and they moved her here to help them get more girls."

"Seriously, Ethan, what kind of world do we live in that someone pretends to be your friend in order to turn them into a sex slave." It wasn't phrased as a question. After all, she wasn't expecting an answer he couldn't possibly provide.

"For every bad deed, there is a good deed. You proved that. She trusted the wrong person, but you rescued her. If there wasn't the good with the bad, there would be no purpose in life."

"I had some help in getting her out of there."

"But you risked your life to get her to the hospital. Your good act outweighs the bad act."

"Maybe. But it isn't enough. Not nearly enough."

"It has to be. For now, it has to be. Those good deeds, no matter how small, are what gets me through the day. You have to promise me that you will not do something like this again without asking me to help you out. If anything had happened…" He stopped talking abruptly and swallowed, having revealed too much. Even though she had already confirmed in the parking lot that she saw through his charade, it was still too much, and he swiftly changed the subject. "Kara wanted me to remind you that you have lunch plans with her."

Quinn looked at the smart watch on her wrist and seemed startled at the time.

"Guess I don't have much time, then, so I better get a move on."

"I'll walk you out. Don't argue with me. I know you're about to. I realize you can take care of yourself. I realize you've been doing that for a long time. However, just humor me and let me be the testosterone-filled Neanderthal for a few minutes, and I'll escort you to your car. It would make me feel better, and I don't care if I just lost my man card by admitting that."

His comments startled a laugh out of her, and suddenly, the most brilliant smile he had ever seen cross her face sucker punched him. There was no doubt in his mind that he was falling hard for the hardheaded, petite, blonde woman who had just lit up the room and his world with one smile. But he hadn't been joking with her about escorting her to her car. Not really. Sure, he wanted to make her laugh. But he was concerned for her safety. Even with all of her training in martial arts, not to mention her record on the shooting range, and the girl was a better shot than Kara, which said something. Even though she was short in stature, if someone got the drop on her, she could hold her own. Kara had killed two psychos when they got the drop on the officers taking them down. In the end, Ethan would put his money on Quinn. He just didn't want to risk it or her.

Quinn had looked at him so long that the smile started to slip a bit, but then he smiled back, and her lips turned into a full-on grin. Her eyes twinkled and her cheeks got a little red and he was utterly smitten by the whole package. There was nothing he wouldn't do for this little firecracker. He just needed to convince her of that fact.

"All right, studly man, you can walk me to my car if you so choose. But just remember, I could take you in a fair fight." She smirked and sashayed around him toward the elevators.

There wasn't a doubt in his mind that the spitfire in front of him could take him or just about any other person down. He shook his head, smiling from ear to ear at the thought of rolling around on a mat with her. Immediately he was swallowing hard and trying to think of things that didn't have his body responding to the lush curves in front of him. Except, one whiff of her perfume when the doors closed in the elevator, and he was once again in trouble. Distraction—he needed a distraction.

"How are things going at the center?" Swift. That didn't sound lame at all.

"Actually, really good. We have plenty of people donating time, money, and supplies. All of which are appreciated and needed to keep the center running at the level we expect. The level I expect, the level I owe it to Kara to maintain." Her smile had become serious, and her eyes were downcast.

On some level, he hated that look as if she didn't want to disappoint Kara. In the end, though, that look meant that Quinn respected her work so much that she didn't want to fail. Ethan could respect that. It was what he had come to expect from Quinn, who was so much like his sister, yet also very different. It really was no secret that Ethan idolized his sister, and if one looked really closely, they would see he also idolized Quinn. The two most amazing women he had ever had the privilege of knowing.

"You know, Kara thinks you're doing an amazing job, and you should ease up on yourself. She has no complaints about you whatsoever."

"That may be, but I still have my own standards."

"We all know that, and that's why we will never say you don't care about the center. Just give yourself a little leeway to live a little. There's more out there than the center."

"Really? And what might that more be?"

Holy crap! If he wasn't mistaken, Quinn Sanders was flirting with him. No way. He had never seen her even give a man a sideways interested glance, much less flirt with one. All of his dreams had just come true; well, maybe not all of them. He had a lot of dreams built up over the last months, ever since that night that Quinn had sat and held his hand while his world was falling apart. That day had done something to him, and he no longer had any interest in playing the field. He hadn't dated anyone since then. At first, he had no clue why he had lost interest in not just women, but sex as well. The fact that the only time the notion even popped into his head was when he was around her set him straight in a hurry. His little man was only interested in one woman, and it just took the big man a little longer to figure it out.

"I guess I meant dating. I mean, I've never heard you talk of a boyfriend. That doesn't mean there isn't one out there, does it?" Smooth, real smooth. Could he sound more like a buffoon?

To her credit, she didn't laugh at him. Actually, she blushed a bright red. Suddenly, Ethan was worried that he had embarrassed her. He shouldn't have pried into her personal life. What the hell had he been thinking asking if she had a boyfriend? Maybe she preferred to keep it private, or maybe she was humiliated because she wasn't dating someone. A selfish part of him liked the latter option better. Ethan was still considered a player, even though that wasn't the case, and she probably thought he was hitting on her so he could have another notch in his belt. When, really, he was just trying to find out if she was available for him to hit on. Man, he was ridiculous.

"Nope. Not seeing anyone. I mean, I don't date. Too busy at the center to take the time out of my schedule to find someone worth spending time with. I guess I sound kind of picky. But the men I come across usually aren't worth my time."

"That's because you spend all your time at the center and rarely see any men that aren't abusers."

"I see plenty of decent men at the center, but I don't mix work and pleasure. I know it sounds boring."

"Actually, I was thinking it sounds lonely," he said quietly.

They had made their way to her car and were standing, somewhat awkwardly. He had done that, he had created that awkward feeling, and he was furious with himself. After all the careful planning and patience, he had blown his shot in one fell swoop.

"It is. A bit. It doesn't mean I wouldn't suspend my rules if I find the right man. I just don't have the time to search." Her eyes were locked on his, trying to read him in a way he couldn't figure out. "Anyway, I need to get going. See you around?"

"Yeah. I mean, of course." He turned to walk to his car before spinning around to remind her once again the message from Kara. "Don't forget your lunch plans or Kara will blame me."

"How could I have forgotten? You just reminded me a few minutes ago." She looked frustrated with herself and then shook her head and smiled, though it didn't look genuine. "Thank you for the reminder." As he turned to walk away, her hand caught his wrist, and he turned to look at her. "Ethan?"

"Yeah?"

"I, um, I meant what I said."

"About?" he asked, genuinely confused.

"About suspending my rules for the right guy."

Once Quinn was in her car and Ethan had walked away, she lifted her hands to the steering wheel. She was still shaking. What in the ever-loving-world had she been thinking? There was no way he could have misinterpreted what she had said. The fact was she wasn't sure if she was reading his signals right or not. She wanted him to be interested in her, didn't she? Of course, she did, even if it made things complicated. After all, she wasn't really able to date. Although, that wasn't really true—she was able to date. She just wasn't in the position to commit.

That didn't mean that she couldn't date him, did it? She could have fun and then move on. Who was she kidding? That wasn't who she was. She couldn't just give him a good time without getting invested in him, and he was the kind of guy she wanted to be invested in, but she knew he had a reputation of loving and leaving. Which would play well into having fun and running, if she were that kind of person. She really didn't believe that he was as much a player as the rumors said, though. Sure, she wasn't naïve. She knew the man had dated plenty of women. He looked like Alexander Skarsgård, for Pete's sake. He could probably just gaze at a woman, and her panties would combust, fall off, or magically disappear. Or maybe just hers would.

Lowering her head to her steering wheel, she jumped when the horn sounded. With a deep sigh, she lifted her head, started her car, and backed out of her spot. She had a little time until lunch, and she needed to run a quick errand. She had barely enough time to get that done before she had to be there. She pulled into her parking spot with a minute to spare and dashed toward the restaurant.

"Quinn!"

Kara's voice from behind her had her turning around to greet her friend.

"I'm sorry, I was running behind."

"Me too," she said, and she seemed slightly out of breath.

"Did you run here from the hospital?" Quinn asked, amused.

"I didn't find a parking spot like you did, so I had to park a couple blocks away. I had an appointment run late, and I was worried I would be late, so I ran the two blocks. I guess I'm a little out of shape. How embarrassing," she said, laughing.

"I get it. I haven't had time to really condition myself recently, and I'm not a newlywed." With a roll of the eyes, Kara smiled her adorable grin at her.

"First, there is no way you are out of shape. Not when you run that many miles a week and teach martial arts to the people at the center. Second, we are hardly newlyweds anymore."

It was Quinn's turn to roll her eyes at her friend.

"Right, you sure behave like you are, though." Kara looped her arm through Quinn's and marched them into the restaurant.

"Are you sure you have time to sit down? I mean, you work in the ER."

"I have extra staff on today. The new interns are rotating through, too. Lots of extra hands today. This group is pretty impressive. I'm hoping at least one or two decide to practice ER medicine and that they stick around. We could use them." She attempted a smile, but it fell short.

"That bad?"

"Just that shorthanded. Therefore, today is a good day. And I'm hungry, so let's eat."

They found a table and ordered. The conversation flowed like normal until Quinn decided to pry into that morning.

"So, how are things with you and Mr. Hot Detective? I mean, you both seemed a little off this morning. Did you have your first marital fight?"

With a chuckle, she shook her head and took a drink of her water, and Quinn couldn't help but note that Kara looked like she wanted to avoid the question.

"Kara? Seriously, what's going on?"

"Nothing. Caleb is just protective."

"Well, yeah, he has a reason to be, and you deserve some protection as long as it isn't overbearing."

"No, nothing like that. He's worried because I haven't slept much."

"No offense, but you can tell. You look wrung out. Any chance you can take a vacation?"

"Not right now, too shorthanded. Hopefully soon, though. Anyway, enough about that. Let's talk about Ethan," she said with a sly smile on her face.

"What about him?" Quinn threw back at her.

"Oh, come on. You aren't fooling anyone. We all see the sparks flying. So, what's going on between the two of you?"

"Nothing, really. We're friends. He's your brother."

With a burst of laughter, the Kara she had been used to since Caleb came into the picture peeked through.

"Well, if you are waiting for me to object, you will be waiting a while. I'm completely okay with the two of you exploring things. You're both big kids and responsible. I'm pretty sure you can explore without jeopardizing your friendship."

Quinn opened her mouth, closed it, opened it again, and nothing came out. The waiter brought their food, and she thanked the food gods for the timing. With single-minded attention, she focused on her food and changed the subject to the center. Which was safe territory for them both. She knew that she hadn't pulled one over on Kara, but a subtle, yet obvious, truce had taken place, and they had both gone to their corners waiting for the next round. After all, neither seemed to want to discuss the two men for the moment. As they walked outside, Quinn took a deep breath and looked over at her best friend.

"I feel like a walk. How about I walk you to your car?"

"But you're parked right there," she said, pointing to Quinn's car in front of the restaurant.

"Just the same, I feel like a walk. It isn't that far."

Before Kara could argue, they headed to her car. Quinn didn't know why, but she had a weird feeling and didn't want to leave Kara alone until she was safely in her car and on her way back to work. Call it a sixth sense, but she felt eyes on her and didn't want Kara in the line of those eyes. She had been through far too much as it was. Judging by the sideways glances Kara was giving her, she hadn't fooled her with the lame excuse of wanting to take a walk. They had rounded the corner to the street where Kara's car was parked when a noise caught her attention, and with barely a second's hesitation, Quinn had thrown Kara to the ground just as a car came careening around the corner and jumped the curb. Quinn jumped out of the way, barely avoiding being hit before the car tore off.

8

"Son. Of. A. Bitch. That hurt," Quinn muttered as she rolled to her knees, swaying with pain from her dive to the pavement.

Her left wrist and shoulder were screaming at her, and her knee was on fire. Suddenly remembering that Kara had been with her, Quinn lurched to her feet and swung around looking for her. About two feet away, Kara was on her knees and climbing to her feet. She was rubbing her hip, and her face was ghostly pale.

"Crap. Kara, are you okay? I'm so sorry for shoving you like that!" There was a ringing in Quinn's ears, and she was aware she was talking louder than she needed to be.

"I'm fine. Just a little dazed. What the hell was that driver thinking coming around the corner that fast? If you didn't have such good reflexes, he or she would have hit us both!" Kara was talking really fast while she continued to rub her hip and looking around.

"I don't think it was an accident." She tried to modulate her voice, finding that where a minute ago, it had been too loud, now it was too calm because she was pretty sure that if it had been only Kara walking, the car wouldn't have tried to hit them.

"You don't think...?" She paused, thought a moment, and then obviously reconsidering, she looked at Quinn with a terrified look on her face. "Quinn, you think that was on purpose, don't you?"

"I don't think it was a coincidence. Gah, my wrist hurts, and my shoulder and knee are on fire."

"We need to get you looked at."

"We both need to get looked at," she said, and she was in serious need of a place to sit. She crumpled to the ground; the pain was suddenly too much.

"You're right. Can you make it to my car? It's right there." Quinn knew the moment that Kara realized she wasn't really in any shape to get up, not yet, at least. She crouched by her and looked her over. "You fractured your wrist, and your shoulder is already swelling. Your knee has a wicked abrasion. Did you hit your head at all?"

"I don't think so." Quinn blinked several times as Kara checked her eyes, saying they were equal and reactive.

"Shit, there is no way we can keep this quiet from Caleb and Ethan." Kara cursed softly.

"I seriously doubt it, not if my wrist is broken. I can pretend you weren't with," Quinn said. But no sooner were the words out of their mouths than they heard sirens coming. They were close and coming fast. Simultaneously, Quinn became aware of a man quickly approaching her. Without thinking, she hopped to her feet, pain be damned, taking a protective stance in front of Kara.

"Are you two ladies all right?" The man was out of breath as he approached, holding a cell phone to his ear. "I saw the whole thing from a block away. I called 911."

Two things came to her mind at the same time: The man in front of her was not a threat, but rather a very elderly man who was being a Good Samaritan followed by, there was no way that Caleb and Ethan weren't going to find out that Kara was with her. In fact, she was sure they already knew. The call had gone over the radio system, and the two men would have figured out that this was right by the restaurant they were going to for lunch. Along with the description that the man in front of her had surely given to the 911 operator, there was just no chance they hadn't put it together or at least weren't going to check it out to make certain.

"Damnation!" Quinn bit out and judging by the look on Kara's face, she had deduced the same thing. "Thank you for coming to our aid, but we're fine. She's a doctor, and we're going to just head on over to her work and get checked out."

"Young lady, that car tried to run you down. I saw the whole thing, that wasn't an accident. Not by a long shot." He paused. "What? Yes, they are both responsive. The blonde says the brunette is a doctor."

Hellfire, the good Samaritan definitely had given them a description. The operator on the phone certainly wouldn't have given out a description over the radio, though. Right? The sirens were close. Within a few seconds, she saw the ambulance coming down the road looking for them. Mr. Samaritan stood on the road and waved it down. Good grief, could the guy be any more helpful?

"Yes, they're here now. Yes. All right, thank you for responding so quickly."

"Thank you, Mr. Samaritan—I mean, what was your name?" Quinn managed to ask, tripping over the words as she saw the unmarked squad car that was most definitely familiar to her pull up along with another marked car.

As it was, Quinn was going to have to explain this to the first responders. She really didn't want to have to tell Caleb and Ethan that she had let her guard down with the most important woman in both their lives and almost got said woman killed. Drawing in a breath and sucking it up, she squared her shoulders and waited for the barrage of questions that were going to be aimed at her.

"Samuel Cumbers."

"Excuse me?" Quinn asked, distracted by the two exquisite displays of male testosterone getting out of the car in front of her. One zeroed in on Kara and the other on her. Gulp. Clearly, Ethan had been tasked with reprimanding Quinn.

"My name. It's Samuel Cumbers."

"Yes, yes. Of course. Thank you, Mr. Cumbers for coming to our aid," she babbled while shaking his hand, but her eyes never left Ethan's.

Except Ethan didn't look mad; neither did Caleb. Both men looked terrified. Of course, that made sense. Kara was their sister and wife, respectively. The call on the radio must have been horrifying and then to see that it was her and not some other woman must have been a terrible shock.

"Listen, Ethan, let me explain–" Her words were cut off when he roughly pulled her into his arms. She sucked in air as excruciating pain engulfed her, but she was overwhelmingly relieved that he wasn't yelling at her. Suddenly, he released her, and she almost toppled over.

"Shit, Quinn, I shouldn't have grabbed you like that. Can we get that medic over here?" he barked over his shoulder. With his shouted order, one medic ran to Kara and one to her.

"I'm fine. Kara checked me over. No worries."

"The hell you are. You obviously have a fractured wrist, judging by the angle of your arm. Not to mention the bloody knee you're sporting." He paused and looked at Caleb who was tending to Kara, and Quinn was shocked at how scared he looked. As bad as he had when Kara had been kidnapped. "How's she doing, bro?"

Caleb didn't seem to hear him; he was in a war of words with Kara. Words she was only catching parts of, but she definitely did not imagine one word that he said over and over. Baby. Sweet mother of God! It all made sense. The tired, drawn look, and how neither were really part of the conversation that morning.

"Wait, what?" Ethan said, obviously hearing what she had heard. "What baby?"

Kara's head snapped toward Ethan and her, then she whispered something under her breath that sounded like an f-bomb.

"Kara? Caleb?" Quinn asked, looking bewildered.

Ethan didn't know what to do. The person who he had cherished from the moment she had been brought home as a squealing baby was nearly struck down by a car, and apparently, she was pregnant. The woman who had become the center of his universe, whether she knew it or not, was standing shaking like a leaf, barely able to hold herself up and quite nearly tipping over, and now she looked even worse—the blood draining from her face.

"Well, we, um…we weren't ready to say anything," Kara said, looking pointedly at Caleb.

"You peed on four sticks. I need your cute butt in the ambulance, and I want you completely looked over. You and the baby."

Ethan and Quinn had moved a step closer and were completely focused on the conversation that had been happening in tandem to their own. Except Ethan had only thought Quinn had taken a step closer with him. In reality, she hadn't. Out of the corner of his eye, he saw her swaying and was reaching for her, as the medic that had stood to the side when the drama started to play out rushed forward. Ethan was faster and had his arm around her in a nanosecond.

"Baby? I almost got you and your…your baby killed?"

Without another word, Quinn slumped against him, the shock of the moment had hit her like a ton of bricks and, alarmingly, she began to cry. Delicate tears slid down her face. When Ethan or Kara cried, they were ugly criers. But Quinn was just gorgeous and heartbreaking. He had never seen her show an iota of weakness. Seeing it now gutted him. With an arm around her waist and her body cradled to his, he gently helped her to sit on the stretcher that the medic had brought over. Both women needed to be looked over, but from first blush, it appeared that Quinn was the more urgent of the two. However, Kara being pregnant was a game changer. With her being thrown to the ground by Quinn, according to the radio chatter, she could have harmed the baby. But that wasn't Quinn's fault. In fact, Quinn had probably saved both of them from serious injury or worse.

"Quinn, there's nothing you could have done to avoid this."

"We both know that isn't true, Ethan," she said sadly, and he knew she had put together what he had, that this wasn't an accident. That she had been targeted for helping rescue Becky Plummer.

"You're not responsible. Right now, I need you to go to the hospital. Without an argument." He was quick to add the last sentence when she opened her mouth to protest. Then he stood from the crouch he had been in and walked toward Caleb, who was hovering over Kara as she was arguing about getting in the ambulance.

"Ma'am, Dr. Montgomery, I need you to get in the ambulance so we can have you and the baby looked at properly. I'm aware that you appear to only have minor injuries, but we both know that with the fall to the pavement, you need to be looked at."

Kara was clearly disgusted. While she was a phenomenal physician, she was a horrible patient, but finally, she listened to reason and grumpily allowed the medic to take her vitals. Ethan took the opportunity to talk to Caleb.

"You got her, right?" Ethan didn't even flinch when Caleb sent him a look that could have killed a lesser person.

"The fuck? Of course—she's my wife." On the last word, Caleb's voice cracked. "And she's carrying our child."

Ethan looked away when he saw the moisture pool in Caleb's eyes. Not because he thought less of him, but because he knew that he was close to falling apart himself.

"Listen, we both know this wasn't an accident. I want to go with Quinn in the ambulance. She's pretty banged up and really upset. She's blaming herself." That revelation got Caleb's attention. He apparently hadn't heard her declaration about nearly getting them killed. "But I know I'm not going to get you to separate from Kara."

"Not a chance," Caleb ground out between his teeth.

"Ease up buddy; you know how Kara gets. You're going to piss her off, and you won't get lucky for a month." Caleb smiled at that thought.

"Nah, I'm irresistible."

"Whatever you think, bro. Anyway, I think that I should go with Quinn in the ambulance and that leaves our car here. I know that you're not leaving her side."

"We established that. What's your point?"

"After the medic checks her vitals, I think you should take her in the squad to the hospital." Ethan saw Caleb's hackles come up. "Hear me out. She can refuse an ambulance ride, and judging by the stubborn set of her chin, she's about to do just that. She knows as a doctor what to worry about. The hospital is only a short distance away. Knowing Kara, she picked this restaurant because it's close to the hospital. With lights and siren, you can get her there in less than a minute. Same as us. And she'll think that you're letting her win."

Caleb thought it over for a second while watching Kara get checked over and then nodded his head.

"Fine. I know you're right. I'm just—"

"Terrified, I get it, I do. If anyone understands, it's me. Granted, the whole baby thing is a new development. But I know how it is to be consumed by fear for someone you love."

"I know you do. All right. Thank you. I needed to hear it."

Ethan patted him on the shoulder, but before he turned to go back to Quinn, he looked at Caleb and smirked.

"So, I'm going to be an uncle, huh?"

"Yeah, man. How do you feel about that?"

"It's freaking crazy, wild and wonderful. You?"

"Same."

"Kara?"

"Complicated," he said and walked away.

Ethan didn't know how to take that statement. He was going to get to the bottom of it, and soon, but not until he knew that Quinn was okay. Kara was in good, capable hands. Caleb would do anything for her. Quinn didn't have anyone like that in her life. Not that he knew of, but he fully intended on being that man for her. He turned and looked at her slight figure on the stretcher. She was scowling at the medic while blinking away tears. Not from pain, but from feeling like she let her friend down. Ethan needed to get that thought out of her head. If anyone was forgiving about something like this, it was Kara. She knew that Quinn didn't do anything wrong. In fact, Kara was also in on the rescue, so she may have been a target, as well.

"I told you, I'm fine. I don't need to be strapped to this blasted thing," she said, sniffing.

"Ma'am, there is no way that your arm is not broken in at least one spot, probably two. Your shoulder took a beating, too, it may be dislocated, I can't be sure. As for the knee, that's going to need to be cleaned up. Are you up to date on your tetanus?"

Quinn stuck her tongue out at the medic's head, which was down, busy applying a bandage to staunch the bleeding on his uncooperative patient's knee. Ethan couldn't help but smile at that display of sauciness. That was the Quinn he was used to. Assertive. Reliable. Confident. Strong. Not the tiny woman crying on the stretcher. As if she could hear his thoughts or sense him near, her head snapped toward him and her eyes locked with his.

"Can you tell this blowhard that I'm fine and I can ride with you to the hospital?"

"Absolutely not. Sorry—tough as you might be, you get the full ride to the hospital. Kara is going to ride with Caleb in the squad. Not enough room in the ambulance for all of us."

"All of us?"

"Caleb isn't going to let Kara out of his sight, and I'm not letting you out of mine. We compromised," he said with a shrug.

"Compromised? Did you think to ask the poor, weak little ladies their opinion?"

"No need to." The medic, he thought his name was Eric, smirked while tending to her. "You *are* getting a ride in the ambulance; I'm going with you and getting your statement. The patrol officers who responded are going to stay and secure the scene while another set of detectives and crime scene technicians come in to investigate."

"You mean you aren't going to investigate?" she asked, shocked. He couldn't help but feel good that she wanted him to do the investigation.

"We can't. We're connected to you both. Captain wouldn't allow it. Kara is going to ride with Caleb, as I just discussed with him. The squad has sirens. The medic is checking her out, assessing her, and monitoring her vitals. Once they're done, she'll get a chariot ride, too, but she doesn't need her arm stabilized."

"She's pregnant!"

"True, and my niece or nephew will get a full checkup, as well. But she's not the one who is wobbling on their feet and in need of the stretcher. Also, judging by the look she just sent your way, she would prefer that you not yell that across the city." Quinn looked properly chastised and quickly looked over to see Kara glaring at her.

"I guess she'd prefer to tell people they're expecting versus my shouting it out, huh?"

"Looks that way. So, are you going to be a good patient or the lousy one you're being right now?"

"Oh, stuff it. Fine."

"What was that?"

"Fine, I will go in the ambulance."

"Good. We just about set here?"

"Yes, sir. All set and it looks like your friend is on her way, as well."

They both looked up to see Kara shaking off Caleb's helping hands as she climbed into the squad car. Ethan chuckled. Stubborn. Always and forever. Ever since she was a little girl, especially when she was a little girl, when she was trying to please their parents she was still stubborn, only they had almost beaten her down and beaten it out of her. They hadn't won though, and that's what saved her, because Kara was a survivor. The thought made Ethan sober, suddenly he suspected he knew why Kara's feelings were complicated about the baby.

9

Once Quinn accepted the fact that she was going to be forced to go the hospital and was set on the stretcher, the pain and severity of what had happened hit her. Not only did she almost lose one of the only people she could honestly call a friend, but she was responsible. Whether Ethan wanted to believe it or not. The thought that this was all her fault was almost too much. Even though Quinn knew that she wasn't the one driving the car, she still felt responsible, but she also knew she would help Becky again. Just like Kara would help her with Becky again. It was in their nature to help people, maybe because of what had happened to them or maybe because they were just built that way. Quinn thought it was a little of both.

The worst part of the whole situation was letting Ethan, of all people, see her cry. Quinn knew she was a proud person, one who prided herself on being strong, never letting emotion get the better of her. But this had just been too much, and she'd crumbled. Not only that, but the pain had set in, and she knew that she needed medical attention, but that whole pride thing got in the way again.

Should she be embarrassed that Ethan wanted to go with her or should she be furious? Right now, all she could drudge up was happiness that he was willing to ride with her. Not just happiness, but an all-encompassing feeling of finally belonging somewhere. That her friends cared enough to take care of her. Providing that was why Ethan had said he was riding with her, it could have been out of work duty. Then again, the way he looked at her like she was the only thing in his orbit made her think otherwise and it curled her toes and made butterflies flutter in her stomach.

"All right, all set. It'll probably hurt when we move the stretcher. The jostling will hurt all those parts you didn't know were bruised from where the container flew into you," the EMT told her.

What container? Confused, she looked around and saw a garbage can laying on the ground. It had a dent in it and was laying by a small smear of blood, probably from her knee. That had hit her? No way. She'd have known that, right?

"That didn't hit me."

"Yes, it did."

Quinn turned her head and saw Samuel Cumbers still standing there, holding his hat and twisting it in both hands. For the first time, Quinn really focused on the frail elderly man whose face looked so ashen. He had to have been terrified, and he had come to their aid. She had thanked him, right? Of course, she had, but it wasn't enough. The man deserved better than what she had given him for a thank you.

"You're still here! I mean, I thought you left. I-I didn't thank you enough for helping my friend and me." His face blushed slightly, and he smiled shyly.

"Young lady, there is no need to thank me. I'm just happy I could be of service to you and even happier to see you listen to that fine young man about going to the hospital." Mr. Cumbers nodded toward Ethan who was talking to a patrol officer who had sectioned off the street, so they could investigate the accident. "You have yourself a fine one there."

"What?" she asked, confused, and then realized what he meant. Flushing, she quickly tried to set him straight. "Oh, he's just a friend. The brother of the other girl who was hurt."

"If you say so, young lady, if you say so. Seems to me, though, that he has deeper feelings than friendship for you. You better get going to the hospital and get yourself properly looked at. No offense, sir."

"None taken," the EMT said, smiling, and then he began to move her stretcher toward the ambulance.

In the blink of an eye, Ethan was at her side. He climbed into the ambulance after the EMT situated her inside. Eric the EMT hadn't lied—it hurt everywhere when the stretcher was jarred. Breathing deeply, she gritted her teeth through the pain. At least it was her left side that was the most damaged. It would be a real treat to take care of herself with a broken right hand. As much as she hated to admit it, she knew they were right. Her wrist was definitely broken. As if an ER doctor, detective, and EMT would be wrong on that account? A warm hand brushed her face, and she was startled to see Ethan leaning toward her looking worried.

"You okay? You got really white there."

"Just trying to breathe through the pain. No more being a tough girl because, even if I jumped out of the way, it feels like that car hit me."

"Well, the garbage can did hit you. It hit you pretty hard judging by what the witness told us."

They rode the rest of the way to the hospital in silence, Ethan watching her intently the whole way. A couple times he reached for her hand and then pulled away when he noticed the brace on her arm. Once at the hospital, she was wheeled into a room and assumed he was going to check on Kara, but she was surprised once again when he followed her into the room she had been moved to.

"You can go check on Kara."

"She has Caleb with her, and right now is a sensitive time while they check on the baby."

"Still, I don't need a babysitter, and I'll have to get an x-ray."

"Not going anywhere." He sat in a chair in the room and placed his left ankle on his right knee. "There is nowhere I would rather be right now."

She blushed. What was wrong with her? Quinn Sanders did not blush, did not cry, did not show any emotion, and yet that's all she'd been doing all day long. She jumped when a doctor—a very attractive doctor—entered the room with a couple of younger people following her. They must be the interns Kara had been talking about.

"Hello, Ms. Sanders, I'm Dr. Aderhold. I have two interns with me today if that is all right with you?"

"That's fine." She wondered what she would do if she said no. She almost laughed at the thought.

"Wonderful. Now, you were nearly hit by a car?"

"Correct. Well, I don't know how close it was. I jumped out of the way and landed wrong on my left arm and knee."

"The EMT gave us the rundown. So, you know we'll be sending you for x-rays on that arm. But I would also like to do a CAT scan to rule out any other injuries. It's going to be a little bit if you need to be somewhere, Detective Vanderbilt."

"I'm good. I'll wait here. I can catch up with some gossip while I wait," he said, flashing a smile at her.

"Suit yourself." She shrugged and turned her attention to Quinn. "Let's take a look at your knee. The EMT didn't think you would need stitches." She put on some gloves and gingerly took off the bandage. Gently, she examined the cut. "Doesn't look too bad, a deep cleaning should be good enough. Not our number one concern, though. I want to make sure you didn't suffer a head injury."

"I didn't. I landed on my left side."

"All the same, I still want to rule it out. It would be negligent of me if I didn't. They'll be down shortly to take you up for the x-ray and scan. Make yourself comfortable, detective."

Dr. Aderhold wasn't kidding when she said they were going to be there a while. It hadn't taken long for Quinn to be wheeled back into the room, but they were still waiting for the results of the tests and, admittedly, Ethan was getting a little stir crazy. He didn't mind sitting in the room and waiting. What he minded was not knowing if Quinn had any other injuries or how Kara was doing. A quiet knock sounded on the outside of the room, and as if conjured from his very mind, Kara walked in with Caleb following close behind her.

"How's the patient?" she asked quietly while glancing at Quinn.

"Out. They gave her some pain medication in an IV to help with her pain level."

She had finally fallen asleep about fifteen minutes ago, and he had been quietly playing on his phone and silently cursing the doctor for not coming back to give him an update. It crushed him to see her in that hospital bed. She looked so tiny and fragile. Kara was a petite girl, but Quinn was smaller in stature by an inch. Yet both girls could kick butt and take names later. Which, if he was honest, was a huge turn on for him.

"That's good. They're kind of slammed right now, and I'm sorry it's taking so long, but another trauma patient just came in. It shouldn't be much longer. I've been ordered to go home, so I can't help right now," she said, glaring at Caleb. It was clear to him who had ordered her to go home. Since she was the attending doctor in the ER, no one could really send her home, unless it came from above her.

"How's everything with you?" he asked hesitantly.

"Good. We got to see the little one and hear the heartbeat. Everything is as it should be," she said, smiling, but the smile didn't reach her eyes.

"Kara, I'm only going to tell you this once. So, I need you to listen very closely. Are you listening?" he asked. Out of the corner of his eye, he saw Caleb grimace and lean his hip on the counter.

"Save it, Ethan. I don't want to hear a lecture."

"I'm not lecturing you. But I'm going to tell you something important. You and I are not our parents. We never have been, and we never will be. This baby is going to be beyond loved by you, Caleb, me, and everyone else. There is not a doubt in my mind that you will be a phenomenal mother and that someday I will be an awesome dad." And darn it if his voice didn't catch.

"You don't know that, Ethan," Kara said, and damn it, she was blinking back tears. Caleb moved to go to her side, but Ethan lifted his hand to stop him.

"I do know that."

"How can you?"

"First, you have a mother you never knew—who loved you. We figured out she wanted you back, and that's why Constance killed her. There was no reason to kill her because simply taking you from her was torturing her. We all know Constance was sadistic. But your mother deciding she wanted you back wasn't acceptable. How would the Vanderbilts explain a child that wasn't completely theirs? You came from a kind woman, not that monster. Second, I see you. I see you with the kids at the center, with the patients you help at the free clinic you established there. I see you with Ava, Alex, and Arabella. I see you. You aren't fooling me or anyone else. You will be an amazing mother because you are an amazing aunt and person."

"I second that," came a whispered reply from the hospital bed. Apparently, Quinn hadn't been sleeping after all. "You're a damn fool if you don't already know that. Because of your parents, because of the way they were and what you fought to become, you will be the best mother out there. Now go home and get some rest, but can you first tell that doctor who looks like a model to cast my arm or whatever, so I can go home?" Kara giggled at the last comment and walked over to the bed, kissing Quinn on the forehead.

"How are you feeling, tough one?"

"Like I got hit by a car. Imagine if it hadn't missed us." The joke fell a bit flat, and the already sober room became even more so.

"I can take a look at your chart quick." When Caleb opened his mouth to protest, she waved him off. "I'll look at her chart and see the results to help them out, then I will go home, and you can wait on me hand and foot if that's what you so choose. Deal?"

Everyone in the room knew that she wasn't really giving him the option to say no. Like a good boy, Caleb nodded his head yes and leaned back on the counter to wait. Kara left and returned a few minutes later.

"Sounds like the CAT scan came back good. You have a dislocated shoulder and what we call a Galeazzi fracture, which is a fracture of the radius accompanied by a dislocated radioulnar joint. Common with a fall. Unfortunately, it means you'll need surgery. Depending on when they can get you in and how you do afterward, you may be able to go home without an overnight stay. But I'm not promising that."

"Any chance you can call in some favors and have me out sooner?" Quinn asked. Ethan could tell she was fighting sleep.

"I'll see what I can find out about available surgeons and how long an operating room will take. Like I said, they have their hands full down here. It might be a bit before they can get you in. I would just prepare yourself for an overnight visit." Ethan could see panic fill Quinn's drug hazed eyes, and the sleepy expression started to fade.

"I can't stay overnight."

"You can if you have to. I know better than anyone the feeling associated with staying in a hospital," Kara said, her voice soothing.

"And yet you became a doctor," Quinn said, and as if that was enough, the panic seemed to subside a bit.

"I'll ask around, report back to you, and then," she said, looking at Caleb, who had sighed quietly, "I will let my impatient husband take me home. Where he is going to make me my favorite supper and rub my feet." She smiled wickedly at him.

"Deal." His voice was grumpy, but the look on his face was anything but. Kara left the room again and came back a few minutes later.

"Looks like the surgery will be a little later. They're going to get you prepped, Dr. Vandehei is available to do the surgery, but they want to wait a little bit since you ate not that long ago. It isn't ideal to do surgery after eating. At least you've been waiting down here a while, so it really shouldn't be too much longer, but since your injury isn't life threatening, they weren't going to rush you into surgery."

"Thank you," Quinn whispered.

"I didn't do much, just called to ask how long it was going to be. They were already prepping everything. I would love to stick around—"

"Not going to happen." Caleb cut her off when her searching eyes reached his. "No offense, Quinn."

"None taken. Take her home, even if you have to drag her out kicking and screaming. I'll be fine. I'll see all of you later."

Ethan didn't budge. He knew when he was being dismissed, but he was choosing to pretend he didn't notice. He calmly picked up a magazine and flipped through the pages. After Caleb and Kara left, Quinn looked at him with a look of irritation, and if he wasn't mistaken, relief on her face.

"You better hurry up; they aren't going to wait for you."

"No worries. I wasn't going anywhere anyway."

"You don't have to stay. I mean, if they leave, you won't have a car."

"Caleb drove Kara here this morning. Their car is in the hospital parking lot. He left the keys to the squad on the counter over there. I'm all set."

"Don't you have plans?"

"Yep."

"Then you better get to them."

"I am."

"What?"

"My plan is to sit here until they come down to get you. Once they get you, I will move into the waiting room for surgery. Once you're out of surgery, I'll find out if you're going home or staying here."

"And then what?"

Ethan shrugged, flipped through a few more pages.

"Ethan?"

"If you have to stay, I'll stay here, maybe hold your hand. Kind of like you did for me. When you get to go home, I'll drive you there."

"You can't be serious. There is no way I'm allowing you to sit here all night. It's ridiculous of you to even think I would allow that. If I have to stay the night, I can get Taylor or someone else to drive me to my car in the morning."

"Not happening."

"And why not? I'm sure you have somewhere better to be."

"You're not getting rid of me."

"Why are you being so heavy-handed?"

"I'm not being heavy-handed. I'm looking after you. Taylor is gone for a few days, which, if you weren't in excruciating pain and on narcotics, you would have remembered. Also, you won't be able to drive because you'll be on the same narcotics, and you'll not be permitted to drive yourself home. I assume you will need a prescription to be picked up, so there is that, as well. And the matter of your car."

"What's wrong with my car?" Her voice had raised in pitch and Ethan almost felt bad that he was being so overbearing. He knew it, she knew it, but for some reason, he couldn't stop himself. He needed—no, he wanted—to protect her. To take care of her like she needed to be. He had waited patiently for months, and now he just wanted to be part of her world, not sidelined as a friend.

"Nothing is wrong with your car. I had an officer stop and get your keys while you were getting checked out. He drove it home. Therefore, your car is safely at your house, and I will take you to it and your car when you are released."

With that statement, he leaned back in his seat, propped his ankle over his knee again and began flipping through the magazine he had looked through, from cover to cover, half a dozen times already.

10

Quinn had never had surgery. That didn't mean she had never had a broken bone. On the contrary, she'd had her share of injuries in her life. Even so, she had never required surgery. There was a doctor who made house visits all those years ago. He came in, made sure she wouldn't die from her latest lesson in life, and then he would leave. Amazingly enough, nothing had ever been life-threatening. Then again, her abuser knew how to hide the marks, how to make the most of the injuries without seriously harming her.

The thought of trusting someone to do surgery on her made her want to jump out of her skin. To be put under general anesthesia and trust a doctor to take care of her and not do any harm to her was exceptionally hard for her to allow. It wasn't long until she started to feel herself panic, and her breathing came in shallow gasps.

"Hey, are you okay?" Someone was talking to her.

No, not just someone, but Ethan. Ethan's voice came through the haze of her panic. An anchor, someone she knew and trusted, leading her home. Taking a deep breath through her nose, she held it like she had read about and taught herself to do. In through the nose, out through her mouth. Over and over until she felt better.

"Quinn?" Ethan had sat gingerly on her bed in the ER, and she opened her eyes and looked up at him.

"I'm fine. Just got a little panicky about having surgery. I've never had surgery. It's more nerve-wracking than I thought it would be."

"Dr. Vandehei is pretty awesome."

"You know him?" she asked and then winced at the stupid comment. Of course, he knew him. He probably knew most, if not all, of the doctors at the hospital.

"Not really. I mean, I guess I know him. He's the one who performed the surgery on me when I was in the car accident."

The idea that the doctor who saved Ethan would be performing the surgery on her was more reassuring than just about anything could be at that moment. Which was a good thing, because a few moments later they came to get her prepped for surgery. Ethan squeezed her hand, the hand she didn't realize he had been holding. She looked up and smiled at him.

"I'll be waiting when you get out."

Then he stood up and moved out of the way so they could move her bed out of the room and into the elevator. She didn't know what to expect and was trying to go with the flow of things. They had stitched up her knee before she'd fallen asleep. Whatever they had given her made her feel out of it, and she didn't like the feeling, but it was better than the terrible pain in her arm. After all the waiting around, when she wanted things to slow down, they didn't, and before she knew it, they were wheeling her into the operating room, and she was being talked to by a doctor with a soothing voice before she was out for the count.

Groggy, she woke to the sound of a woman's voice telling her that she had something for her to chew on once she woke up enough, and then she fell back under, only to open her eyes a few moments later to the same soft voice.

"Well, there you are. It took a bit to get you to wake up…" Quinn blinked long and slow and tried to focus on her words. "…adverse reaction to the anesthetic…"

"How long?"

"The surgery went well, in and out in no time. Getting you to stay with me has taken a lot longer, but I see you're with me now. The doctor will pop in and talk to you about it. They will make a notation in your file about your reaction. You'll want to let any medical professional know about it."

Quinn hoped they'd go over this with her when she was more coherent. It was really hard to follow what the woman was telling her. She could hear the concern in her voice and knew that she should feel anxious about it but was still too lethargic to care at all. Bit by bit her head cleared, and she started to feel more focused. It must have become apparent to the woman who was still talking to her in that soft voice because she placed a cracker in her hand and asked her to take a couple small bites. Her mouth was so dry, like the Sahara Desert had invaded her mouth. She could hardly find any saliva to swallow, but she listened anyway and took a tiny bite.

"I know it seems strange to give you a cracker, but it's easier on the stomach after surgery. That young man is going to be so relieved that you're awake." Young man? Obviously, she must be talking about Ethan. "He was ready to tear down the walls to get to you. We're going to get you in a room and then he can come see you."

"I can't go home?"

"Afraid not, honey. It's pretty late. They weren't sure about letting you go home to begin with, but with you struggling with the anesthesia, they'll want to keep you for observation. It would be irresponsible to send you home. My understanding is your young man has already stated he won't be leaving. Such a sweet man."

"He's not my young man."

"Hm, seems he wouldn't mind the job. I think I would take him up on the offer, if I were you."

"He should go home."

"Nonsense. He had a scare, what with it taking so long for you to wake up." As if sensing she'd said too much, the woman became quiet.

"That bad, huh?" Quinn asked. "I have to admit, it is kind of scary."

"I imagine it is. All right, how are you feeling? I think we're all set to move you into your room. How does that sound?"

"Since I don't have a choice, it sounds just lovely."

The kind woman, who looked just like a gentle grandmother, had the decency to ignore the sarcasm in her voice. Granted, it was pretty pathetic, since she was still out of it. While she chewed slowly on her cracker, she felt the bed start to move, and the feeling was a little disconcerting. She closed her eyes tight and chewed her cracker. It was still hard to swallow; her throat was so dry.

"We'll get you some water once you're in your room. But you can only have some small sips." She must have looked confused because she continued. "You said water."

Quinn hadn't realized she had mumbled the word, but obviously, she had. Once she was in her room, all she could think about was the promised water, and as if a magic being had conjured it, the top of the bed was lifting, and a cup was in the lovely silver-haired lady's hands, straw bent over, calling to her. After a couple of small sips, she smiled and sighed.

"Thank you, so much…"

"Jackie, you can call me Jackie, and there is no need to thank me. I'm going to leave this water at the bedside. A nurse should be in shortly, but I imagine that young man will be here before then."

As if on cue, there was a quiet shuffling noise and then a whispered conversation, two male voices that appeared to be somewhat arguing, until one finally acquiesced. The door that was slightly ajar opened all the way and in entered Ethan. His hair was standing on end and messy, his face drawn and pale, dark rings around his eyes. The whole picture reminded her of the night that she sat with him. He looked the same way when he'd been worried about Kara.

"Oh my God, is Kara okay? The baby?" He stopped, obviously confused by her questions.

"What? No, I mean, as far as I know, they're home and everything is just fine."

"Then why do you look so…so…discombobulated?" she asked.

"Woman, are you serious?" He huffed out a laugh and charged toward the bed. Poor Jackie scooted out of the way at the last second.

Once he was next to the bed, he suddenly stopped and stared down at her, long enough it eventually made her want to squirm.

"What is wrong with you?" She heard Jackie quietly laugh.

"You honestly have no idea what I just went through, do you?"

"Well, I was in surgery, so you're right. I have no idea what is going through your head or what you went through. What happened?"

"What happened? What happened?" he asked while running his hands through his hair, which was obviously why his hair was so disheveled.

Without another word, he plopped down into the chair by the right side of her bed and put his head in his hands. He was trembling, and Quinn was genuinely terrified of the scene unfolding in front of her. What in the world was going on?

"Ethan?"

"You have no idea the thoughts that were running through my head. They weren't telling me anything. They couldn't because of HIPAA. I was going mad not knowing if you were okay." He looked up at her then, his eyes tortured.

"I...I don't know what to say. I'm sorry?" And she knew how dumb that sounded.

"You're sorry? For what? For them not being able to tell me what was going on?"

"I know it sounds stupid; I don't know why I said it. Maybe I should have given them permission to tell you what was going on. But I didn't; for that, I'm sorry."

"You have nothing to be sorry about. I'm going to want to know what the heck happened, though. They were sympathetic, but their hands were tied."

"Well, I'm okay. You worried for nothing." She tried to put a brave smile on her face but seeing him so shaken up had her finally seeing the gravity of the situation for him. "Hey, I'm okay. Thirsty. But otherwise, I'm fine."

He looked at the bedside table and picked up the glass.

"Small sips," Jackie said quietly. "I have to get going, but I see your nurse is here to check you over."

"Thank you, for everything," Quinn said to her as she moved to leave.

"Nothing to thank me for."

After she left, an attractive man entered the room, obviously the nurse that she assumed Ethan had been talking to in the hallway.

"How are you feeling?" he asked.

"Better now, not as groggy."

"I need to check your vitals. Your boyfriend can stay in the room, but I will need access to your right arm since your left one is in a cast."

"Oh! He isn't my boyfriend," she said, flushing.

The nurse said something under his breath that sounded like, *you could have fooled me.* Her mind was racing, putting together the conversation with Jackie and now this comment. Apparently, people thought they were an item—attached and in a relationship. Wouldn't that be something? But it wasn't the case. Not even in the cards. Besides, Ethan only flirted with her. He would never want more than that, would he?

Ethan didn't know what to think of Quinn's hurried response to the nurse's statement. Part of him was thrilled that the nurse thought they were an item, even if it wasn't true. The other part of him, the part that second guessed himself, was hurt that she seemed so adamant about them not being an item. Almost as if she was embarrassed by the idea. Maybe she didn't want the good-looking nurse to think she was attached? It wasn't a proud moment when he discovered how jealous that made him, but it did, and he had never been jealous of another man before.

In the end, it didn't matter if she couldn't think of him that way, or did it? He knew the answer; the answer was that he would be crushed if she didn't want to be with him. Ethan considered himself a strong and confident man, but on this item, he wasn't. Not now that he had finally decided there was someone he wanted to spend his life with, someone that he was excited to see. He had Kara back, firmly back in his life, and she was happy, married, and pregnant. For that, he was grateful. Now he wanted a chance at *his* happy ending. He knew in the back of his head that he had closed himself off from all women because of his sister. It took more than a few sessions with the police psychiatrist to narrow down that he wasn't as happy as he thought and that his happiness was joined to her happiness. The psychiatrist had called it survivor's guilt, that he was holding himself back out of guilt for what Kara had been through and the fear that his being happy would hurt her. It also didn't take long for the same psychiatrist to tell him that bedding every woman with two legs was his way of not focusing on what was missing in his life. Namely, what was missing was a meaningful relationship with a woman that he could love and spend his life with.

Ethan could remember that meeting when the doctor had said she had figured it out. Why he had been so unwilling to be in a personal relationship, why he was very cautious with who he trusted, but when he did, he was all in. When he met Quinn, and they were instantaneously friends, he trusted her completely, but nothing clicked into place until Kara had returned home and that night where Quinn sat with him. Now she was so tied to the present, and he hoped to the future, that he felt like he hadn't taken a deep breath since the moment he had gotten the radio transmission that there was a situation. Then the end of the transmission called out Caleb and Ethan's badge number and told them to check their messages, which was the way that dispatch discreetly let officers know a family member was involved. Now that Quinn was safely out of surgery, the band that had been wound tightly around his chest seemed to loosen by small degrees.

Standing looking out the window in the room, he had been so lost in his thoughts he didn't notice when the nurse had left until he heard the door shut and a soft moan. He swung around to see Quinn grimacing and holding her arm. In two long strides, he was by her side, assessing her or hovering over her. Whichever way you shook it, he was there, ready, and able to do what he could.

"What is it? Are you okay?"

"Yeah, I just bumped my arm on the handrail. As many drugs as I have in me, it still hurt like a son of a gun."

"Do you want me to get him back in here?" His voice sounded nervous even to his own ears.

"No. It's starting to subside a bit. No, actually, that is a complete lie," she said and tried valiantly to smile. "But it doesn't matter. He told me that I can't have any painkillers for a bit. I guess it'll be a long night."

"Is there anything I can do to distract you? Do you want to play cards or watch a movie or something?" he asked, indicating the TV.

"Cards? What, you have a pack of cards in your pocket?" She giggled.

"Well, no, but I'm sure I could find some." He ran his hands through his hair and smiled ruefully. "I guess that was a dumb suggestion, huh?"

"No, it wasn't dumb at all. I would play cards with you if you had a deck in your pocket." Again, that smile flashed across her face, and he realized he would do just about anything to keep it there. "What would we play? Go Fish, Crazy 8, Old Maid?" Immediately, he knew she was picking on him. The little minx still had her humor.

"Not exactly. I was thinking more along the lines of Rummy or Poker."

"Sorry, not in the mood for strip poker." Instantaneously, her cheeks flamed red, and he smiled from ear to ear.

"No?"

"Um…I blame it on the fact that I just came out of surgery. You can't hold anything I say against me."

"What can I hold against you?" he asked, aware his voice had gone husky.

"Well…um, geez, I don't know…"

Hands down, she was the most adorable woman he had ever met. But he would put her out of her misery and give her a few moments to put herself back together.

"I'm going to see what's on the TV. If we can't agree on something, I'll see if I can hunt down some cards."

The awkward silence slowly segued into a friendly banter session over what she was willing to watch and what he was willing to watch. He suspected that she was playing a game with him, that she just wanted to see how far she could go before he would relent. After all, she was the patient, and he was trying to please her. Finally, after the tenth time through all the stations, she suggested House Hunters, which happened to be the first show he suggested, and his suspicions were confirmed that she'd been messing with him when she declared how much she loved that show. After an episode, the food staff dropped off a tray of liquid supper for Quinn to eat, and she looked miserable when she stared at the options. He smiled sympathetically at her.

"I remember that; liquid diet after surgery is the pits. They have their reasons, though."

"Not that I'm a picky eater. But I hate most of the food on this table. If you can call broth, juice, and Jell-O food, that is."

"I hear you. I'm more of a meat and potatoes kind of guy."

"Mmm, steak would be so good right now."

"How do you like your steak done?"

"A little pink is fine. But I'm not embarrassed to be girly and refuse to eat something that has barely been cooked," she said in between sips of broth.

"Ah, the big manly man loves red, juicy steak," he said, pretending to pound his chest. "But in all honesty, I prefer it a little more done myself."

"You have to be starving. Or did you eat when I was in surgery?"

"No, I didn't. I waited to hear about you. But I'm fine. I miss meals often when I'm on the job. Not that this is a job, but you know what I mean, right? I can go a long time without eating…" He stopped talking when he saw the big smile cross her face, the same one that had knocked him off his feet that morning. Had it only been that morning?

"Point for me."

"Huh?"

"You got me flustered earlier, point for you. Now it was your turn to be flustered; point for me."

"I didn't know we were keeping score."

"Oh, we are definitely keeping score."

11

Quinn was overwhelmed by Ethan's attention to her every need. If she was thirsty, he brought her water; if she was uncomfortable, he tried to help make her more comfortable. Too bright in the room, he'd turn off the lights. The TV too loud, he'd turn down the volume. She didn't care what they watched on the TV. She just enjoyed messing with him over what to watch, mainly to see how far she could push him before he would throw his hands up and say, *forget it*. But he didn't say forget it or anything else. In fact, he sat quietly doing her bidding, even if she didn't ask, and he held her hand when she sucked in a breath because she bumped her hand again. Hell fire, but it hurt. Yet, she had never been this happy in her adult life. Even in pain, this was the best night of her life for as long as she could remember, and it got better when the nurse reappeared and said she could finally have some painkillers.

Once they were alone again, the mood in the room seemed slightly different—almost sad for some reason—and she couldn't quite put her finger on it. It took her a moment as the painkillers slowly started to work, but she finally figured it out. She had been having so much fun with Ethan, and she hadn't allowed herself to have fun in a long time, if ever, and the nurse coming in had dampened that fun. The pause had effectively allowed the events of the day to slowly trickle back into her mind, and worry had lodged itself next to her heart. She would be a liar if she said she wasn't scared because she was; but she was also a strong woman who had overcome a lot to get where she was, and nothing would take that away.

"What's wrong?" Ethan asked quietly.

"Nothing."

"Liar. If I had to guess, I'd say the day finally caught up with you, right?"

"Yeah." She sighed.

"You know, I've been told that I'm a good listener. Go ahead and talk, and I'll listen." She only hesitated for a moment before spilling all of what she was thinking.

"It isn't a coincidence, the near hit-and-run. They might not have meant to hit us, but they definitely wanted to scare us. The timing is too coincidental, and I don't think they meant to kill me, but they definitely wanted me hurt and scared."

"I'm not going to lie, I think you're right. Only I think they weren't trying to scare you. Whoever is behind all this doesn't mess around and doesn't leave loose ends."

"You think they meant to kill me?" She was proud that she managed to say that without choking on the words. "The thing is, it's a ridiculous waste of energy. I mean, I don't know anything that can take them down."

"The thing is, they don't know that."

"I guess. I mean, Becky did give you a starting point this morning. At least we know where you can start looking." Quinn had been playing with the blanket on the bed and looked up when Ethan didn't say anything. Instantly, the hair on her arms stood up at the look on his face. "What? Just say it; don't hold back to protect me. You found something out, didn't you?"

"Not really. It's what we didn't find." He looked at her with a sober expression on his face.

"Just say it. I would rather know everything, so I know what I'm up against and can prepare myself for whatever may come."

"First, I don't like the sound of that. Second, I will tell you what I know. I just, crap…" He ran his hands through his hair again. "I hate to dump this on you now when you need rest."

"Let me decide if I need rest or not, okay? I've been taking care of myself for a long time."

"Right, well it doesn't hurt to let someone take care of you once in a while." He paused, but before she could say a word, he continued. "We drove by the house that Becky told us about—"

She cut in. "You just drove by? Why didn't you stop and ask questions?"

"We would have if there was a house left to visit."

"What? What do you mean?"

"The house is gone. It wasn't until we drove to the house that I remembered why the address sounded familiar. The house had been burned down, and there's an ongoing arson case. The house was demoed not long after they gathered all the evidence."

"What did the investigation find?"

"It was definitely arson, but they knew that without the investigation, but you can't just run a case on conjecture. They had to follow through with all the bells and whistles even though they knew what they'd find."

"Why were they so certain?" she asked. Something in the back of her head was struggling to break through like she'd heard a similar story recently.

"There were a half-dozen bodies found inside the home when the flames were extinguished. They hadn't died from the fire; they were all executed with a bullet to the head."

She sucked in a breath, and as hard as she tried to hide her reaction, she couldn't, because she had figured out why the story sounded familiar. There was no way anyone within the state of Wisconsin could have missed that case. It wasn't every day a house burned down taking six lives, and it was even less likely that all of the people inside would be victims of execution. All of the victims had been young, late teens, and all had been women. She wanted to cry, wanted to scream, but she wouldn't. She had already cried once that day out of fear and guilt over nearly getting Kara killed. And even though she wanted to scream and cry over the realization of what Becky had led them to, she couldn't. She needed to keep a level head.

"I remember that fire; I remember it well. Those kids—I refuse to call them adults even if they were 18—had all wandered through the center at one time or another. We tried to help each of them, but we weren't able to stop them from the path they were going down. Becky's friend was probably one of them. Of course, we have no way of knowing unless we show her pictures of the kids that died in that fire. She was being held in a dungeon when that fire happened. Someone needs to tell her. I want to be there for her when she finds out."

"I think you're right that there's a good chance that her friend was one of the victims. We were able to identify them all, which you know. We can show her the pictures of them and ask her if any are her friend, but it really won't help the case. That's why they were killed. Cutting ties in the easiest way they know."

Quinn nodded, suddenly beyond tired as the painkillers coupled with the day she had sapped the last energy from her. With a huge yawn, she looked at him, and without thinking about it or overanalyzing what she was about to do and say, she reached for his hand, twined her fingers with his and squeezed.

"Thank you."

"For what?"

"For staying here all day with me, for keeping my mind busy so I wouldn't think of the pain or meltdown from the day, and most of all, thank you for telling me the truth about what you found out. I appreciate that honesty." She released his hand and reached for the controller to call in a nurse.

After the nurse appeared, she asked if there was any way they could get a cot for Ethan to sleep on. The nurse smiled and said he would be right back. He returned a couple minutes later with a cot and asked her if she needed anything else. She said nothing other than some sleep, and he left.

"I didn't need a cot."

"You need some sleep, too."

"I can sleep in the chair. I don't mind."

"I do, go lie down. I'm beat, and I promise I'm going to close my eyes and sleep. But do you mind if I keep the TV on for some background noise? I know they're really quiet out there, but even the slightest noise might send me through the roof, which would definitely hurt."

"I don't mind the white noise. Get some sleep," he said.

"Yes, sir." Her words were soft and slurred as she closed her eyes and sleep claimed her.

Ethan woke with a start and was momentarily confused about his surroundings until he remembered that he had stayed at the hospital with Quinn—the tough, funny, and smart woman that he wanted to take on a proper date. Only the evening was nearly perfect, other than the whole hospital room, broken bone, surgery, and narcotics thing, but if you took all those things out of the equation, it was pretty magical. He sat up cautiously so as not to wake her.

"About time you woke up," came a sleepy sounding voice.

"What are you doing up?"

"They came in to poke and prod me a few minutes ago. When they left, you woke up. Some cop you are sleeping through an intruder like that," she said jokingly. "You must have been beat."

"Yeah, I guess I was. I've been working a lot of long days recently. Crime doesn't rest and all that good stuff."

"You shouldn't work so hard," she said.

"Look who's talking," he said back.

"I guess you're right. But the center is kind of what I have going for me, and I enjoy what I do for a career. I don't even think of it as work because for me, it isn't work. But, yes, I do spend too much time there. I know that just like you know you spend too much time at work."

"Like you said, it is kind of what I have going for me."

"Riiight," she said, drawing out the word.

"What's that supposed to mean?" he asked, his hackles rising.

"Nothing. I just find it hard to believe that the amazingly sexy Ethan Vanderbilt has no social life." One, two, three, and there was the flush he had come to expect when she said something she didn't mean to say.

"You think I'm sexy?" His smile was devilish. "Well, believe it. I work too much to devote a lot of time to dating, and I don't want to date just anyone anymore. I see how happy Kara is with Caleb, and I realized that I want that."

She swallowed audibly but didn't say anything else for a moment. Just when she was about to say something, there was a knock at the door and in walked Dr. Brennen.

"Ethan! What a surprise," she said.

Almost as big a surprise as it was when he found out that Vanessa was related to Caleb. With all the time he'd spent at Caleb's parent's house, he had never run into her. A crazy small world, and yet mere seconds on more than one occasion when they were at the family cookouts had kept them from discovering that his best friend's aunt happened to be the one that had saved Kara. Part of the life of being a cop, working odd hours and not always getting to spend very long at family get-togethers, and Vanessa herself worked long hours and didn't make it to enough family functions. Even so, it still seemed almost impossible that they had never run into each other.

"Hello, Vanessa, how are you?" he asked as he shook her hand.

"Quite good, thank you for asking. Yourself?"

"Not bad at all."

"I was shocked to see Quinn's name on the board this morning, but even more shocked to find you here with her."

"He refused to leave me alone. That whole protective, testosterone, 'I'm a man' gene he has going for him."

"Ah, yes, I know it well. Caleb has a bit of it in him, as well. In fact, I had to talk to him this morning. Kara called begging me to beat some sense into him. They told me you know, also—wonderful news about the baby."

"It is absolutely wonderful. Did she seem a little calmer about the whole thing? With Caleb going all alpha male, she looked a little over-whelmed," Quinn said.

"She was doing pretty good. Sounds like Ethan might have gotten through to her." Vanessa smiled at Ethan. "Thank you for that."

"I know the wheels were turning; there's simply no way she could turn into Constance."

"None, indeed." She smiled warmly at him. "How are you feeling this morning, Quinn?"

"Not bad. I slept fairly well, but still in quite a bit of pain."

"Unfortunately, that will probably continue for a few days. The good news is that you're free to go home this morning. I have the discharge paperwork here. I wanted to give it to you myself and say hello. Also, I wanted to reiterate how important it is that you let any surgeon who operates on you know that you had an adverse reaction to anesthesia."

"No worries there."

"Don't be a stranger; it's been too long since the last time we got together."

Ethan had almost forgotten that Quinn had basically been adopted by Vanessa. It shamed him that he hadn't kept in touch with her over the years, especially since he was practically part of Caleb's family. Now he had a chance to make up for that. Since she was also close friends with Kara and related to Caleb, it was easy to keep in touch. The darkness Ethan had found himself enveloped in when Kara had been taken and the years after had slowly started to retreat, allowing him to finally make lifelong friendships.

"That's fabulous news! Not about the not getting together, but about the getting to go home," Quinn said, flushing again, and darn it but he wanted to kiss her every time that flush crossed her face.

"Do you have a ride home?" Vanessa asked, pointedly looking at Ethan.

"Yes. Mr. Heavy Handed over there not only insisted on staying here all night but in driving me home. Some malarkey about my car being delivered home, that I shouldn't drive on narcotics, and I have a prescription to fill."

"All sound advice, if you ask me."

Ethan grinned from ear to ear when Quinn's bottom lip stuck out a little. She looked like an insufferable little girl. Not for the first time, Ethan wondered how old she was. He figured she was close to Kara in age, but the pouty lip had her looking somewhat younger, though not by much.

"Gah, it's like you two conspired to set this up behind my back."

"Not at all. You are on pain medication, you don't have a car, and I do have a prescription ready to call in for more pain medication. It's all very clear to me. No car, plus drugs, and need to stop for more, equals ride from someone."

"I could call a friend or take a cab." Again, with the pouty lip, and Ethan was almost undone.

"Why, when you can have one of Darkness Falls' finest, not to mention most attractive, detectives take you home? I say this is a win-win for you." With a sneaky smile, Vanessa handed the paperwork outlining care instructions to Quinn, briefly went over all the high-lighted points, and then with a pleasant goodbye, was on her way to make her rounds.

"She's so...so..."

"Amazing? Awesome? Intelligent? Compassionate?" he offered.

"Any other superlatives you want to use to describe her?"

"Such big words, Ms. Sanders." He smiled from ear to ear. "I'll be right back."

Ethan walked out of the room as she was winding up to throw her empty cup at him—at least, he thought it was empty. A laugh escaped him, and he shook his head. The banter between them was more fun than he'd had in a long time. Walking up to the nurse's station, he asked if there was any chance they had some spare scrubs that Quinn could wear home since her clothes were trashed in the accident. He told them that he'd have Kara return them. One of the nurses said she would see what she could do, but when she returned, she had a bag in her hand and a twinkle in her eye.

"Apparently, Kara had these sent up when she started her shift this morning. There's a note attached."

I assumed that big, macho brother of mine didn't leave your side long enough to think of clothes for you to ride home. We're about the same size, no rush to get them back. They won't be fitting me soon, anyway. Tell Ethan it isn't polite to read notes meant for someone else. All my love, Kara

"Sorry, I admit I read part of the note," she whispered conspiratorially. "It was hard not to; she left it on the outside of the bag."

He just smirked and nodded his head. Knowing his sister, she left it on the outside on purpose to call attention to her perceived notion that he should have thought to get Quinn some clothes. The joke was on her; he *did* think about it, just too late to make a difference. His step was light when he went back to Quinn's room to give her the clothes, but when he entered the room, his light mood disappeared. Quinn was staring at the TV with a look of horror on her face. He looked to see what she was watching and saw the Breaking News bulletin.

The Darkness Falls Fire Department and other local stations are currently fighting a structure fire in the upper east side of the city. The house is in the gated community of Lake Henrietta. It is unknown if anyone is inside. A neighbor has told our reporter on the scene that she believes the homeowners to be away on vacation. Stay tuned for further details.

"Quinn?" he asked. She shook herself and turned to look at him.

"I-I don't know for sure, but I think that's the house that Becky was being held at. I mean, I met him at the back side, so I can't be sure, but I think it is."

Ethan was sure she was right. Whoever had sold Becky to the owner of that house wanted to make sure that all evidence that Becky was held there was destroyed, and they'd done a good job of it. From the images that had been on the TV, the house wasn't going to be saved. He would be surprised if anything was left.

"I think you're right. I'm going to have to go in to work and check it out. But I have enough time to drop you off and get that prescription. I have some clothes for you here. They're from Kara," he added when she looked confused.

He handed the bag to her, and when she smiled, he took a deep breath. At least she could still find the good in the bad. She peeked in the bag, and when she looked up, she was still smiling. It wasn't one of her thousand-watt smiles, but it would do for the moment.

"She is so thoughtful. She even made sure to send something I wouldn't struggle to get on." Her voice broke a bit on the last words, but in true Quinn fashion, she pushed it back.

He left the room to give her some privacy with instructions to call out if she thought she might need help, and he would send in a female nurse. But he knew, without a doubt in his head, that she would rather bite off her tongue than ask for help. He asked a passing nurse if there was anything else they had to do before they left, and she said no, but that she would be back with a wheelchair—which he figured Quinn would argue about. By the time the nurse came back, he was starting to worry about the lack of noise coming from the room until Quinn called out quietly.

"Okay, I'm dressed."

It almost broke him completely seeing her sitting on the edge of the bed, so small and proud, but clearly in pain from fighting her way into her clothes.

"I have your chariot here," he said, indicating the wheelchair, and surprisingly, she didn't argue at all, but gratefully sat in the chair. Which indicated how much pain her body was in from the day before.

It was a beautiful sunny morning when they walked outside. The hospital valet had gone to get their car from the parking lot, and they stood in companionable silence. Ethan was scoping out the area, looking for any threats to Quinn or himself. He was looking to his left when someone bumped into them from behind. He whirled around as Quinn let out a little gasp.

"Sorry, man, I was looking at my phone and didn't see you sitting there. Is she okay?" The man asked, looking concerned.

Something seemed off. It didn't sit well with him, but he could hardly drag the guy in for questioning because he bumped into them. After all, they were parked in front of the doors, and he very well could have been looking at his phone. It wasn't that implausible of a story. Even if he couldn't haul him in, that didn't mean he had to like it.

"No harm, no foul," Quinn answered.

Ethan managed a brisk, "No problem."

"Really, I mean it, I wasn't paying attention. Sorry." And then he was off, rushing to the parking lot.

"What an odd man," Quinn said in a distracted way.

"Yeah," Ethan said, as he watched the guy put his phone to his ear and disappear. Ethan definitely did not like that guy. There was something really off with him.

"This better be good; you're disrupting me, and I was about to sample the goods."

"I think you're going to want to hear this, boss," he said quickly, knowing that his boss might hang up at a second's notice.

"You have five seconds of my time, starting now."

"I found the missing package."

Talking in code sometimes was more complicated than it was worth. They used burner phones. It would be hard to trace them, but the boss wanted them to use code words, so they did. After a short time, the silence had Paulie on edge, and when he was about to say something, the man finally spoke.

"You better be damn sure."

"I'm fairly certain," he said, hoping he was right. She definitely looked like the girl they had been instructed to find at all costs.

"You need to be certain. Where did you find it?"

"I found it in Darkness Falls. You won't believe this, but you know that package you wanted us to get rid of?"

"What about it?"

"It's the same package you've been looking for all this time." His boss laughed, and Paulie relaxed.

"You mean the package has been right here under our noses this whole time?"

"Well, I don't know how long the package was here."

While the sadistic man he called boss had lived there for years, he never left the compound. All of his needs were brought to him by his carefully cultivated staff. The man was uber paranoid about being found and carefully vetted anyone he allowed inside the compound walls. He had many people working for him who had never been let in that palace of brick and mortar. Unfortunately, Paulie wasn't one of them. He was allowed in there and would rather not see what he had seen on previous visits. Likewise, the man usually didn't bother himself with details when he ordered someone taken out—like he had Quinn Sanders. He didn't bother with finding out any details about the person. It was easier to deny if he knew as little as possible about those he marked, and the man rarely got his hands dirty. However, this one person was one whom he wanted to get his hands dirty with. They had been told if they ever found her to bring her directly to him.

"Should I grab it? The package is damaged right now so it would be easy."

"Not yet. Find out where the package is being delivered, and we'll keep a close eye on it to make certain."

The tone of his voice made Paulie's skin crawl. It wasn't the first time he regretted a decision he'd made, but this time, he regretted it immediately, because he wasn't willing to kill the Sanders woman or bring her in to his boss. There was a reason she survived the day before. The man hadn't intended to hit her—only scare her. Though his boss couldn't know that, for now, he needed to think that Paulie was merely inept at the job. The man didn't know Paulie at all if he thought Paulie would kill an innocent woman, but he had to keep all his options open a little bit longer.

12

After the one quick errand, Ethan dropped Quinn off at home. He wasn't about to leave until he had her situated on her couch with water, snacks, TV remote, and pain medicine within reach. Once she was settled and mostly comfortable, he kissed her on the forehead and turned to leave, then froze in place. He was absolutely appalled that he had just kissed her on the forehead like he was her father.

"Thank you," she said shyly, and he turned to look at her.

"I almost forgot your cell phone; I should get that for you." He walked briskly to the foyer where he had set her purse and grabbed the phone out of it. "You have my phone number programmed into your phone in case you need to call or text me for anything, right?"

"Yep." She yawned and smiled. "I think I'll be sleeping a bunch, though. The pain medicine seems to make me drowsy."

"Which is why you won't drive yourself anywhere while taking it, right?"

"Yes, Detective Vanderbilt." She saluted him with a dopey grin on her face. He laughed and turned to go.

"I'm going to lock the front door. I'm sure I don't have to tell you to be careful answering if anyone stops by?"

"I know to be careful, Ethan."

"All right, I have to go to work. I want to follow up on a couple of things."

"I understand. You're not responsible for me. Though I do appreciate your being with me last night." Another yawn.

"If all goes well, I'll stop by in a few hours."

As he was walking to the front door, he saw her keys hanging out of her purse. He was tempted to take them to ensure she wouldn't drive but decided that Quinn was too smart to do something that stupid and she wouldn't appreciate it—even if he was only being protective, not controlling. It dawned on him that he would need the house key to get back in to check on her.

"I'm going to take your house key so when I stop by later you won't have to get up to answer the door."

"Sounds good," she said while trying not to yawn.

Ethan hesitated a little longer before he finally left. He figured she was going to sleep just like she said she would. It didn't stop him from worrying though. He didn't like leaving her alone while on that medicine. Her only bathroom was up a flight of stairs; she could easily stumble and get hurt—he'd noticed that the pain medicine made her wobbly. Ethan wanted to call Taylor but remembered she was still out of town. Then he thought of Evie Montgomery. Climbing into his car, he picked up his phone and dialed her number.

"Hello, what a lovely surprise!" Evie answered, knowing it was him because his number was also programmed into her cell phone.

"I was wondering if I could ask a favor of you? I mean, that is, if you aren't busy this morning?"

"I have no plans at all. What did you need me to do?"

"My friend Quinn, you met her at Caleb and Kara's wedding and a couple of other times at the center, she got hurt yesterday in a near hit-and-run."

"Caleb called to tell me. That poor girl! He also said Kara was involved, but not hurt. Though he made her go home and take the night off."

"That he did," Ethan said, a smile in his voice. "I was wondering if you wouldn't mind stopping by and taking care of her for a while. I have to go in to the office for a little while, and to my knowledge, she doesn't have any family around. Taylor is gone, and Vanessa and Kara are at work."

"Absolutely. She has been such a blessing for Taylor and everyone else that goes to the center for help. I'll bring over some stuff and make her a nice breakfast and lunch."

"You don't have to do that. I mean, I think she'll probably just sleep."

"Nonsense. Can you let her know I'm stopping by, though? I don't want to surprise her and scare her."

"Good idea. She's pretty wobbly on the pain medication, so if she has to go to the bathroom or anything, she might need help, even if she tries to be proud about it."

"Hm, I know a little about proud people. Don't worry about her at all. I raised three kids; she's in good hands."

"Her front door is locked, and I don't want to make her get up to answer the door, so you'll need a key to get in. How about I meet you at the convenience store by my place? I have to run home and that isn't too far out of the way for you."

"I think that'll work just fine."

"Thank you, Mom." He noticed the small intake of breath on the other side of the phone, and he realized he'd called her mom, and he liked the sound of it.

"Thank you."

"For?"

"For asking me to help and just for being you. I love you, you know?"

"I love you, too. I'll see you in a bit."

After they hung up, he stared at his phone. It should have felt like a betrayal to call another woman mom, but he didn't feel that way at all. Kara called James and Evie, mom and dad, but he had hesitated. Even though he knew them longer, she was married to their son, so it seemed natural, but Ethan now knew that he had come to think of them as his pseudo parents. He was about to text and then thought better of it. If he texted her, she might not see the message. He was still sitting in his car, in her driveway, and could have gone and knocked on the door, but he didn't want to make her get up. The only other option was a phone call.

"I'm fine, Ethan. You can go to work and stop hovering in my driveway."

"I'm about to leave. Listen, I know you're probably not going to like this, but later you will thank me."

"I don't like the sound of that."

"It's nothing bad. I just asked Evie, Caleb's mom, to stop out and keep you company."

"You mean you asked her to babysit me."

"You can call it what you want, but you know you're not steady on your feet and might need some help. You hit the pavement pretty hard yesterday."

"Fine, fine. I hope she's okay watching me sleep. I would have been sleeping by now if you weren't hovering in my driveway."

"I was just talking to her on the phone. I'm going now. Like I said, if you need anything, let me know. But I feel better having Evie there to help you if you need any help." She was quiet for a bit before she sighed.

"I do appreciate it. Thank you."

"No need to thank me. Get some rest."

A huge yawn and then she mumbled something that sounded like, *I plan to.* He disconnected the phone and then backed out and headed to the station. Deep in thought, he almost missed the conversation that a distraught woman was having with a rookie at the front desk. But a few words stopped him in his tracks, and he stopped to listen to what was being said.

"Ma'am, I understand you're upset. But right now, there's no information that would suggest your daughter did anything but stay out overnight."

"You're wrong, sir. My daughter is a good girl. Kimora wouldn't have stayed out all night. She wouldn't worry me like that. She's a good girl."

"I'm not disagreeing, but…"

Ethan took a few steps toward the African American woman. She was tall and slender, somewhere in her mid-thirties and was wearing scrubs like she had just come from a shift at the hospital or was about to go to work and had stopped here on the way in. It was obvious she was upset, as tears were streaming down her face. His stomach clenched at the sight. When he was home from college one summer, Kara had told him that he was always a sucker for a crying girl. She had been right because it tore him up to see anyone in distress.

"She's only thirteen. If she were a white girl, from a middle or upper-class home, you'd be doing something." The woman's voice was soft and so broken.

Officer Babiarz was about to say something when Ethan lifted a hand to silence him. With a slight gesture of his head, the officer went silent and took a step back. The mother turned to look at him with her red-rimmed eyes narrowed.

"Are you going to t-tell me the s-same thing?" she quietly asked through her tears.

"Not at all. I would like to take you into a quiet room and get a description of your daughter and details about the last time you saw her. If that's all right with you?"

"I would appreciate that," she said, swiping at a tear on her cheek.

Ethan led her down the hall to an office that presently didn't have an occupant because they were still going through applications to fill the job. He wasn't about to make her sit in the hectic bull pen or an interrogation room. Once inside the office, he indicated that she could have a seat in one of the chairs by a small table in the office, and he shut the door for some privacy. Searching through drawers, he finally found a notepad that had been left by the previous occupant of the room, and then he settled in the chair on the other side of the table.

"I know your daughter's name is Kimora, but could we start with your name?"

"Keisha Washington."

"It's nice to meet you, Keisha, even if it is under dire circumstances. If you could tell me as much as you know about the last time Kimora was seen, it would be really helpful."

"I saw her off to school yesterday and went to work. I work at the hospital as a nurse's aide. After school, she's supposed to come straight home and do her homework, start supper, and tend to her younger brother." She paused and swiped at another tear. Ethan looked around and saw a box of tissues that had been left behind. He grabbed the box and set it on the table for her to use.

"Take your time. I have as much time as you need."

"My son called when I was done with my shift and on my way to my night classes—I'm taking classes to become a registered nurse. It's been a rough road. Kimora ends up doing more than she should at her age, but I'm almost done with the schooling. He called because Kimora always gets home before him. But he lost track of time. Davon tends to get sucked into his video games when he gets home. It's all Kimora can do to get him to actually do his homework. He admitted that when she wasn't there, he took advantage of it and played his video game. Then he noticed the time and called me right away."

"Did you call any of her friends?" he asked gently.

"I did. She has a new friend who she walks home with every day."

Ethan's instincts kicked in, and a warning bell sounded at that revelation. What are the chances that Kimora would have a new friend right before she went missing? It was entirely possible, but also coincidental, which he didn't like.

"How long have they been friends?"

"Just a few weeks. I haven't met her, but Kimora says she's a really sweet girl. She has a rough home life, so she always walks home with Kimora to delay going home herself."

A similar story to the one Becky had been told. Ethan didn't like the coincidence. Keisha's eyes had dried, and she now looked wary. Ethan knew that she had picked up on the reason for his question.

"Did you call this friend?"

"I did."

"Were you able to get ahold of her?"

"Yes. She said she walked with her to our house and then went home."

Ethan jotted down notes as Keisha spoke. The scenario was reminiscent of Becky's disappearance, and he didn't like that thought at all.

Human trafficking was becoming an alarmingly large problem across the US and Wisconsin was no different. Milwaukee was fast becoming a hub. Recently, Darkness Falls had seen an alarming increase in the grooming of minors. Hence, why they'd put someone undercover.

"What did you do after you spoke to her?"

"I called all of her other friends. But…" she trailed off abruptly.

"But what?" he prodded, that warning bell ringing again.

"All of the girls she's friends with said that recently she was different. She had turned away from them and was only hanging out with the one girl."

"What was this friend's name?"

"Bridget. I don't know her last name. Kimora didn't share much about her, other than that her home life wasn't the best. I know she's white."

"Is she the same age?"

"She's a year older; she was held back a year."

"I have a few tough questions to ask, and it's just routine. So please don't think I'm judging you." He paused while she nodded, her chin tipped up slightly as if prepared for a fight. "Why did you wait until this morning to come in?"

"I called the police as soon as I tracked down all of her friends and she still wasn't home." Her tone was still quiet, but a bit accusatory. Ethan's stomach felt like a rock was in it. "They told me that if she didn't return home by the morning to file a report, and then that young officer was implying she was just out having a good time or that she had run away."

"I do apologize if you were made to feel that way. I assure you, I'm taking your daughter's disappearance very seriously."

"You had another question?"

"I have to ask, and I once again apologize, but has she ever stayed out like this before?"

"No," Keisha said emphatically.

"I knew that would be your answer, but I still had to ask. Is there any reason she would stay away?"

"No, not anything I can think of. I mean, I'm strict with both of my kids. I want better for them than I had growing up. Kimora and Davon both do good in school, but I know I'm not home enough. They both know that's so I can better myself and hopefully make our lives easier, and so I can spend more time with my children before they become adults and leave for their own lives." Her voice broke at the end, and tears filled her eyes once again.

"If you have a picture of Kimora, I'll start getting it circulated immediately."

"You believe me, then? That she didn't just run away?"

"Yes, I do believe you, and unfortunately, I also think time is of the essence."

Quinn woke slowly and blinked her eyes several times. She struggled to sit up. Remarkably, her body hurt worse now than it had when she left the hospital. The nurse had mentioned that she might be sorer as the day went on. That was an understatement—Quinn felt bruised on every square inch of her body.

"How are you feeling?" The lovely voice of Evie Montgomery floated into the room from the entrance to her living room—she'd almost forgotten the woman was there.

"I have definitely felt better."

"I imagine. I'm making you some lunch. You slept through breakfast, so I put that in the fridge for tomorrow."

"Evie, I appreciate it, but I told you not to bother."

"Don't be silly. My son called and asks for a favor that isn't really a favor. It isn't every day one of my kids asks me for help."

Quinn felt such warmth in Evie's words. What would it be like to have the love of a woman like Evie Montgomery? She imagined it was pretty magical—the woman was such a beacon of light and love.

"I love that you think of Ethan as your son."

"I don't think of him as my son, Kara and Ethan are as much my children as Grayson, Caleb, and Taylor. They deserve parents that care for and love them."

"I couldn't agree more." Evie looked at her with an all-knowing look, the look of a woman who had seen it all, her lips curved into a sad smile.

"Why don't I help you up to the bathroom? I'm sure you need to go, and then you can eat the tomato soup and my famous grilled cheese. It has a secret ingredient. A simple lunch, so you can't yell at me," she said with her palms up in a placating gesture. "I could have made you my world-famous chicken dumpling soup and homemade bread, but I figured that would be a bit too much."

That got a chuckle out of Quinn, and she felt more at ease than she had all day. As nice as Evie was, it was still unnerving having someone that she barely knew taking care of her, no matter how honest and pure their intentions were. Ethan had been extremely thoughtful to think about having someone come sit with her, even if it was annoying. Deep down, she appreciated the gesture. Since she didn't have any family around and didn't want to burden any of her friends—they all had lives of their own—she really didn't have anyone to call.

Her earlier attempt to sit up had been an epic fail, so she decided to tackle it a different way this time and swung her legs off the couch with the hopes that would make it easier. It didn't. She was winded from the effort and felt foolish. For the love of all things holy, she had fallen down. It shouldn't be this painful, should it? Evie was at her side in a flash, her eyes worried.

"Did you crack or bruise a rib?" she asked sympathetically.

"I'm sore everywhere, but the only broken bone is on my wrist. I know that it's awful when I try to get up. It sucks the breath right out of me."

"It sounds like a bruised rib, but it could just be that you're bruised in general. Ethan didn't mention what injuries you have."

"I broke my arm, obviously, had to have my knee cleaned up, and my shoulder was dislocated. Nothing major, but you're probably right, I'm just one big bruise. We were lucky. I keep hoping maybe they were only trying to scare us. It was pretty awful. Apparently, a huge garbage can hit me, and I didn't even know it."

"Ethan and Caleb didn't mention that, but they did mention you pushed Kara out of the way."

Quinn tried to shrug her shoulders, but she was still lying awkwardly on her right side with her legs off the couch. She didn't have the right leverage to get herself up, and Evie was hesitating, clearly wanting a cue from Quinn that she indeed wanted help. Sucking it up wasn't something Quinn was used to doing, and her pride didn't want to let her ask. The tug of war was real, but in the end, she knew when it was best to let your cards lie where they were and ask for help.

"As much as I dislike asking…"

Before she could finish the sentence, Evie had her arm under her right shoulder and was gently lifting her, so gently that it hardly hurt at all. Quinn allowed herself to lean into her until she was sitting completely upright. Dizziness took control for a moment, and the room spun. A combination of lying down and pain medicine contributed to making her feel off. After a moment, the dizziness went away, and she was ready to stand up.

"You know, I can't imagine how I would feel if that car had actually connected."

"Dead," Evie quipped.

Quinn snorted out a laugh, completely taken by surprise by the comment that had come from the sweet woman still holding onto her shoulder as she stood up.

"You're funny," Quinn wheezed as she held onto her ribs. Even laughing hurt.

Now that she was vertical and on her feet, she took a deep breath, in through her nose and out through her mouth. If she got up and moved around, maybe her tight muscles would relax a bit. When she shuffled to the foot of her stairs and looked up, she lost any determination she had just mustered to keep moving. She never thought twice about her stairs, but right then and there, they seemed like the most difficult task of the day, and she knew, she just knew that the only bathroom upstairs was going to defeat her. Sure, she could make it up those steps once, but twice, three times? Not a chance.

One excruciating step at a time, she climbed to the top, and by the time she was on the landing, she was exhausted. Evie was quiet the whole time as she walked up those stairs with her, and once she had been safely left in the bathroom, she sat gingerly down to relieve herself. Of all the injuries Quinn had gone through in her life, this was by far the most painful to date. After she was done, she slowly made her way back to the stairs and sighed heavily.

"There is no way I can do this again today," she grudgingly admitted to Evie.

"Oh, thank God, I was hoping you would say that!" The response startled Quinn.

"But it isn't like I have much of a choice; it's the only bathroom in my house."

"I hope you aren't mad, but I texted Ethan while you were in the bathroom. I told him that I didn't want you trying the stairs again today. His apartment is on the first floor of a house. I suggested that he bring you there after he's done for the day. I would bring you home with me, but I'm leaving for a few days with James. Taylor is gone, too, but you knew that." Evie was speaking so quickly that in Quinn's drug-induced state she could hardly keep up.

"I can't ask that of Ethan."

"You don't have to. I did, and he agreed that it was a good idea. I'm going to get you down those stairs and seated in the most comfort-able seating option you have, which, at this point, I think, would be your recliner. Once you're situated, I'm going to go pack you a small overnight bag, if you just let me know what you want and where to find it."

Quinn was sunk. She knew this was the smarter option at least for one night, but she didn't want to leave her home. It wasn't much, and it was in a bad part of town, but she paid the rent on her own. However, those stairs were not going to happen again today, and Lord knew her bladder would need the bathroom again at some point. Without any other option, she acquiesced, and once they were down the stairs, she let Evie help her into the recliner and bring her a tray of food which smelled amazing. Even if she wasn't a big fan of tomato soup, today it smelled amazing.

"Just sit there and eat. Do you need anything? Something to drink other than water?"

"I suppose wine is out of the question?" she said sarcastically, and Evie smiled at her bad joke.

"Let me go pack that bag. It sounded like Ethan was wrapping something up, and then he was going to come get you."

"He doesn't need to come right now; I can wait."

"His text was brief, but it sounded like he has time now, and then would have to go back to work after he gets you comfortable."

"Well, if there's anything I know about Ethan, it's that once he makes his mind up, he doesn't change it."

"I wonder who that sounds like?"

13

Ethan wrapped up his conversation with Keisha Washington and was in the process of sending over the missing person report to the local news stations when his phone buzzed. He glanced down and saw it was a text from Evie.

Quinn is not going to be able to do these stairs again today. Body is very sore. Better option? Perhaps your house?

Ethan didn't like the sound of that. He really wanted to run to her house and make sure she was okay, but he knew that she was in good hands with Evie, and he couldn't get away right now if he tried. . Not until he got Kimora's picture uploaded and shared to as many places as possible. They couldn't issue an Amber Alert, which he thought was wrong, there should be some kind of alert available for something like this, but his hands were tied. Without proof that she had been taken against her will, he had to follow the proper channels. He could ask the news to air her disappearance and hope they would. Thankfully, Ethan had a good relationship with the press and was confident he could get some air time.

Agreed. Wrapping something up. After that, I have some time to pick her up.

It would have to be good enough because he knew that Kimora's disappearance was linked to the same group that had taken Becky. He didn't know why or by whom, but there wasn't a doubt in his mind that it was connected. The mere idea that there was some syndicate taking root in his town made his blood boil. And the realization that this wasn't an easy fix made it run ice cold. There had to be a faster way to get to the heart of this sex ring before another person was sucked into the ugliness of it all. He knew Black, and he respected him. Even if Caleb still had a hang-up with him, Ethan didn't. Ethan was able to look at the situation and realize it was a colossal mistake, but it was only a mistake. Even though Black was a damn good cop, it was a tall order they were asking of him.

Black had infiltrated the network quickly, but he still wasn't the inside man they needed. It took time to become trusted by the inner circle, which meant that he had to be extremely careful if he wanted to get out alive. Going that deep undercover could change a person. Black was immersed in a very dark world right now. Ethan wouldn't trade places with him for anything in the world.

"Vanderbilt! I need a word with you," Captain Bob Wickman shouted from his office.

Ethan wondered why he sounded so agitated. Bob was one of the calmest people he knew, but something had him fired up. He looked around the squad room for Caleb and didn't see him anywhere. As a matter of fact, he hadn't seen him all day. Which really wasn't odd; it was their day off. Ethan had only come in to do some leg work on Becky's case and had inadvertently ended up helping Keisha Washington, or at least, he hoped he'd helped her out. The only way he could really help her is by finding her missing daughter.

"Hey, Cap, what's going on? You sound upset about something."

"What? Oh, sorry about that. I just got off the phone with the mayor." Uh-oh.

"And?"

"He was mad that he didn't get a heads-up that Becky Plummer was found. SOB wants to turn it into a political game to get him votes. Between you and me, I hope his opponent beats the crap out of him at the polls."

"You and me both," Ethan said. "She genuinely seems to care about this community, not votes. Maybe with her, we can get some money back in the budget." Bob grunted.

"Wouldn't that be nice? Anyway, I didn't call you in here to complain about the current mayor."

"Yes, you did," Ethan said wisely. Another grunt escaped Bob. "What did he want? Other than to yell at you because we didn't tell him about Becky?"

"That was about it. He didn't seem to care that we didn't know about her until she was at the hospital or that she is a minor and we can't just run to the media. Granted, I'm pretty surprised her family hasn't announced her return."

"They just got her back, and they don't want her in the limelight. I can understand that. She's been through a lot, and to be honest, they weren't sure she would make it through the night."

"He didn't seem to care about any of that."

"I forgot what an asshat he is."

"Yeah, that's an understatement. Anyway, I was peeved because he was being such a jerk about it, and I didn't mean to take it out on you. I also wanted to know how Kara and Quinn are."

"Kara is good as far as I know. I haven't seen her today. Caleb managed to keep her from work yesterday."

"Today, too, from what I hear."

"Really?" Ethan's eyebrows raised at the revelation. "I guess that's why he didn't show up here today—if they're both off of work and all."

"Probably. What about Quinn? I know she took the brunt of it all and that Kara was basically unscratched because of Quinn's quick moves."

"Her arm is broken. They ended up doing surgery to repair it. She also has a dislocated shoulder and a nasty abrasion on her knee. Other than that, she's banged up and bruised pretty much everywhere. In fact, if you don't mind, I was going to run to her house and pick her up and bring her to my place."

It was Bob's turn to lift his eyebrows.

"It isn't what it sounds like. Right now, Evie, Caleb's mom, is watching her and just sent me a text message. Quinn's home only has one bathroom, and it's on the second floor. Evie said that she's struggling with the stairs. My place is on the first floor."

"She doesn't have any family?"

"None that I know of, and I think Evie and James are going out of town. Taylor is out of town, Caleb and Kara have other stuff going on."

"His being over protective and watching over her being the main stuff?"

"Yep. Anyway, I'm the logical choice. I don't want her trying to go up those stairs by herself and getting hurt worse than she already is. I can bring her to my place and come back; she can rest pretty comfortably there."

"You know, you are off today, you don't have to come back. You could just hang out with her and help her out if she needs any help."

"I caught a case this morning when I got here. It seems connected to the human trafficking ring. I'm not sure I should take the afternoon off after all."

"What case is that?"

"Missing thirteen-year-old girl. Name's Kimora Washington. Her mother was just here, distraught over Kimora not coming home last night. Keisha, the mother, said that her daughter has never done this before, and when she called around to talk to her friends, she found that her daughter hadn't been hanging with them that much recently. She has a new friend she hangs out with. I was going to try to track down the new friend this afternoon."

"Why do I have the feeling you won't find her?"

"Probably for the same reason I don't think I'll find her. This case sounds too similar to Becky Plummer. Good girl, solid family home, a new friend in the picture, and now she's missing."

"Sounds like she was being groomed to me."

"I thought the same thing. Regardless, I'm going to go through the motions and try to find her and talk to her. Maybe she hasn't fled yet, or maybe she isn't involved at all."

"Maybe."

"Your doubt is noted."

"You know as well as I do that isn't going to be the case."

"Like I said, I still have to try. I owe it to her mother, and maybe something will pan out. Maybe I'll get some inkling to where she went."

"Good luck. Keep me posted and be careful. If she's caught up in this whole situation, well, we all know how ruthless the people who deal in sex trade can be."

Ethan had filled Bob in about the house that Becky's friend had taken her to while Quinn had been in surgery. They all know how ruthless this group is, and Ethan wasn't going to let his guard down, not for one second, not when his sister and the woman he's crazy about were both involved. Caleb had probably tried to spirit Kara away on a much-needed vacation to get her away from the danger. The good news was, that for the most part, Ethan thought Kara wasn't even a blip on their radar. Quinn was a different story. She was definitely in their crosshairs, and Ethan wasn't going to let her get hurt again. Not if he had anything to say about it. Ethan checked his watch when he left Bob's office and realized he needed to hurry if he was going to get to Quinn's, get her settled in at his place, and still have time to get some work done on Kimora's disappearance.

Evie let him into the house when he got there, and he found Quinn sitting in the recliner. He noted that she had a tray of unfinished food and that she wasn't looking as good as she had when he left her that morning. Her skin was flushed and almost looked like a rash had started to form. Alarmed, he looked at Evie, who was wringing her hands.

"The rash just started a few minutes ago. I don't know what it could be."

Ethan crouched in front of the chair that Quinn was sitting in and grabbed her wrist to check her pulse. It was racing.

"Quinn, do you have any known allergies?"

"Just avocado."

He heard Evie gasp from behind him. When he turned to look, she was covering her mouth with her hand.

"I made her grilled cheese, and I added avocado to it. It's all the rage now."

"How severe is the allergy?"

"I didn't eat that much of the sandwich. I noticed the avocado right away, but I didn't want to hurt your feelings. I get hives from a small taste of it—not a big deal. It looks worse than it is. An allergy pill should help."

"Oh, you should have told me. I just feel terrible. Now I know why you weren't eating it. I thought you didn't like it because of the extra ingredient. Not everyone does, but you were trying to be polite by pretending to eat it," Evie said, with tears in her eyes.

"It really isn't a big deal. It isn't a life-threatening allergy, just annoying."

"Well, next time try not to be so tough, and just tell me. It wouldn't have hurt my feelings. It would have been more hurtful if you ate it even if you hated it."

Quinn felt like such a jerk for not saying anything, but she hadn't wanted to hurt Evie's feelings. She had worked so hard to take care of her and made her such a thoughtful lunch. It wasn't like there was much she could do once she ate some of it. The damage had already been done. The hives were definitely annoying and uncomfortable, but like she said, they weren't life-threatening. Evie's eyes widened, and she turned to leave.

"What's wrong?" Ethan asked.

"Nothing, um, well the breakfast I made for her and put in the fridge has avocado in it, too. I'm going to go throw it out."

"Good idea," Quinn said, laughing. Evie smiled, and Quinn felt better right away. She had felt terrible that this woman, who had been nothing but nice, was feeling guilty.

"Well, other than the hives, how are you feeling?"

"As good as can be expected. For now, it's manageable, but the pain ebbs and flows all day. It hurts the most when I try to get up and move. Sucks the breath right out of me, but after I'm up for a bit, the stiffness goes away a little. Do you think there would be a problem taking a pain pill with my allergy pill?"

"I wouldn't think so. But I can call Kara, if you want?"

"Actually, if you don't mind? At this point, I think I should be cautious."

"I completely agree. Give me a minute, and I'll find out."

Ethan left the room to call Kara. While he was gone, Evie flitted around the room straightening things, and folding the blanket Quinn had used in her vain attempt to sleep. It wasn't very long until Ethan returned to the room with a smile on his face.

"Good news, you can take both. Kara made sure to emphasize if the allergy pill didn't seem to work we should bring you in just in case it's a reaction to the pain medication and not the avocado. Speaking of pain medication, I think you're due to take a pain pill now. I'll grab one for you before we leave."

"It has to be the avocado. It's the same reaction I have every time I eat it, and the pain medication they prescribed is the same stuff they gave me in the hospital. As far as taking another pill, I think I'll take the allergy medicine and forgo the pain medicine until we get to your place. That way I won't be as wobbly or fall asleep on the ride." Her voice sounded self-deprecating, even to her own ears.

"You know, it wouldn't bother me if you fall asleep or if you get wobbly and need a hand. If the pain is too much, I would prefer you stay on top of it and take the pills," he said as he handed her an allergy pill and glass of water then turned to place the pain medication in the bag that was on the floor by her chair.

"I can manage...for now." She added the last part because she knew that the threshold for what she could handle was just about at its max.

Looking at her skeptically, Ethan picked up her bag and slung it over his shoulder while Evie moved the tray out of the way so he could give her a hand up from the chair. Part of her wanted to protest, but the meek side wanted the help, needed the help. Her body hurt, and her mind was exhausted. All she wanted to do was climb in a soft bed and sleep for days. Which really didn't seem to be something that was going to happen for her. The couch at her house that she had always thought was comfortable was nowhere near comfortable when in pain. Maybe Ethan's couch would be a more pleasant experience.

"I'll stick around and clean up the dishes before I leave. If that's okay?" Evie asked.

"Absolutely not. You shouldn't have even made me lunch, much less clean up after me!" Quinn protested.

"Don't be silly. You can hardly wash dishes one-handed."

"I have a dishwasher."

"Just let me help you," Evie said quietly.

At that moment, Quinn saw it, saw how easy it was to fall in love with this woman. With her family. A woman who took the time to come and play nursemaid for someone she hardly knew because someone she considered a son had called and asked her to do so. The woman standing in her living room was amazing and a force to be reckoned with, and Quinn was already attached to her. She hoped that Evie's children realized how utterly amazing their mother was. Of course, she knew they did. There was no doubt in her mind that Caleb thought his parents walked on water. While she didn't have as much contact with Grayson, she knew the same could be said for his feelings about his parents. As for Taylor, she worshipped both her parents. So much so that she tried to hide how much her rape still affected her severely. But, because they were good parents, she couldn't fool them, and they knew.

"You collect abandoned puppies," Quinn whispered.

"Excuse me?" Evie responded with a confused look on her face.

"I just, well, I mean you find and collect stray or abandoned people and adopt them, bring them into your home, and make them part of your family. It's nice that you do that, make people feel so included, so at home, at peace. You have a gift."

There was no doubt in her mind that she sounded stupid and she had a hard time making eye contact with Evie, but it was how she felt, and Quinn made it part of her daily practice to be honest about everything with the exception of, and probably because she couldn't share, her past. That big black part of her life festering inside her with no outlet made her honest to a fault about everything else. Well, not everything, since she was still lying to herself about her feelings for Ethan.

"Well, thank you, that means a lot."

Quinn looked up when she heard the thickness in Evie's voice and was shocked to see the older woman had tears in her eyes. Rewinding the moment in her head, Quinn tried to think what she had said that made the woman cry and found herself suddenly embarrassed, thinking she must have said something wrong.

"Um, well, anyway, I can clean up tomorrow when Ethan brings me home," she stammered in a ridiculous attempt to change the subject, her eyes darting around the room as she shifted from foot to foot.

"Nonsense, it is the least I can do after such a lovely compliment." Evie sniffed a little and patted her cheeks, appearing embarrassed by the sudden emotion, but then she smiled at Quinn and gave her a hug and kiss on her cheek and whispered in her ear, "I hope you allow me to find you and make you part of my family, too."

14

Quinn was feeling sentimental over the words that Evie had whispered to her. She couldn't remember ever feeling so included. Her memories of her parents were nonexistent. There was no way to know how old she was when she last saw them. Given the opportunity to see them again, Quinn would walk the other way. There had been a time for them to be parents, and they had failed. Evie was what she would have wanted for a mother: loving, a protector and nurturer for her family. It was obvious that she was the glue that kept her family together, the center of their universe.

"You're awfully quiet," Ethan said softly. "Are you feeling okay?"

"Yes. The allergy pill took away the itchiness."

"So, care to tell me what's wrong?" His question was tentative.

"Not really." Realizing how rude that sounded after all he had done, she quickly continued. "I'm sorry. I didn't mean it like it sounded. It's just, well, Evie whispered something to me when we were leaving, and I was thinking how nice it would have been to have a mom like her when I was growing up."

"You weren't close to your parents?" Another tentative question from him.

"Not really. I mean, I don't remember them. I think I was really little the last time I saw them."

"When was that?"

"No idea." Quinn shrugged.

"You don't know the last time you saw them?"

"Nope."

He must have sensed that she didn't want to talk about it anymore because he didn't push, and she silently thanked him for not pressing her to talk about what was clearly a painful topic for her. They rode in silence for a bit until they pulled into a driveway in a middle-class neighborhood in the city. The house he lived in was humongous. Even though she knew it was split into apartments, it was still impressive to behold. It was an old Victorian house that some entrepreneur had decided to refurbish, make into apartments, and rent out. Whoever had done the work knew what they were doing.

"This house is gorgeous. It must cost a fortune to rent here."

"Not really."

"Come on, the rent has to be terribly high. The neighborhood is top-notch, and the building looks completely renovated."

"It is."

"And the landlord doesn't charge premium dollars for it?"

"Nope."

"Nice guy. Maybe you could introduce me, and if an apartment ever opens up, I'll have a better chance at getting in."

"I thought you liked your house?"

"I like that it's close to the center and that the clients can stop at any time, but…"

"But, you also live alone, and the clients' exes could stop at any time?"

"It isn't that so much. I mean, it is. On more than one occasion a pimp stopped by my house looking for one of his workers who'd quit the trade. Those situations can get dicey, and before the center it was a necessity. Now that there's a place for them to find me that is safer, more controlled, I've been thinking about moving and keeping the address confidential."

"Would you sell your house?"

"I actually rent, and the lease is about up, so now is the time to do it if I'm going to."

"Not a bad idea and good timing for you. The building is recently renovated, so none of the apartments are filled yet. There are a couple with one bedroom and one bath."

"Really?" She got excited at the thought of moving into this beautiful house. It really wasn't that far from the center. "Could you introduce me to the owner?"

"Sure."

"That would be great. I suppose I'll have to wait until I'm feeling better, probably wouldn't look great showing up like this."

"Pretty sure he wouldn't care."

"He's probably really busy." She looked out the window again and sighed. "It would be nice to move in here, though."

"Safer neighborhood, and there is an added bonus of living in the same building as a hotshot detective." He winked at her.

"When do you think I could meet with him?"

"How about now?"

"What? No way, look at me. Anyway, how would that work? Does he live here, too?"

"Yep."

"Really? I would think he would live somewhere else, somewhere fancier."

"It makes it easier to maintain the building if he lives on site. I'm sure he wouldn't mind meeting with you."

She looked at him, indecisive, knowing if she waited, she might miss a huge opportunity.

"All right, if he's home and doesn't mind."

"Great! I'll help you get settled and then get him. I'm sure he has pictures of the apartment to show you. It's on the second floor, and you're probably not up to climbing those stairs today."

"Probably not. Pictures would be great."

"Sounds like a plan."

Opening his car door, he walked around to the back and grabbed her bag before coming around to her side. She had opened the door, but he was already there ready to help her out of the car. Her body yelled at her, but she just ignored it and pushed up and out of the car only leaning on him slightly. As they walked up the sidewalk to the front door, she took in the gingerbread trim and warm colors that the owner had used to make the house a home—not just an apartment building. The man had an eye for architecture and renovation, or at least, the team he had used did.

"This house is just breathtaking. I have always loved Victorian houses."

"I'm glad you think so. I love it, too."

Once inside, Ethan helped her settle on the couch in his living room. She had to admit that she had stereotyped him to have the epitome of a bachelor pad, all contemporary and leather. But his apartment was a delightful surprise. Warm and cozy, the couch was beyond comfortable, way nicer than her own couch and she knew she would have no problem getting some sleep on it.

"Let me get you a glass of water so you can take that pain pill now." She opened her mouth to protest, but he held up a hand, silencing her. "Don't pretend you aren't in pain. I saw you get out of the car, the look on your face, the grimace and pain in your eyes. Pain pill or I won't get the owner."

"Oh, fine."

After he returned with the water, he grabbed the pills out of her bag and handed her one. She dutifully took it and settled back into the couch. She began to have doubts about meeting with the owner. She was beat and wanted nothing more than to take a nap.

"I'll be right back; make yourself comfortable. Never mind, looks like you're doing just that," he said with a smirk as she yawned.

After he left, she closed her eyes and rested her head on the back of the couch, waiting for the pain pill to take effect. As much as she didn't want to take them, because they made her feel groggy, she also welcomed the reprieve from the sharp pain in her arm. The door opened quietly, and she sat up and tried to smooth her hair and clothes.

She was confused when she saw only Ethan, but she was also happy. She had decided having this meeting now was not a good idea.

"I thought you were going to go get the owner. Wasn't he home?"

"He was home."

"Is he busy?"

"No."

"Then, where is he?"

"You're looking at him."

───────────

"Wait, what? You're the owner?"

"Yep. I just had to go grab my mail and I have a small office in the foyer where the tenants can drop off concerns, if they have them. I also have a portfolio of pictures in the office and wanted to grab it to show you."

"Why didn't you just tell me you're the owner?"

"I did."

"Well, yeah, but just now. I mean, you could have said so when I first started asking questions."

"I could have, but you didn't really ask the name of the owner."

"You stinker. You're totally enjoying this right now, aren't you?"

"A little bit. It got you out of your funk, didn't it?"

As soon as Ethan said it, he regretted it. She *had* been out of her funk. Had being the operative word. As soon as he drew attention to it, her brows narrowed, and the sad, haunted look returned to her eyes. Ethan wanted to kick his own ass. Why did he have to go and say that? He knew better and was usually more charismatic and attuned to what needed to be said and done to reach a person. But he had blown this one, and his only excuse was that she did something to him to make him feel off center. This wasn't the first time, and he doubted it would be the last time that he'd say or do something stupid around her.

"I'm sorry. Listen, I shouldn't have said that."

"No, you're right. You did get me out of my funk, and I appreciate it. I'm sorry I got all weird in the car. Memories, or the lack thereof, sometimes get to me."

"If you ever want to talk about them, I'm a good listener."

"I know. But for now, how about we look at the pictures?"

With a single nod, he walked over and sat next to her on the couch, purposely sitting closer than he needed to, because he just wanted to be close to her without being obvious about it. It was like she was a magnet, and he was being drawn to her. Not for the first time, he wanted to know what was going through her head, and if she felt even an iota about him of what he felt about her. Trying to play it cool, he set the album on his knees and opened it up at the beginning and started flipping to find the page with the apartment pictures on it but stopped when her hand came to rest on his, effectively stopping him from moving or breathing.

"What?" he managed to ask.

"I know you need to get back, and I would like to look at them all. These are from the renovations, too?"

"Yeah." And damn if he wasn't embarrassed. "Technically, I don't have to go back to work. It's my day off. I just need to get moving on a case that I picked up this morning. A thirteen-year-old went missing. Her mother came in this morning, and I overheard her explaining to a cop about her daughter. She was on her way to work at the hospital."

"Oh, no! What's her name?" Quinn's eyes searched his, worry filling them. Ethan realized that Quinn knew so many people in the neighborhood that the Washingtons lived in.

"Kimora Washington." Her hand flew to her mouth, and she started shaking her head back and forth.

"No, not Kimora. I know their whole family. Her mom, Keisha, helps at the free clinic one weekend a month. Kara knows her, too. Kimora wants to be a doctor, so sometimes she helps her mom at the clinic, as well."

Shit and double shit. It was bad enough that the young girl was missing, but this made it even more personal. The urge to get going and try to find her was strong. Ever since Kara had gone missing, he had this drive to find every missing girl or boy out there and bring them home. It was so strong that sometimes it consumed him and that was when he put on the cocky swagger as a defense mechanism to protect himself from other people figuring out how much it affected him.

"Go. You need to go; I can see it in your eyes. I can look at these pictures later. There's no rush, and I'm tired anyway."

Glancing down at his watch, he was surprised to see it was almost 3 p.m. He still wanted to try to locate the friend that had last seen Kimora. If he found her in time, he might find Kimora, or at least a lead to her. But if she was involved and had gone underground, it would be almost impossible to bring the young girl home to her mom and brother. That scenario was simply unacceptable to Ethan.

"Are you sure? I hate to just drop you off and run out the door."

"I'm certain. In fact, I would be disappointed in you if you didn't go and look for her."

That was all the answer he needed from her. She got it. She understood the maddening drive in him more than just about any person could. Still, he sat and stared in her eyes longer than necessary, before he leaned forward and brushed a hair from her face.

"I have an APB out for her. But, I need to track down her friend. Today, before she disappears on me."

"Disappears?" Quinn paused a moment, her eyes widening, too smart for her own good. "She's connected to Becky, isn't she?"

"I honestly don't know. What I do know is there are similarities."

"Then you need to go now. Don't waste any time with me. I'll be fine. I can figure out where the bathroom is. Just go, find the friend."

"I'll be back with supper. Okay? Any requests?"

"I just really want a cheeseburger and fries. But don't worry about me. If you get a good lead, run with it, I can find something in your cupboards."

"Good luck with that. I haven't had time to shop in about a week. You might find cereal."

"Good enough for me."

"But you won't find any milk." She just laughed and swatted at his arm.

"Go. I'll be fine. Like I said, I want to take a nap anyway."

Even though he hated to leave her, he knew he had to. It was his job to help find Kimora Washington, before she got sucked into the underbelly of a bad world. With a nod of his head, he stood up and walked to the door. He was almost out the door when he looked over his shoulder at her. She looked so tiny and fragile sitting on his huge couch, but he knew better.

"I'm going to dead bolt the door. Other than Kara, I'm the only one who has a key. Get some rest. Hopefully, I'll be back in a few hours with good news."

Paulie's phone ringing startled him out of his thoughts. His single-minded concentration on the task at hand had him distracted and he wasn't expecting the phone call. But he knew who was on the other end. It was the only person who used that phone as was his rule. Swallowing once, twice, Paulie grimaced as he placed the phone to his ear.

"Hey, boss, what's up?"

"How's the assignment going?"

"Not as far on the homework as I wanted to be."

Paulie chose his words carefully for two reasons. Reason one being, you never knew who was listening, and reason two, he didn't want to piss off the man on the other end of the phone. No one who pissed off the boss lived to tell about it. Paulie didn't want to be one of the many that made it into the landfill or buried in some one-thousand-acre forest where some hunter might stumble on his remains one hundred years from now. He liked life too much, even the current horror show he got himself tangled up in.

"What, exactly, does that mean?"

Shit. He sounded mad. Paulie started to shake. Not for the first time, he considered running and never looking back, but he knew that the psycho on the other end of the line would find him. It didn't matter how long or how far he ran, he would never get out from under him.

"Just that we still only have the one. I need more time."

"You don't have more time. The order is for ten, not one, and we need them tonight. The customer will not accept another delay."

"I can't fulfill the order tonight. There are too many obstacles in the way to finish the assignment tonight. Not if you want the product willing to go." It was getting harder to choose the right words. Hopefully no one was listening.

"I could give a shit if the product is willing. I need nine more tonight. No excuses."

"Sir, with all due respect, I can't get nine, not from here and not in one night. They're already watching our operation closely." The young girl at the warehouse was already all over the news.

"Then branch out. Go to Milwaukee. There's enough product there to fill the order and then some. Go, now, and get me the rest of my order, and be damn careful. I know things are already hot around here. Make sure to pick what won't be missed."

No, shit. Paulie knew all too well how hot things were around here, and he also knew that if they got caught, he would take the blame while the boss walked around scot-free, because he couldn't rat him out and expect to live past the first day in prison if he told the police who the head of this operation was. If they got caught and he stayed quiet, what could he look forward to? Being someone's bitch in lock up, that's what. Unless he turned state's evidence and demanded witness protection? It seemed like the best option. He didn't have any family or friends he needed to keep in touch with, and they didn't take kindly to pedophiles in prison. Even if *he* wasn't a pedophile, he was party to selling girls and boys to plenty of people that were.

"Are you listening?"

"Yes, sir. You can count on me. I'll fill the order tonight."

Without another word, the bastard hung up, and the line went dead. Maybe witness protection was the way to go. If he took the fall and didn't say a word, he would be out of the game and have a roof over his head but being semi-free to do what he wanted was better. But, most importantly, he wouldn't have the sociopath controlling him any longer. He wouldn't have to run and hide. He would be in plain sight and not have to do the dirty work anymore. Even if he became some

129

guy's girlfriend, that wouldn't be so bad. Anything would be better than the mess he got himself into. One mistake, one freaking error in judgment, one moment of weakness with a girl who was just south of sixteen, and he was beholden to one of the evilest people he had ever met in his whole life.

15

Ethan was exhausted. Three hours and he couldn't find Kimora Washington's friend. Bridget was a ghost in the wind; she was nowhere to be found, and Ethan was frustrated. As he sat at a red light, he hit his steering wheel with his fist. If there was one thing his job had taught him, it was that time was running out for Kimora. If they didn't find her soon, they either would never find her, find her dead, or find her with only a semblance of herself remaining. He just couldn't let that happen. He couldn't let her be lost or have her life ruined.

The light turned green. When he didn't notice, a car honked behind him, and he inched forward into the intersection. The car flew around him. He switched on his lights to warn the jerk and then turned them off. In that moment, Ethan wanted nothing more than to be a beat cop again and pull over the arrogant jerk who had just torn by him and give him a ticket, to take out his irritation on the impatient ass. In the next instant, he was grateful that he wasn't that beat cop, because his anger was not controlled right now. Ethan prided himself on being calm, cool, and collected; while he knew he would never harm a person for merely speeding, he wasn't sure if given the opportunity he wouldn't smash in the head of the person who took Kimora, the person who had hurt Quinn, or the one who had hurt Taylor. He'd never gotten the chance at

Kara's abductors. That was probably a good thing. It was disgusting how long the list was of people he wanted to hurt for all the atrocities they had caused. In the end, he knew that wasn't him, that he would never hurt someone if it wasn't self-defense. He knew it, didn't he?

About a block from his house, he realized that he'd forgotten supper for Quinn, so he circled around and headed to his favorite burger place. When he walked in, the bartender, Jonny, nodded at him, and before Ethan was even seated, he had a cold bottle of beer in front of him. He gladly drew a long pull of the beer. On a day like today, he would allow himself a beer. Normally, he didn't drink much at all. With his job, he never knew if he would get called in, and he had seen too many friends fall victim to the bottle. In their line of work, it wasn't that hard.

"Rough day?" Jonny asked.

"Could have been better. I need to order a couple cheeseburgers and some fries to go."

"Hungry?" Jonny's eyebrow was raised.

"I have a friend convalescing at my place. She's craving a cheeseburger and fries, just make sure no avocado comes close to it. She has an allergy."

Jonny laughed and walked away. Knowing the bartender well, Ethan wasn't sure if he was laughing about the avocado comment or that he was bringing supper home for a woman, but he didn't give a rat's ass what Jonny or anyone else thought was going on. Of course, he would also set them straight if they even thought to say something about the integrity of the woman, who was hopefully sleeping on his couch. Which reminded him, when he got home he was going to correct that little error. No way should she be sleeping on his couch when she was still healing. He slammed the last of his beer and stared at the label thinking how good that beer tasted and how badly he wanted another, but before he could act on it, Jonny was back setting a bag on the bar in front of him.

"How much?"

"On the house."

"Bullshit, how much?"

"Listen, I want to buy the meal for the woman who finally tamed the heart of Casanova. You do know that's what people call you behind your back, right? Casanova or Cas. Anyway, it's about damn time someone got your attention." Before Ethan could muster a response, the gossipy bartender had walked away to help another patron. Was he really that transparent?

Ten minutes later, he was unlocking the door as quietly as possible, hoping not to wake up Quinn if she was sleeping, but when he walked through the door, he saw that she was sitting up and looking through the album of pictures he had left on the table. Her skin still had remnants of the allergic reaction from earlier, but she looked better already.

"Hey, I thought you'd be sleeping."

"I did for a bit, then some noise woke me up."

"What noise?" he asked, his teeth on edge.

"Relax, it was just a cat outside. Pretty insistent one, too. I think she wanted in here."

"Ah, yeah, that would be Cat." He ran his hand through his hair, embarrassed.

"I realize it was a cat; I just said a cat wanted inside." She rolled her eyes at him, and he couldn't stop himself from thinking that she looked adorable.

"No, I mean, her name is Cat."

"You named the cat Cat? Are you kidding me?"

"No, I mean, yes, I named the cat Cat, and no, I'm not kidding you. Kara dropped the stupid thing off one day. She thought I needed a friend. She gets this big manly dog to bring everywhere and gets me a freaking kitten." Her answering smile left him conflicted. He felt turned on and embarrassed at the same time. "What are you smiling about?"

"Your sister gave you a kitten, and you named it Cat. That has got to be a first for me. I mean, you could have named her Black Widow or Pepper or something manlier."

"Are you listing off comic book names?" Now she was blushing, which he liked just as much as the smile.

"You're missing the point."

"And what's your point?" he asked, leaning a hip on the counter while crossing his arms across his chest.

"I don't know, just that you could have picked any name, and you picked that. Even Socks would have worked. I mean, she has white feet. I find it funny, that's all. Anyway, I'm glad to know that Cat is your cat."

"Why is that?"

"Because she wouldn't shut up, so I let her in. I mean, I saw the litter box when I went to the bathroom, so I assumed she was yours."

It was then that he noticed that there was a gray ball of fur blending into the blanket that she had wrapped around her. The traitorous beast was curled up, no doubt purring like crazy, next to the woman that he wanted like none other, and all he could do was smile that they were getting along. How lame was that? Then he realized that to let in Cat, she would have had to open the door and go into the hallway to open the front door. That thought made his blood run cold.

"She's a sweetheart, by the way."

"You unlocked the door and went into the hallway to let her in? In the shape you're in?"

"Whoa, easy, Mr. Overprotective. First, I can take care of myself. Even in this shape, I'm not helpless. Second, she was sitting on your porch, so I just opened the window to tell her to quiet down, and she hopped in."

"Oh, because that makes it so much better, you opened the window and let her in. Did you lock the window when you were done?"

"Yes, I let the cat in through the window. What's the big deal? Listen, I live in a pretty crappy part of town. Like I said, I can take care of myself just fine."

"The big deal is that someone tried to run you over yesterday. As in one day ago, as in twenty-four mere hours ago. Self-preservation isn't a bad thing. I'm just asking you be more cautious."

"I'm being cautious. I let the cat in, locked the window, which wasn't locked by the way, and closed the blinds."

"What do you mean it wasn't locked?"

"It wasn't locked. Not hard to interpret that statement. Now that I think about it, why don't you have a screen on the window? If I wasn't on drugs, that would have seemed strange earlier. What? Why are you looking like that?"

"Like what?"

"All freaked out and in cop mode."

"Why? Because I wouldn't leave my window unlocked. Come to think of it, I don't remember letting the cat out. Stay here."

Without a glance back at her, he left the apartment and locked the dead bolt behind him. He wouldn't put it past her to try to follow him, but he hoped that she was smarter than that. Walking around the front of his porch, he took out the pocket flashlight he carried with him. It was small, but it would do the job. It didn't take him long to examine the porch and see exactly nothing. The windowsill looked fine; it didn't look jimmied, but then he didn't expect it to look out of place. The question was, had he been stupid enough to leave his window unlocked? He had let her in through the window before. With a bad feeling in the pit of his stomach, he went inside.

"Find anything?"

"No, and to answer your question, I removed the screen a week ago. It was warped and needs to be replaced. I haven't gotten around to doing it. Too busy, and to be honest, I was being lazy. It's easier to let Cat in through the window when she cries in the middle of the night. She likes to come and go."

"That is a silly habit to let her get into with winter not so far away."

"You let her in through the window, too."

"Well, she was driving me crazy with the meowing at the window, and I didn't have it in me to walk to the front door."

Ethan had stupidly forgotten that her body had been put through an ordeal. Looking at her, he obviously couldn't forget she had been injured, but he forgot that it might be taxing on her to walk that far. Which was dumb on his part. After all, that was the reason he'd brought her to his apartment, wasn't it? Nope, not entirely. He'd also brought her there so he could keep her safe. So far, he was doing a terrible job of it.

"I should have thought of that, how your body is sore. I'm sorry. I also should have told you I have an annoying cat."

"Named Cat." She chuckled a little, and then her eyebrows narrowed, and she looked at him with a serious expression on her face. "Full disclosure?" He wasn't sure he liked the sound of that.

"Always."

"I was also scared to go to the front door."

That realization nearly tore Ethan in two, and the inner possessive Neanderthal wanted to break out and barricade his apartment with Quinn safely inside.

Quinn hated that she had revealed that she was scared. No doubt Ethan had already ascertained that, but admitting it was not something she was thrilled about doing. She was totally going to blame it on the blasted drugs. It made her mind tired and her mouth sloppy. Of course, it could also have something to do with the mouthwatering man who was currently standing and staring at her like he would tear apart the next person who came through the door to protect her. Yikes, the man was sexy on any given day, but all testosterone filled, he was a sight to behold. Even if she didn't normally care for the overprotective type, it was nice to feel…feel, what exactly? Liked?

"I shouldn't have left you here alone."

"Don't be ridiculous. You needed to go search for Kimora. I shouldn't be putting my own fears and worries in front of the fears and worries of Keisha, who just wants her daughter to come home. I'm ashamed to say that I forgot that was where you went."

"You shouldn't be ashamed. If you can distance your mind from it all and get some rest, then I say good for you."

"I still feel like an awful person. But you're right, I did manage to get some sleep. I guess that's a win. At least, I slept until Cat kept meowing and woke me up. Then when I let her in, she cuddled up in the middle of the couch, taking up all the space." Quinn rubbed the cat affectionately.

"Yeah, she is kind of a furniture hog."

While he spoke, he walked to the kitchen and rummaged around. She angled herself so she could watch him and saw that he was getting plates and silverware. It wasn't until that moment that she focused on the amazing smell that had filled the room. Whatever container the food had been in had managed to mask most of the delicious smell, and her mouth began to water at the aroma as Ethan walked in with two plates full of food. He set one on the coffee table in front of her and one in front of the chair that was next to the couch. Then he went into the kitchen again and came back with two tall glasses of milk

"I would offer you a beer, but I don't think that's a good idea with the drugs you're on. Unfortunately, I only have milk and water to offer, and I decided milk is good for bones—broken bone and all." His smile was wicked.

"I thought you said you didn't have milk?"

"I stopped and got some."

"I went through your pictures. You did an amazing job on the place."

Without asking, he placed the plate on her lap and then sat down. She glanced at the humongous cheeseburger on her plate and then looked at his plate and immediately felt foolish when her eyes stung with tears, because he had cut her cheeseburger in half to make it easier for her to cat, and for some reason, that small gesture was enough to undo her. Blinking furiously to push back the tears that threatened, she picked up the cheeseburger and took a bite and immediately moaned. Now she wasn't worried about tears, because when she looked up at Ethan, he was frozen with his cheeseburger halfway to his mouth, and he was staring at her.

"What?" she asked, suddenly self-conscious.

"Um, nothing."

If her eyes weren't deceiving her, Ethan Vanderbilt, stud-muffin-extraordinaire, was blushing. She set her cheeseburger down, and while she chewed, she reached up and rubbed her eyes. Clearly, she was exhausted. It was obvious that she needed sleep if she thought for one second that Ethan was blushing. But when she opened her eyes, she saw the same pink cheeks. Even though he was now studiously ignoring her and focusing with single-minded attention on his own food, she could still see that he was embarrassed. Over what, though?

Sweet mother above, she had moaned when she took a bite of the cheeseburger. It was an annoying habit of hers when she bit into something good; especially if she was extremely hungry, she often found herself moaning out of sheer pleasure from the food. Kara had once told her that it sounded like she was orgasming. Oh, God, had she really done that in front of him?

"You liked the pictures of the apartment, then?"

"Huh?" she asked, confused.

"The apartment?" he prompted.

Right, the pictures. She'd mentioned she was looking through the pictures before she went all food porn on them. Focus. She needed to focus on the conversation, so she didn't look like a complete moron.

"Yeah, I mean, the pictures are awesome. But, I really am more impressed with how you rehabbed this house. You did a great job."

"I can't take the credit. I mean, I knew what I wanted, and I helped. But I hired people to do a lot of the work, and Caleb and his family helped quite a bit."

"You can tell."

"Tell that they helped? How is that?"

"I can just tell from the pictures of before and after that a lot of love was put into your home. That's all."

"Thank you—for noticing how much this place means to me. I know you haven't had much time to think about it, but I really think that you should take the apartment. I actually talked to Kara about it when the renovations were complete. I was trying to figure out a way to approach you without…" He paused.

"Without what?"

"Without having you think it was a handout. I know you're a proud person, but Kara and I both worry about you in that house by yourself.

That isn't a safe part of the city, and like you said before, you help people that have volatile relationships." She took another bite of the cheeseburger and chewed thoughtfully for a moment before replying.

"I can't argue with that logic. You're right, I'm a proud person, but the time is right for me to move, if I can afford the place."

"Well, you see, that is why I hadn't approached you yet." He hedged.

"What do you mean?" Her heart sunk a little because obviously, the apartment was more than she could afford.

"It's just that Kara and I agreed that we want you to have the apartment at no charge."

"What?" Quinn shrieked and sat up straighter and then winced, she caught that Ethan noticed the pain that had crossed her face, but she blazed on. "No charge? Are you out of your ever-loving mind? Why would you do that?"

"First, because Kara knows you deserve more than the center can pay you. Second, because you deserve a safe environment to come home to, and what better place than here where a cop lives? Not to mention, I don't need the money. Kara and I own this place free and clear, thanks to my trust fund, a trust fund that I feel pretty strongly should be used to make the world a better place for people who have been victimized."

"You're crazy. You know that, right?"

"I don't think I'm crazy at all. I just want to help people like Kara and Taylor and you." He added the last part quietly. "We want this to be a benefit for you, since you run the center single-handedly, and I also talked to Kara about subletting the apartments to families trying to get on their feet again. The only problem is figuring out who to let have the apartments. Ideally, we would like you to help us decide who should get the apartments."

"You mean you want me to help pick families to live here? I don't know if I could choose. There are so many in need."

"I know. That's one of the reasons we haven't done it yet, but I don't want to drag my feet any longer. Think on it. But just know that if you move into the apartment, I won't accept a dime from you for it."

He quietly stood and collected their dishes. When he came back, she steered the subject away from the apartment.

"Did you find Kimora's friend?" she asked.

"No. She's in the wind. Just like I expected her to be. Which is part of the reason I'm later getting home than I had planned."

"I was really hoping that wasn't the case." A huge yawn caught her off guard, and Ethan stared at her, his eyes full of concern.

"I'm going to go get my bed ready for you."

She opened her mouth and closed it a few times, unsure what to do with that statement.

"There is no way I'm letting you sleep on the couch. I'll sleep on the couch tonight, and you can have my bed."

After he walked away, she thought about how her core had tightened and warmth had spread to all the right places at the mere mention of Ethan's bed. Oh dear, even in the shape she was in, he turned her on. She was definitely in trouble where Ethan Vanderbilt was concerned. Even if he was a bit high-handed.

Kimora was scared, and even though she was blindfolded, she could sense the room she was being held in was dark and cavernous. Her body was trembling. It was still summer, but she was frozen to the bone. Why had someone taken her, and where was she being held? She just wanted to go home. She would do anything to go home and hug her mom and listen to her brother talk back to her. Tears streamed down her face as she thought of the last words she had said to her mom, how she had snapped at her about her responsibilities to watch her brother. Kimora would do anything to take those words back. Her mother worked so hard to make ends meet, to take care of Davon and herself. It would devastate her mother to lose her only daughter, but she wouldn't let it break her. Her mother was too strong for that.

A noise had her jumping, and she strained to hear where it was coming from. She was almost sure it was coming from in front of her, and it sounded like a door rolling up and then closing. Had someone found her? Was it the police there to rescue her? She could only hope that was the case, but when she didn't hear someone call out, she felt the small surge of hope flicker and fade. A dragging sound had her body tensing and straining against her bindings. Then a thud, a wet sounding thud, and a whimper.

"I brought you some friends to keep you company for now. At least until we transfer you to your new home." The male voice sounded almost remorseful. "I'm really sorry about this. You probably don't believe me, but it can't be helped."

The sound of footsteps retreating and then returning while dragging something or *someone* else had the hair on her arms standing on end. Kimora had held on to the hope that she was going to get out of there, but when the footsteps retreated a second time and returned dragging another object that she could only assume was another person, the flicker of hope completely died. There was no chance she was getting out of wherever he had her held. At least not to go home to her mom and brother. He had said he had brought her a few friends until she was transferred to her new home. Oh, God, what did he mean? But she knew. Down deep, she knew what he meant, and it chilled her to the bone.

Paulie hated this job, hated what he was being forced to do, but the self-preservation he felt was more important to him than the three girls and one boy that he had stored in the warehouse his boss owned. If he could find a way around it, he would. For now, he had to collect five more girls and one more boy, and the order would be filled. Unfortunately, he couldn't grab them all from Darkness Falls or they would have an even bigger target on their operation. As if it could get much bigger than it already was. He couldn't chance it, though, so the other six teenagers would have to come from nearby Milwaukee. He only hoped that he grabbed the right ones so that they were less likely to be missed right away.

Glancing nervously at the clock, he did the math and realized he only had a couple hours until he had to be back with the order. He needed more time in order to be picky about who he grabbed. He swallowed hard. There wasn't much he could do but grab the kids and run. Not ideal, but he would do what he had to because he was not going to end up in an unmarked grave.

Pulling the van to a stop, he watched a group of teenagers that were out way later than curfew. Grab the whole group or just a couple? It'd be hard to grab the whole group. Waiting to see if the group would break up, he was rewarded after only ten minutes when he saw two girls wave goodbye and head down the alley next to where he was parked. Now he only had to wait for the rest of the group to leave. When they lingered for a moment, he began to get discouraged, but then they, too, began to leave, walking away from the van. It was perfect, as if fate had directed him to the two girls.

He got out of the van with the stun gun and quietly followed, looking both ways before he entered the maw of the dark abyss of the alley. When he saw no one else, he picked up the pace and was on them in a matter of a couple long strides. One girl was down before the other even knew what was happening. The second girl dropped to the ground a mere few seconds later. Maybe he had used too much juice because they were out almost too easy. Shrugging, he picked one of them up. Five minutes later, he had both girls bound, gagged, and stashed in the back of the van with blankets thrown over them. Two down, four to go. If the night continued in this way, he would be back to the warehouse with his new acquisitions with time to spare.

16

Quinn woke up sweaty and confused. She'd been having a bad dream, and the awful sensation lingered, even after she blinked the sleepiness out of her eyes. She blinked a few times more until her eyes adjusted to the darkness in the room, but it still took her a full minute to remember that she was at Ethan's place and that she was in his luxurious bed. Smiling a little, she did a full body stretch, much like a feline, and then she felt the little engine purring next to her. Cat had snuggled in by her after she had fallen asleep. Lying there, she realized she was wide awake, and there was no chance she was falling asleep anytime soon.

Thirst and an aching arm had her gently pushing back the blanket, so as not to disturb her bedmate. Her feet touched the plush rug that covered the impeccable hardwood floor. Slightly dizzy, she waited a moment before standing up to quietly search for a glass of water. Her search was short-lived when her eyes alighted on the glass of water, pain pill, and a note on the table by the bed. Turning on the bedside light, she squinted through the soft glow at the note.

I figured you might end up needing one of these and didn't want you to have to search for it. No need to be a tough girl. Ethan

If there was anything Quinn had learned in the last day, it was that she wasn't very tough at all. Not if judging by the fact that she whole-heartedly agreed to take the pill sitting on the table, but she knew that she wasn't going to allow herself to take them that much longer. It wasn't just the way they muddled her mind and her movements, but the fact that she led a fairly clean lifestyle and didn't allow herself to even drink alcohol. She had seen too many addicts and had a healthy dose of fear of addiction.

After placing the pill in her mouth, she took a long swallow of the water and then another. It was so cold and refreshing, and the pills made her mouth so dry. After another long sip, she realized that the water was much colder than it should have been if Ethan had put it on the bedside table shortly after she had fallen asleep. Which led her to believe it hadn't been that long ago since he had set it there. Of course, he could have just put ice in the glass, but she found that she hoped he was awake, since she couldn't sleep. After she guzzled down the rest of the water, she tiptoed to the door. If Ethan was sleeping, she didn't want to be the reason he woke up.

Slowly, she turned the doorknob and silently slipped out of the room. Walking as lightly as possible wasn't all that easy when she was still slightly unsteady on her feet. Her normally graceful gait was wobbly at best, but she somehow managed to get down the hallway without crashing into the walls. Of course, it helped keeping her hand on the wall to guide her way. Before she knew what was happening, though, the wall disappeared, and she stumbled forward, her flailing limbs propelling her until she crashed into the back of the couch. Her right arm shot out and stopped her from toppling over the back—or worse, falling and causing more damage to her left arm. It didn't take her long to ascertain that Ethan was not asleep and that her right hand had landed in a very precarious spot.

Embarrassment flooded her as she tried to regain her footing, but it wasn't until she could see Ethan's body shaking with his attempt to hide his laughter that she finally gave up and busted out laughing herself.

"So much for sneaking out of the room and not waking you up," she said between gasping breaths for air.

"First, I heard you open the door. Second, you were far from stealth like in your trip down the hallway," he replied after he was able to control his laughter. When she didn't immediately respond, concern etched his face. "Are you okay?"

Was she okay? If ever she had heard a loaded question, this was the time. Physically, she was fine, other than the racing heart and the sudden pooling of heat in the middle of her legs. Because Ethan was very much nearly naked on the couch, and the blanket he had been using was covering the only part of him that appeared to be clothed, which left some, but not much, to the imagination, and currently that imagination was taking in the V of his torso and distracting her on a whole new level. It didn't help that her hand was brushing up against something that was getting harder by the second.

"Quinn? Hey, Earth to Quinn, are you okay? You didn't hit your wrist, did you?"

"What? Um, no, um…I just…" She was rambling but couldn't stop herself. Staring at his chest and that blessed V had her girly parts in a frenzy. A frenzy she had never in her life felt—not once. Try as hard as she might, she couldn't drag her eyes away from it or him. No matter how much her brain told her to *look away, look away now*, it wasn't computing to her actual eyes, which were apparently paralyzed because of the kryptonite that was his abs—his washboard abs. Seriously, how much time did he put into those things?

"What is that saying? 'Take a picture, it'll last longer'?"

Darn it. She could hear the smirk in his words and that was all it took to get her eyes to snap to his face and break the trance she had slipped into. But even though he was smirking, it didn't quite reach his eyes. His eyes had gone dark, and his voice, while cocky, was also husky, and she was terrified he could sense, or worse yet, smell, the dampness between her legs. Was the arousal that was apparent to her, equally obvious to him? Or was he simply reacting because he was Casanova and a scantily clothed woman had nearly fallen into his lap? Worried that was the case, she fell back on the tried and true Quinn persona. Somehow managing to pull her hand away from dangerous territory, she pulled herself up to her full height.

"Why would I want to do that? Oh, that's right, Mr. Every-

Woman's-Wet-Dream thinks all women fall over themselves with desire around him." Truer words had never been spoken. He sat up then, and his face was mere inches from hers.

"If that's how you want to play it, then prove it."

Before she could say anything back, his mouth was on hers, and she was melting into his arms. She put up a fight for all of two-point-two seconds, and then her mouth parted on a gasp and allowed his tongue access to her mouth where it pillaged. It wasn't Quinn's style to be outdone, and while she was not an accomplished kisser, she gave as good as she got. Her good hand reached toward him and ran up his chest and into his hair, tugging him closer to her, with the back of the couch between, she couldn't get close enough to him. She only partially noted that the blanket had fallen down to pool by his knees. He deepened the kiss on a moan. The sound only encouraged her, and she rubbed her chest on his. Even with the shirt separating them, it was apparent that her nipples were hard as diamonds. His hands slipped down to the hem of her shirt and hesitated before he reached under and caressed her stomach with his fingers.

Stomach muscles quivering from the contact, she gasped as he released her mouth and kissed his way down her neck until his mouth landed on that too-hard nipple, and he sucked it into his mouth through the shirt. Her body arched into the touch as she tried to will the couch between them away. The naughty mouth that had soaked through the shirt and taunted her nipple made its way to the other nipple, which was eager for the equal opportunity clause of the night. Those sneaky fingers were inching up the hem of her shirt when Cat jumped onto the back of the couch and scared the ever-living crap out of her. Quinn jumped backward guiltily, as if she had personally affronted the feline intruder.

"Holy crap, Cat! You scared the bejeezus out of me." Quinn was panting as her hand flew to her chest, and Ethan pulled away, clearly startled himself. One look at the expression on his face and the spell was broken. Stumbling, she retreated as fast as she could down the hallway with a hasty good-night as he called after her to come back, but she didn't turn around. Once safely ensconced in his bedroom, she crumpled onto the bed ready to figuratively lick her wounds, because if she wasn't mistaken, that was a big dose of *regret* on Ethan's face, and that is exactly the opposite of what she wanted to see on the face of the first man she had ever gotten that hot and steamy with.

Ethan wanted to kick his ass after he saw the expression on Quinn's face. Cat had broken up one of the happiest moments of his life, sexually speaking, and while he wanted to kill the cat, he also wanted to thank her for stopping things before they went too far. Not because he didn't want to sleep with Quinn. He was pretty sure he would walk over hot coals to do just that, but she was still healing from nearly being run over, and she wasn't ready mentally to make love to him. She was getting there, but if he slept with her tonight, he was almost certain it would end up being a one and done because Quinn would regret it immediately after. Which is exactly the opposite of what he wanted to happen when he finally made love to her. What he wanted was to convince her that it was not a one-time deal.

The buzzing of his phone caught his attention and gave him a much-needed reprieve from the turmoil churning through his head. Glancing down at his phone, he cursed under his breath. The text was short, and it was definitely not the kind he wanted to get in the middle of the night.

Two girls. One boy. Missing within minutes of each other.

What the hell was going on? He threw a quick text back at him.

Any link to Kimora Washington? The answering text was fast and to the point.

Unknown. Probable. Report in. ASAP.

Ethan was already dressed in the clothes from the previous day and on his way down the hallway. Even if his captain hadn't told him to go in, he would have. Three kids missing on the same night was not a coincidence. He would lay money down that they were taken for nefarious reasons and that they didn't have much time before they wouldn't be found. Regretting the fact that he had to barge in on Quinn's privacy, especially after what had almost happened in the living room, he gently knocked on his bedroom door.

"I don't want to talk right now." Her voice sounded miserable, and Ethan once again wanted to kick his own ass, but he didn't have time for that.

"Quinn, listen, I'm sorry; I know we need to talk, and I know now isn't the time. Even if it was, I wouldn't have time. I hate to disturb you, but something just came up and I have to leave. I didn't want to leave without telling you, and I hate to—" The door swung open before he could finish his sentence. He stared at Quinn like she was his life-line and could heal the sadness that had engulfed him at the thought of three more kids missing.

"What's happened?" she asked intuitively.

"Three kids went missing tonight. We aren't sure if it's connected to Kimora or not, but I'm going in." There was no use keeping any of it from her. She moved to the side and opened the door for him to enter.

"You need your gun." It wasn't a question, she knew he had put it in his gun safe before they went to bed.

With a brisk nod, he strode to the gun safe that was under the bed. He stood and turned and saw her looking at him with a lost expression on her face, and it was almost more than he could take. Without thinking about what he was doing, he took two long strides toward her and kissed her with all he had in him.

"I want you to lock the door behind me, dead bolt, too, and do me a favor—don't argue with me—but I want you to check the window locks for me. I'll be back as soon as I can, and when I get back, we'll have that talk." He covered her mouth with his in desperation when she opened it to say something and continued to kiss her until she kissed him back. "Promise me."

"I promise. Be careful. I'll be waiting for you when you get home."

He pulled her in for another kiss before he finally released her. She followed him to the front door and he waited in the hallway until he heard the dead bolt click into place. Good enough. It had to be, because as much as he wanted or needed to be, he couldn't be in two places at once, and he had to trust that she would be the smart woman he knew her to be and keep herself out of harm's way while he was gone. His instincts were screaming at him to not leave Quinn alone, but he had a job to do first. It was more important now than ever because, while Ethan couldn't explain the feeling buzzing along his nerves, he knew—just knew—the shit was about to hit the fan.

The cell phone in his hand vibrated as he was getting in his car. No doubt Caleb asking where the hell he was. Ethan had sent him a text that he would pick him up in ten minutes, but he was running a couple minutes late. Good thing they lived close to each other. He sent a quick message that he would be there in five and climbed in the car. He glanced at his front window before he backed out of the driveway and saw Quinn holding Cat while she checked the lock. She waved stoically at him and pulled the curtain shut.

Exhaustion seeped into his bones, nearly incapacitating him, but he'd done it. He'd managed to get all ten acquisitions in time for the transfer. Hopefully, things would go down smoothly, and his boss would be none the wiser about what he had to do to get the children. Of course, he still had to get the packages to the actual rendezvous point, but once that was done, he deserved a vacation or something for his troubles. He pulled the van into the warehouse and cut the lights. Quickly exiting the vehicle, he made his way to the storage area where he had left the other four kids hog-tied and gagged. He breathed a sigh of relief when he saw all four huddled together. For some reason, he had a bad feeling that they wouldn't be there when he got back. That something or someone would figure it all out and get them out of there. Paulie laughed under his breath, just superstitions, there was no reason to worry. None at all.

One by one, he dragged each kid to the van, but he waited to use the stun gun on them until they were in the van. He was too tired from driving around all night grabbing the other six kids and dragging their butts into the van. He couldn't drag another four unconscious kids around, even if it wasn't that far. It was far easier to have them conscious. Even if they were fighting him, they weren't dead weight, and since the order was for petite children *not yet through puberty,* it wasn't that hard.

After they were all in the van, he shut the door and jogged around to the driver's side of the van. He had rigged the door so it could only be opened from the outside, so he wasn't worried they would be able to get out. He was more worried he would be late, and he knew from experience not to ever be late for this particular client. The one and only time he'd been late, the buyer had almost walked away, and his boss had nearly killed him in a blind rage for almost losing him his best customer. That was the only time Paulie had messed up, and he was damned certain he wasn't going to let it happen again. He had decided a long time ago that if he was going to be late, he would just keep driving and not look back. He'd be dead either way, but at least he'd go out on his own terms.

A quick glance at the clock on the dash had him swearing under his breath. It was going to be close, but if traffic cooperated, he would be there with about ten minutes to spare. Paulie did the sign of the cross. He knew it was wrong to pray for help in delivering these children to a monster, but he was raised in a very religious family and the habit was ingrained in him. Besides, he needed the extra help if all was going to work out like he wanted. If his mom knew what he did for a job, well, it was a good thing she was six feet under because even if she were rolling over in her grave, she wasn't here for him to see the disappointment in her eyes, and that was a very, very good thing. In fact, it was the only thing that allowed him to sleep at night.

Black watched the van pull out of the warehouse and disappear down the road, the lights off. Paulie wasn't a novice and knew how to get in and out with little detection. Unfortunately for him, his luck had run out when Black went undercover. If there was one thing he was good at, it was trailing people. Undetected. He had discovered right away how to get the fastest results, and that was by following Paulie, which he'd been doing for months. It was so much easier to get to him than the head guy.

Black had been told to infiltrate the network, find the head of the sex trafficking ring, and get in his good graces. It hadn't taken as long as he thought it would to find out that the person in charge was Vance Duprey. It had taken much longer to work his way up the food chain and accomplish the latter part of his directive, and even though he'd begun to earn the trust of the man, he hadn't met him face-to-face. Few people in his inner circle got to meet him. Things had begun to heat up in the operation over the last few weeks. There was a power struggle going on, and someone was trying to take a cut of the pie for themselves, which was making the big guy livid. For now, Black had been told to hold his ground and observe unless something crucial changed.

There was no question in his mind that something crucial had changed. The timetable for this current order of children was short, as if the buyer was testing the capability of the purveyor of his goods. It made sense, since Black had been quietly working to undermine this particular operation for weeks, and part of the power struggle was a direct result of his machinations. But the tight turnaround was not a good thing for their operation. However, it was great for his operation, because it meant that mistakes were being made. Paulie had been sloppy for weeks. He had no idea what had been happening all around him. Another point for the good guys. Paulie knew his days were numbered, and it was definitely good timing for him to figure that out. It helped Black gain his trust, which was why Paulie had reached out to him.

It was a good thing Black was good at making himself invisible. Tonight might be enough to end it all. All he needed to do was follow him until they got to the rendezvous point so he could ensure that they took down the buyer and got those kids because there was no freaking way he was letting those kids into the hands of a monster. His left hand tight on the wheel, he grabbed the burner phone and speed dialed his handler.

"Got word of movement." His tone was clipped. He wasn't alone and able to talk freely. Even if he were alone, he would still be cautious. Black wasn't the only one who was good at his job. His handler was one of the best.

"Be ready. I have eyes on the shipment. Keep the line open. I'm not sure of the exact rendezvous point. I will get you coordinates."

"What's your position?"

"Currently traveling south on Jefferson." He disconnected. It would have to be good enough for now; he couldn't keep the line open forever.

———

The line went dead and the man on the other end of the phone took a deep breath, hoping they would get the coordinates in time. For now, he would have to be happy with calling in Black's location. He stressed over the phone call that they had to go in silent. They weren't sure of the exact location, and if they all converged on Jefferson with lights and sirens, they would tip their hand before it was advisable and fuck the whole thing up. But he didn't have to wait long until he got word by text.

Old Dump Rd. Two miles S of CTY TRK B.

Now it was time to call in the cavalry and hope they got there in time.

17

Surprisingly, all the vehicles converged at the right time, but even more surprising was that no one had come in with lights and sirens on. Even though the edict had gone out saying everyone should come in sans all the bells and whistles, messages get lost and the chance that someone would have come in hot and loud was pretty large. Ethan sighed a breath of relief. He was hoping that they were about to find Kimora and get her returned to her family. If that was the case, he was hoping she would be relatively unharmed, since she hadn't been transferred to the third party who had requisitioned her kidnapping.

They were supposed to stand down until they saw the exchange begin. They couldn't take down the buyer without some indication there were actually children in the van and that the people in the other van were there to purchase them. There was no question that they had the seller. After all, how would he explain having ten minors tied up in his van? Ethan watched impatiently, waiting for the freaking buyer to get out of his car. They had been waiting for five minutes. For what, he didn't know. Maybe the buyer suspected something was amiss or maybe he was just being a world class jerk and making the seller wait.

Finally, after what seemed like hours, the door to the other van opened, and a woman got out. Not a man, like Ethan would have expected for an exchange with so many bodies to control, but then the passenger door of the van opened, and the muscle got out. Apparently, there was a tag team on the buyer side, but the lone seller stood waiting. From his position and due to the pitch-black night, it was hard to make out the faces of the people on the road. But he could tell that the seller looked fidgety and with good reason. He just wanted to transfer the kids and get the hell out of Dodge. Smart man—well, not really. After all, he'd just kidnapped ten kids and not very expertly, since he was surrounded by police.

They were at the dangerous part of the exchange. They couldn't afford one of the officers to get jumpy and open fire, not with a van full of kids in the cross fire, but that wasn't their only obstacle. If they waited until one of the kids was taken out of the van, then it could turn into a hostage situation with a child for a shield. They had to take down the three people quickly. Once the order was issued, they would converge from all sides and take them out of the scene.

What the hell were they doing in there? Just get out of the damn van already and take the kids. Hell, take the van they were currently in and leave. Paulie would be willing to walk the five miles to his piece of shit apartment. He could get a new van. Once he finally saw movement, he relaxed a fraction. About damn time. He got out of the van, eager to get this show on the road so he could get the hell out of there.

"I have your order." He knew it was a stupid statement. They knew he wouldn't have shown up if he didn't have the kids. Judging by the look on the female's face, she was thinking the same thing.

"The money will be transferred as soon as we see the product," she said briskly, all business, as if she were talking about microwaves and not children.

"Hurry up. We don't have all night. The boss is in a hurry for his product," the meathead muscle demanded.

Paulie thought to himself, *listen asshole, you're the one delaying things*, but he just nodded his head and moved to open the van. The quicker he got out of there, the better. His hand was on the door handle, and he had just opened it when a noise behind him distracted him, and he stopped mid-motion and turned to look over his shoulder in time to see first the woman, then the man's head turn to red mist, and a fraction of a second before the bullet cleaved his head. He barely had enough time to regret his decision and to think of his mom before it was lights out for Paulie Romano.

———

The man had just walked around to the van, and Ethan was ready to spring into action when all hell broke loose. The man heard a noise at the same time Ethan did. It was coming from the far side of the road, but before he could fully process the pop, the woman's head was gone, then the beefcake, then the driver of the van holding the kids. Three rapid shots—pop, pop, pop, and they were all down. What the hell had just happened? The silent field turned into chaos. He could make out several voices yelling *stand down*. He knew the shots that were fired had not come from one of them. But they didn't want somebody light on the trigger finger to shoot up that van.

In his ear, he heard the team leader shouting, *"Everyone. Stand. The. Fuck. Down! No one shoot. I need the northern position to move on that van. We need those kids out of there before this turns into a war zone."* That was his cue to move; he and Caleb were positioned the closest to the van. They were both covered in full tactical gear, but even that might not be enough if there was a sniper out there. Staying low to the ground, they rushed the van, not even looking at the bodies that were laying in triple pools of blood. At that moment, he had never been more thankful that they had taken the SWAT training. The city didn't have enough money to have a full-time SWAT team, and Darkness Falls didn't really require one. Thankfully, instances like this were few and far between. Therefore, SWAT was comprised of officers from throughout the force that doubled up on work duties when the need arose. So far, it worked out well.

Ethan slid open the door of the van as Caleb watched his six and was greeted with two feet to the face. One of the kids was ready for their abductor and wasn't going without a fight. He would find the time to be proud when he stopped seeing stars. The kid sure packed a punch behind those feet; he could taste blood in his mouth. If only the kid had aimed for his Kevlar protected chest.

"Darkness Falls PD, we're here to help, but we need to get you out of this van and to safety," he said quickly.

The young kid was pulling back his feet to kick again but stopped and assessed Ethan before his face crumpled and he began to cry. Shit, the young boy looked to be only eleven. The blood in his veins boiled at that realization, and he had to tamp it down as he looked at each of the scared faces.

"Listen to me and listen closely. I want you all to stay put for now. We need to secure the scene, and then we're going to get you out of here and back to your families. Copy that?" He watched, his stomach sinking as he realized there were ten kids in the van, and all ten of those heads bobbed up and down in unison. "Good."

There was crackling in his ear and then he heard, *"All clear. We found where the SOB was hiding, the grass and brush are trampled. Whoever it was is a professional, not to mention a jackass. Left the gun behind, guess he knows that won't net us any evidence."*

"All right, we got the all clear to get you out of here. But I want you to stay tight to me. I'm going to take two of you at a time and bring you to the other good guys. Got it?" He watched as once again, all the heads bobbed in unison.

There was no need to get too gutsy. Even if the shooter had left, there was still a small chance they were lying in wait somewhere else or that they had an accomplice. After he sliced through the bindings, he helped two of the kids from the van, leaving Caleb behind as he made five trips to the police caravan waiting. It was a long process, but easier to control the scene if all eyes were trained on the van and him escorting the children two at a time. They didn't want to have too many kids to watch if the shooter was still out there. Though Ethan figured whoever it was had made like a ghost and vanished.

Once all the kids were safely inside the police vehicle set up to take them to the hospital, he climbed in and looked at all of their faces again. Now that he had good lighting, he wanted to see if Kimora was among the group. He was about to give up hope when his eyes landed on the last girl huddled in the group, and his eyes stung when he saw that it was Kimora.

"Kimora, honey, your mom and brother sure are going to be happy to see you," he said and watched as her face broke and she began to cry. She had been stoic until that point; the only child who hadn't been in tears he noted as he glanced around the van one more time. "We are going to get you all home to your families as soon as possible."

A tap on the side of the van was his cue to get out so they could get moving. He climbed out and stood by Caleb as the van pulled away. His captain walked up as soon as the taillights were no longer visible.

"Kimora Washington one of the kids?" Ethan nodded and he continued, "I suspect that you would like to be the one to tell Ms. Washington that her daughter has been found?" Another nod. "Then get out of here—the kids are going to the hospital. I need you to find out the names of the other kids so we can get them home tonight. I have more than enough officers here to help me clear this crime scene. Caleb, go with him. The work will go faster if you both work on finding their parents. The faster you're done, the faster that you get home to that beautiful wife of yours. I hear congratulations are in order. You, too, Vanderbilt. I hear you may have finally landed that girl you've been pining over." With a chuckle, he turned and started barking orders at the other officers on the scene.

"How does he know these things?" Caleb mumbled.

"I imagine it's one of the reasons he has the job he has, and you know that he considers Kara a daughter. Hell, he stole my job and walked her down the aisle along with your father." Caleb grunted at Ethan and smiled, shoving him in the shoulder.

"You know damn well she wanted you at the end of the aisle standing next to me. The two most important men in her life."

"Yeah, I get it. Let's get going. there are a bunch of people that are in need of some good news tonight."

"Don't think I didn't hear his last comment. I'll let it slide tonight."

They drove in silence, both on that adrenaline high that happens after a takedown. The same adrenaline high that wouldn't get him far and that he was about to crash from. He didn't sleep well for starters, and having Quinn in the same apartment was playing havoc on his dreams. When she came out in that ridiculous set of pajamas that covered too much skin and that was probably supposed to not look sexy, but did exactly that and much more, he almost lost it. Then she nearly fell in his lap, and he *did* lose it. That kiss. Man, that kiss, the spark from that kiss was enough to light a thousand fires with its intensity. Not for the first time since that earth-shattering kiss, he found himself cursing the cat. If it wasn't for her, he'd have had the woman he wanted in his bed with him in all their naked glory.

At least the cat was smarter than he was. She put the brakes on for him when his horny mind couldn't, but the look on Quinn's face was enough to deflate any joy or hard-on he had after that kiss. She looked confused and then terrified. He had pushed too soon and too fast. He'd have hated himself if he'd slept with her right then. Not only was it too fast for her, but then the text came, and he had to leave. Nothing says I love you like, *hey, sorry to rev your engines and run, but you know, a person has to work. Catch you later.*

They were pulling into the parking lot as dawn was breaking. The van would have beaten them by a few minutes, and for the first time in a while, Ethan didn't feel dread when he got out of his car to go into the hospital. There was a lightness to his step because today was a good day. Not only did he kiss the girl of his dreams, but he was also going to return ten kids to their homes, and three monsters were put down in the process. The only downside was that the bad guys weren't alive to help take down their leaders.

"What. Happened?" he shouted down the line.

"I don't know, sir. One minute the exchange was going down smoothly and then the next brains were spraying all over, and then the pigs were everywhere."

"You mean to tell me, that the cops took out the best procurer of our product and the best client we had?"

"No."

"What do you mean 'no'?" His teeth were clenched so tight that his jaw ached.

"What I mean to say, sir, is that I don't think the cops took them out."

"You don't think? I don't pay you to think. I pay you to know."

"It's just, judging by the way they were behaving, they got caught with their dicks out. They were just as surprised when Paulie got it as I was, and they were everywhere. I had no choice but to bail." At least the little pissant had the balls to sound scared.

"I want to know who the hell killed them and cost me that paycheck. The sooner, the better." He disconnected the phone and then picked it up again.

"Bring up one of the new ones, boy or girl, I need to let off some steam." He disconnected again and cracked his knuckles. He almost felt bad for whoever they brought up. Well, not really. If he had a soul he would care, but since he didn't, it wasn't his concern.

That greasy son of a bitch needed to die. Harrison Black wanted to be the one to make that happen. Paulie didn't know that his boss had put a tail on him. He thought that Black was only there because he wanted him there, but he didn't know that the boss was starting to feel jumpy about his capabilities. It had worked in his favor to play both men against each other. Black had done a good job planting seeds of deception, but it hadn't been enough, not yet anyway. The old man was still reliant on Paulie. Unfortunately for him, poor, dumb Paulie had his run of luck come to an end on a dark deserted road. The question that remained was who killed him. Black had two theories, but it was just that. A theory. Either the buyer took out Paulie or Paulie's boss did before he became a liability. Something about the man's reaction to the news was slightly off. It was another piece of the puzzle that needed to be solved soon before more people were sold or he was discovered.

Black being discovered was simply not an option; at least, not until this was finished. He had work to do, and he wasn't going to be taken out in this hellhole of an environment until that work was done. And what about after? He had already decided that once this case was done, he was going to reevaluate his life goals. He felt much older than his thirty-four years on this planet should have him feeling. The time was coming for him to make a decision, because he was bone tired of the evil he encountered and how too often his hands were tied by the rules of his job.

There was also the matter of a young woman he'd met not that long ago who invaded his mind at the darkest moments and made the shadows disappear before they could take him under and strangle him. That beautiful woman was about all he had to anchor himself to the real him: the person he knew he was but that he had almost lost playing this game. A game he was damn sure ready to be done with. One way or the other, Black was going to get what needed to be done, done.

It was only a matter of time and he was going to have to take some major risks, but it needed to be done because he wanted to get back to the light and those hauntingly, beautiful blue eyes that saw too much. That saw him—the real him—and didn't shy away. Even if he might not be the match others would want for her.

Quinn was going stir-crazy sitting in Ethan's apartment with only Cat to keep her company. Cat was great company, cuddling with her and purring, but she needed to know that Ethan was okay. He had somehow become an integral part of her life, and he stirred feelings in her that she didn't even realize she had. That kiss, the kiss that set her underwear on fire and nearly melted them off, was enough to make her forget all her reasons for never getting involved with a man. It was enough to make her say to hell with it all, live for once, Quinn, just once. Then Cat decided to put a kink in it all. It was probably for the best, though. Probably. Maybe?

The fantastic news was that her pain level wasn't worse. The bad news was it wasn't much better, either. Regardless, she got up and made herself move. Sitting around was not helping, so she might as well keep her muscles moving. Her restlessness brought her to the kitchen, Cat hot on her heels. She scrounged around to see what was in the cupboards, fridge, and freezer. Ethan had said there wasn't much there. He wasn't exactly wrong, but there was enough for her to make a decent supper for them both. She found some potatoes and a pot roast. She figured she could handle the simple meal, even with a broken arm. At least, that's what she told herself.

An hour later, she had potatoes and the pot roast in a crock pot. Quinn was exhausted, and her mind was still whirling. After a bit, she decided she could turn on the TV or play on her phone. Wandering into the living room, she grabbed her cell phone off the table and glanced down, her brows knitting together when she saw she had a bunch of text messages. She hadn't heard her phone chime at all, but then she remembered Ethan had put her phone on silent when she was resting yesterday morning, and she had been too out of it to really pay attention to her phone's silence.

None of the messages was urgent, but the most recent message sent her pulse sky rocketing.

Good news. Kimora found safe. Caleb and I are fine. Will fill you in when I get home.

Home. The word made her feel warm and welcome. Even though she knew he was referring to the fact that he was coming to his home, not hers. Although, if she decided to move into the apartment, then she would be able to call this beautiful place her home. She still couldn't believe that he had offered to let her live there rent free. It was crazy, but also something she would be completely one hundred percent nuts to turn down. What were the chances anyone would offer something like this again? Slim to none. A safe place to come home to with a police officer living in the ground floor apartment. One that she knew was a great guy, whose sister she loved as if she were her own.

Like a lightning rod, it struck her that she wouldn't turn down the apartment. Not a chance. It was a dream to be able to live there, and the fact that Ethan and Kara wanted to offer the other apartments to struggling families made it even harder to say no. Ethan really was an outstanding person, and she knew that she was in dangerous territory with this man. She was still trying to work through her feelings about that kiss when she heard a knock on the door. The unexpected noise had her nearly jumping out of her skin. She walked as quiet as humanly possible and peeked through the peephole in the door only to find a smiling Taylor with a bag in her hand standing on the other side. Without hesitating, she swung the door open to allow her admittance.

"What are you doing back so soon?" she asked, a grin splitting her face. "Ethan isn't here right now."

For some reason, the idea that Taylor was there to see Ethan made Quinn feel odd. It was something akin to jealousy. Quinn stomped on the feeling and pushed it back, way back into the recesses of her mind. There was no reason to ever be jealous of Taylor and Ethan. They were like siblings, and she'd never seen Ethan look at Taylor with anything other than the same adoring look he gave Kara.

"I'm not here to see him, silly! I just came from making sure Kara, and my new niece or nephew was indeed healthy, as reported to me via Mom. Now I want to see with my own eyes that you're okay. Like Mom told me you were."

"I'm not going to lie. I've felt better. I can't believe your mom told you about it."

"Are you kidding? The Montgomery clan has a telephone chain when something like this happens to one of our own." With a shrug, she added, "I cut my trip short."

"Your work trip? You cut it short to see that we were fine? After you were presumably told we were fine?"

"Ah, yeah? Why?" Taylor said, looking sheepish like there was something else to the story. Something she wasn't willing to tell her parents.

"Come in, have a seat. You might have to fight Cat for a spot."

"Cat?" Taylor asked with a lifted brow.

"You haven't met Ethan's cat?"

"Well, I heard Kara gave him a cat, but the way you said that…"

"Yeah, Ethan named the poor thing Cat. He is quite insufferable at times."

"You're telling me." Taylor chuckled.

After Taylor settled into the chair, Quinn gratefully sunk down onto the couch. Cat quickly got up and rubbed her warm little body on her.

"It smells great in here. What is that smell?"

"Just a pot roast and potatoes. It was all I could find in his kitchen to make, and I was feeling antsy. It was harder to do than I expected, with one arm in a cast. Ethan had to go to work, in the middle of the night. I couldn't fall asleep after he left."

"Mm-hmm, for some reason, I feel like there's more to this story. Spill it, Sanders."

18

Taylor, always the clever one, the one who would sit back and watch everyone was too intuitive for her own good, but she was also a very close friend and confidante. Next to Kara, she was one of the few whom she trusted. But she couldn't share how she was feeling with Kara, not about Ethan, because while Taylor was like a sister to Ethan, Kara *was* his sister, and it wasn't that they were fiercely protective of each other. It was just weird to talk to her friend about her brother when it came to all the confusing feelings she was having. Kara had told her she was okay with it, but that didn't mean she wanted intimate details about what was going on.

"Fine, I'll spill if you tell me the real reason you came home from your work trip early." Taylor blinked once, twice, and then slowly nodded.

"Fine. It's a deal."

"Ethan didn't want me staying at my place alone. You know how over the top protective he can be."

"Yeah, it is pretty adorable. Caleb and Ethan are both over the top like that."

"You think it's adorable but try being on the receiving end of it. A little trust I can take care of myself would go a long way. Anyway, my bathroom is on the second floor at my place, and yesterday I struggled with the stairs to go use it. Your mom was leaving town with your dad, and they colluded to have him take me to his place."

"Colluded?" Taylor's eyebrows lifted. "That's a million-dollar word if I ever heard one."

"It may be, but that is exactly what they did. After they colluded, he brought me here, but there's a case he's working that's kind of tricky, and he had to leave. He came back around supper last night and then got called out in the middle of the night to work the case." Quinn looked at the purring furball curled up next to her, working hard to not look Taylor in the eyes.

"What else?" Taylor asked with a smile in her voice.

"What? Nothing else. He left, I couldn't fall asleep. I got up and started rummaging around in his kitchen. End of story."

"You decided to make a pot roast, because you were bored? Quinn, I know you better than that. You cook when you're stressed out or trying to figure something out. Which one is it? Stress or are you trying to figure something out?"

"He kissed me, and…and I kissed him back."

"Finally!" Of all the words in the English language that Taylor could have said, that wasn't the one that Quinn was expecting.

"Wait, what?"

"You mean, you have no idea? That boy has been moping around like a lost puppy for months drooling over you."

"No way. It was just one of those moments where an opportunity arose for him."

"Not hardly. Why would you think that?" Taylor asked, scoffing at her statement.

"Well, I mean, he has a reputation for being a bit of a Casanova."

"Psh," she said, waving her hand. "That's all an act. He's definitely been with women, but all of his relationships ended amicably, and even if he used to be a bit of a player, that was before he fell for you, and even then, he was starting to tire of the game. Not to mention, he only slept with all those women out of self-preservation."

"Why and how do you know all this?"

"He was scared to let anyone close. Look at his parents. They weren't really good role models, and I know because I watch. I see how often he actually dated, which was pretty much not at all. All of his relationships didn't last much more than a couple dates, and he wasn't going to bring any of them around my family—that would mean he actually wanted more from them. That was, until you."

"Me?" Quinn was confused and a little dumbfounded by the conversation.

"Don't be naïve. How can you not see how he feels about you? Granted, he didn't figure it out all at once. I saw the change in him after he was in the hospital, the way he looked at you. Almost like he was confused and looking for an answer. Then it was like it clicked. He has it bad for you, has for months; he just doesn't know how to tell you, and I suspect he's being cautious."

"Why would he be cautious? He isn't the type to hold back. If he sees something he wants, he'll go for it. That is, if what you say is right, and he wants me."

"Oh, he wants you, but he's being careful with you. Ethan treats Kara like she might shatter—not as much recently, but he still does it. Because of his job and what he sees, he's very careful around people who are victims. Even if you haven't shared your story with me, I know that you're a victim of something, and Ethan senses that, too."

The two women sat in silence for a moment. Taylor was clearly giving her some time to digest what they had just discussed. A soft sigh pulled Quinn from her reverie, and she looked up to see Taylor looking sadly at her hands.

"Do you want my unsolicited advice?" Taylor finally asked.

"Do I have a choice?" Quinn answered sardonically.

"Not really." Taylor paused, took a deep breath, and let it out. "Whatever is holding you back, whatever you have in your past, just let it go—or better yet, tell Ethan what it is. I know he won't care. Not one iota."

"I think you should practice what you preach," Quinn said quietly.

"Just call me pot, and I will call you kettle." Quinn continued to look deeply into Taylor's eyes until she shrugged. "I know I need to declutter my past, too, and I may have found someone worth doing that for."

"Oh, really? Do tell."

"That is a story for another day, but I think this is a good time to tell you why I'm home early. I figure you're the safest one to tell at this point, and maybe you can help me explain to my parents."

"That doesn't sound good," Quinn said, wincing when she tried to shift to a more comfortable position.

"Are you all right? Do you need anything?"

"I'm fine. I needed to readjust. Sitting too long in one position tends to draw attention to the aches in that part of my body." She waved her hand as if to brush it off. "Don't think that you can change the subject twice on me. What's going on?"

"I quit my job."

Quinn didn't get surprised often, mostly because she didn't allow herself to be in unpredictable situations, but Taylor had surprised her more than once in a small span of time. First, with her *not* being surprised that Ethan kissed her, and then, with the quitting of her job. She knew exactly what Taylor's parents would think, and it was the opposite of what Taylor thought.

"It's about time." It was Quinn's turn to surprise Taylor. "I'm not surprised that you quit. I'm surprised that you did it so soon, though. I saw this coming for a while. You aren't happy at your job, Taylor. You know it, I know it, and your family knows it."

"You think they won't be upset, then?"

"They'll be concerned about your reasons for quitting, but they won't be angry, if that's what you're worried about. If I know anything about your mother, I know that she's very intuitive to her children's needs."

Tears sprang to Taylor's eyes, and she blinked furiously to stop them from brimming over and spilling down her cheeks, another thing the three friends had in common—hating to cry, to show any weakness. Often the weight of holding it all in became too much, though, and the emotions spilled over. Quinn made sure she was usually alone, or in the martial arts class she taught when her emotions got the best of her. Then she took it out on her sparring partner.

"You don't think they'll be mad?"

"Not at all. They love you. Once you tell them and explain your reasons, they'll understand. I'm not going to lie and say they won't worry. They're going to worry that you're back on drugs, but you'll explain that this is for your mental well-being. That you quit because it isn't what you want out of life. That you aren't the girl that you were when you had wanted to be a graphic designer. You're different now. Explain that to them, and they'll understand it's part of your healing."

"You know me too well, like you can read my mind. But that's a good thing, I think."

"You should also explain to them that you didn't quit your job until you knew what else you wanted to do."

"Again, with the eerie mind reading ability."

"I'm not doing any mind reading. Like you said, I know you and that you wouldn't just up and quit your job without a backup. You wouldn't do that to your family; you wouldn't worry them. You fought too hard to get where you are."

"Just like you. Just like Kara."

"Exactly. When do you want to start?" Taylor just shook her head and smiled.

"How long have you known?"

"A while. You spend every moment you aren't at work at the center, and we need another full-time person. Someone to help teach the self-defense classes, among other things. The pay sucks, but I did get the board to approve a full-time position. I've been waiting for you, so I could fill the spot."

"I know it'll be a bit of a pay cut. That was part of what took me so long. I'd like to go back to school and get my therapist license, and I was hoping to be able to move out of my parents' house soon. This will delay things a bit."

"Hold on to that thought. I have an idea, but I need to talk it over with someone first."

The wheels in Quinn's head were already turning. She knew Ethan wanted to sublet to women getting on their feet. Either Taylor could move in with her, or she could take one of the other apartments. Something told her that Ethan wouldn't hesitate for a second.

The reunion between Kimora, Keisha, and Davon Washington was worth the bone-weary feeling Ethan had when he got out of his car. Seeing the sheer joy and relief on Keisha's face when she embraced her daughter was enough to keep Ethan going for days, maybe even weeks. Coming home to a house that smelled heavenly and a gorgeous woman snuggled in his armchair with his cat could keep him going forever, and seeing that exact scenario when he came through his front door was a sucker punch, because he knew that Quinn fit in his life, and he didn't want her to leave. Even if it was only in the upstairs apartment.

It would be a lie if he said that offering the apartment to her wasn't partly a selfish move on his end. What he told her was true; he did want to open it up to people who needed help, but he also wanted her close. If not in his apartment, at least in his building. He didn't like her in that run-down house in that high crime neighborhood. Not with the job she had. All other thoughts stopped when she looked up and smiled that thousand-watt smile at him.

"I was starting to think I might have to put leftovers in the fridge for you."

"Sorry about that. We had ten kids to get back to their families, and it took some time."

"Did you say ten kids?" Her face went from startled to ferocious in a heartbeat. "I hope you killed the son of a bitch who had them." Ethan knew that she meant it, and he was inclined to agree with her, except that meant they had no one to question.

"Not me, personally; but yes, he's dead. Along with two others."

"Officers?" He could see her whole body tense.

"No, the people that he was selling the kids to. And not by an officer's hand. They're still there trying to piece together what happened."

"Somebody executed them to keep them quiet, didn't they?" Her voice had gone cold.

"We don't know; it's possible, but it's just as likely that it was someone who's competing for territory or someone who wanted to take advantage of ten kids ready to be sold. Unfortunately for them, we were in position at the time. Fortunate for the children, though. The youngest one was eleven and packed one hell of a kick." He rubbed his jaw; it was still a bit sore.

"Thank goodness for small favors." His wry smile had her eyes going wide. "I mean that you were in place, not that you got kicked in the face."

Ethan couldn't stop himself from laughing at the look of mortification on her face. He could have teased her some more, but she looked so embarrassed that he couldn't bring himself to do it. His stomach unabashedly growled, and his mouth was salivating from the aroma of the food that was cooking.

"What smells so good? It smells like pot roast."

"Probably because it's pot roast."

"Where in the world did you get that from?" he asked, genuinely perplexed.

"Your freezer. It was the only thing in there other than pizzas."

"You made it?" His eyebrows lifted in surprise.

"I most certainly did. I know how to cook."

"It's not that. It's just, well, you're laid up with all kinds of injuries. I mean, you have a broken arm."

The sound that came out was less than ladylike, and the gesture she sent his way was even less so. He chuckled, and she flung a pillow off the couch at him. He swatted it away efficiently and smiled from ear to ear at the indignant look on her face. She went to pick up another pillow to throw at him and winced at the movement. He was crouched in front of her in a second, looking deeply into her eyes.

"Are you okay—?" He didn't have a chance to finish the statement before she moved on him, securing him around the waist with both legs as she battered him over the head with the pillow that was in her hand. "Uncle, uncle!" he shouted through his laughter.

"Had enough, big boy?" she asked and burst into a fit of giggles, but it was his turn to move on her, and he had her off the chair and pinned under him in a flash. Another wince had him pausing until he saw the sparkle in her eye. The little harpy wanted to play.

"Not. Even. Close," he said as he pinned her good hand above her head.

A flash of fear crossed her face but was quickly extinguished and replaced with another look, and if he wasn't mistaken, it was a look of lust that floated into her eyes. Without conscious thought, he leaned in and brushed his lips against hers and ignited a fire. While his mind knew that he needed to be careful with her healing body, the other part of his body that was rock hard and pushing against her warm entrance took very little time to even consider the bruises on her body. Her lips opened, allowing him access to her mouth, and his tongue swooped in, tangling with her eager one. He did his best to keep his weight off her, but she tugged him closer.

A moan escaped her, and her hips gyrated up and into that hardness that needed to be rubbed. He desperately wanted to sink into the welcoming warmth between her legs. The kiss deepened, and his hand was tangled in the hem of her shirt. So much of him yearned to let go, to take what he wanted to be his, but he knew that he still needed to be cautious. She was healing, and he could barely contain himself. Tentatively, he reached under her shirt and skimmed his fingers across her belly, only to be distracted by the knocking at his front door.

"Ignore it," Quinn panted into his mouth. He kissed her again and again. Damn right, he was going to ignore whoever the hell had made the mistake of coming to his house right then. But the knocking continued—louder and more insistent.

"Quinn, it's Taylor, are you all right? I left my phone. Answer me, you're worrying me, please answer me!"

Ethan stopped kissing Quinn and sighed, resting his forehead against hers. After another heavy sigh, he got to his knees. With a glance down at her kiss-swollen lips, he groaned with displeasure. Damn Taylor. This time the moment felt right like there was nothing but him and Quinn in this world. Enter Taylor, a sister to him, but not who he wanted to see right now. Beyond grumpy, he stood and reached down to help Quinn up off the floor. Carefully, he adjusted himself, hoping to hide the evidence of his arousal from Taylor.

Opening the door harder than necessary, he stood staring at the young woman who was clearly startled either by the way he had opened the door or that he opened the door and not Quinn.

"Hello, Taylor."

"Oh, hi! I didn't know you were here. I was here earlier and left my phone." She looked over his shoulder at Quinn and blushed. "I got a little worried when Quinn didn't answer, but it looks like you were, um, occupied? I'll just get my phone and leave."

With a huge grin on her face, she pushed past Ethan and walked over to the chair that Quinn had been snuggled in when he got there. She looked at the pillows on the floor, and her grin turned wicked. After a quick glance around, she found the phone, pocketed it, and walked back to the door she had just come through.

"Well, I would love to stay, eat, and chat, but I really don't want to interrupt."

"Too late," Ethan muttered and shut the door on her laughter as she sashayed out of his apartment.

There were many reasons he didn't want to turn around and face the woman standing behind him, but Ethan was never one to shy away from difficult situations. Taking a deep breath, he turned around. He wasn't prepared for the look of sheer panic on her face at getting caught by their friend.

"I'm sorry about that."

"What? Oh, no, there's nothing to apologize about. I just, well, I'm sorry for losing control."

"Losing control? You didn't lose control."

"Trust me, I did."

"Did I hurt you?" His voice was laced with fear.

"No. I mean, my body is still really tender, and I shouldn't have provoked you, but you didn't add any injuries to me. I actually feel a lot better today. We should probably eat; the pot roast is going to be dried out if we wait much longer." With that, she turned and walked toward his kitchen.

The full moon and cloudless sky made visibility perfect; however, when one wanted to be inconspicuous, it really was a bitch. Black was currently deep in the woods tracking who he hoped was the killer from the previous night. If he could find out who the shooter was, he might be able to get out of this particular case before he turned ninety. Clad completely in black, he blended in, but not good enough—not by far.

Melting into the night as best he could, he hunkered down behind a fallen tree. His NVG firmly in place, he peered over the top of the tree trunk at the two figures standing in the trees. They were arguing about the merchandise, which he assumed was the kids the police had rescued, and the discussion was getting more heated by the second. Bad guy number one shoved bad guy number two, and number one pulled a gun. Number Two put his hands in the air in a placating gesture. But it was too late. Number One shot Number Two between the eyes, and he crumpled to the ground. A noise behind the gun bearer had him spinning around, and bad guy number three walked out of the cover of a nearby tree.

"What the fuck, man? I told you to get information from him. I didn't tell you to kill him. Did he know who the fuck killed our best two transporters?"

"Not likely. It sounded like he was pretty low on the ladder. It doesn't sound like it was anyone in their organization. The boss on their end is as furious as you are. Apparently, the guy that lost his brains was their best, too."

"That's a small consolation."

"You're telling me. What are we going to tell him?"

"I have no idea, but we have an order to fill, and if we don't bring him something, we might end up like those poor suckers last night. I'll have to see if I can buy us some time. He won't be pleased if we're spinning our wheels. I might be able to pull some girls from the massage parlors, but they're going to be older than he was looking to buy."

"They're definitely going to be more seasoned. I thought he wanted ten pure kids."

"There are some new recruits in one of the massage parlors in Green Bay—they're young enough. It'll have to do. We can't go grabbing them off the street like that dumb shit did yesterday, and we don't have time to get another purveyor to find them for us."

"No kidding. Even if his brains hadn't been blown all over, it wouldn't have been long until the cops caught up with him."

"Which is why we need to be smarter, I think we might need to take a road trip to Chicago to fill the rest of the order. If we hurry, I think we can get it done in time. There just won't be enough time to sample the product."

The two men walked away, and Black had to stop himself from charging them to put a bullet in their heads. Did they actually say they were going to sample the product? Like they were talking about freaking wine or vodka, when in reality, they were talking about children. The two men walking away were living monsters, and their days were numbered because Black had them in his crosshairs and had given them an expiration date.

19

After Taylor left, Quinn felt like she was another person. She wasn't one who did crazy and impulsive things like roll around on the carpet with an insanely attractive man. Every inch of her was beyond embarrassed and didn't know what to do about it, but every inch of her was still turned on and wanted to jump Ethan's bones. While she should be aching from the tumble, she actually felt better than she had all day. Must have been the endorphins from the near sexual encounter. Quinn wasn't used to the feeling. She was used to her life revolving around the center, and she wasn't free to be with Ethan, not really, at least not the way she wanted to be. She was no longer able to deny it. She wanted Ethan, in every way possible. He had her hook, line, and sinker. The only thing she could think to do was go into the kitchen and put the food on some plates for them, but the insufferable man followed her, and when she went to get plates, he beat her to it, placing a hand on hers and turning her to look at him.

Silently, she backed up a step and allowed him to fill their plates and carry them to the large table—a table that was far too large for a man who lived alone. A table that also had ample space that they didn't need to be seated next to each other, but that is exactly what he did, placing the plates in front of two chairs. He pulled out one chair and waited for her to sit down. Quietly she did, feeling like a little girl on her first date. In theory, one could argue that is exactly what was happening.

"What did Taylor have to say when she was here earlier? I didn't know she was back in town."

Thankful for the bone he was throwing her, she felt herself relax ever so slightly. Taking a little bite of the pot roast on her plate, she chewed slowly, considering what to tell him and what not to tell him. She settled on not giving any real details from the conversation.

"Apparently, your family called her, and she came back to check on Kara and me. We caught up after I convinced her that I'm fine, just a little banged up."

"I thought she was at a work thing. Are they okay with her coming back early?"

Dangerous territory—was it betraying Taylor to tell Ethan? Taylor hadn't told her not to tell him. It wasn't like it was her parents she was spilling the beans to about the fact that Taylor had quit her job. After a little bit, she decided to not tell him. It was up to Taylor to tell him why she was home so soon.

"I think she'll have to tell you that story. It isn't mine to tell."

"Fair enough. You know, you're always the counselor who listens in confidence. It's a good trait."

"It helps people trust me. Not to mention the whole professional therapist thing; you never know when someone is looking for free advice."

"Even the toughest case will trust you. It really is a remarkable talent."

"I don't know about that. Anyway, she stopped to see me, and we talked for a while before she had to run off. But there is one thing I wanted to run by you."

"What's that?" He took a bite of the food and closed his eyes. At her chuckle, he opened his eyes and smiled. "This is amazing. I guess you aren't the only one that goes a little goofy over good food when you're starving. You were saying?"

"Just that I was wondering if the offer would still stand if I wanted a roommate for the apartment you offered me?"

If she wasn't mistaken, Ethan's eyes got a little cold, as if he didn't like what she had just asked. Surely, he didn't care if she wanted a roommate? What would be the big deal? He kept talking about her being in a safer neighborhood, and a roommate is a logical move to make her safer. Then it occurred to her that perhaps he thought she meant a man, but they had already discussed how there wasn't a man in her life, hadn't they?

"I don't think you would want to share the apartment. It's a one bedroom. Unless…" And there it was; he absolutely was worried about her inviting a male to live with her.

"I guess a one bedroom would be tight quarters. Judging by her wardrobe, there would be no room for any of my clothes." She took a bite of the potatoes to hide the sly smile that was fighting to reveal itself.

"The closets are pretty big—wait, what? Her who?"

"Taylor."

"Taylor?"

"Yeah, Taylor. Who did you think I was talking about?"

"Honestly, I don't know."

"You kind of looked like you thought I was going to invite a man to live with me. No worries there; no man to invite." She could have sworn he let out a breath that he had been holding.

"If you had someone to move in, I would allow it, though. I mean, the offer would still stand."

"I told you, I don't have anyone in my life like that."

"Well, just so you know."

"Duly noted."

"Why is Taylor interested in moving in? I thought she was happy living with her parents?"

"She's in her twenties, and believe me, she doesn't want to live at home with her parents. That doesn't mean she doesn't love them. She just wants to spread her wings. We talked about it, and she doesn't really have the funds yet."

"Well, in that case, she can absolutely move in. I would feel better having her here if she's considering moving out. She can have the other apartment on the second floor."

"Are you sure? I mean, that's great! Taylor really could use this fresh start."

"Fresh start?" Ethan said, narrowing in on those two badly chosen words she'd spoken. "What do you mean a fresh start?"

"Oh, nothing, you know the whole living at home thing—"

"Save it, you can't bullshit a cop. What do you mean 'a fresh start'?"

"I can't believe…I didn't tell her I wouldn't say anything, but I feel like it isn't my news to share."

"Spill it."

"I just can't. But can you just trust me when I say that she isn't in any trouble, and she's safe? She needs this move and will share with you when she's willing." He looked at her shrewdly for a long time and then slowly nodded his head.

"Yes, I can trust you. There isn't a doubt in my mind about that. I don't like that I don't know what's going on. Taylor isn't just *like* a sister to me, she *is* my sister. I know you understand that I would do anything to keep her safe, just like I would for Kara, Caleb, and Grayson."

"I do understand that. I just don't know if she spoke to me in confidence, and I want to respect that. I will talk to her and feel her out. Maybe she's fine with my telling you—"

"No, I said I trust you, and I also trust Taylor to make her own decisions. She'll tell me when she's ready. As long as I know she isn't in trouble or her life isn't in danger, I can wait. I think you'll find that I'm a very patient man," he said and then looked down at his phone and stood. "I have to take this."

I think you'll find I'm a very patient man... What the hell did that mean?

"Vanderbilt," Ethan said as he walked down the hallway, his phone pressed tightly to his ear.

"Yeah. I got some information tonight that might be useful."

"I'm listening."

"Sounds like the buyer is a go-between. They buy from our guy and sell to another guy."

"Why don't they just do it themselves, so they don't have to share the profit?"

"I don't know. Maybe because it's easier to distance themselves? They're doing more than middleman work. They have massage parlors in Green Bay, for sure."

"Great. Just what we need. Sounds like they're trying to make a claim on some territory. I'll contact the sergeant heading the division up there."

"That's not all, though. They didn't kill the people last night. They're pissed that their two best transporters got made into red mist. They killed a guy trying to get information. I didn't know it was going to go down that way, or I would have stopped it."

"And compromised the case?"

"If it hadn't happened so fast, I could have distracted them somehow."

Ethan believed him. Black was solid and would have done something, much like Ethan would have, to stop it from ending in bloodshed. Recently, they'd been a step ahead, but just barely. It was getting frustrating that they weren't getting where they needed to be. Eventually, they weren't going to be a step ahead but a step behind instead.

"Do you know who they killed?"

"Low man in the operation. They called him Digger. They seem to think that the head of this ring is the one that had my CI killed."

"Any chance of that?"

"I don't know; it's possible, he's pretty crazy. But he also relied heavily on him."

"They're having trouble IDing him at the station. Remarkably, he's squeaky clean and no prints on file. The bullet did a number on his head, and they're trying to go with dental records. But if you could give us a name, that will help tremendously."

"Paulie Romano. I've gotta go, but listen, one more thing, there were orders issued to send someone to watch your place. I don't know what that's all about, but watch your back." Then the line went dead.

Why the hell would they be watching his place? Because they knew that Quinn was there and that she had helped get Becky out of her hellhole, or because they knew about Black being undercover and had tied him back to Ethan? Either one was not a good scenario. All he knew was that he had to double up on protecting Quinn.

"If you were so trusted, what the hell did you do to get yourself killed, Paulie?"

"Paulie? As in, Paulie Romano?" Quinn asked from behind him. He flinched and turned to face her.

"You're pretty quiet when you sneak up on someone."

"I wasn't sneaking, I assumed you had gone into your bedroom, and I need to use your bathroom. I'm sorry. I didn't mean to get up in your space."

The look on her face was a cross between pissed off and devastated. Like she didn't know if she should be mad or hurt that he would accuse her of sneaking up on him. The reality was, he knew she hadn't snuck up on him, but not only had she busted him in the middle of a call with his undercover officer, but he'd also slipped and said information out loud that he'd gotten from the said officer. Shit and double shit.

"It's not that, it's just…crap." She started to turn to walk away, and he grabbed her wrist and stopped her. "You don't understand. You're here as a guest. You can go anywhere you want. It's just that phone call was confidential in nature."

"I understand that. You said you trusted me before, right?"

"I did."

"Then trust me enough to tell me what you know. I'm not going to run around and tell everyone what you tell me. I want to stop this madness as much as the next person, and I might have information you need."

"There are some things I can't tell you."

"I know you were on the phone with the same person I was helping the other night."

He didn't say anything, just stared at her. How could she have possibly figured that out? Ethan knew he couldn't confirm it, but he didn't have to. Judging by the look on her face, his hesitation was all the confirmation she needed.

"Good enough. I'm not going to tell you how I know or what tipped me off. Just know I have known for a bit now that you're his handler. I asked you to go with me that night because I trusted you, but also because I suspected you were his contact. But that's neither here nor there. I might have useful information for you regarding Paulie Romano. That is, if you were talking about him. But I need to know why you were talking about him."

"What makes you think his last name is Romano?" he hedged.

"I don't." She shrugged. "But he is the only Paulie I've heard of and a bit of a legend at the center, so it fits that it would be him."

"What do you mean a 'legend at the center'?" He did *not* like the sound of that—not one bit.

"I told you there've been weird things going on at and around the center. Kids whispering, et cetera."

"I recall that you mentioned something about that."

"Well, there is one thing that is a connecting point in all the strangeness. The name Paulie Romano."

"How so?"

"He's been chatting up some of the kids, especially the ones that come from more complicated home lives."

"You mean the ones that would be less likely to be missed."

"Exactly. But Paulie is smart; he's never seen by an adult, only the kids, and he sticks to the under sixteen crowd. Especially if they are prepubescent and looking for a big brother or father type in their lives."

"How long has Paulie been in the picture? Do you remember when you started hearing his name?"

"I want to say it's been about six months. I didn't really think much of it at first. Which is weird, because things like this usually get my hackles up, but he was clever and very helpful. I just thought that he was basically acting in the capacity of a big brother."

"What changed?"

"Kids that he'd been talking to stopped coming in to the center, and when I called them at home, they were short with me. I tracked a few of them down, and they wouldn't talk to me anymore. All the rapport I had built with them was gone. They looked at me like I was an alien and I couldn't be trusted. What's worse is I think a few of them had turned to the streets and prostitution, but I didn't have anything more than a name to go with. No description. I didn't even know what color he was—though, with a name like Paulie Romano, I would have guessed Italian ancestry."

"He was trolling the center for disadvantaged kids?"

"That's my guess. They were easy pickings for a charmer like him. I have to admit that I spent many nights thinking of ways to castrate the son of a bitch."

"Sorry to be the one to burst that little fantasy of yours," he said wryly.

"Why?"

"Because he's currently residing in the city morgue. He's one of the three that had their heads sprayed all over last night."

"He was one of them trying to sell those kids?"

"Afraid so."

"Was he the seller or buyer?"

"Does it really matter?"

"Nope, they're both pond scum, but I want to know."

"He was the seller."

"Then I'm glad he's going to be worm food soon."

Ethan swallowed and considered his options. He knew he could trust Quinn, and he also knew that what he was about to do was all kinds of wrong as far as protocol went. But he also believed in tit for tat and knew that Quinn had given him valuable information. Before he could change his mind, he decided to trust his gut.

"Paulie had become a CI for Black," he said quietly. "Last night was supposed to go down an entirely different way, but someone must have found out that Paulie was switching sides and beat us to the punch."

That useless piece of shit was dead. While there was a downside to that, there was also a glorious upside. The buyer had been brought back into the fold, and they weren't holding him liable for the death of the two transporters, as well they shouldn't. Not if they wanted to live to see another day. He would have liked to have seen their expressions when they found out that not only did they lose two of their people, but the ten kids they were trying to buy. Vance had known for a while that they weren't the real buyers; he wasn't a dumb man by any means. As far as he was concerned, they got what they deserved for trying to pull one over on him, and if they didn't stop sniffing around his territory, they were going to get an even bigger attitude adjustment. They told him they were starting to scope out other vendors. The threat was empty in Vance's eyes. He wasn't against taking them out. He had other people that would buy what he was selling. They just happened to be his most lucrative clients. The death of Paulie wasn't great. After all, he was stupendous at the job, but it had stopped him from going too far astray.

Of course, Vance calling that idiot Manuel himself to apologize and offer four of his private stock to them went a long way to smooth ruffled feathers, as well. They didn't need to know how used up those four were. All they needed to know was he was giving them at no charge as an apology for the mishap. They jumped at the offer. Yes, Vance wasn't a stupid man. He had them all eating out of his hand. Even though his new go-to guy had reported back that they had killed Digger, he didn't care. That guy wasn't going to work out anyway. He took too many chances, and in this business, you could only take calculated risks. Not to mention, he wasn't as charismatic as Paulie had been. However, the guy who had updated him on Digger's demise? That guy could be the second coming for this organization. Good-looking, built, and smart. Exactly what he needed.

Vance had worked too long and hard to let some pencil dick screw him over. If he even caught wind that someone was getting soft, he made sure they disappeared. If someone didn't keep control of the assets they got from him, they were taken care of swiftly. Which reminded Vance that he needed to make sure that asshole couple who'd lost custody of Becky was taking a long drink in the ocean, or his fixer was going to have some explaining to do. That one Vance would have a hard time letting go. He was extremely competent and had been in his employ for well over ten years. But even *he* was expendable.

Just like the last fixer had been when he failed to find and extermi-nate an asset. He had given him time to locate the asset, and when he hadn't, Vance hired a new fixer, and he exterminated the one who'd become obsolete, and he'd been working exclusively for Vance ever since. No one crossed Vance Duprey. No one.

20

Apparently, sleep be damned, Quinn thought as she lie staring at the ceiling. Her body was feeling much better, and her wrist was downgraded to a constant throb. She'd been waiting longer in between painkillers, but the dull throbbing pain wasn't what was keeping her up. The wheels in her head, trying to figure out what the hell was going on was what had her staring wide-eyed at the ceiling nearly all night long. Now the sun was starting to rise, and she was fed up with lying in that bed, as comfortable as it was, and pretending nothing was wrong. There was a hell of a lot that was wrong, and she needed to help figure it out.

With renewed resolve, she got ready and marched into the living room. Ethan was already in the kitchen. Two plates heaping with food and two glasses were set on the table. He was carrying milk and juice toward the table when she came bounding in, hell bent on telling him that he wasn't keeping her locked up in that apartment one more day, but the smell and appearance of the food had her stopping in her tracks and moaning out loud.

"Where did all this food come from?" she asked.

"I couldn't sleep, so I went to the store a little bit ago and filled the fridge and cupboards with food. Sit down and fill up. I know you have something on your mind, but I want you to eat first."

A grumbling sound emanated from her stomach. She was usually not one to turn away food. Especially food that smelled that good. Telling Ethan what she needed to could wait until after she'd eaten copious amounts of scrambled eggs, American fries, and bacon. Only *then* would she be ready to talk. She looked up when she heard Ethan laughing. He was staring at her with his fork midway to his mouth.

"What?" she asked.

"Nothing, I just love how much you enjoy food."

"That's good because I'm not going to apologize for it. I like food."

There were reasons for eating like she did and years of seeing a therapist hadn't assuaged the feeling that she needed to take advantage of food when it was around, but when you were starved at one point in your life, you know how to never undervalue food. Ethan nodded once as if he somehow knew what she meant and proceeded to eat his own food. A few more moments passed as they ate in companionable silence. Finally full, she set her fork down next to her plate and took a breath, expecting a fight.

"I want to go to the center today. I need to be doing something. I can discreetly talk to some of the kids about Paulie. I know how to ask them without looking like I'm too interested, and I have a martial arts class I was going to instruct today." She paused to take a breath. The words were tumbling out so fast that she was short of breath.

"I know."

"Don't get all uber-protective—wait, what?"

"I said, I know. If I hadn't figured as much out last night when I could hear you pacing in the bedroom and then tossing and turning in my bed, I knew the second you came stomping in here with a mission clearly in place."

"And you aren't going to yell at me and go all cop mode?"

"No, I'm not going to yell at you. Yes, I'm going to go all cop mode. That is, if by cop mode, you mean that I'm going to insist on dropping you off and picking you up and that I'm also going to insist you stay at the center at all times, and if anything seems off that you will let me know right away."

"That's definitely what I mean by cop mode."

"If you agree to those things, then I won't argue about you going in to work. I understand what it's like to feel like you aren't contributing, and if I were to be honest, which I try to be as much as possible, I would admit we need answers—and fast. I think the kids at the center might be the way to get some answers."

"I agree with everything you just said."

"Good. Now that we have that settled, we can head out as soon as I get the dishes put in the dishwasher."

"Let me. It's the least I can do after that great meal." She stood and carried the dishes to the sink, rinsing off the food remnants before placing them in the dishwasher. "I appreciate you trusting me enough to take care of myself. I'm not a weak woman who needs someone to hold her hand."

"Trust me when I say I would never underestimate you or any woman for that matter. Women aren't inferior because of their gender." His voice was like silk, and she jumped slightly when he spoke, not expecting him to be so close. "I forgot to mention that I like your new haircut; it suits you."

Bracing herself to face him, she was surprised, once again, when she discovered he was no longer standing behind her. He liked her haircut? Was his comment just a compliment or was it his way of letting her know that his cop eyes missed nothing? She was known for changing her hairstyle frequently, but she really liked the short pixie cut with the highlights and thought it suited her and hoped that she could keep it longer than usual. For the first time ever, she felt like her personality was showing through. Of course, cutting her hair short meant that it would be harder to change the style, and maybe when she did it, she'd been challenging herself. After all, it was an old habit, and she couldn't break herself of it. Even though it had been fourteen years, and she had no reason to believe she was anything but safe from her past, cutting and coloring one's hair was such an easy way to change a person's appearance. That and glasses.

Even though Quinn had no need for glasses, she had several pairs at her disposal that had clear lenses. Every once in a while, she would add them to her routine, telling people her contacts were irritating her eyes.

Quinn hoped that he'd meant it as a compliment. Mostly because she wanted him to be attracted to her. She knew that now, but also because it wasn't good if he was questioning her constant change of appearance. Up until now, people had accepted it as part of her personality. They assumed she liked to keep her look fresh. Had he figured out there was more to it than that? Shaking off the disturbing thought that Ethan was more attuned to her than she had realized, she wandered into the living room to find him standing in the center of the room, deep in thought.

"Ethan?"

"What? Sorry. I was just thinking about something."

"What's that?" she asked apprehensively.

"Just how much I hate letting you go to the center. I do believe you can take care of yourself, but it's just against every moral fiber in my being to let you be out of my safety zone."

"But even if you leave me here, I'm not safe. Anyone can get through that door or the window. You know that. I need to feel useful, and right now, I don't feel useful. What's more, I need to go to work and see my clients. They rely on me. I'm the one constant in a lot of their lives."

He turned to study her and took a step toward her; then, as if he thought better of it, he took a step back. But for some reason, she countered his backward move with a forward move of her own...and another...until she was standing only half a foot in front of him. Not knowing what was controlling her when she reached her hand up and brushed it across his cheek, she heard him swallow, but her eyes were locked on his bright blue ones.

"I'll be fine. You need to go to work, kick some ass, and take names later. I need to go to work and do what I can to stop this monster from taking any more of my kids. Trust me to take care of myself, like I trust you to take care of yourself. I'll do my part, and you do yours. I need to know you're focused on this case and not worrying about me. Promise me."

"That's impossible for me to guarantee, but I will promise if you promise not to leave that building and to not take any unnecessary risks."

"Deal." Before she pulled her hand away, he turned his face into it and kissed her palm. A blush crept up her neck and burned her cheeks.

"Ah, I like that," he said, his voice husky.

"What?" His statement confused her.

"If you only knew what it does to me to see you blush." She took a hasty step back. "Relax, I'm not going to attack you, but I think tonight we have some things we need to talk about."

After Ethan dropped off Quinn at the center, with further instructions that he knew annoyed her, he left and went to the station. When he walked into the bull pen, there was a hive of activity unlike any he'd seen in a while. He made a beeline for Caleb who had his cell phone to his ear, but when he saw Ethan, he ended the call abruptly.

"What's going on?" he asked without formality.

"They just raided a Green Bay massage parlor off an anonymous tip. It was one that they were watching for the last few weeks after reports that more than massages were happening inside."

"I assume they found something?"

"You could say that. Not only did they find half a dozen underage and undocumented immigrants, but they found none other than Manuel and Luis Hernandez."

"And those names should mean something to me?" Ethan asked, hedging his bets that Caleb didn't know the anonymous tip had come from him and hoping to hell those were the two men that Black had seen in the woods.

"Because they're the owner and operator of that massage parlor and many others. They're also slippery as hell, and Chicago PD has been looking for them for months."

Score one for Black. Good thing he'd texted a description of the two men to Ethan so when he called it in to Bob, it was easy to know who they were looking for. With the best performance of his life to date, he kept a straight face and let Caleb tell him how it all had gone down.

"Why the hell am I just hearing about all this right now?" he asked, only mildly irritated. He was a little mad he didn't know the takedown was happening, but since he had helped orchestrate it, he wasn't all that upset. After all, he'd been busy having breakfast with Quinn, and currently, he was trying really hard not to think of her caramel eyes.

"It all just went down a few minutes ago. GBPD was keeping everything really close to the vest, and Cap just came out and told us what went down. I was calling you when you walked in a few minutes ago."

"Oh." He tried to look chagrined and hoped he pulled it off. "Sorry about that, man; I should have known better."

"Don't worry about it. I know you have your head on other things right now." Caleb clapped a hand on his shoulder.

"What other things?" Ethan knew his voice sounded a bit belligerent, but he couldn't stop himself.

"Don't be like that, dude. I just meant keeping Quinn safe—and don't bullshit me. We've all noticed how you look at that woman."

"And how's that?" This time his voice was full-on belligerent.

"Don't give me attitude. You are head over heels for that woman. I know, because I have given that same dopey look to your sister, and you've called me on it or rolled your eyes at me countless times." He started to make his way to the meeting room, then turned to look at him. "For what it's worth, it's about damn time. You have Kara's blessing, too. You coming?"

Caleb walked away before Ethan could respond, so he just followed him with his tail between his legs. Was he really that transparent? Apparently, the answer to that question was yes. He slid into a chair next to Caleb and sat brooding a little bit. If Caleb could see it so easily, how was Quinn so oblivious? Unless she wasn't oblivious. Which would mean, what? It meant she wasn't interested. No, he didn't believe that—not for one second. He felt how she responded. There was absolutely interested, but there was something holding her back.

"All right, settle down. I know there's a lot of energy right now, but we need to go over what I know right now," Captain Bob Wickman said from the front of the room. "Acting on an anonymous tip we received several hours ago, we contacted the GBPD with credible evidence that a massage parlor in Green Bay was currently in operation with underage persons involved. Acting on said tip, the GBPD choreographed a sting operation in which they infiltrated the building where they found an illegal sex business with underage girls and boys was operating. Some of which were undocumented citizens, some that were not. During the raid, the Green Bay police, with the help of the human trafficking division, brought in two men, at first believed to be clients. However, after they were brought in and booked into the system, it was discovered that they were actually Manuel and Luis Hernandez." There were some whispers in the room, and Bob held up his hand to silence them.

"Judging by the whispering, some of you are familiar with those two names. For those who aren't, the two men are brothers and rising stars in the human trafficking world. Chicago PD has been looking for them for quite some time. As a matter of fact, rumor is that while they are grateful, they're also steamed that they weren't told of the operation. Never mind that we had no idea the two brothers would be there."

"Screw 'em," someone mumbled, and a bunch of officers nodded their agreement.

"Can it. You know as well as I do, Stuart, that if it was flipped around, we'd feel the same way. Although, we weren't really included in the takedown, either, but that's beside the point. There's a lot of red tape to go through to be in on an operation out of our jurisdiction. Anyway, the hope is that the two Hernandez boys will sing. As of now, all intel has supported that they're more the middlemen between buyers and sellers. What we know from the Cook County report from the data they collected from 2011 to 2016 is that, more often than not, buyers are Caucasian males, aged thirty-one to forty. Keep in mind that this is not always the case."

Bob pointed to a pie chart that came up on the projector. It showed the breakdown of ethnicity and age of buyers. Caucasian and Hispanic men made up sixty-nine percent of the chart. Fifty-three percent were aged thirty-one to fifty. Other slides showed that almost half had a high school diploma or GED, almost half were married, and ninety-one percent were employed. The next slides dealt with the victims.

"As you can see, African Americans are more likely to become the victim with an alarming sixty percent compared to twenty-nine percent being Caucasian. Nearly half of these people were under eighteen when the prostitution began. Even more disturbing is that nearly ninety percent reported some kind of abuse in their life. This is just a small smattering of what we're up against, and I thank Cook County for giving us this report. This is a growing problem, and it's touching every corner of this world. We're fighting a battle, and we're losing badly. We need to stop the SOB who was nearly able to sell those ten children last night. This operation has been officially given top priority. These are no longer faceless victims. They have families, they have friends, and we need to do what we can to stop the putrid evil that has been invading and spreading."

No one said a word as they let the charts sink in. It was more real when you actually saw it in black and white or on a colorful chart. Guaranteed, there were a lot of people in that room at that moment who wanted to kill the buyer and seller. Ethan was really surprised there weren't more vigilantes taking out these oxygen stealers.

"What do you need from us, Cap?" Stuart asked.

"Unfortunately, right now, we're in a holding pattern. We wait for word from Green Bay. Hopefully, they'll call with good news that the two Hernandez boys have told us how to find either the buyer or seller. Until then, we need to pound the pavement and see what we can find out…if we can find anything. Prostitution has changed a bit. They don't just hang out on the corner anymore. With the advent of technology, they now use websites like *Backpage* to find their Johns. Let's use that against them. Stuart and Sanchez, get on *Backpage* and the web and see what you can come up with. Set up some meet and greets, and see if you can find out any information. Tell them you won't bring them in if they can tell you anything useful. Montgomery, Vanderbilt, hit the streets. See if you can track down Kimora or Becky's friend."

Ethan didn't know if he would rather surf the web, but he really didn't want to drive around town chasing his tail. He hoped that Quinn was having better luck than he was. It was going to be a long day, and he wanted to be able to pick her up and bring her home sooner rather than later. She seemed much better this morning, but she was still recovering, after all. However, after the Captain's stirring speech, he knew it was going to be a while before he got to pick her up. He just hoped she held to the promise she made and didn't take any risks.

Black was busy trying to get close to Vance, but the man had shored up his walls and was making it really hard to get anywhere near him. Now that word had trickled down the line that two men had been arrested and that those two men were Vance's biggest clients, the man had gotten even more difficult to see than before. It didn't mean that he wouldn't keep trying. Eventually, Vance was going to need someone to trust. Even if the man was beyond paranoid, he wasn't going to be able to maintain his business on his own, since so many bodies were falling around Vance. Black hoped that his days were numbered.

His burner phone buzzed, and he found a secluded area where he knew there were no cameras to check it. The message was short and sweet:

Hernandez x 2 @ GB raid

Holy shit, if that message meant what he thought it did, they had taken down two of the biggest names in the area. Black had heard Vance mention their names several times, but he had never let on that those were the buyers. In fact, he regularly talked about how they were major competition and trying to step in on his business. Had Black inadvertently gotten rid of his competition and not just the buyer? For some reason, he didn't think Vance would be all that upset since the man said more than once how he tolerated his buyers even when they became difficult. Even though these two were his best customers, if they were stepping in on his territory, the man would brutally cut ties and had only been biding his time. Black typed a fast response.

Will wait for fallout

Stuffing the phone back in his pocket, he continued his route around the compound. He'd been hired as muscle. They actually thought he was dumber than a box of rocks, but that was all by design. It was much easier to watch your prey if they underestimated you, and that's exactly what they were. Prey.

21

So far, nothing had really come of Quinn going into the center. She had to relay what'd happened to her so many times that she wasn't able to actually ask any of the kids about Paulie Romano. She noticed that some of the regulars were nowhere to be seen, but that didn't necessarily mean anything. At least, that's what she kept telling herself. It was a mantra that had played in her head since she found out that someone had been preying on her center. *Just because they aren't here doesn't mean they're in danger*. It replayed in her head so many times, she was sure she was losing her mind with fear.

Mid-morning, she reminded herself that it was a school day, and even though some of the missing kids had a habit of being truant and trying to spend the day at the center, it didn't mean that was the case today. Maybe today they had gone to school. A couple of them had been warned that they couldn't miss more days without a valid reason. Like that would matter. When you had some of the family situations these kids did, idle threats weren't going to do much. It had taken months to build up a relationship with many of the people who frequented the center.

There was nothing she could do to locate them without actually leaving the center, and she had promised Ethan she wouldn't leave, not to mention she had a self-defense class to teach. She wouldn't be as hands-on today, but she could still teach the class. As a matter of fact, teaching the class in her current state might not be such a bad idea. Maybe it would instill confidence in some of the battered women that you *could* fight back even if you're knocked down.

The group had started to assemble when one of the kids she'd been looking for showed up with another girl—one who Quinn didn't recognize. They were deep in conversation and didn't notice her watching them intently. The conversation seemed serious, or at the very least, very animated, and Quinn felt warning bells sounding in her head. Carefully, she moved toward the girls so they wouldn't notice her yet. Pretending to organize the brochures, she overheard snippets of the conversation.

"…haven't seen her in days…"

"Maybe she ran away…"

"I don't think she would…she promised…"

"Maybe her dad was touching her again…said she would leave if he did."

"Shhh…Ms. Sanders is over there."

Busted. Nonetheless, Quinn kept arranging the brochures like she hadn't noticed them. The silence stretched on so long that she almost gave up and approached them. But then she heard the girl she didn't know trying to convince Shawna, a girl who came in all the time, to talk to Quinn.

"We should ask her. I mean, that's why you dragged me here, isn't it? You say you can trust her. So just ask her for help."

"I don't know, it would be like betraying her."

"Not if she needs help. What's the worst that can happen? If she doesn't want to be found, and we find her, she can tell us to get lost."

Quinn had moved on to one of the plants that had some dried leaves and began to pick off the dead leaves.

"You can quit pretending you aren't listening, Ms. Sanders," Shawna said. "We knew you were there the whole time."

"Did you, now?" she asked, playing the game that Shawna wanted to play. She knew the girl hadn't seen her at first and wanted to save face in front of her friend for getting caught. "Why don't we go in my office where there are fewer ears around?"

Once they were inside her office, she told them to have a seat and then asked if they were comfortable with the door open or if they wanted it shut. Being alone in a room with an underage person could prove to be dangerous territory. She knew that Shawna and her friend would want to have some privacy, but this opened her up for someone to accuse her of impropriety.

When the center was built, this concern was voiced. Because of it, they tried to put safety precautions in place. It was suggested to put in a window, so she was visible. This was the easiest solution, but also problematic. Some of the people that came through there wanted to speak with her on condition of anonymity—having a window might scare some of them off. But, in the end, the window stayed. They also placed a camera in the room. All of the people who came to the center knew that there were several cameras throughout the building. At first, they'd thought it would deter people, but it had done the opposite because the people who were victims of violence felt more secure knowing cameras were there monitoring the whole building. Some of the kids were still skittish, but it was a necessary precaution. There were also recording devices. Those tapes were logged and secured in a locked vault, as an added security blanket. Only she and Kara had access.

It was useful in case an angry spouse showed up, as well. They couldn't falsely accuse their spouse of something because everything was recorded and could be released if needed. Because Quinn counseled rape victims, she'd made sure that she was a licensed therapist. It made it more difficult to force her to testify against one of her clients because she was licensed, but she also knew that videos could help prove her client's innocence if a manipulative spouse wanted to try to stir up trouble.

"What's going on, Shawna?"

"We can't find Jasmine," the new girl spoke over her friend.

"This is my friend, Kaylee," Shawna said, looking affronted. "Like she said, we can't find our friend, Jasmine."

"How long has she been gone?" Quinn asked, choosing her words carefully, making sure not to use the word *missing* and create a panic. Even though Quinn was feeling a bit panicked herself.

"I haven't seen her in two days. I know that isn't long, but still. She doesn't have a boyfriend to hang out with, and with Father Romano nowhere to be found, we thought it best to come to you," Shawna blurted out, almost entirely in one breath.

The hair on Quinn's arms stood on end. *Father Romano*. That was a new twist to his scheme, and it was clever on his part. Too bad for him that he was killed before he was able to really use it and no doubt that was why the girls couldn't find him because there was no way that Father Romano wasn't Paulie Romano.

"Who's Father Romano?" she asked, hoping she sounded casual.

"Just some priest who tries to talk to kids like us and help us to make better choices," Kaylee responded while shrugging.

Sure, by gaining trust so he could take them under his wing and then turn them into prostitutes, she thought sourly.

"Why haven't I heard of him before?" Quinn asked cautiously.

"What do you mean? Why would you have?" Kaylee was suspicious, and Quinn needed to be careful how she proceeded.

"No reason. I just figured since we both have the same goal, he might have stopped in and introduced himself. That's all."

"Paulie—I mean, Father Romano—doesn't trust establishments like this."

Red flags bounced up all over that statement. What priest would allow kids to call him by his first name? I guess it really wasn't unheard of, but coupled with his distrust of *establishments like this*, she definitely heard warning bells. Normally, a priest would partner with a place like A Place to Hope. Nevertheless, she chose to ignore the slip of the name and focus on the second part of that admission.

"Why not? This center is a safe haven for people who need it. Rape victims, domestic abuse victims, people who are on the street and need a warm shelter, people who would just like to learn how to protect themselves and countless others come here because it's a judge free zone."

"I don't really know why. I mean, he never really told me, but I think he maybe sought help at a place like this and was turned away."

Shawna's eyes met Quinn's, and she knew the girl was speaking mostly truth, at least as far as the truth that Paulie had given her. But she was holding back more of his cover story. But, why? To protect the man from Quinn? That seemed preposterous but totally believable. Grooming at its finest—turn them against all they trust, so they feel there's nowhere left to turn.

"Surely, he must know not all places are like the one he was at?" When she saw that both girls were becoming agitated, she decided to back off. "Back to Jasmine, what makes you think there's something wrong?"

"Even if she ran away, not sayin' she would, but if she did, she'd contact Kaylee or me. The three of us are tight."

"Does she have a cell phone?" The girls nodded. "And I assume that you tried calling her?"

"A bunch of times, it just goes to voicemail."

"I have a friend I can call and see what he thinks. I won't mention your names," she was quick to add when she saw how nervous the girls got. No doubt the girls knew that her friend was a police officer. It was no secret that she had many friends in the DFPD.

"You'll let us know if you hear anything?" Shawna asked.

"Absolutely, just give me a phone number to reach you. I also need a picture of her."

"Why?" Kaylee asked, chewing on her nail.

"So they know who they're looking for. We know what she looks like, but the beat cops don't. Jasmine is relatively new to the center; I'm not sure how tall or what her weight is. She's your age, right? That would make her sixteen?"

"Yeah. She's a little shorter than me, and I'm five feet three. That means, she would be about five feet two. I don't know about her weight. I know that we can't borrow each other's clothes. I'm stick straight, no curves, but she's very curvy."

"I'm sorry I don't remember her very well; she was so new here and very quiet around me."

"It's okay. There are lots of us who hang out here. We can be hard to keep track of. I was wonderin' what happened to you. Your boyfriend beat you up for steppin' out on him or somethin'?"

"No, I don't even have a boyfriend."

"But I thought Paulie said you were dating that cop—" Kaylee was cut off when Shawna grabbed her wrist and tugged her out of the chair she'd been sitting in.

"We better be going now," she said hastily, grabbing the bag she had set on the ground.

"Wait, what do you mean that Paulie, Father Romano told you I was dating a cop? How would he know that if I haven't ever met him?"

Kaylee was chewing her nail again, obviously refusing to speak further out of fear she would mess up again.

"I don't know why he told us that. You'd have to ask him." And with that, she nearly dragged Kaylee out of Quinn's office.

Quinn followed them, but she was still clumsy, and her clothing got snagged on her desk. By the time she'd freed herself, they were long gone. Why would Paulie have told them that? Was the man they were talking about Ethan? And, if so, when would he have seen them together? One thing was for certain, she needed to see a picture of Paulie and fast. Because if Paulie knew her, maybe she knew Paulie.

"We're just spinning our wheels, and it's freaking frustrating as hell. I need to accomplish more than just driving around and talking to people that know nothing." Ethan was in a foul mood, and he knew it, but he couldn't stop himself. Every second that ticked by was another that Quinn's life was in danger, and that was unacceptable to him.

"Listen, E, I realize that you're all in love and stuff and that testosterone-filled head of yours is in super protective mode, but you know that police work takes, well, work, right?"

"Yeah, stuff it. First, I'm not in love—" When Caleb snorted, Ethan gritted his teeth. "And if I were, what would be the big deal?"

"If?" Caleb was smiling.

"Yeah, if I'm in love, like you say, I would prefer that the first person I admit it to is the person who I feel that way about." Geez, he sounded like a schmuck.

"Good Lord, man. You know that's as good as admitting it, right?"

"Whatever. Anyway, I don't remember you being such a calm person when it was Kara whose life was in danger, and you were drooling all over her. What I remember is a lovesick dog and someone who was devastated when she went missing. Even in my drug-induced state, I saw that. I felt it."

"Yeah, look, I'm sorry."

"I never told anyone this, but the night Kara went missing?"

"Yeah?"

"Quinn came to the hospital and stayed with me while Kara was gone. She held my hand, didn't say a word the whole time. She just came in, sat down, and held my hand. The. Whole. Time. And when Kara came to see me, she just got up and left."

"Damn. That's, um, I don't know what to tell you, man."

"She hasn't figured it out yet."

"Figured it out?"

"That she loves me. I'm going to make her see it. I told myself to give her time and wait for her to come to me, but screw that. I'm tired of waiting."

"About time, man. I'm tired of you pining away for her, too. At the very least the female population needs to know you're off the market for good. I think Quinn just needs a little shove in the right direction."

Was that the case? Was he off the market for good? Hell, yeah, he was. Quinn was it for him. She was the end all and be all that he wanted to wake up next to every damn day. The person he wanted to fight with, have make-up sex with and have children with. She was his beginning, middle, and end; he just had to get her on the same page that he was. Maybe Caleb was right, and she just needed a little shove.

"She's holding something back. I think once she gets past that, she'll see me finally and what I can be for her."

"And what's that?"

"Her future."

Caleb just smiled and then reached into his pocket, pulling out a picture.

"Since we're sharing good news…" He handed it to Ethan. "Here's my baby's first picture. Lay your eyes on your future niece or nephew."

Ethan would definitely call that good news. The little baby in that picture was a sign that good could come from evil. He stared for a long time at the picture, he couldn't wait to be holding a similar picture to share with Caleb someday. Hopefully, soon. He wanted nothing more than to have children. He especially wanted them to grow up with their cousins close in age, and he couldn't wait to welcome his niece or nephew. He needed that close familial connection for his own family that they were deprived of as children. But he needed to stop himself from putting the cart before the horse and needed to get her to admit that she was actually interested in him. For now, he needed to focus on his damn job so they could have that happy ending.

"Let's go back to the office. We aren't accomplishing anything out here. We can stop and get some lunch and then help Stuart and Sanchez filter through the filth online."

"Good plan. Not sure how far it'll get us, but it's worth a try," Caleb said.

"Now who sounds like a crab?"

"Just a realist. I agree about the spinning our wheels comment. We need to get those brothers to talk. They're the quickest way to link the actual buyer and seller."

"Getting them to flip is going to be next to impossible. Unless the state goes after them and they're facing hard time. Even then, they're going to aim for self-preservation. Squealing on their business partners wouldn't be a wise move."

"Unless it comes down to life in prison or telling all," Caleb surmised.

Once they'd picked up lunch, they made their way to the station. As soon as they walked in, they could tell something had happened. The chaotic energy from earlier was subdued and almost somber. Not only had something happened, but whatever it was, it wasn't good. He looked at Caleb, and he could tell from his expression that he also could feel the tension in the room. They weaved their way through the bull pen to their desks. Stuart looked up from his computer, his eyes bloodshot from hours of staring at the screen.

"What's going on?" Ethan asked.

"Nothing good. I'm not really sure, but Cap got a phone call and hung up swearing like I've never heard him swear before, then he slammed out of here—hasn't been back for thirty minutes." As if the words had conjured the very man they were talking about, Captain Bob Wickman came stomping back into the room.

"Conference room. Now!" he bellowed. No one questioned him; they all just got up and walked into the conference room and took a seat. Without preamble, he began to speak. "Both Hernandez boys were found dead an hour ago." A chorus of voices began shouting questions.

"Be quiet, and I'll tell you what I know." Everyone promptly shut up. "They found Manuel shanked and Luis hanging in their cell. All hell broke loose. They aren't sure what the hell happened."

"Or they aren't ready to share," Stuart mumbled.

"GBPD is a good group. If they knew what happened, they would tell us. Right now, they're running off the following three scenarios: either Luis killed Manuel to keep him silent and then killed himself; someone killed Manuel and hung Luis to make it look like he killed Manuel, or someone killed Manuel, and Luis was devastated, so he killed himself. Either way, they're both dead, and neither gave up any information before they bit the big one. We're back to ground zero, folks."

"How the hell did someone get to them?" Stuart's voice was frustrated. They all were frustrated.

"For some damn reason or other, they weren't in a locked cell block."

"They let them around the gen pop?" Ethan asked, incredulous. "They had a target on their backs for dealing with kids. That's basically asking for someone to take them out."

"Where did he find something to hang himself?" Sanchez asked.

"That's a damn good question. Which is what leads us to believe it was another person in the cell block. The boys were too new to have gained access to a shank, let alone something to hang themselves with. We need to finish this and finish it ASAP." With that, he walked out of the room.

"He's pissed off," Sanchez mumbled.

"I'm sure he has people breathing down his neck. There are a lot of bodies piling up, and it's starting to look pretty bad. With an election coming up, the mayor is going to want to clear this case in a hurry," Caleb said.

Ethan just got up and headed to his desk to try to figure a way out of this whole mess. Hours later, he stood and stretched, then grabbed his phone. He was surprised he hadn't had any messages all afternoon. He assumed he'd been so absorbed in what he was doing that he had tuned out any noises from his phone, but when he looked at his phone, he found numerous missed messages. He'd accidentally put it on silence. Real smooth, great time to make that kind of mistake. Flipping it back to ring, he scrolled through the messages. Most of the messages were nothing important, but his pulse ratcheted up when he saw that several were from Quinn.

From three hours ago: *Hey, I'm ready to wrap it up for the day. Probably overdid it with that self-defense class. Any chance you can swing by and take me back to your place?*

Two hours ago: *You must be busy, let me know if you can't take me back so I can find another ride.*

An hour later: *Kind of scaring me a bit. Hope you're just busy. I'll wait a little longer. Just message me, please.*

And then thirty minutes ago: *Never mind, Kara just showed up. She said she'll give me a ride back, she has your key and is going to let me borrow it.*

Ethan wasn't thrilled that Quinn had left with Kara. He understood, but he didn't like either of them exposed like that. He felt terrible that he hadn't been able to leave work to take her home. She was probably exhausted from being at work all day; she still was nowhere near one hundred percent. Glancing at his desk, he decided to call it a day. He could sit there for another twelve hours and continue with what he'd been doing, but it hadn't netted him any kind of solid leads anyway. He would call in his backup plan to cover her until he got there; he was about to tell Caleb that he was ready to head home when his cell phone rang. Looking at the screen, he saw Quinn's name. Relieved, he answered the phone, and the floor dropped out from under him when he heard the terror in her voice.

22

Quinn let herself in the front door to Ethan's building with the key Kara had given her. It seemed everyone close to Ethan had a key to the outside door, but only Kara had the key to his apartment. Kara explained that the locks were keyed, so his key opened all the locks in the building, but all of the apartment keys only opened the front door and their apartment.

When she'd come to his apartment the other day, she was kind of loopy and didn't pay close attention, so it took her a second to find the light switches to turn the outside light on for Ethan. When they had left, it'd been light out. She was inserting it into the lock when Cat came out of nowhere and crashed into her legs. Quinn jumped and looked down at the furry beast.

"Geez, you know how to make an entrance, huh? Where did you come from?" She was certain that the cat had snuck outside when they left, but they hadn't had time to track her down.

Her heart was racing fast as Cat did a figure eight around her legs and sat down. How had she gotten back inside? Had Ethan stopped by and let her in? Quinn noticed two things at the same time: Cat had started to lick her paw. Her red paw. And there were what seemed to be a trail of paw prints on the floor where Cat had run toward her. The hair on Quinn's arms stood on end, and she backed a step away from the door of the apartment. She was undecided what to do. Go to the apartment or leave? All she knew for certain was she wanted to scoop up the cat, but she thought that was a bad idea. The smartest choice was to call Ethan. Reaching into her purse, she pulled out her cell phone and punched his name in her contact list.

"Vanderbilt."

"Ethan, it's Quinn." Something in her voice must have alerted him to trouble because he instantaneously asked what was wrong. "Um, I need you to come home, there...well, Cat's paws are red, and she's licking them and...and there are red paw prints all over."

"Quinn, you aren't making a lot of sense right now," Ethan said, his voice strained.

"I...I think it's blood. Ethan, I think she walked through blood and tracked it all over."

"Are you still in the apartment?" When she didn't answer, he shouted, "Quinn!"

"No, I-I'm sorry. I'm in the hallway. I never went inside. She startled me as I was putting the key in the door. Should I leave?"

"No! Go upstairs to the second floor. Knock on the door on the right. I want you to wait there with the officer in the apartment. Stay with her until I get there." Either Quinn was too scared to think straight, she had misheard him, or it was Ethan's turn to be talking in riddles.

"What? Who?"

"I'll explain later. Just go up there and stay on the phone until you're in the room with Officer Rodriguez. Do you understand?"

"Yes." Quinn climbed the flight of stairs as she spoke. Halfway up, she missed a step and tripped. As she regained her footing, she stopped dead in her tracks. She had wondered where Cat had come from. It was clear from the paw prints that she'd been upstairs. They were darker and more noticeable farther up the stairs. "Ethan...there are bloody prints on the stairs."

"Quinn, we're a few minutes away. Don't go upstairs, I need you out of that house. Now!"

"But Officer Rodriguez, you told me to go to her."

"Ignore what I said. Get out!"

It dawned on her then. In her fear, she hadn't thought about how the officer could be the source of the blood.

"What if…what if your officer needs help?"

"Quinn, get out now! Don't go up those stairs!"

Quinn wasn't listening, or at least, she couldn't hear. Her heart was pounding hard, and the blood seemed to be thrumming through her ears. There were two arguments waging war in her head. Fight or flight. Go check on the officer or run with her tail between her legs? It was just as likely the red wasn't blood, wasn't it? Maybe she'd gotten into paint? But she knew that wasn't the case. She took a hesitant step up the stairs, thinking of all those times in scary movies that the person ran up the stairs and got killed because of it, but the more she looked at the paw prints, the more she realized that it was just as likely the reason for the blood could be innocent in nature. Perhaps the officer had fallen and gotten hurt? Or maybe if someone had attacked her they were long gone. The fighting side of her was clinging to the former of the two. She tried to convince herself that there was nothing to worry about as she took another step and continued up the stairs. Ethan was yelling in her ear, but she kept going. At the top, she saw the door on the right was slightly ajar, enough for a cat to get through, and the paw prints were coming out of that room.

"Ethan, the door is ajar."

"Damn it, Quinn, I told you *not* to go upstairs. Do *not* go in that room."

"What if she needs help?"

"We can help her. I'm begging you to go back down the stairs. We're almost there."

"What if I could make the difference and save her?"

Knowing how extremely stupid it was, she slowly pushed the door open and saw the officer lying on the ground, blood coming from her head and stomach—a lot of blood. More blood than was good for a person to lose. Without really thinking, Quinn entered the apartment, and her first aid training kicked in. She knew better than to go in that room, but she also knew the officer was bleeding out. Falling to her knees next to the fallen officer, she checked her wrist for a pulse and felt a relatively strong one. The wound to her stomach was still bleeding profusely from what appeared to be a knife wound.

"Officer Rodriguez, can you open your eyes?" She could hear the tinny voice of Ethan coming from the phone she had set on the floor and sirens in the distance as the officer's lips started to move. She leaned forward to hear her. Her ear was nearly pressed against her mouth. "What did you say?"

"Get…out…behind…you…" The words had her blood running cold. She turned to look over her shoulder just as she heard the noise of approaching footsteps.

Years of self-defense kicked in, and she spun, sweeping her leg out. The hulking man crashed to the ground, but he was limber and up on his feet in an instant. The sirens were closer. The masked man looked around before he lunged at her, shoving her to the ground. She was in a crouch and lost her balance, falling to the floor before he was on top her. He slammed her head into the ground once, then whispered, "Consider this your lucky day," before he slammed her head into the ground again, then he stampeded out the door and down the stairs. Breathing heavily and seeing stars, she flipped onto all fours and threw up. Then, remembering how badly Officer Rodriguez needed her help, she crawled to her and applied pressure to the wound on her abdomen.

Ethan was driving like a bat out of hell, screaming at Quinn to get out of the house when he heard a shuffling, a thump, and then a male voice speaking. The words were quiet, but he could hear them, and Ethan's stomach tightened. He punched the gas as he heard another thump.

"The bastard's still there!" he shouted.

Fear clawed at him. What was the thump he'd heard? Was Quinn all right? Was she dead? Did he just hear her murder over the live line? Would they miss the suspect by mere seconds? All of these thoughts were cascading through his head, and he thought he was going to lose his shit. There was no way this was going down this way. He finally had the woman of his dreams. He wasn't losing her—not now and not like this.

"Ethan, you can't take that last turn this fast."

"The hell I can't," he spat back as they rounded the corner on two tires. Caleb swore a blue streak next to him as the car righted itself. He skidded to a stop half on the sidewalk and threw the car door open.

Running up the walk, he ran through the wide open front door. Caleb was hot on his heels, watching his back since he wasn't thinking straight at the moment. Taking the stairs two at a time, he flew through the apartment door and found Quinn, alive and applying pressure to Officer Angela Rodriguez's stomach. Quinn appeared to be okay, but she looked pale and shaken. Officer Rodriguez was another story. She needed help. Fast.

"Go see if you can track the son of a bitch!" Ethan shouted at Caleb as he knelt by Quinn and dialed for an ETA on the rig he'd called for.

Gently, he tried to remove Quinn's hands so he could take over, but she wouldn't let him. She just shook her head and stared at Rodriguez's face, talking softly to her, telling her that she was going to be okay, that help was on the way. Rodriguez opened her eyes and closed them a couple times. As they could hear the ambulance approach, she seemed to relax and give into the pain and lost consciousness. Ethan squeezed her shoulder. He had told them on the phone to be careful approaching, that the scene may not be secure. He could hear Caleb downstairs, and he needed to clear the other apartments.

"I'll be right back, I need to clear the apartments before the EMTs can come in."

"Hurry," was all she said.

He left the room and saw a couple of uniforms coming up the stairs.

"Clear the upstairs. I'll check this floor."

"Detective Montgomery is clearing your apartment downstairs. He found her key on the floor."

With a nod, Ethan dismissed the officers and went back to the apartment to clear the other rooms. He didn't want Quinn in that room until he knew there was nothing else that could harm her in there. It was unlikely that there was anyone left in the building. They would have left after they had her down, but they still needed to be sure. For all he knew, there was a bomb in the building. After he cleared the apartment, he told Quinn he was checking the one across the hall, the one he intended to have her move into as soon as possible.

Once he was satisfied that the floor was secure, he called out the all clear. Caleb called back that Ethan's apartment was clear and that Cat was locked in the bathroom. The officers on the third floor called down a moment later, and then Ethan called down to let the EMTs up. They came in quickly, intent on getting to their patient.

"Apartment to the right," he called out and waited for them to enter the apartment before he went in to collect Quinn. At first, she was resistant to leaving until he told her the room was too crowded for the stretcher with that many people.

They were standing in the hallway, watching from the door as the EMTs worked to stabilize the young officer. Quinn was trembling beside him. Likely an adrenaline crash, he drew her close to him and held on when her body tensed. There was no way he was letting her out of his arms, not right then. Right then, at that exact moment in time, he needed her next to him, a concrete person, not just the dream of what he wanted in life. He had been so close, so unimaginably close to losing her, and he now knew how Caleb had felt. Ethan had been grief-stricken while Kara was missing, but the soul crushing feeling he'd felt when he was on the phone listening to the attack had been earth-shattering, to say the least.

"Are you all right? Did the attacker hurt you?"

"He slammed my head into the ground a couple times, but I'm fine. I didn't black out. I did throw up, but it could have been the adrenaline that caused that to happen."

"We should make sure that you don't have a concussion before they leave."

"Their priority is Officer Rodriguez."

"True, but it won't take more than a second of their time."

"Ethan—"

"Quinn, don't argue with me. I asked you to stay at the center. You didn't. I need you to let me have you checked over."

"I can check her over," Caleb said from behind. Ethan visibly jumped; he hadn't heard Caleb approach. "I've been learning from Kara what to look for. First aid training, et cetera. It's useful for this line of work, don't you think?"

"Yeah, I think you're right. Let's go down to my apartment. We'll need a statement from you, as well," he said, looking at Quinn who was still staring at Rodriguez.

"I'm not moving until I know her status."

One of the EMTs heard and responded, "We need to get her to the hospital, but she's stable for now. She'll be heading into surgery for sure. I'm sure Captain Wickman will have them update Detective Vanderbilt with her status."

"All right. Good enough. For now. Thank you."

Taking Quinn's arm, he escorted her down the stairs behind the stretcher. She insisted on watching as the ambulance left. Her body was still trembling slightly, and he knew she needed to decompress.

"After Caleb takes a look at you, I want you to go take a bath or shower. We can get your statement after."

"No. I'll give my statement first." He knew she had no idea that she was covered in the officer's blood.

"Are you sure you don't want to get cleaned up first?" he asked gently.

She looked at him, confused, blinked, and then looked down at her hands.

"Oh, yeah, I guess I should go clean the blood off. I'll give the statement after. Will you give Cat a quick rinse while I'm in the shower?"

Ethan waited as Caleb checked her over and deemed her concussion free before she went to go get cleaned up. After a brief word with Caleb, he followed her into the bathroom and stopped short. Quinn was clutching Cat to her chest, swaying side to side and whispering in her ear. The scene before his eyes was too much. He watched as she stood there looking lost, and he didn't know what to do to comfort her as she clung to his cat, and now wasn't the time to load more on her.

"I didn't see Cat when I got here. Caleb said she was trying to sneak out when he came in, so he locked her in here. I didn't realize how covered in blood she was. I would have taken care of that so you wouldn't have to see her like that again." A dry sob shook Quinn, and he stepped toward her. "Let me try to get the blood off your injured arm, and then I'll get a bag over your cast so you can shower. Once you're in there, I'll give her a bath in the laundry tub."

She didn't move, so he gently pulled Cat out of her arms and set her on the floor. The cat didn't move from Quinn's feet while he moved her toward the sink and began to wash her left hand. Once he had the plastic bag over her hand, he went and turned the shower on. She still stood there, not moving.

"Quinn, honey, I need you to get in the shower. I'll wash your clothes, okay?" Nothing. No response whatsoever. He gently began to nudge up her shirt, and that was enough to get her back into her own body.

"I-I've got it. Thank you. Sorry, I was reliving it. Um, I'll be out in a bit."

"Leave the clothes on the floor, and I'll get them after your shower."

"Okay."

Closing the door behind him, he brought Cat to the laundry room and rinsed her off. To say the feline was pissed was putting it mildly. He towel-dried her and set her on the ground then made his way back to the kitchen where he found Caleb leaning against the counter.

"How is she?" he asked.

"In shock, I think. At least, I don't think it's the head injury making her spacey. You said there's no concussion." He ran his hands through his hair. "Jesus, Caleb, I don't know what I would have done. When I got up there, she was covered in Angela's blood and on her knees next to her, swaying. I didn't know if any of the blood was hers."

"It wasn't, though, right?"

"I don't think so. It was hard to tell in the bathroom. I mean, I couldn't see where her clothes covered her. But I think it was all Angela's. I doubt any was his, but I'll bag the clothes and send them off to evidence."

"She held her own against him. Even injured."

"Yeah, imagine what would have happened if she was fully locked and loaded and not sporting a broken arm."

"Yeah, no kidding. But she's fine. Remember that. Don't go all crazy and try to be overprotective."

"Easier said than done."

"I know, man. Trust me, I know. All I want to do is wrap your sister in bubble wrap and lock her in a room where no one can get near her. The feeling is worse now that she's pregnant. But I also know that it's the exact opposite of what I should do if I actually want to keep her in my life. And I would give up every prized possession I own before I give her up."

"Even your collection of football cards?" he asked with a sly smile on his face.

"Hell, yes, even that. I know you're kidding, but all that's just stuff. She's what matters, and you know that."

"You make her see that, and the rest will fall into place."

"She's got to be running out of hot water by now," Ethan said, glancing at his watch.

"Just let her be. She'll come out when she's ready. Remember, it's hard for her to do basic things with a broken arm. I assume she hasn't really gotten to shower properly since she got hurt. Listen, I know you're upset that she came here. Alone. I'm not all that thrilled that Kara drove her home, knowing someone is after her. But we both know how stubborn these women are."

"Foolish is another word to describe them, but you're right." Ethan felt like a complete ass. Of course, she needed time alone to process what had happened.

They waited another five minutes before they heard the water turn off, and after fifteen minutes of pacing with pointed looks from Caleb to knock it the hell off, she came slowly into the room. She was dressed in her pajamas, and the sight was intoxicating. Which made him a complete shit, considering what she'd been through. *Down, boy,* he told himself.

"Sorry it took so long; I needed a moment." Her voice was so quiet he had to strain to hear what she was saying. "I just, it took a bit to process what all had happened."

"Quinn—" he began, but she cut him off.

"You can't talk your way around this; it's my fault that Officer Rodriguez was hurt. I know it, you know it, everyone knows it. And they wanted us to know it. And that sucks. But even though I know that, I can't change it. I can only make damn sure it won't happen again. So, let's get this statement down so I can move on with my life."

Move on with her life. He didn't like the sound of that, because for some reason, he got this sneaky suspicion she was going to run, and he was terrified of that possibility. After the statement was taken, it was time for him to finally put it all on the table, because he was damned if he was going to let her walk away. Not now. Not ever.

23

Never in her life had Quinn felt so beaten down, but she wasn't going to let whoever was behind the attempts on her life win. That wasn't who Quinn was, at least not the adult she had grown into. After she was finished answering all their questions, Caleb said good-night and told Ethan that he would bring the statement in, telling him that he would handle the paperwork and that Ethan was off the hook. She wasn't dumb. There was man code in there somewhere, but she was just too tired to care enough to decipher it.

"Quinn, we need to talk," Ethan said as soon as the door closed behind Caleb. Definitely a set up.

"Ethan, I'm tired. Can we do this in the morning?" Suddenly every-thing was too much, all of it—the lies, the chaos, the macabre amount of bodies piling up around her. "I'm just so frustrated. I try to be strong, but I don't know how much more I can take, and I hate that, I hate feeling inferior, weak. Like…like a useless person who can't take care of herself, the exact opposite of who I am and who I want to be."

"You aren't any of those things, and you know it. You're just in overdrive. The events of the last few days are a lot for even a seasoned cop to handle. I know I'm having a hard time rebounding from it all."

"Except it isn't happening to you!" she exclaimed, exasperated and the moment the words were out of her mouth, she hated herself for them.

Covering her face with her hands, she ran. Into the living room and out the door, spooking Cat, who chased after her. The hallway was still covered in bloody paw prints, and that alone was enough to make her want to laugh hysterically. She was losing it, completely losing it. Flying down the stairs, she stopped abruptly when she realized Cat had taken off. It gave her pause, and she suddenly wanted to slap herself. What was she thinking running outside when someone was clearly trying to make a point that she wasn't safe, and when had it started raining? In the recesses of her mind, she knew how stupid she was being, but she just didn't care. She spun in a circle in the rain and flung her arms out as if to say, *you want me, come and get me, I'm done hiding.*

"Quinn." She jumped at Ethan's voice; some tough girl she was. "Come back inside. Don't let what happened tonight change things between us. I mean," he ran his hands through his hair the way he often did when he was feeling particularly stressed out, "how things were before this all started."

"It's not just tonight, Ethan. Everything has just been a mess for so long, and I'm just fed up with shoring up and handling it all by myself. I have to, and I'll manage, but I won't hide—not anymore. If they want me, they can come and get me. As a matter of fact, I would prefer that to some other innocent child being harmed."

"Don't talk like that."

"Like what?" she asked, blinking rain out of her eyes. The slow trickle had become a steady rain, and she was becoming more drenched by the second.

"You know that they'll keep taking kids if they manage to get you. Also, stop with the whole you don't matter crap and don't act as if this isn't affecting me as well because it is. Anything that affects you affects me, and a whole myriad of other people."

"I'm not trying to be all melodramatic, 'woe is me, nobody loves me.' But let's be real here. I don't have a family. I barely have friends, and my life isn't more important than Kimora Washington or Jasmine Browne."

"Jasmine Browne?"

"Another missing girl, from the center. *Father* Romano was grooming her as well as Shawna and Kaylee. God, how did everything get so messed up so fast, or was it there all along and I just missed it all? Some therapist I turned out to be."

"You're a phenomenal therapist, the best we have."

"Then I feel sorry for you because I missed so much. Too much. Hell, my own life is a mess. How am I supposed to help anyone else?"

"So much of what you're saying is misguided and wrong. There are people who care about you—a lot of people. You might not have blood family, but you have family and friends, so many friends that you couldn't count them all if you tried. There are people who rely on you who need you in their lives. There are people who try to reach out, and you push them away so effectively that you don't notice they're reaching out to you, begging you to let them in. I can understand if you regret that I kissed you if that somehow messed things up between us, but there is just, something about you. I can't put my finger on it or explain it."

Quinn heard the words and didn't know what to say, what to do. She had reasons that he didn't know about that made it impossible for them to be more than just friends. Didn't she? Maybe there was something she could do, some way she could change things and then she could live her life the way she really wanted to.

"Ethan, my life is such a mess…"

"You said that already. Do you think my life has been all sunshine and roses? Come on, you know my back story. But I'm not shutting myself off from the world. I don't know what your history is, and I don't care, I just know that I don't want you to shut me out."

"I'm not shutting you out, I just can't…"

"Can't what? Can't give me a chance? Can't feel something for yourself for a change? There's more between us than you want to admit. Tell me you feel it, too?" His voice sounded desperate, and she looked at him, chewing on her bottom lip.

"I consider myself a pretty straight shooter. I'd be lying if I said I didn't feel it, too." He let out a breath and took a tentative step toward her.

"I'm happy to hear you say that, because I'm a pretty straight shooter, too, and I need to get some things off my chest regarding you and me."

Uh-oh. Quinn took a step back, but he countered her move. The rain had long ago soaked through her hair, dripping down her face. She swiped at the sodden mess, pulling it back from her face, but when she saw the look in his eyes, she was suddenly immobile.

"You see, like I said, I think there's something about you that draws me to you, like a bee to honey. I need to be near you, with you. I can't think straight if I'm worrying about you. Somehow you have become the center of my world, and I need you. No, I want you to take a chance on me. On us. I'm standing in front of you, getting soaked, asking you to see me. See me standing here, holding out my hand, hoping you will step forward and grab it and hold on for dear life."

As if he were a magnet and she was drawn to his words, she took a step forward and reached toward the hand he had outstretched, but she hesitated, just a moment. The look on his face was enough to crush her under the weight of the expression. Quickly, she shook her head and looked at him, really looked at him, allowing him to see her. The truth that she needed him to see, that he was more important than she had intended him to be, and it crushed her that she couldn't let him all the way in.

"I want to. Oh, how I want to just reach out and grab your hand. Let you shoulder the weight of the world with me." Another step was taken toward her, and his fingers grazed hers for just a brief moment. "But I just can't; I'm so sorry." Tears streamed down her face, mixing with the rain. She only hoped that he couldn't see them.

"Why? Tell me why. I deserve to know the reasons why you won't give me a chance. I know you're attracted to me."

"It has nothing to do with chemistry or how I feel about you." Her voice caught on the last word.

"If it has nothing to do with chemistry and nothing to do with how you feel about me, then what is it?"

"I can't…"

"You owe me that."

"I don't owe you anything." But that wasn't true, was it. Didn't she owe him her life? Hadn't he been watching out for her? Not just the last couple days, but for weeks and even months. Hadn't he checked in on her at the center nearly every other day? "No, you're right, I do owe you an answer, but I'm not free to give you the answer you deserve. Just know that I can't pursue things with you."

"What do you mean, you're not able to pursue things with me? You aren't dating anyone. You've told me that again and again. Are you just saying this to let me down easy? Trust me when I say I want one hundred percent brutal honesty. Tell me why." Another step toward her, and she could feel the heat emanating from him. "I thought you were a straight shooter, one that doesn't hold back when it gets tough. A person who doesn't back down to a challenge. I didn't figure you for a coward."

"I'm not a coward, but I'm also not a free woman."

"I don't understand what you're saying."

His breath was coming hard and fast, and Quinn felt utterly lost and confused, not knowing what to do. Before she could change her mind, she blurted out the words that had been unspoken for too many years.

"I'm m-married," she choked out on a sob.

"Married? What the hell are you talking about you're married? You don't wear a ring, and you don't live with anyone." She could see the anger and confusion battling each other. He paused and then seemed to really think about it. "Is he dead? Is that what it is? He died, and you can't get over him?"

"He's not dead." She stumbled over the words, feeling like they were strangling her just by saying them.

Ethan stared at her. His eyes bored into her, and she could see the moment he figured it out. Without giving her a moment's notice, he grabbed her hand and tugged her toward the front door, out of the rain and into the foyer of his beautifully renovated home, through the hallway to his front door and into his apartment, closing the door behind them quietly. Stoically, he removed his shoes and waited until she did the same. Squaring his shoulders, he looked up until he met her eyes and held them. She wanted to squirm but saw nothing but compassion and empathy in those crystal blue eyes.

"If he's not dead, then the only other possible option is that you ran from him." His voice wasn't harsh or mean, but it wasn't a question. "This conversation is long overdue, and I would prefer it in my apartment, not out on my front walk."

The fact that he knew with certainty restored some of her strength, his knowing she wouldn't lead him on, that she wasn't an adulteress meant more than words could show. Even so, she stood mute. The words seemed to escape her. Standing in his foyer, dripping on his floor, her teeth chattering, she couldn't make the words come. Instead, she just nodded her head up and down.

"How long have you been hiding from him?"

"F-fourteen years." Between the cold she felt from the air-conditioned room chilling her skin and the fact that she'd kept the secret for so long, it was nearly impossible to say the words.

"Fourteen years? But you can't be older than thirty?"

His shocked face was nearly too much, and when she didn't say anything, his eyes became sad, so utterly devastated as he did the math in his head and realized something wasn't quite adding up. That either she looked really good for her age, or she was entirely too young to have been married fourteen years ago.

"You're right, I'm thirty. I w-was sixteen when I ran away."

"How long had you been *married*?" he asked between gritted teeth.

"T-two years." She was shivering hard and couldn't seem to stop.

"Two years? You were married when you were *fourteen-years-old*? How old was he?"

"I...I don't know. If I had to guess, the late twenties."

"That's criminal." He was shaking, but Quinn realized it wasn't because he was cold. It was unbridled rage.

"Ethan..." She reached out to him, but as her fingers grazed his skin, he flinched away, and she took a step back. Though her tears had dried, a sob jerked out of her. "I knew I shouldn't have said anything. I knew you would look at me differently…"

The clouds that had been circling in his eyes seemed to clear as he focused on her, reigning in his anger, and when he seemed to actually see her, he shook his head as if to push out the dark thoughts that had been circling. With a savage breath, he took a step forward and grabbed her, crushing her still body to his. Quinn had no idea how long they stood there. She just knew that the warmth and strength of his body seemed to lessen the trembling of her own. He kissed her temple, her brow, her cheek, her eyes tenderly, wiping away the rain on her face as he did so.

"You just don't get it, do you? I'm angry, but not at you. I'm angry at the son of a bitch you were supposedly married to, and I'm sorry I flinched. Quinn, honey, I need you to look at me. Open your eyes and really look at me."

Begrudgingly, she listened to his words and opened her eyes to see him staring into her very soul so hard that she felt naked, stripped and bared to him by the intensity in his expression and she wanted to look away but found she couldn't. A tear slipped down her face, and he brushed it away.

"There's no part of me that is looking at you differently; there is no part of me that's condemning you or judging you for your past; there is no part of me that is angry with you for keeping this secret. There's understanding, so much understanding and compassion. I understand more now that I know and there is a large part of me that wants to hunt that piece of scum down and wipe him off the face of the Earth. A large, scary part of me wouldn't even care one iota that I was killing him in cold blood. Do you see me, understand me?" She shook her head as he gave her body a little shake. "When I flinched from your touch it was because I was angry at him and that anger was consuming me so much so that I was worried you would take the brunt of it."

"You would never do that—" Her words were cut off when his lips brushed hers.

"You're right, because I'm not him, and I'm not finished. If you think that I'm going to run with my tail between my legs after this big revelation, you have another thing coming. I'm here, in it for the long haul. I promise you that I will not stop until I figure out a way to nullify that marriage."

"I…but, you can't!"

———

Ethan was startled by the outburst. She had been almost emotionless, and then she looked like a deer caught in the headlights. Her eyes had gone wild, and she tried to back away from him. He stopped her from moving out of his arms, but he continued to hold her gently so she wouldn't retreat into herself, and he could sense she was dangerously close to doing that very thing.

"What do you mean, I can't?"

"Do you think I didn't look into it? Do you think I didn't research how to sever all ties with him? I did, but the only way I can without serving him papers is Divorce by Publication."

"Well, then we'll do that."

"You don't understand," she said, shaking her head back and forth while trying to get away from him. But he still held her slight figure against his with little effort. He knew that she was well-trained in evasive maneuvers. Even banged up, she could get out of his grasp without a problem, which meant she wasn't trying that hard to get away.

"Obviously, I don't understand, but I'm desperately trying to understand what is going on. Please tell me what I need to know so I can grasp this."

"Ethan, my husband is an evil man. It took me a long time to be brave and strong enough to escape him. And I did escape. He didn't let me go out of the goodness of his heart. I ran in the middle of the night with barely more than the clothes on my back. I know he's still looking for me, and if he finds me, he will kill me. He won't let me go quietly into the night because even though I was barely sixteen, I outsmarted him. Hell, I don't even know my real age because of him." She swallowed hard and paused.

"You've lost me again, how do you not know how old you are? I feel there's a lot more to this story than should be told while we're dripping wet practically in my doorway. Why don't we get into some warm clothes and then go sit down, and you can start from the beginning?"

"No. If I change clothes, it'll give me time to change my mind, and I need to get this out. I need to tell you all about it before I chicken out. You deserve that."

There was no doubt in his mind that she would back out, lock herself back behind that wall of privacy, and he wasn't going to let that happen. He wanted her to trust him enough to tell him everything. If that meant they stand dripping wet at the entrance to his apartment, then so be it. He wasn't about to force her to do anything she didn't want to do, but he wanted to make her more comfortable.

"How about we sit at the kitchen table?" She nodded her head, and he moved to the table and pulled out a chair, but she stayed on her feet and began pacing, chewing on her bottom lip until she seemed to come to a decision and stopped and looked at him, then slowly sat down in the chair.

"You bring emotions out in me I don't know how to handle. I pride myself on my strength, in how I came out of that forest a better person, but when I'm with you, I feel weak."

"You're not weak. I'm helping you to feel, to let the toxins out of your system from all those years of holding it all in."

"I don't remember how old I was when I was first given to him. I know that he kept me around for years. Grooming me would be the term they use these days. I would call it old-fashioned brainwashing. Then one day he deemed me ready to marry him. He waited until I was twelve before the real hands-on training started, but it wasn't until my menstrual cycle started that he started to really become interested in me, and it wasn't until I was fourteen that he told me it was time to marry him. He told me I was officially a woman, and because of that, it was time for me to take a husband. Like I said, until then he had done…things to me, but we never had intercourse." She choked on the last word. He didn't miss the use of the cold, clinical term.

"He systematically convinced me that without him I would cease to exist, that I needed him for food, shelter, *love*. I thought I loved him. It took me years to realize that I didn't love him, that what we had wasn't even remotely close to love. As soon as I figured that out, I knew that I had always hated him. I hated him so much that sometimes I could hardly stand it, but at the time he was all I had, so he was all I had to love me."

"What changed? What made you run?" he whispered.

"He brought another little girl home. He was saying the same things to her that he said to me. That was the first wake-up call. Suddenly, I knew it wasn't right, that he wasn't right, but I still thought that was what love was."

"How were you to know any different?"

"He was telling me how I was her mother now, and I had to take care of her, that he was the only one that cared about her, that when the time was right, he would make it legal and take care of her. I knew…I knew he was getting ready to get rid of me, to sell me."

"Sell you?" the words were an angry whisper of sound this time.

"Like he did the girl before me, the one who had been told she was *my* mother. He only kept her around until I started my menstrual cycle, and then he deemed her old enough. We didn't know what that meant, until one day a small group of men came out, and he auctioned her off to the highest bidder. He told her he was divorcing her and that she was going to go live with the other man. She left kicking and screaming. The new man beat her in front of all the others, and no one said a word. The man that bought her was in a uniform with a shiny badge. I didn't know what that meant at the time."

Son of a bitch! The bastard was a cop. How could she even stand to look at him? Or to think of him as anything other than a monster? Her whole world was skewed to the point where she didn't know what was right, what was moral. Then a man who should have helped her wasn't more than another monster in a world full of them.

"He told me she had been bad and that was why he divorced her, that I would be a much better wife. Then he came home with this little girl. It took a while, but I started to realize that he would only keep me so long. The men that had been there that night had been pure unadulterated evil. Maybe even worse than he was." She got up from the table and began to pace again.

"I decided I would leave, even if he found me and killed me. It would be preferable to being given to someone worse than him. At the time, I was brainwashed by him into believing that the beatings, the raping, was all his way of showing me how to be better, how much he loved me, and if I just did everything the way he wanted, he wouldn't need to beat me. He liked to tell me about the other men and the things they did to the girls he sold to them. I was terrified and knew I needed to get out of there."

Ethan felt his blood boiling. If there ever was doubt in his mind before, it was gone. He would kill this man if given the opportunity, and he wouldn't even blink an eye. If anyone could get away with it, it was him.

"Go on."

"I began to devise a plan to get away. It took longer than I had expected to get enough money from the loose change I found all over and to hide away some food that would keep without him noticing, but finally, everything I had waited for fell into place. I waited until he was gone on one of his business outings. When he left, I sprang into action. It had been a while since he'd locked me up. He trusted that I wouldn't try to leave, that I was so controlled by him that I wouldn't even try. I was almost out of the house, with what little food I had scrounged up when I realized that I couldn't leave the girl."

Of course, she couldn't. Not the Quinn he knew. That girl would rather die than let someone else be a victim. It was one of the many things that he loved about her. He had seen her with countless victims, anger under the surface, but compassion, always one hundred percent compassion for the person telling their story to her.

"He had her locked up, but one of my jobs was to take care of her. I had access to the key. He even trusted me with that. I got her out, got her dressed in some of my old clothes. They fit but were baggy, and we left. I didn't know where we were. I had no idea how to get us to safety. I just knew that I had to be careful, and I started walking. With this little girl, who was maybe five. When she got tired, I carried her. Eventually, I found a road and followed it, but I stayed in the tree line, far enough in that I didn't think I could be seen, but not so far that I lost sight of the road. When I got to a small town in North Dakota that was, ironically, named Hope, I left her at a gas station and asked the woman attendant to call the police—that I had found her wandering in the woods. The woman tried to stop me from leaving, offered me food and water. I took what she offered and then left. I risked checking the news once, after I was safe, to see if she made it home. All I could find was an article about a young girl being left in a rural town and that they were appealing to the public to help find her parents. I never was able to find out what happened to her and then, later I was too scared to even chance looking for her."

"What did you do after you left her there?"

"I kept walking until I couldn't walk anymore, and I was sitting, lost, tired, and hungry, on the side of the road when an old woman saw me. She stopped and asked if I needed help. She told me she could get me some if I wanted it, and I should trust her to get me out of there. I got scared, and she said she wouldn't call the police, that the local police weren't to be trusted. I wasn't sure what the police were, but I told her I didn't want her to call anyone, and she took me to a center like ours, and I lied about everything. She knew I was lying, but she didn't care. She knew how much I needed to disappear."

"So, she helped you."

"Yes. She gave me a new identity, complete with an ID and birth certificate. She helped me change my appearance, and then she moved me to a friend's house who lived in Wisconsin. That friend happened to be an amazing woman who took me under her care and got me the education I needed. I didn't know how to read or write, but she taught me how. I was able to get my GED and go to college all because of her."

"Your real name?"

"I can't tell you that, not today. I know that changing my identity by those means was illegal—"

"As if I would care at all about that. I'm not talking to you as an officer of the law right now."

"I appreciate your silence."

"You don't need to appreciate it. I wouldn't compromise your safety."

"Thank you. I will tell you my name, some day. I just can't while the wounds are still so open."

"Fair enough. How long were you with him?"

"Best guess is nine or ten years. Any other questions that you need to be answered today? Otherwise, I think I'm going to take a warm shower, if you don't mind?"

"How did he get you all those years ago? Do you know where he found you?"

"I can only go off what he told me."

"Did you believe him?"

"I had no reason not to believe him." She shrugged and moved to leave.

"What did he tell you?"

"That my heroin-addicted parents sold me to him for the price of their next fix."

24

Quinn was emotionally exhausted and just wanted to curl up under a blanket and sleep for a week, but as she turned to leave, Ethan stood and stopped her with a hand on her arm. When she didn't move or turn to face him, he gently turned her himself, but she didn't look up, her eyes locked on his chest.

"I know that you were just on an emotional roller coaster. But don't walk away, don't shut me out. I want you to know how much you mean. To everyone at the center, to Kara, to Taylor, to me. I won't tell anyone what you told me tonight. That's between you and me. Your identity is safe with me. There *are* good men, good officers of the law out there, and you can trust me. If you're actually married to him, as hard as it is, I won't force you to divorce that son of a bitch, and I won't hunt him down and kill him." Because he knew now how important it was for her to stay hidden.

"You know then, why we don't have a future, why we can't have a future?"

"No. I don't know that."

"What?" she asked, taken aback. "I just told you I'm married, and I can't divorce the monster, or he'll find me. What part of that did you not understand?"

"Oh, I understood it all. Be assured that the *only* reason I'm not going to hunt him down is because of the slim chance I would get caught and be taken from you. I also think there are other legal avenues we can pursue. After all, you were only fourteen at the time. How could he marry an underage person?"

"My parents signed off on their parental rights, and we lived in a state where it was okay to marry at fourteen if your parents gave permission. I checked that, too, hoping that the marriage wasn't legal."

"Something still doesn't add up. First, it's disgusting if a parent can say it's okay to marry at fourteen. Second, if he was given legal guardianship then how could he still marry you? He would, in essence, legally be your father."

"I don't know the answer to that. Maybe he gave the guardianship to someone else. I just know he was smart enough to cover all his bases, and I don't want to find him to ask him. I never want to see him again. In fact, I hope he's dead and rotting somewhere, but I'm too scared to even search for him, and even if I did search for him, I doubt I'd find him. A smart man would have changed his identity by now, just in case."

"Even if you are legally married to him, in the end, I don't care."

"But we can't ever be legally married without my divorcing him or at least finding out if he really is legally tied to me, and I'm too scared to even search for him. I mean, if we gave this a shot and things progressed to that point."

"You're right, legally we could never marry. But I don't care about that. I just care about having you in my life, in my arms, in my bed. A piece of paper means nothing to me if you are here, beside me."

"Even if I can never tell you my real name?"

"Even if you can never tell me your real name, I hope you will someday, but it's not a deal breaker for me because you will always be Quinn Sanders to me." With a small tug on her hair, he wrapped his arms around her and pulled her fully into his arms, kissing her softly. Almost reverently. "And nothing, no matter what, will stop me from loving you."

The walls around her heart were crumbling, and she felt herself falling head first, but it took her a moment to actually register the words that he had spoken to her because he was busy kissing her neck, her ear, her brow, and she couldn't focus. Finally, the statement rang through her head repeating itself: *and nothing, no matter what, will stop me from loving you.* And then her mind focused on the most important part, *loving you,* loving her. All the synopsis finally connected, and she sucked in a gasp of air and pulled away, just a bit, to look at the man holding her in his arms.

"Wh-what did you just say?"

"Damn it, you heard me. I love you. Every part of you, every flaw, every imperfection, every proud, blessed part of you. I want it all to be mine. It doesn't matter what's behind you; I'm in front of you, begging for a chance." His eyes, such a beautiful shade of blue, searched hers. "Tell me you'll give me that chance. That you won't let what he did stop us—"

Whatever he was about to say was expertly cut off by her mouth crashing into his. All thoughts of why she shouldn't be doing this flew from her mind as she melted into him, kissing him like her life depended on it. Maybe in some small way it did; maybe it was the fact that she was willing to finally trust someone enough to bridge that void in her heart that had developed after she'd escaped. Maybe it was that she suspected she finally knew what being loved the right way was like. Either way, she was so lost in the moment, that she didn't realize right away that he'd tensed. Confused, she pulled back from him.

"You don't have to do this if you don't want to. I didn't tell you that I love you to get you to sleep with me," he said, his breathing ragged. Ever the gentlemen, that was her Ethan, and he was one hundred percent hers.

"You selfless, foolish man. Don't you know by now I don't do anything I don't want to?" A hesitant smile quirked up one corner of his mouth. "I haven't since the day I got away. Since that moment, I've lived life my way, and I think I finally know what love is. I love you, too. You do know that, right?" His face seemed to relax, and he sagged a little against her, his forehead to hers.

"I hadn't dared to hope, but God, I can't tell you how good it is to hear you say that. I thought I would have to wait an impossibly long time to hear those words if I was ever fortunate enough to hear them."

She reached up and touched his face. She slid her hand into his hair and tugged his mouth down to hers again. There was no guilt for kissing a man while she was legally bound to another, nothing but regret that the monster was still lurking in her past. But she wouldn't let him control her any longer. If Ethan could look beyond that one thing, admittedly it was a huge thing, she could do the same. With a passion she didn't know could exist, she kissed him, holding his head to hers, not allowing him to break away again because she needed him. Oh, how she needed him. He groaned and pulled her hips tight to his body, they were now touching from their knees all the way to their chests, and her very erect nipples were in serious competition for the hardest object on their two bodies.

Warm hands glided to the hem of her shirt, and ever so slowly, he pulled the still sopping wet pajama top up and off of her, careful not to bump any still tender spots. Following his lead, she tried to pull his buttons out of the holes but found it clumsy with only one hand to do the job. He reached up and touched her hand, indicating for her to stop. With an infinitesimal step backward, he made quick work of the buttons, and with a flip of the wrist, he discarded the shirt, throwing it to the floor to join hers. Those nimble fingers of his made their way to her pants, sliding them down her legs and waiting for her to step out of them. She raised each foot, and he tugged the material off as he trailed kisses up her inner thighs, until he buried his face in the juncture of her thighs. Her body shook from the contact, and her knees nearly buckled, but then he was back, kissing her mouth with such fervor that she thought she would pass out from lack of oxygen.

While his mouth plundered hers, he unbuckled his belt and shimmied out of his own pants, no small effort considering how wet the denim was and how hard he was, and they stood, once again, pressed together. Without knowing what he was about to do, he had scooped her up in his arms and turned to go toward the bedroom, grumbling under his breath.

"Our first time damn well better not be on the floor of my kitchen." And then his mouth was back on hers.

With barely a moment to register what was happening, she was laid gently on his bed, and then her legs were spread wide and he was on top of her, still kissing her as if she were the very air he needed to survive, and then that talented mouth made its way down to her breast, where he licked and nipped and teased through the lacy fabric of her bra. She had a moment of fear that she had on her granny panties and then thought, who cares, as those talented lips found their way to her belly, just above the promise land. Her muscles quivered as he kissed a trail to the fabric covering her treasure trove, and he licked and nipped through the lacy undergarment—definitely not granny panties—and even though she was fully on board, she tensed as he moved the fabric slowly down to allow him better access.

He paused a moment, which allowed her body to relax before his mouth was on her again. Her body bucked and arched off the bed when his mouth found her clit. A sensation unlike any other was building in her and much sooner than she had wanted. Her body tensed with the explosion as she rode out wave after wave of the most intense orgasm she had ever had. A small chuckle escaped her, and he looked up, his eyebrows raised.

"Not exactly the reaction I was hoping for," he said wryly as he kissed the inside of her leg, her lower belly, her ribs, making his way to her mouth.

"It's not that. It's just, I was thinking how much better that was than my magic wand."

Clearly caught off guard, he stopped in mid ascent and laughed before he seated himself between her spread legs. Never had she felt like this, like a wanton woman. Somewhere along the way, he had lost his boxer briefs, and suddenly he was there, pressing against her. Sucking in a breath, she felt her body go taut with anticipation. Misunderstanding, he immediately stopped and began to pull away, but she locked her legs around his hips and held him tight.

"No, don't pull away."

"I don't want to rush you." His words came out choppy, his breaths ragged. The man would have stopped even if it used up every ounce of willpower, and as hard as it was if she said to stop, he would have. If she didn't know she loved him before, she knew it with every fiber of her being at that moment.

"I love you, Ethan Vanderbilt. You aren't rushing me. I want you, I want this. It got real, but that was my body anticipating what was to come. Nothing more. Please don't pull away from me, from this, from us."

"Quinn, I could never pull away from you. I love you. Let me show you how good it can be when there's nothing but love in the room."

Slowly, his mouth lowered to hers, and he was kissing her slowly and tenderly, and as the kiss deepened, he sunk into her by slow degrees, allowing her body to adjust to him. Her fingers dug into his arm, her injured arm resting on his shoulder, as he withdrew, and slowly, ever so slowly, filled her as far as he could. Then he pulled out and pushed back in, again and again, until a rhythm was set, and she was meeting him thrust for glorious thrust, and still, he was kissing her, loving her as he filled her over and over. She felt that wonderful tingling begin to build again and broke the kiss, biting his shoulder as her climax ripped through her. His tempo picked up as she crested that glorious wave of sensation once more, while his body finally found its own release.

Relaxing, he lowered himself onto her for the briefest of moments, before he rolled to the side tucking her into his body. He pulled the blanket up and over them as they both tried to regain control of their breathing.

"That was amazing," she breathed. "I never knew…"

He was kissing her neck and drawing lazy circles on her shoulder when she sat bolt upright in bed, drawing the blankets up and around her body as if they could shield her from what had just occurred to her.

"What?" He sat up, instantly on high alert.

"How stupid. Oh, I can't believe I didn't think of it. I was just so lost in what was happening, it never dawned on me."

"What are you talking about?" he asked, bewildered.

"I'm not on birth control."

Ethan had been terrified when Quinn sat up, nearly knocking him off the edge of the bed, until the moment she said what had freaked her out. Instantly, he relaxed, his body once again melting into that after-sex feeling of euphoria. He gently tugged her down, once again tucking her body against his. As far as he was concerned, she could stay right there for the rest of their lives; that is, if they didn't need basic essentials, like food, water, and bathroom breaks. Her body was rigid as he resumed kissing the place where her shoulder met her neck.

"Is that all?" he asked, once again lazily circling her arm.

"Is that all? Is that all?" she cried out.

"I don't understand what the big deal is. Unless you're worried about STDs or STIs? Because I'm regularly checked. With my job, there's the constant danger of coming into contact with bodily fluids. So, there's no need to worry about that on my end."

"No, it's not that. I mean, that's good to know, I guess. Though in the end, it wouldn't matter to me. I love you no matter what. You don't have to worry about me. I, um, I mean, I haven't had a partner in a long time."

"How long?" he asked hesitantly, a little concerned what the answer would be.

"Fourteen years."

He was silent for a moment as he let that realization sink in.

"So, when you said that was so much better than your magic wand. You really meant it?"

"Yes, I really meant it." She burst out laughing but immediately sobered. "Does that bother you? That I don't have a lot of experience?"

Try no experience, he thought.

"No. I would be lying if there wasn't a small part of my inner selfish male doing cartwheels right now, but I wouldn't care if you had a dozen partners. It's just I would have gone slower this time."

"I think the pace you set was just fine." The statement was tongue-in-cheek. "I didn't abstain from sex all these years out of fear. Like I said, I don't do things I don't want to, and I hadn't found someone I wanted to have sex with until you came along. Then all I could think about was having sex with you. That magic wand got a hell of a work out the last few months." Now it was his turn to laugh.

"Thank you?" he responded.

"Yeah, that's a compliment, and you know it." She pinched his arm. Her voice went serious. "Aren't you worried we might have just made a baby?"

"Nope. Not at all."

"You're that certain it didn't happen? The timing is right, for me, as far as my monthly cycle."

"That's not what I meant."

"Then you *are* concerned?"

"Nope."

"I'm lost."

"What I'm trying to tell you is that I don't care if a baby was just made. In fact, that would make me extremely happy."

"You mean, you wouldn't care—at all—if we conceive a baby? Even if I can't marry you and give that baby a normal upbringing?"

"Who says it isn't normal? Plenty of unmarried people raise children as good, if not better, than married people. As long as that baby has parents who love them, that's all that matters." His voice had gone distant as he clearly was thinking of Kara and his parents and how they hadn't loved them, especially Kara, the way they had deserved to be loved.

"I just meant, I would want to do it the traditional way."

"Then we have to find that son of a bitch and take him out of your life once and for all. You know that if I find him, I won't let him near you, right?"

"I know that you would do your best. I also know that he would find a way to get to me if he knew where to find me. After this much time, I wouldn't be able to press charges."

"At the very least, we could dissolve any legal ties there might be."

"And then what? I would have to explain my fake documentation."

He sighed. He knew she was right. Of course, he knew that, but he also knew that there had to be a way out of this nightmare she was forced to endure, but now wasn't the time to discuss it. They could talk about it all night and still not come up with any kind of solid answers, and he would prefer to spend that time on other things.

"For now, I don't want to talk about him. I don't want you worrying about him, and I damn well don't want him ruining what we have going on here and now. I want to celebrate that I finally broke through those walls you erected around yourself and claimed you as mine."

"Claimed me as yours, huh?" she asked, pinching him again.

Fast as lightning, he rolled on his back and pulled her on top of him. It was a good thing that her body had started to feel better because she suspected she was going to feel every inch of this night in the morning, as she was shocked to feel the erection that was evident against her bottom.

"Yeah, claiming you as mine. Got a problem with that?" he asked as he hooked a finger in the cup of her bra and dragged it down, leaving her breast exposed to his hungry mouth.

"How can you...so soon..." Her question was broken, and he smiled wickedly at her dazed expression.

"Are you complaining?"

"Huh?" She blinked down at him a few times as he rolled his hips under her.

"That I'm so attracted to you that I'm ready and able to go again?"

"Not complaining. Not even a little bit. Mmm, do that again," she said when he tugged on her nipple with his teeth.

A groan escaped her, and her head tipped back as she allowed herself to succumb to the sensations. He growled and sucked her nipple into his mouth, nipping it again. She arched into him, allowing him easier access, and he happily took advantage of the angle. While he licked and played with her nipple, his hand slid between her legs and teased that tender, swollen nub. Another moan slipped past her lips. He placed his hands on her hips and gently lifted her enough to help guide her to him. For a moment, the trance was broken, and she looked at him bewildered.

"I don't know if I can..." Her voice was shy and so unlike the strong, assertive Quinn he knew and loved.

"Yeah, you can." He released her hips and let her slide onto him. Her lips parted as she sat there a moment, and then he gently encouraged her to move.

As if a switch was flipped, she took the reins and brazenly rode him, her eyes locked on his the whole time as she moved up and down, until her body went rigid with her orgasm and he took that as his cue to thrust up and into her once, twice, before he bucked as his own orgasm took over his body. She slumped against him and lay on top of his body. And he felt like he was home, for the first time in his whole life.

25

A huge yawn shook her whole body as she lay curled up next to Ethan. Her eyes were so tired, but she didn't want to fall asleep. Not yet. Right then, she wanted to bask in the moment—the exhilarating moment of making love for the first time in her life. Her legs were tangled with his, and the sheets were just as tangled, but she felt untangled for the first time ever. No emotional tangle in her heart, her head. Just one hundred percent bliss. Through that bliss, a thought reached into her sleepy mind. She stood up and stretched.

"Where are you going?" he asked as she threw a T-shirt on. His T shirt.

"I'm going to put some food outside for Cat. Hopefully, that'll encourage her to come back."

"Good idea. Let me throw on some pants; no way I'm letting you go out there alone."

Not willing to argue, she went into the kitchen and filled Cat's food dish. It struck her then that she wanted him to go with her outside. She was still jumpy, not to mention she wasn't completely healed. It felt good to have someone want to bear some of it with her. While she acknowledged that, she also knew it didn't make her weak. What it made her was a woman finally willing to share her load and her life with a man versus being the one to do it all alone.

"You never told me why Officer Rodriguez was up in that apartment," she said as they walked outside to put the bowl on the porch. "You should install a kitty door here and in your apartment if you're going to let her come and go."

"I'll look into doing that. Remember, I hadn't planned on owning a cat, to begin with. As for Officer Rodriguez, I would tell you that we can talk about it in the morning, but technically it is morning, albeit the wee hours, but I know that you won't sleep until I tell you."

"You're right. On both counts."

"I got a phone call and was told that my apartment was being watched. The only reason I could think of for that to happen is because you're here. I got nervous about it and had a conversation with my captain where I demanded that someone be put here to watch you since I can't be here at all times. We're spinning our wheels on this case. Even with someone on the inside, we still aren't getting anywhere."

"Surely you have enough to take him down?"

"Not really. He's clever and keeps layers of people around him to protect him from prosecution."

"He has fall guys?"

"And women and someone who cleans up the loose ends." He sighed.

He watched as she set the bowl down and then he pulled her into his arms. They lingered on the porch for a moment. She didn't want to go inside yet, and she was secretly hoping that just being outside would be enough to get Cat to come in. After a few minutes, when it became clear she wasn't coming, they turned and went back inside, back to the bed that was still slightly warm from their body heat. She curled against his body, feeling more at ease than she could ever remember.

"Green Bay arrested two men—the ones who were trying to buy the kids."

"That's great."

"They were killed while in holding."

"What? How is that possible?"

"We don't know; we don't even know what happened. We just know one was knifed and the other was hung. They weren't even there twenty-four hours."

"You know that the one didn't kill himself."

"Yeah, I know. The police never got to interrogate them fully. Even worse, the couple that had Becky were reported missing by their family. We were hoping that they just went on the lamb."

"They're dead." She was certain. She didn't know how she knew, but she did all the same. "Whoever's behind this doesn't leave anyone behind to lead the police to him. He's smart."

"No one is too smart to get caught; he *will* mess up. There'll be something that's his kryptonite. But, you're right. The people who had Becky were our best chance to nail him."

"This is so frustrating. There has to be something we can do before it's too late for Jasmine and who knows how many others. Paulie Romano was pretending to be a priest. A *priest*. It's disgusting. I'm not sorry he's dead, and that makes me feel like a bad person."

"No, it makes you human. He wasn't a good guy. He made decisions he didn't have to make. You always have a choice to pick the right side, and in the end, he realized that. But the damage was already done, and it was too late. He gambled and crossed the wrong person and died because of it. Had he not made that one mistake in working for this asshole, he'd probably still be alive."

"I just don't understand what makes people so evil. Can you tell me that?"

"No. I can't. If anyone knew the answer to that, I'd be out of a job."

"I can't believe you freaked out and forced Bob to put detail on me."

"Yes, I freaked out, and I'm not going to apologize. For what it's worth, I didn't force him. He agreed and said to hell with the mayor's budget. The bodies are piling up, and it's only a matter of time before one of the good guys gets added to that pile."

"I think plenty of good guys have been added to that pile already if you consider all the innocent kids who've been taken and gotten rid of to hide their tracks. Even if they *do* get away, they're forever changed."

"You're right, I'm sorry. It was insensitive of me. I was thinking how we've been fortunate to not have lost an officer. It was a win getting all those kids back, but you're correct; they're changed forever. Even if we got to them before major harm was done, their innocence has been shattered."

"I think a lot of the kids they targeted already had their innocence shattered, that's why they were selected, but you shouldn't feel bad. You got those kids home, and that's a win. If their parents get them help, they'll do fine. Unfortunately, in some of these cases, that won't happen. I was thinking of all the other kids, and even adults, people we don't know about that have been taken or conned into getting involved in this lifestyle, just thinking of the bigger picture. In a lot of these cases, the kids who go missing are already fighting to survive to adulthood. I just want to neuter every last one of the people who buy or sell them."

"You and me both. That's why we need to stop this before it escalates."

"Then what? Someone else will move in to take their place."

"Maybe. It'd be naïve to say no, but that doesn't mean we shouldn't stop this particular person from continuing with his operation."

"You're right. Sorry for being so pessimistic. It sometimes just feels like nothing we do is good enough. You know?"

"Yeah, I know, but that's why we chose these jobs because we know even if someone else is standing in line to take over being the new resident bad guy; someone has to try to stop them, or they will completely permeate the whole system."

"It's just so widespread, it's impossible not to feel overwhelmed by it all. Even so, I'm not washing my hands of this and walking away. They deserve a chance to have a good life, not the one that they're being forced into."

"I agree, but you need to know that you can't win them all. I started this job thinking I could, and I was really close to burning out."

"What did you do to survive?"

"Women. I filled the sleepless nights with women. Mostly one-night stands, no commitments. For the most part, they knew what they were getting into, but every once in a while, there was a woman who wanted to try to save me or get me to commit."

"But not anymore?"

"Not for a while now."

"What changed?" But she thought she knew the answer.

"You. I haven't had another woman in my bed or elsewhere since that night where a fierce little pixie came into my hospital room and held my hand without saying a word. From that night on, I didn't need all those women to fill the sleepless nights. I had a pair of amazing hazel eyes and a girl that changed her appearance so often I got lost trying to figure out which look was my favorite."

"About that…"

"You had me fooled, everyone fooled. We just thought it was your quirky personality. Now, I know better—it's a way to hide in plain sight."

"At first it was to help me stay hidden, but when years went by, and the danger seemed to dissipate, it became a habit I couldn't break. Like a security blanket. You had your one-night stands, I had my Clairol or whatever version was on sale."

"For what it's worth, I wasn't lying when I told you I like this look. I think it's my favorite so far. I wouldn't mind it sticking around, but someday I would like to see the real Quinn, without all the smoke and mirrors."

"Funny you should say that because this is my real color. The eye color has been mine for a while. I used to dabble in colored contacts but really hated them. I guess I was slowly weening myself off the disguises in recent months. This is me without the glamour. I was finally feeling comfortable, safe even. Guess I jumped the gun on that one, huh?"

"No, you're still safe, and you should still feel comfortable. I won't let anything happen to you. If I did, it would be like letting myself die. You've become that important to me."

How had she found this man, and why had she waited so long to let him into her life and into her heart? Rolling toward him, she swung a leg over him and trailed a finger down his chest toward the sheet that covered him from the waist down. Her hand snaked underneath to find him aroused again.

"All those sweet words. I think you're just trying to get me to do naughty things to you." She nibbled on his ear.

"Not at all, but if sweet words are all it takes for you to get turned on, then I'll keep it up." She quirked an eyebrow at his choice of words.

"No pun intended?"

"Oh, I definitely intended it."

With a growl, he rolled her onto her back and with one fluid move, he was inside her, driving away all the sad thoughts and filling her with a joy she didn't know could exist. She clung to him like she was sinking, and he was the only thing keeping her from going under. Somehow, he had become a lifeline for her, one she wasn't going to give up, because she finally realized she had done nothing wrong when she ran for her life and, damn it, she deserved to be happy.

When he woke up, the bed was still warm next to him. He was disappointed to find that Quinn wasn't there. He stretched and breathed in deeply. He closed his eyes and then reopened them, rolling onto his back to stare at the ceiling. She had asked him what he did to survive. That was a loaded question; what hadn't he done? He hadn't gone to booze like so many did; he hadn't resorted to violence, which also happened. But he also had his vice to get through the turmoil of all the cases. He was relieved that he had confided in Quinn, that he had told her the reason behind his one-night stands.

His stomach growled at the aromas coming from his kitchen. The woman was going to make him fat if she kept cooking for him. Of course, his eating food on the fly wasn't really great for his waistline either. He was sitting up when he saw her come through the door carrying a tray.

"You're awake! Fantastic, I made breakfast. I thought we could eat it in bed while we snuggled. Unless you prefer to eat in the kitchen."

The sight of her walking toward him wearing one of his T-shirts was enough to make his mouth salivate. How could such a simple sight make him as horny as a teenage boy on prom night? Because he was in love; that's why. There was no worry that he would gain weight from her cooking if he was busy burning it off rolling around in bed with her. She sat down next to him and held a piece of bacon up to his mouth. When he hesitated, she frowned and took a bite of it, chewing slowly and moaning that amazing way she did when she was eating something she considered delicious.

"You don't like bacon?"

"I like bacon. I was just frozen by your beauty. Oh, God, do that again," he whispered. "Take another bite. When you moan like that…" He grabbed her hand and placed it on the evidence of what that moan did to him.

"You are quite insatiable, Mr. Vanderbilt."

"You have no idea." Gently taking the tray from her, he set it on the bedside table and rolled her underneath him.

"You're going to be late to work."

"I'm willing to risk it."

"Our breakfast will get cold."

"Worth it."

They were interrupted by his cell phone ringing, and, apologizing, he looked at the screen. The number was unknown, and he knew right away that it was Black calling. Quinn just smiled, grabbed a piece of bacon, and stripped off her shirt on the way to go take a shower; her adorable behind sashayed away.

"Vanderbilt."

"I don't have a lot of time to talk, but something big is going down. I don't know what. All I know is that The Fixer is coming in to town to take care of a few problems. Apparently, he'd been dispatched to take care of something big and has been told to get back. All I know is someone important has been located, and the head honcho wants them brought to him and taken care of in front of him. Normally, he wouldn't call his main clean-up guy back into town for just anyone. He has other flunkies that he can get to kill people on the fly, so whoever it is, he really wants them dead, and he wants it to be soon."

"Any idea who it is? Can we move on them to get them protection?"

"No clue. I just know it's someone he's been looking for, and he wants them gone."

"Thanks for the information, keep your head down. I think things are about to boil over, and we need to be ready to move when the time comes."

"I hope you're right. I'm ready to be done with this."

"Soon."

"It won't be soon enough." The phone went dead.

Ethan would be lying if he said he wasn't worried about Harrison Black. With each phone call, the man sounded more strained. He wasn't sure how much longer they had until he was at his breaking point. Undercover work was hard and dangerous; you had to give yourself over to the world you were immersed in and walk a fine line between good and evil. Some could never get back from that.

"That's how you were at the hospital so quickly that night," Quinn said quietly from the bathroom door, a towel wrapped around her.

"Yeah."

"Surprised it took me that long to figure it out. I mean, I knew that you were his contact, but I didn't realize that he had you in the loop that night."

"It's been hard because Caleb isn't in the loop. There are hard feelings when it comes to Black."

"Why? I didn't even know that he knew Kara until the night he delivered Becky to me."

"He was the officer that was bringing Kara home the night she was abducted. He got called out on a bogus call."

"Oh, no! He was the one that let her go with that psycho? She never told me that."

"Right, and Kara never blamed him. There wasn't anything he could have done differently."

"How did I not know it was him?"

"Kara didn't want anyone to know. She said he wasn't to blame, and that was it. In the chaos that night, and probably to protect me, Caleb never told me who'd slipped up. When Kara was rescued, she told Caleb to zip it about Black, and he listened. It wasn't until later that Black told me he'd been the one to let her go with that asshole. He was torn up by it. I talked to Kara about it after I talked to him. She said there was no reason for him to still feel guilty. He didn't intend for it to go down the way it did. She also told me that Caleb was still holding a bit of a grudge and to try not to bring him up for now."

"That's why he went undercover." It wasn't a question.

"Yes, when the need to put somebody deep undercover came up, he volunteered. I think he feels this is his way to finally make amends."

"That's why he risked himself that night to get Becky out. It wasn't safe for him to do that. He took one hell of a risk. Honestly, I was surprised he didn't get caught that night."

"I wasn't sure he could handle the job. He isn't in the best of places mentally, and the guilt is overwhelming for him. I convinced Cap to let me be his handler, and he agreed. The one condition being that Caleb wasn't allowed to know that I'm his contact."

"Caleb is a good man."

"Caleb is the best man I know. However, he's blinded by his love for Kara, and I know that he's almost to that point where he can forgive Black, but we just couldn't risk letting him know. Not yet."

"He's going to be mad at you."

"He's going to be royally pissed, but he'll get over it. Family forgives each other for the small stuff, and we're family."

A little later, they were both fed and dressed and on their way out the door. Quinn was going to go to the center again and try to get some work done. She hoped she'd find out some more information about

Jasmine, but she wasn't holding her breath. Ethan held her hand the whole way to the center, and she smiled lazily while she stared out the window of the car. He insisted on walking her into the building, and they were standing in the center of A Place to Hope talking to a couple of volunteers when she heard a scream. Whipping around, she saw a bloodied woman stagger through the door and collapse. People rushed to the crumpled form, and she had to push her way through them to get to the hurt woman. Once she broke through the outer circle, she knelt beside the prone form as Ethan knelt on the young woman's other side. He reached for her wrist and checked for a pulse without hesitating, even though there was blood everywhere. It took a while for Quinn to recognize the person in front of her because she was so badly injured. She wasn't a woman at all; she was a teenager. The very teenager she had been worried about.

"Jasmine, can you hear me?" Ethan was on the phone with 911, and his eyes snapped to hers when he heard her call the girl by name. "Jasmine, honey, please stay with me."

It was obvious what had happened. Someone had beaten her and brutally raped her, if the blood smeared down her inner thighs was any indication. Quinn blinked back tears of rage and focused on the girl in front of her. The girl who was only sixteen, the same age Quinn had been when she had escaped her own private hell. She reached out and held the girl's hand. Things looked really bad for her, and she wasn't sure the ambulance would make it in time. A scream sounded from behind her, and she heard Shawna yelling Jasmine's name. Jasmine's eyes fluttered and then opened.

"Ms. Sanders..." She licked her lips and closed her eyes.

"Shhh...honey, we're getting you help, just hold on."

"He told me...to give you a message."

"Who told you?" Quinn was instantly on high alert.

"He said to tell Jenny he's coming for her...he knows where she is...and she can't hide."

Jasmine lost consciousness again, but Quinn hardly noticed. She released her grip on Jasmine's hand and swayed to the side. The room seemed to fade around the edges, and all she could hear were the two words resonating in her head, *tell Jenny*. Quinn, the fearless, was no longer fearless. Quinn, the brave, was now trembling from head to toe because only one person could have sent that message. The monster had reared its ugly head and found Jenny. Found Quinn. She didn't feel the strong hands on her until she was lifted by them. She didn't see the kids staring at her or hear their whispers; all she heard was that name over and over in her head.

Jenny. Jenny. Jenny.

An awful keening moan sounded, and it took her a moment to realize it had come from her. She didn't hear Ethan whispering to her, asking her what was wrong. The room was spinning when she felt her body sinking and then rocking back and forth. The calming motion coupled with the sound of Ethan's voice finally started to break through her panic, and she blinked, looking around the room. Her office…they were in her office.

"You back with me?" he asked, kissing her brow.

"What? How did we get in here?"

"I carried you in here before you fainted in front of all the kids."

"Jasmine?"

"The EMTs have her right now. They got here just as you—"

"Started to panic."

"Yeah. Jesus, Quinn, you scared the shit out of me. You got white as a sheet and then swayed. For a second, I thought you were hurt— shot or something—but I didn't hear a shot or see any signs of an injury. I didn't know what was going on. Then the EMTs showed up. I grabbed you as you started to breathe erratically. What the hell happened? What did she say to you?"

"You…you didn't hear what she said to me?"

"No, I mean, I was on the phone with 911. I was giving them her vitals and the rundown of what was going on when I saw her talking to you, and then you just checked out. Your face went blank. I watched you swaying, torn between helping her or catching you. Thankfully, the station is just down the road. Their response was insanely fast. What did she tell you?"

"The person who did that to her gave her a message for me."

Ethan's whole body tensed against her. She didn't know how to soften what she was about to say. She didn't know what to do at all anymore. The fearless Quinn had disappeared the moment Jasmine had spoken that name. Had she ever been fearless at all? She doubted it, because one word, and she had retreated into that scared sixteen-year-old she had left behind. She could hear the words Jasmine said, but it wasn't Jasmine's voice. It was his. The way he said Jenny had always creeped her out, even when she had thought he loved her. To this day, she would recoil when she heard the name. The feeling had never disappeared, and she worried that the next Jenny she came across would wonder why she had behaved so oddly when she was introduced to them.

"Quinn?"

"Wh-what?"

"You spaced out again. I asked what the message was and why was it for you?"

"'Tell Jenny he's coming for her, he knows where she is, and she can't hide.'"

Was that voice really hers? It sounded so far away and foreign. It couldn't possibly be her voice, but it had to be, right? The words were the ones she was thinking, and she felt her mouth moving, but it felt so alien to her.

"You lost me. Is Jenny from the center? Why would he tell Jasmine to tell you something that was meant for Jenny?"

"Because I'm Jenny."

26

"Wait, you mean...son of a bitch, it's him? He's here?"

"That would be a big hell yes."

"How did he find you?" It was his turn to sound panicked.

"My guess is by accident. Fate can sometimes be cruel, but Karma is a bitch and if he thinks he's going to uproot me...well, Karma's coming for him."

"There's my Quinn. You had me scared for a bit there."

"Oh, you should be scared. I mean, I'm terrified, but I'm not running. It's more important now than ever to stay put because I know who your big, bad, ugly guy is. I can identify him, and he doesn't like loose ends."

"Oh my God, how did I not connect it right away? I'm the cop, not you, but I didn't see it. Paulie was chatting Jasmine up. Paulie worked for the guy we're trying to take down."

"Bingo. My worst nightmare happens to be your guy. Isn't that lovely?"

"All right, at least we have all the cards on the table now. The big question is: what are we going to do about it?" he asked.

"Oh, we're going to take him down and get our town back. That's what we're going to do." Quinn replied, venom in her voice. "He's not going to come in here and hurt my kids, this center. No way. No matter how scared I am of him, I won't let him hurt anyone else. I know who he is, and I can help take him down. I freaked out for a second there, but I'm back."

"You may be back, but now I'm freaked out, and I'm not sure I'm on the same page as you. I want you away from this case. I'm going to arrange for you to be put in a safe house."

"No way. Been there, done that, not going back."

"I'll go with you." He knew his voice was pleading, and he was on the verge of a full-blown panic attack. Her calm was also terrifying to behold.

"Not a chance. Ethan, they're taking children off the street in broad daylight. However they found me doesn't matter. What matters is that they have been messing with me for days. First, they tried to run me over. Then they hurt Officer Rodriguez. She nearly died because she was there to watch over me. Now they raped and beat Jasmine and brought her here to deliver a message to me." She stood up and looked down at him. "I need you to let me do this."

"You don't need my permission, Quinn. You're going to do what you want, no matter what I say." His voice was tight, and his face was set in stone.

"Ethan, I know I don't need your permission, but I do need your understanding and acceptance. This is my decision to make. Mine. I know we are two parts of a whole—at least, I like to think we are—and after this is all done, we *will* have an equal say in everything. But, right now, for this one thing, I need to make the decision. Please understand."

"I understand; I don't like it, but I understand. Quinn, can you honestly tell me that next time you won't do the same thing? If you hear a child is in danger, you'll stand by and let the police handle it?"

"This is different, you know that. I need to set this right. If I would have done something all those years ago, maybe this wouldn't be happening."

"We don't even know for sure if he's the one behind all this."

"Yes, we do. At least, I do. I know it's him. He's smart. All these years he's immersed himself in shadows, but I would know him anywhere, even if fourteen years have gone by. He is the monster in my recurring nightmares; he is the boogeyman in the shadows, but I *will* stop him. It's time I do a little damage by breaking those shadows."

"What if you can't? What if something goes wrong? Then what? I don't want you to be bait because I'm selfish. I need you here, safe, out of his reach."

"I know, but what would you do if I told you that you had to give up your job or lose me forever? Your job is dangerous. I will constantly worry about you."

"Is that what you want? For me to quit the force? Because I will if it means I get to keep you."

"No! That's not what I'm saying. Ethan, you're an extraordinary detective. I would never ask you to give that up, and you can't ask me to not see this through. I love you, and we'll get that future together—the one with the white picket fence and as many children as we can manage—but we need to end this. I need to get him out of my life. I want what we deserve, and we deserve a future with no shadow looming over us. Our future children deserve that." She took a step toward him and brushed her finger against his cheek. His face softened, and he grabbed her around the waist and pulled her close.

"If the opportunity presents itself, we'll talk about it, but for now we'll carry on as usual. Don't go off half-cocked. Let us discuss this and do it the right way. I can't lose you."

"You won't lose me." His mouth sought hers in such heated passion that her legs felt like Jell-O. There was a soft knock on the door before Caleb walked in and cleared his throat.

"What are you doing here?" Ethan asked, his voice uncharacteristically clipped.

"Hello, to you, too. I was driving by with Cap when we heard the call come over the radio."

"Whatever you two think you are agreeing to, you can get it right out of those pretty little heads of yours. The DFPD does not use civilians as bait." Bob's booming voice came from behind Caleb, and he stepped around the man who dwarfed him to stand toe to toe with Ethan.

"Bob, with all due respect, if this is the way to end it, then we end it. Tonight." Quinn said wearily.

"Not a chance. I said we don't use civilians as bait. I won't allow it. I've worked for Darkness Falls my whole life, and I plan to retire here. I also plan to leave this place with a good track record. I don't do bull-shit things like sending a civilian in to do a job like this. End of story. You are dismissed."

"Um, Bob, this is my office. You can't dismiss me from my own office. You know, that whole civilian thing you were just lecturing me about? Yeah, that. If you want, you can leave?" Quinn smiled sweetly at the older man but didn't back down one iota.

Ethan gave her credit for bouncing back so quickly and for the fact that she was telling Bob Wickman to get out of her office. Bob handed Ethan a sheet of paper and then turned to leave. Ethan glanced at it, and as Caleb and Bob walked out of the office, he fed it into the shredder.

"What was that?" she asked.

"Nothing for you to worry about."

"Ethan, don't shut me out."

"I'm not. Trust me on this one, okay?"

Quinn had told him there was no one she trusted more than him, and even though he could see the wheels turning at a hundred miles an hour, she nodded her head in agreement. Without any explanation, he grabbed her hand and started to tug her out of her office, but appar-ently, that was more than she was willing to allow because she dug in her heels and refused to move.

"What are you doing?"

"We have somewhere to go, and we need to run to my place and get cleaned up. We both have Jasmine's blood on us."

"Where are we going after we get cleaned up?"

"I'll explain later."

It wasn't until they were in his apartment and he had stripped her naked and shoved her in the shower, only to climb in behind her that he explained what was going on.

"The shower should drown out our voices, but talk directly into my ear. The piece of paper Bob gave me had the address where Becky is. We have her in a safe house until this is over. Even I didn't know where she was."

"Are they being guarded?"

"There is a bodyguard that I called in to help out. I would trust him with my life."

"A bodyguard?"

"The department couldn't spare an officer right now, so her parents wanted to hire someone. I suggested my friend's company for the job. I trust him to watch over her. The safe house is his, and he's doing this as a favor to me, and per my request, he was told to contact me through Bob, and only if it was necessary. It was best that as few people as possible know her whereabouts. No one other than my guy and his trusted few knew where they were. Until now. Something important must have happened for him to tell Bob the address."

"Why contact you through Bob and not just contact you?"

"Bob's more removed from the case. It's far less likely they're going to pull him off the street and try to torture the address out of him. Not to mention, it would be crazy to pull in someone with his ranking. That would bring the whole thing toppling down on their head in a hurry. Every cop in the city would be going after them, but even Bob doesn't know whose address it is that he handed me. He just knew that he was given an address to give me and that I was to shred it once I saw it, but he does know it's connected to this case."

"Why the cloak and dagger act in the shower?"

"I'm being overly cautious. I don't like that this guy knows where you are. I don't like that he's been watching this apartment and having you followed. I also don't think that the man the other night came in here strictly to hurt Rodriguez and send you a message."

"You think they bugged the apartment?"

"Possibly, and if they did, your office is probably bugged, too. I'll have someone sweep both places. They know you're digging into this, so we need to tread lightly, and for now, let's keep our conversations about your favorite color on the down low." He hoped she understood he was referring to Black and how they had to make sure not to give out any information regarding him.

His mind raced back to the few conversations they had about Harrison Black in this apartment. They never used his full name, and his undercover persona had a different name. If they were being listened to, at most, they would know someone had breached their network. Maybe he was just paranoid, and the apartment wasn't bugged. More than likely, they were only watching the apartment and following her, but he didn't want to chance it. They'd already said too much regarding Black.

"I'm not sure that's my favorite color, after all. I'm kind of fond of blue." God bless the girl for being able to play along. She kissed his ear and pulled back, blinking water out of her eyes, and he knew she completely understood what they had to do to protect the undercover officer. "Why did he tell you where Becky is?"

"I don't know. The note said her name and address and to shred it immediately. I imagine we'll find out when we get there."

"Then we better get a move on so we can find out what's going on. Something tells me we should hurry."

———

After their very fast shower, where they didn't get to enjoy the luxuries of exploring their wet soapy bodies, they dressed quickly, with whispered promises that next time they showered together, they would make better use of their time. The unspoken statement being, once this case was done, they could actually enjoy life a little more. Quinn put some hair gel in her short hair, slipped on her shoes, and rushed out the door behind Ethan. A small meow from the front porch had her stopping abruptly. She dropped to her knees, and the cat flew at her, rubbing her body all over Quinn while she purred so loud that she found herself chuckling.

"I missed you, too. How about we get you in the apartment with some kibbles and some water?" She looked at Ethan. Her darn eyes stung with relieved tears, and he was smiling from ear to ear.

"Good to see you came back. I should call you a traitor for running straight to Quinn. But if I had to decide, I would choose her, too." He rubbed the cat between the ears, and she purred even louder.

Once they had her secured in the apartment with food and water, they left to go see Becky. Quinn worried since she had just come back, and now they were rushing out the door, and she hoped she didn't feel abandoned. She was just so relieved to see her back. Seated in the car, she turned and looked at Ethan.

"I think you're rubbing off on me."

"How so?"

"All I want to do is lock Cat in your apartment and never let her out again. I want to keep her safe. Who do I sound like?"

"Me. And you know what? You won't, just like I won't lock you up."

"Because you can't cage a person or an animal, it isn't fair or right, but that doesn't mean I'm not going to firmly lecture her for running off. I know she was freaked and everything. Of course, maybe she did come back sooner, we were gone..." Ethan glanced at her and started the car.

"You carry so much guilt."

He saw through her so easily, and he was right. If it wasn't about the cat, it was about how she'd not gone to the police all those years ago. She'd wanted to believe that when she fled, he got scared and stopped what he was doing, that he didn't want to get caught, so he changed his ways, but she knew now that wasn't the case. That was wishful thinking, a fairy tale she had told herself to help her sleep at night, and she was going to have to endure the guilt of what she'd done for the rest of her days, but she wouldn't let him go on. Even though she was freaked out, she couldn't be locked up and hidden away. It would be easier because isn't that exactly what she'd been doing for the last fourteen years? If she had gone to the police back then, she would have stopped his reign of terror. Instead, she ran and hid herself away and allowed him to prowl the streets, taking more and more children.

"I can practically hear your thoughts, and I don't like them." His voice was so soft, like he was talking to a frightened doe.

"I'm not sure what you're referring to." She tried to play the dumb act but failed miserably.

"You're thinking that if you had gone to the police all those years ago, none of this would be happening."

"Well, damn, you're good at that whole reading minds thing," she quipped.

"I can tell you this: there is no way to know what would have happened if you went to the police. First, one of the police officers was a client of his. If you had gone to the police in that town, they might have returned you to him. They would have said you were a runaway."

"I—"

"Let me guess, you never even considered that, did you? I can almost guarantee that's exactly what would've happened if you went to the police there. Even if you went to the police in the neighboring community, the same results might have happened. He's smart, or he wouldn't have evaded the law this long, and he had paperwork to prove he had legal claims to you, right? At the very least, he would have shed doubt on what you'd said, and you would've been returned to him…or maybe not. But he would've known where to find you, and in the end, he most likely would've been left to continue roaming the streets and building his business."

"Maybe, but maybe he would have been locked up."

"It would've been the word of a sixteen-year-old against a man who had clients that were respected members of the community. I think you know, down deep, that you wouldn't have survived if you went to the authorities, and I know it's a burden you have to carry on your shoulders, but there is no way to know if the outcome would be any different than it is now, and there's no way to change it. Kara has the same guilt."

"Kara's guilt is different."

"Is it? You both have survivor's guilt. She still thinks that if she would've done things differently, those other girls wouldn't have died, but there's no way to know for sure, is there?"

"Well, no, but that's totally different."

"How so?"

"She thought he was dead. She didn't know there were two people."

"Didn't she? She said she thought that he was two people."

"But she was told that her abductor died. She had no way of knowing."

"You're right, but she also never talked about it until many years later. She made a choice she needed to in order to go on, to live. She has regrets, but she's working on it. You made a choice you had to in order to survive. You were a young girl. There is no one on this planet that if in the same shoes, would judge you."

"What about the parents of the children he's hurt since?" Her voice shook with frustration.

"Those parents might be angry, but if you were their child, and if they sat back and considered it, they would want their child to do exactly what you did. They would've wanted them to run, to survive. Quinn, you didn't just run, you helped a small girl get away. You carried her for part of your journey."

"Anyone would have done the same thing."

"No, I don't think they would have."

"But we don't know that, and we don't know if I changed her life for the better."

"Her name is Megan," he said quietly.

"What?"

"The girl you saved. Her name is Megan."

27

"How do you know that?" Her heart was racing, and her hands had gone clammy.

"I searched for her when I was at work. You said that she was in the newspaper, a little girl in a rural town, that they were looking for her parents. I found that article and the follow-up one from a couple weeks later. They found her parents, and the little girl told them an incredible story of a fairy princess who carried her through the woods and left her with a nice person, and the fairy princess told the person that she had found her in the woods. That the fairy princess had saved her from the monster." A single tear slid down her face as he spoke.

"Because she was so little, and you said she was found wandering in the woods, they called Child Protective Services and the police. I assume the police weren't willing to return her to him because the person had already called CPS as well. She was taken into custody until they were able to find her parents. It only took a few days for them to find them. The parents had a reward to find the fairy princess who returned their daughter to them. Do you want to know what became of Megan?"

She nodded her head.

"She graduated from high school a year ago and is currently

enrolled in college at Yale University. She's studying prelaw. She was valedictorian, and in her speech to her graduating class, she thanked the girl who rescued her, the fairy princess, and said that she was going to become a lawyer with aspirations to become a district attorney and that she planned to also work on cases, pro bono, for parents with missing and exploited children. She is doing all that because of you. You are her fairy princess, and I bet she would love nothing more than to meet you. Would you like to meet her when this is all done?"

"I would like that very much." She brushed the tears from her face. "Thank you."

"For what?"

"For finding her, for telling me her story, that she's doing well. It's what I needed to hear right now to help me focus on the task in front of us."

"I didn't tell you that story to encourage you to do something stupid."

"I know, but I needed to know that I did something right back then. Even if I hid like a coward afterward."

They had pulled up to the address they'd been given, and he turned to look at her. His hands came up to cup her face, and he tipped her head up until she had no choice but to look him in the eyes.

"Quinn Sanders, there are a lot of words I would use to describe you and not one is coward. Not. One." He kissed her soundly and then released her face. "Let's go inside and see why we were summoned here."

Quinn didn't know why, but she was suddenly really apprehensive. Something, some intuition was screaming at her that if she went in that house, there was no turning back. No way she could cut and run—not that it was even an option. She knew she had to finish this, but she was also struggling to accept that her worst nightmare was happening. *How could this be happening* had been repeating in her head since the moment she'd left the center. The walk to the front door seemed to take an eternity, yet they were there before she knew what was happening. Ethan knocked on the door, and a tall, muscular man opened the door.

"Hey, Cole," Ethan said.

"Hey, man, glad to see you got my message. Thanks for coming so fast." As soon as they were inside, he shut the door behind them. "As soon as we're done here, I'm moving them. My instincts are telling me shit is about to get real. I don't want her near this when it happens."

"And that's why I asked you to watch over her. There are very few people I would trust to keep her safe, and you are the top one on that list. Just don't tell Caleb; he might get a complex." Cole snorted, and Quinn liked him immediately. "Cole, this is Quinn. I guess you would call her my girlfriend, though the word seems inadequate. She's the reason we're here right now."

"Nice to meet you. Too bad it's under such shitty circumstances. After all this is over, I would like to get to properly have a conversation about your intentions with my man here." He winked at her. Yeah, she liked him, all right.

"I'm actually really surprised that Becky is out of the hospital so soon," Quinn said. "I would've thought she'd be in there a couple days longer."

"She rebounded remarkably well once she was given fluids and food. Her eyes are still a bit sensitive and getting her healthy and thriving again is going to take a bit, but the hospital was willing to let her go because I'm a doctor." Quinn turned to look at the woman who had spoken. She hadn't seen her behind Cole. "Once we determined that we didn't feel she was completely safe at the hospital, we contacted Detective Vanderbilt and said we would be moving her. He offered the services of Mr. Davenport."

"What made you feel unsafe at the hospital?"

"Why don't you come in and I'll explain everything and then you can go see Becky. I know you'll want to see her, but then we'll be leaving, like Mr. Davenport said."

"All right, and yes, I would like to see Becky before we leave."

Once they were in the living room, Quinn sat on the edge of the couch, her body unable to relax. Apprehension filled her until she felt consumed by it and she felt a sense of unease that she couldn't pinpoint. Maybe it was the fact that they were summoned to this secret location, which meant something had happened, or maybe it was the look on Becky's mom's face. Whichever it was, she couldn't explain it.

"My husband is packing. We don't have much with us, but he's getting it all ready."

"Time is of the essence, and we don't want to keep you here longer than necessary. Ethan was cautious on our way here, but there's never any certainty that we weren't followed," Quinn said, earning an approving look from both mother and bodyguard.

"Very well. Apparently, a couple of days ago someone visited Becky in the hospital. We didn't know about it. Becky thought he was an employee of the hospital and said he was there briefly, left an envelope, and then was gone. She completely forgot about the whole incident until this afternoon when we started going through the gifts she'd gotten in the hospital. One of the gift bags had an envelope in it." She paused and swallowed, her calm demeanor cracking for a moment. "The envelope is addressed to you, Ms. Sanders. We haven't opened it. It says it should only be opened by you in the event of the death of Paulie Romano."

"What did you just say?" Ethan asked.

"Paulie Romano left an envelope for Quinn in my daughter's room. We had reservations about how safe she was in the hospital because a news reporter managed to sneak in dressed up as a nurse. We had no idea that this man had also been in her room."

"What day was it that he was there?" Quinn asked.

"The day after you stopped to visit her."

"That would have been the day that you were released from the hospital after your accident." He looked at her and saw the moment she'd figured it out.

He pulled out his cell phone and sent a text to Caleb, asking him to send a picture of Romano. It wasn't long until his phone beeped, and he looked down at a picture of the dead man. In all the craziness, he hadn't taken the time to look at a picture of him. In the brief glimpse at night that he saw him before his brains were splattered everywhere, he hadn't appeared familiar. Now, looking at a picture of him with good lighting, he could see it. He turned the phone so she could see the picture.

"The weird guy, when we were leaving the hospital. The one that bumped into me. Remove the glasses, and it's definitely Paulie Romano."

"Yeah, I think you're right. Shit. Remember how he looked at you like he knew you?"

"I bet he told him that he saw me. He would have had the people he trusted in his organization looking for me."

"But they didn't know it was you when they tried to run you off the road. Which means Paulie wasn't behind the wheel?"

"Or he just didn't get a good look at you at the time."

Ethan didn't want to read the letter while they were there. The Plummers needed to get gone and fast, but he also wanted to tear open that letter and see what was in it. He knew that Quinn was feeling the same urge. He glanced at Cole and saw that he was marking the time. They'd already been there longer than he was comfortable with, and Quinn still hadn't gotten to see Becky.

"We need to go. Let's go see Becky fast so they can make like a ghost and vanish."

"You're right. Can we have five minutes, or is that too much?"

"Five minutes, max. We'll get everything closed up here while you talk to her."

They walked briskly out of the living room, making a beeline for the back bedroom. Becky was sitting on the bed, dressed in pajamas, but she was ready to go. She looked better, but she was still weak and fragile. Her eyes went wide and filled with tears when she saw them. Quinn walked over and sat beside her, placing an arm gently on her shoulders. The girl leaned on Quinn and held on.

"Thank you for visiting. My parents knew I needed to see you before we leave, to thank you, and I wanted to tell you that I believe in miracles, but I'm scared."

"I'm scared, too. This letter is the key to all this craziness." Ethan sure hoped that was true, but he didn't contradict her because he knew the girl needed the reassurance that it was going to be all right. "This will all be over soon. I promise." Quinn kissed the side of Becky's head and squeezed her shoulder.

"Are they all set to go?"

"Just waiting on you. Let's make a date to sit down and get to know each other once you're feeling a little better. I'll take you out somewhere to eat—your choice—or if it's too soon for that, I can cook you your favorite meal. Rumor is I'm a pretty darn good cook. Deal?"

"Yeah." She sniffed and wiped her tears. "I would really like that. Could my mom and dad come?"

"Absolutely. I want to get to know the parents that raised such an amazing young woman."

Becky managed a small smile, but it faded when Cole stepped into the room. Ethan knew by the look on his face that something was up. He indicated that Ethan should meet him in the hallway. The two women, one not quite an adult, didn't miss the silent exchange, but Quinn did her best to distract Becky as Ethan left the room braced for bad news.

"What's going on?"

"I think you may have been followed. I have the perimeter wired with an alarm system. One of the back alarms is going off. There's a reason I picked a remote house with a lot of acreage and wide-open spaces. For them to come in, they would have to be really careful or risk being seen."

"Son of a bitch. I was careful. How did they manage to follow us?"

"My guess is they slipped a tracking device on your car. They've known where you are on several occasions."

"You're probably right, which means my apartment probably is clean for listening devices—tracking my car would be easier to accomplish. Can we still get you out safely?"

"Sure." He grinned cockily. "But it's going to be a hot exit. I have a couple guys on the perimeter hunting whoever was stupid enough to try to breach my security. We aren't sticking around to find out how long that takes."

"You need us to lead them away?"

"Affirmative. I'm hoping whoever followed you is an idiot on the bottom of the food chain and doesn't realize that he hit a gold mine here. Two for the price of one. I'm not holding out hope that that's the case. In fact, I think it's the complete opposite." That they called in the big dogs to get to Quinn and Becky.

"Me, too. I would ask you to take Quinn—"

"She won't come. She'd end up fighting it, and that would make her more of a liability."

"You pegged her."

"It's my job."

"We'll lure them away. Are you ready to go?" Ethan didn't love the situation, but there was little they could do to change it.

"Locked and loaded; we just need the little lady in there." He tipped his head to the room.

"She's ready."

When he walked back in the room, Quinn was helping Becky stand —the girl was wobbly. Cole took two strides to her and scooped her up. With another trademark cocky grin sent toward Quinn and a tip of the head to Ethan, he walked out of the room.

"We need to be a distraction for them. Someone managed to follow us here, and I'm hoping to draw whoever it is away from the house so they can get out quickly. But it's possible it'll be a hot extraction."

To her credit, she didn't so much as waiver as she strode to the front door. He was terrified to let her leave that house. Most likely they'd been instructed to bring Quinn in alive. Ethan was collateral damage, but even so, he hoped that they'd been told to leave him alone. They didn't need the heat of a dead detective to bring the whole DFPD down on their heads. Rodriguez was bad enough, but she'd survived. That didn't mean that the other officers weren't gunning for the SOB that had tried to gut her, and it didn't mean that the bad guys wouldn't gut Ethan. He wanted to tell her to tuck and run, but he knew that would tip their hand. Their only option was to walk out of that house like they had no clue what was going down. Before he could overthink it, she took the decision out of his hand, opened the door, and walked outside. He followed, and as soon as they were outside, she grabbed his hand and squeezed.

"What a colossal waste of time. I swear if we keep chasing our tails like this, we're never going to catch this son of a bitch." Ethan wasn't expecting Quinn to strike up a fake conversation, but he went with it.

"I know what you mean. I feel like we're treading water against a current and we can't get anywhere."

They were almost to the car when he heard a noise. A twig snapped, and Ethan spun, placing Quinn behind him, his gun out of his holster. There goes hoping they would let them get out of there without incident because standing behind him were two huge men with guns drawn, looking to take him down and grab Quinn. Hell no! Not a chance that was happening. Not today. He was outgunned and didn't know how to get them both safely in the car. He would have shoved her toward it, but he had the keys and couldn't get them to her while he had both eyes on the assholes in front of him. This wasn't going to go down the way he'd planned. Cole needed to get Becky and her family out of there, and he needed to get Quinn out of there, as well. Panic was welling inside him until he felt Quinn slide her fingers into the waistband of his pants.

"Give us the girl, and we'll let you walk away. Our beef isn't with you."

"You're out of your freaking mind if you think I'm going to let you walk away with her."

"I read the letter while you were with Cole. It has everything you need to take them down and to find me. But be quick about it." Still gripping his pants, she stood on her tiptoes and kissed the back of his neck.

"What the fuck?" he said as she stepped back and around him, her good hand out in surrender, her hand that was still in the cast also raised and Ethan felt his world tip off its axis and go spinning in the wrong direction. "Quinn!"

"You have what you need," she said, and he knew that the cryptic statement was directed at him and not the two heavily armed men she was approaching.

Ethan couldn't do anything without risking injury to her. He watched impotently as she took another step and then another away from him. He still had his gun drawn and pointed at the two men, but there was nothing he could do to stop them as the first man grabbed Quinn, spun her and twisted her uninjured arm up and behind her. Ethan knew that if she wanted, she could get out of that hold in a second. Sweet Jesus, she was sacrificing herself to get the Plummers out of there. She mouthed the words, *I love you,* and *it's okay* as they dragged her backward toward the trees, where they presumably had their car stashed away. Ethan stared until he could no longer see them. When he heard the sound of squealing tires, he stood cemented to the ground. Cole was suddenly next to him.

"What are you still doing here?" Ethan asked with a bite to his tone.

"Everything just went south. They got the jump on one of my best guys. He's dead. My other guy came barreling into the house a minute ago. I sent the Plummers with him. He's taking them to another safe house, and I have several people there ready to guard them. But I have to stay here and see to the business of dealing with a dead employee who happened to be a friend, as well. I called 911, and they're on their way. We'll get her back."

Ethan felt like an asshole for not considering Cole's feelings at the moment. He'd lost an employee and friend, but all Ethan could think about were the words that Quinn had said. In his terror, he'd forgotten that she had fiddled with his pants. At first, he thought she just used it as leverage to keep her balance as she stood on her tiptoes to kiss him goodbye. Realization dawned on him, and he grabbed the back of his pants and tugged out what she had slipped into his waistline. It was the damn letter from Paulie Romano. The envelope was torn open. He grabbed the single sheet of paper out and read it twice. The blessed thing wasn't long. In fact, it was short and succinct and had every bit of information they needed to take down Vance Duprey, but all Ethan cared about was the last sentence. Ethan held the winning hand. The look on Quinn's face as she was hauled away haunted him, but the letter in his hand was all they would need to demolish Vance Duprey. But it was the last sentence that held all the information he needed to know.

28

Not for the first time in the last twenty minutes, Quinn found herself wondering what the hell she'd been thinking. But it didn't take long to remind herself of the answer. She'd been thinking about getting Ethan out of the line of fire. She'd also been thinking about getting Becky out of that farmhouse safely. The girl had been through enough already, so Quinn threw herself on the proverbial grenade. And she would do it again, but the look on Ethan's face had nearly destroyed her will to stick with the plan. The plan she'd made up on the fly as soon as she had heard the two men approaching. She only hoped Ethan understood why she'd done it and that they were able to act quickly because she knew that she didn't have a whole lot of time before her time was up.

They didn't drive long before they pulled into a sprawling complex on the outskirts of town. A six-foot stone fence ran the length of the property. One of the men was driving while the other man was sitting next to her, a gun at her side. When they pulled up to the gate, the driver rolled down his window, and after he entered a code into the keypad, the gate swung open, revealing the sprawling mansion on the other side of it. They pulled up to the front of the house, and the driver got out, marched around to the side of the car, and opened the door. She crawled out after a small shove in the side from the gun.

"Let's go, bitch," Goon Number One said while tugging on her arm that was in the cast.

"Lay off, man."

"What's it to you?" he snarled at the man climbing out of the car behind Quinn.

"Nothing to me, but if you don't deliver her in one piece, I reckon the boss is going to be mighty pissed at you."

Quinn saw that the jerk had the good grace to look uncomfortable about that very idea. Inwardly she smiled, but outwardly she made herself look like the docile little woman, willing to do anything to get out of there alive. She was definitely planning on getting out of there alive, but she was far from a docile little woman.

"I'll take her to her room, and you go find the big guy."

"Yeah, sure, man."

Quinn didn't like the look he sent her way, like he didn't believe for a second that the other man was going to deliver her to the room and keep his hands to himself, but Quinn knew better. There was no way he was going to touch her.

"Sorry about jerking your arm so hard; I had to make it look real," Harrison Black whispered through clenched teeth. If she wasn't standing next to him, she wouldn't have seen his lips move.

"Keep it up. They might be watching us."

"Oh, you can count on that. That SOB sliced one of the guard's throats back there. I couldn't stop him. For that alone, I'm taking him down." That seemed like a very hands-on way to kill someone. Was it The Fixer? Without a minute to process more, he jerked her toward the house. Once inside, he dragged her up the stairs to the second floor. She played right along, tripping and crying out where necessary.

The room he brought her to was dark and small, as if it was meant to be a closet. It had a small window that didn't allow for much natural lighting due to the side of the house that the room was on and the late hour of the day. She could tell that night was fast approaching and suspected that they'd wait for dark to enter the house. Harrison shut the door and pretended to frisk her while loudly asking if she had any weapons or a cell phone on her. She answered truthfully to both questions. She had no weapons, and her cell phone was in her purse in the car. When he was kneeling at her feet, he looked up at her and smiled grimly. After a moment, he stood, and as he turned to leave, he looked at her one last time, and she noted the worry in his eyes. This could go down good, or this could go down really bad. She opted for door number one.

After she was alone, she paced the room. He hadn't tied her up. He'd said there was no need to tie her up—the room was being guarded. All clever words to let her know what she was up against. When she had seen that Harrison was one of the two men behind them at the farmhouse, she'd almost cried out with relief, then she saw that the man next to him had blood on him, and she didn't want to chance that he'd shoot Ethan. She'd looked at Harrison and tried to communicate what she was about to do. He couldn't compromise the operation, and it was clear to her that he was thinking about taking out the other man at that exact moment. Instead of letting that happen, she slipped the letter into Ethan's waistband. Kissing him goodbye was the hardest thing she'd ever done—even harder than leaving that house all those years ago—because now she knew the good in life. But it had to be done. She saw with crystal clear clarity that this was the only way to stop this from continuing.

Quinn walked right toward Harrison, forcing the other man to cover them. Ethan could have taken him out. He could have ended it there, but he hesitated when Harrison stood to the side, blocking the other man slightly. No doubt he was scared he would hit Quinn, but she hated the confused look on his face—the fear that was evident. It was obvious to her that he worried that Harrison had flipped to the other side. She mouthed that she was okay to him, hoping that he would understand that Harrison wasn't a threat, but that they had to do it this way. If Ethan managed to get her out of that situation without injury to himself or her, the Plummers were still in danger, and in Quinn's mind, this was the only way to take down the monster who called himself Vance Duprey.

"What the fuck happened?" Captain Bob Wickman's voice boomed as he climbed out of the car.

Ethan was pacing back and forth as what appeared to be every police car in the city pulled up. He raked his hands through his hair and stopped and looked at his mentor. Where did he start? How did he explain this mess to the man who trusted him to finish this case? Out of the corner of his eye, he saw Caleb's car come screeching to a halt on the lawn. One of his best friends in the world, and he had no idea how much Ethan had deceived him in the last few months.

"We came to talk to the Plummers. They had information that was pertinent to the human trafficking case."

"What information?" Bob demanded, clearly not happy that he had no clue that the address he had given him was to the safe house where the Plummers had been.

"A letter addressed to Quinn Sanders, from Paulie Romano. A letter he snuck into Becky Plummer's belongings at the hospital, a letter that was to only be opened upon the event of his death. Becky found it and Port Investigations owner, Cole Davenport, called you with the address. We came out and gained ownership of said letter. Davenport was in the process of moving the Plummers to a new safe house. He gave us five minutes to talk to Becky. While we were in Becky's room, a silent alarm was triggered on the perimeter. We decided to be a distraction so they could get out."

"What the hell went wrong?" This time Bob's voice was gentler as he sensed the anguish that Ethan was going through.

"As we were walking to the car, two suspects approached from the rear. Quinn felt there was no other option and sacrificed herself to the two suspects in order to get the Plummers out safely. She did so without consulting me. Before she did, she slipped the letter into the waistband at my back. Cap, one of the suspects was our undercover officer."

"Was he going along with the situation because he had no other choice, or do you think there was more to it than that?"

"If you're asking if I think he's switched sides, then the answer is no. I don't believe he's switched teams. One of the guards on the perimeter was killed, and suspect two had blood on him. I believe that the officer had no choice but to go along with the situation, especially once Quinn gave herself over to them. For what it's worth, she walked right to him, without any hesitation or fear. She knows him and trusts him. I believe they were doing what they felt they needed to do to stop this once and for all, and he was gentle with her. It was apparent to me that he wasn't hurting her when he took her away. Quinn did a good job pretending, though, but I know her skill. The officer is tough, but she's slippery when being restrained."

"Why would Quinn sacrifice herself?" Caleb's voice was slightly incredulous.

"In light of the circumstances, I believe that Quinn would understand if I fill you in. We have reason to believe that the man known to us as Vance Duprey is a man from Quinn's past, and the fact that they were here had less to do about the Plummers than it had to do with her."

"How are they connected?" Bob's voice was quiet, and he quickly moved them off to the side where no one could hear them, not that anyone was listening through the commotion.

"Understand that I promised Quinn I wouldn't share this story and that the only reason I am is that the situation warrants it and that I don't believe at this juncture she would care, if it means ending this."

"There's no reason for it to go beyond us if it isn't necessary," Bob said.

"Fair enough. When Quinn was a little girl, her parents sold her to Vance Duprey, and he kept her captive. When she was fourteen, he forced her into marriage with him. When she was sixteen, she escaped, taking with her a little girl who was also being held there. It seems that at the time, he was dabbling in selling children, that his operation was just starting up. She believes he would have been in his late twenties at the time."

"What happened after she got away?" Bob asked.

"She ran and hid. I'm not willing to say more than that."

"You mean to tell me she's still married to that psycho?" Caleb asked.

"I'm going to wager a guess that they were never legally married," Ethan responded. "I tried to convince Quinn to let me look into it, but she was adamant that I not do that."

"You didn't listen, did you?" Caleb knew Ethan well.

"I would have looked into it, but there were certain things that prohibited me from being able to find him."

"Like not knowing his name or hers?" Bob asked intuitively.

"Something like that."

"Vanderbilt, there's a couple things you need to learn in a hurry. One thing is that when I say that this doesn't need to go beyond this point, I mean it. The other thing is you might be surprised to find out that I'm one hundred percent okay with people that are being abused changing their identity and running. Even if the means they do it by isn't considered legal. You know why? Because if it was done legally, there would be a paper trail. I know that you are by the book, but sometimes it's okay if you have to color outside the lines a little for the right reasons." He patted Ethan on the shoulder and pulled him in for a quick hug, whispering in his ear, "You let Quinn know when we get her back that I know how to help people disappear if ever someone comes into the center and needs to do just that. Now let's see that letter so we can get your girl back. In case you didn't know, I really like Quinn. You picked a good one."

Before Ethan could say anything, Bob marched off barking orders at a couple officers to secure the scene, then ordering the rest to gather up so they could plan how to take down a monster, but as he was walking toward the group, his phone rang. A glance at the screen had his heart thundering.

"Vanderbilt."

"How long until the forces are in place? I can't keep him distracted forever, and if you can't get here soon, I'm going to have to make a move."

"Don't move without a word from us. We're gathering the troops right now."

"Hurry. Not sure how much longer I can keep that asshole from visiting her. Trust me, if the rumors are true, you don't want him to."

Ethan's stomach rolled over as the meaning of those words sunk in. The phone went dead, and he pocketed it. Bob caught his eye as he joined the group. There was no turning back from this; it was now or never. As he approached the group, he locked eyes with Caleb and held them. He was going to be pissed, but it couldn't be avoided.

"What did he say?" Bob, always able to see what others didn't, knew who he had been on the phone with.

"That was our guy. He said to hurry because he won't be able to distract the subject from Quinn for long."

Ethan registered the surprise on Caleb's face. Clearly, when he heard Ethan explain that Black had been one of the men that took Quinn, he hadn't figured out that Ethan was the contact for Black. The hurt on Caleb's face was evident, but he covered it quickly. They had been partners for a long time, and Ethan understood the betrayal he was feeling.

"Glad to hear that Black is still with us," Bob said.

Caleb's face went rigid. Shit! He didn't have time for this discussion, a discussion he should have had with him sooner, but his hands had been tied. Bullshit! Bob would have understood if he let Caleb in on what was going on; it would have made things easier. Less sneaking around. He just couldn't bring himself to tell him because he knew that Caleb wouldn't react in a positive way. He'd hoped that eventually, Caleb's feelings toward Black would dissipate, and in recent weeks, it had finally started to seem like Kara had finally gotten through to him. Yet he hadn't said anything to him, and that was on him. Ethan couldn't worry about that now. He had other things to worry about.

Quinn was shoved to the ground and landed hard on her right side, but it absorbed the impact and saved her already injured arm from further harm. If she planned to get out of here alive, she needed to make sure that she was firing on all cylinders and that her body was up for the challenge. The door shut behind her. It was now night, and the room was left in pitch black. Even so, she knew that whoever had shoved her was still in the room with her. She could hear his loud breathing. Vance had always been a loud breather, and she had become adept at recognizing every sound he made.

Why had she stupidly turned her back on the door? If her back hadn't been turned, she might have been quick enough to turn, blitz him, and get out of that too small room. The room that reminded her of the one he'd kept her in all those years ago. It was useful to know, that while his house was bigger, his main operation hadn't changed. He still had the small room to cage his prey in. Breathing in and out, she assessed herself. Other than the burning in her knees, she was fine. She wasn't bound because Harrison wasn't about to bind her, and she knew he could play it off because of the cast. It would be useful for them to underestimate her, and so far, they'd been doing just that, and *that* would work to her advantage. Appearing to be the weak little woman long enough to delay things until the police arrived was the way she would walk out of there alive.

A light flickered on just as she was climbing to her feet. She blinked against the sudden invasion of light. The image of Becky, blindfolded to protect her eyes from the light came to her in a flash. If that light even as dim as it was hurt her eyes after being in the opaque darkness for such a short time, what had it felt like for poor Becky to finally have light hit her eyes? Once she was vertical, she could feel the heat from the other person behind her before he made contact with her body. She flinched as his body pressed up against her.

"My, how you've grown. Little Jenny, my baby doll, has grown into a woman. Tiny but packing lots of curves, aren't you? Though I'm not really into the curves as much as some of my clients."

Her insides went to liquid at the sound of his voice, at his proximity to her body. She had vowed to herself that she would never see him again, but if they *did* ever cross paths, she would never let him see her scared, and it nearly broke her that she had failed on both counts. But she could use that fear against him because even if she was scared, she wasn't giving up, and as much as she hated his touch, she could use that, as well. The longer he wasted time with her, the more time the police would have to breach his walls and get her the hell out of there.

"Don't call me that. My name isn't Jenny."

Careful, Quinn. She had to play this right. The question was would she buy more time if she resisted him or would that make him rush things? She would bet her car that he would get more bang for his buck if she resisted, so she made a split-second decision to go that route. She just hoped it was the right one.

"That's right, you changed your name after you ran from me, didn't you?"

"You didn't think I would keep your name, did you? I couldn't wait to get away from you. I'm only sorry it took me so many years to get the nerve to run."

His body was still pressed against hers, and she desperately wanted to take a step away from him, but before she could, he pulled her tightly against him. She had struck a nerve with that last comment. Good. Keep him unnerved, make him angry. She smiled insolently at him as if she hadn't a care in the world, but let her eyes appear to be frightened. It really wasn't that much of a stretch for her to do so.

"You cost me a good employee when you ran."

"Really? How so?" But she thought she knew the answer to that question.

"I don't have room in my business for failures or troublemakers. When he didn't find you, it was imperative that he be dealt with. Just like you will be dealt with, but not yet, not before I get to play with you for a while."

His hands roamed over her body, sliding up to cup her breasts, where he tugged viciously. There was no way she could hide the shiver of repulsion that ran the length of her body. With one caress, she was back in that house, the terrified little girl who was brainwashed into accepting her fate and who had endured too much before she finally was brave enough to escape. Vance inhaled deeply, laughing, and his laughter was all it took for her to snap back to the present.

"I'm not that little girl anymore. You can't scare me, Vance."

"Oh, I disagree. As a matter of fact, I think you're pretty terrified right now."

"Think again. You know, I do admire the set of balls you have. The fact that you never changed your name or ran. Pretty gutsy, if I do say so myself."

"You would know a thing or two about having guts. It was pretty brave to run away from me. I figured you would go to the local police, and since I had the sheriff in my pocket, it wasn't really a threat, was it? Of course, when you didn't go to him, I remembered that you had seen the sheriff and were wise enough to go somewhere else. Of course, it wasn't like you knew what a cop was, but I still wanted to be careful. Then days turned into weeks. There was really no need for me to run. I did lay low for a bit, though."

"Glad to hear I scared you."

"Only for a blip in time, then I was more confident than ever that I wouldn't get caught. Though, I'm still really pissed at you. Not only did you cost me the money I would have made for you, but you took Megan from me. She was going to be my new play thing, but you stole that from me. The way I see it, you owe me a replacement."

"I would rather die than do any such thing."

"Oh, don't worry, it's only a matter of time, but I guarantee you'll be begging to do anything I ask by the time I'm done with you."

"Don't bet on it."

With a vicious shove, she flew into the cement wall. Her head cracked against it, and she slumped to the ground, blinking back what at first, she thought was tears, but then she smelled the coppery scent of blood. With every fiber of her being, she knew she was going to kill the son of a bitch standing in front of her. It was only a matter of time.

29

They were in position in the woods outside the luxurious house that Vance Duprey called his home. Currently, Stuart was working to take out the hi-tech security cameras that were placed around the perimeter before they entered. Ethan was pacing back and forth waiting for the all clear to breach the walls and go inside and get back what was his. If he had to kill a few people on the road to getting her, then so be it. He wouldn't feel one second of remorse for any of the assholes inside that building. They had made their bed; now, they had to sleep in it. His only concern was getting Quinn out. Helping Harrison was secondary; the man could take care of himself.

"I can't believe you didn't tell me that you were his contact. We're partners, we're supposed to tell each other everything," came a voice from behind him.

"Shit, Caleb, we can hash this out later. Now is not the time."

"I know, I…Well, I just wanted to say I would have been pissed, but I would have understood. I get what you're going through right now, and I just wanted to say, no hard feelings. You did what you had to do, and I wasn't in the right place to hear what you had to say anyway. For what it's worth, I think Black is in there because of what went down with Kara and the fact that I wouldn't lay off him."

"Yeah, you're right that he's in there because of his guilt over how he handled everything with Kara. However, you didn't play into his decision at all."

"I'm not so sure about that."

"I am. What the fuck is taking so long? Why can't we just go in there and freaking get her out?"

"You know how this goes, Ethan. We can't just go storming in. Right now, they're trying to figure out where she is in the building and if there are any other innocent people inside. It's entirely possible he has people in there against their will."

Shit! Ethan had such a one-track mind that he never even considered the possibility that there might be other victims in that house. But it would stand to reason if he took Quinn's story into account about how he had both her and Megan at his house at the same time. Not only did the man sell children, but he also liked to partake in his own business dealings. If there was ever a moment that Ethan didn't want to kill the man, that moment was long gone. He knew they needed him alive if they wanted a chance in hell of taking down his network, but Ethan just wanted him pushing up daisies. His phone vibrated, and he answered on the first ring.

"You better have good fucking news."

"Are you assholes in place?"

"Oh, yeah. Just waiting for them to take out the eyes inside that palace."

"I'm about to help you with that problem."

Black was still speaking when a voice came through the comm in his ear—Stuart's voice telling them that the cameras had gone out and that they were blind inside, and then he mumbled something about it being their lucky day, and he wasn't sure if he liked that the cameras blinked out.

"We just got a little help," Ethan responded through his comm.

Black's voice was there again. "That should be better. Wait for my signal, it won't be much longer. I'll clear you a path to get inside undetected." Ethan wasn't sure what that meant, but he liked the sound of it. He motioned Bob to come over.

"That was Black. He said he's clearing us a path to get inside undetected and to wait for his signal. Not sure what that means, but—" He was cut off by his comm again.

Stuart's voice came over the comm, cursing under his breath. "The gate just opened; more help from the inside?"

"I'm guessing that's our signal. It's go time," Bob said wryly and motioned for everyone to converge on the house.

It's about damn time, Ethan thought. He hoped she knew they were coming for her and hoping that she could just hold on a little bit longer. With a quick glance at his watch, it was his turn to curse under his breath. She'd been inside that house for longer than he wanted, and if one hair on her head was harmed, he wasn't sure how he would handle it because he had let her go with them and it was on him if anything happened to her.

After the waves of dizziness passed, Quinn lingered on the ground longer than necessary. Waiting for Vance to approach her, lulling him into a false sense of security. She didn't have to wait that long as he couldn't keep himself from wanting to touch her, to harm her for getting away and she had been counting on that very thing. Curled on the floor in a fetal position, Vance couldn't tell that she was conscious, much less the fact that she was reaching for the ankle holster that Harrison's nimble fingers had managed to hide under her jeans. Her fingers slid around the handle of the gun just as Vance crouched down to drag her to her feet.

As he pulled her up, she pulled the gun from the holster and shoved it into his gut. She had almost forgotten that he liked to laugh maliciously when he beat her as a child—almost, but not quite. That laughter had finally been silenced as he looked down quickly and then slowly up until his eyes met hers.

"Step. Back. Just one step." He took a step back, and she smiled coldly at him. "That's right. Good boy. Not so nice when the shoe is on the other foot."

Her hand shook as she aimed the gun at him. Swallowing hard, she fought to steady the trembling but settled for stabilizing her shaking hand on her cast. She could not, would not, let him see her shaken. If she was going to die, she would die with the satisfaction that she hadn't gone down without a fight because the bastard that haunted her dreams, the puppet master of her childhood was now standing in front of her with a gun pointed at him. He didn't deserve her fear. He didn't deserve anything from her. And she would do everything in her power to stop him, even if it meant dying. Because she could not live with herself if he harmed another child because she let him walk out of there alive.

The days of Quinn running were long gone because Quinn could live with his blood on her hands. She could not live with another innocent child's. When she had walked away all those years ago, a scared teenager, she had stupidly convinced herself that he would stop, that he would be watching over his shoulder every day terrified that she had told the police and that they were coming for him. Now her naivete astounded her.

"Put down the gun, Jenny. We both know you won't use it on me. My darling little girl. You wouldn't hurt your daddy, would you?"

"You. Are. Not. My. Father," she ground out between gritted teeth. Her anger steadied her hands. "You are just the son of a bitch who bought me from another of your ilk, another monster who was allowed to roam this earth far too long."

The monster of her dreams smiled that perfect reptilian smile and laughed again. If there was anything she wanted it was to silence that laughter, the laughter that made Quinn's blood run cold. Something about the way he was laughing wasn't right. As if he knew something she didn't know. Like he was in on a private joke she didn't know the punch line to. And then he clapped his hands together in glee.

"You never figured it out, then, did you?" He tsked at the look of puzzlement on her face and then flashed that grotesque smile at her again. "Your parents didn't sell you. I took you from them when you were just a wee little one."

"What the hell are you talking about?" *Don't listen to him, he's a master at lying, manipulating people into believing everything he says.*

"Your real parents loved you quite a lot, actually. They were just young and inexperienced and turned their back for just a moment."

"I don't believe you."

"You should believe me. After all, I'm the one who took you. I saw you that day at the park, and I just had to have you. You understand, don't you? I mean, you were such a beautiful little girl. I guess one could say you turned into a beautiful woman, too. If you like that sort of thing."

"That sort of thing? You mean if you like adult women versus children? You sick son of a bitch!"

"You really shouldn't judge something you don't understand. As a therapist, aren't you supposed to help me, sympathize with me, tell me that I can be fixed?"

"There is no fixing you. The only way to humanely stop someone like you is to put them down."

"Darling Jenny, you sure have gotten angry in your old age."

"*Don't* call me that name. Don't you *ever* call me that name! Jenny died in those woods—Quinn emerged, she survived."

The sound of that name on his lips resulted in a flash of anger so profound that her body felt superheated with the intensity of it. Surely, she could use that anger as a weapon. If she'd learned anything, she'd learned that there were many ways to skin a rabbit, and she was looking at the rabbit.

"I groomed you from a young age, didn't I? I raised you, took care of you. I can call you whatever I want. I did such a good job that you never even thought to check after you got away, did you? You never wanted to find them because I told you how terrible they were to you."

She stumbled backward at his words until her back was against the cement wall. Blood was still dripping from the wound in her head, but she barely noticed. She shook her head vehemently as if she could shake the words out of her head, never hearing them. Never know that he had ruined her perception of her parents.

"Liar. You are lying!" she yelled, even though she knew

he wasn't. But she wanted so badly to believe that he wasn't being honest, that she hadn't wasted all these years without loving parents.

"A simple Google search would have netted numerous links to articles where your parents are pleading for your safe return." He glanced down at his nails as if they were the most interesting thing in the room, as if he were bored. "Even on the anniversary of your abduction this year. They still held out hope twenty-five years later that you would turn up alive and well. This year was especially somber since it was the silver anniversary of your disappearance. Though I have to admit, they did sound less believable this year in their claims that you're alive. Of course, you would have had to have known your real name, your real age, where you were really from to find your true identity." Her real name? "Feeding you all the wrong information just in case you ever got away and ever searched was pretty genius. It was also necessary to break you down and make you think your parents hated you. If you had Googled, you would have found the exact parents I told you were yours. Unfortunately, they did have a child go missing, it's also unfortunate that they OD'd. Convenient for me, though, that there are so many stories like that out there. I find it immensely useful when I groom my girls."

Quinn's knees felt weak. Nothing could have sucked the wind out of her sails more than this. It was as if she had been sucker punched. Her parents loved her, had never stopped looking for her, and she had never tried to find them. She had never known her name, their names, their address. Even if she'd wanted to find them, she couldn't. She didn't even know her age or birthday to make an educated guess. He had made sure of that. He had played her so well, she couldn't have found them even if she'd tried.

"Liar..." she whispered. Her denial even sounded phony to her own ears, because she knew every word of what he said was true. As the truth sunk in, she began to feel a renewed will to live. She had to get out of there. If only for the fact that she owed it to her parents to find them, to tell them how sorry she was for not looking for them, for not trying sooner.

"You know as well as I do that I'm not lying. You just don't want to acknowledge that you didn't care enough to find them."

"I would have cared if I had *known* they existed. I would have moved heaven and earth to find them."

"It's all semantics, isn't it?'

"You bastard, you unconscionable bastard. I cared. I would have looked. I *did* look."

She choked on a small sob. All she'd found was the OD'd drug addicts like he'd wanted. It was another secret she'd not wanted to share. The final secret, in a world of honesty amid forced secrets, there was just this one that she hadn't told Ethan. She had bared the rest, but not this, not the fact that she'd searched for her parents, and that all she had found was they had died. Only they hadn't, had they?

"Ah, so my subterfuge did work, then. Lovely. It's so much more rewarding to know that you did try to find them and were blocked by my manipulations."

"You mean your lies!"

"Once again, semantics."

Suddenly a thought occurred to her, and she could have shot him then and there if she didn't still need answers.

"We were never married. If my real name isn't Jenny and you stole me. You asshole, you manipulating asshole."

"All these years you believed that? That really is something else!"

Her hand was no longer shaking, her aim was true as she pointed it at the monster in front of her. There was no doubt in her mind as she clicked off the safety that she was going to shoot him between the eyes and not lose one second of sleep over it, but she needed to know her name first. Her real name. She chambered a bullet and stared him straight in the eye, and for one fleeting second, he looked hesitant, as if he knew she wasn't bluffing and wasn't going to let him out of there alive.

"What's my name?"

"Come now, do you really think it matters? You aren't going to be able to do anything with the knowledge anyway. You're not getting out of here. After all, you're heavily guarded."

"What's. My. Name? You *will* tell me my name before I bleed you dry," she ground out between gritted teeth.

"I love your guts, but you're the one who is going to be bled dry."

"I don't think so. You see, I'm looking at you, so I have a distinct advantage."

"How so?" he asked, sounding cocky once again.

"Because you can't see the red dot on your forehead from the sniper."

His face blanched. He didn't know if she was lying or not. He knew it could be a ploy to buy her more time—she'd always been resourceful. Her acting must have been Oscar worthy because he definitely believed her. The police had arrived, she knew that, but there was no red dot on his head. Pity.

"Ah, you didn't really think I would come here without a backup plan, did you? Judging by the look on your face, you did think that. Such a shame that you always underestimated me. It really is a bummer for you, but I can tell you this much, all those guards you have, they have been systematically disabled for the last thirty minutes while you blabbered on and on."

Quinn was still shaken by the bomb of information he'd dropped, and she hoped that her bluff wasn't really a bluff. Harrison had let her know that he would be working to help her out of there. He had also told her to keep him talking, to do her best to implicate him in her abduction. The room she was in was the one room in the house that didn't have a camera. It was the room he took the girls to test them out. Harrison had whispered to her that while Vance wanted to be able to tape his visits with the girls and boys, he didn't want any photographic evidence. That is, until Harrison slipped one to her before he left the room.

Quinn was no longer terrified of the man in front of her. If anything, she was grateful he had decided to taunt her. Now she knew she had parents to look for. A family, a history, a past worth acknowledging, one that didn't have him in it, because he had already taken up too much of her life. She could also thank him for allowing her to cleanse herself of his very existence.

"How does it feel to be the one in the cage? Huh, Vance? *Daddy.* I suspect that you're just about pissing your pants right now. Good. You deserve it and everything else that's coming your way."

"Stupid girl, nothing else is coming my way. I won't be taken by the pigs you have outside. As long as I have you as a hostage, they won't move on this room."

"Bet me? If that's what you think, then you definitely don't know the detectives out there. Did you know that your network was infiltrated for the better part of a year?"

30

If there was anything that could make her smile, it was the look of pure unadulterated rage and panic on his face. The wolf had now become the sheep, and she loved every minute of it. That expression was all it took for her to realize that she didn't want to kill him. She wanted him to go to prison and get to see the other side of the world for a while. She wanted him to learn what it was like to be prey.

"You didn't know, did you? How was it that you worded it before? Lovely. It really does feel good to have the shoe on the other foot. At least, it does for me. Probably not so much for you, though."

"Impossible. There's no way someone was inside my network and I didn't know."

"Personally, I'm looking forward to putting you away. Rumor is that child molesters and rapists don't have it easy in prison. How do you think you're going to like it when you become some guy's bitch?"

"You stupid bitch, I'm not going to prison."

"Yeah—yeah, you are. Trust me, there is nothing I would rather do than make you worm food, but I think that you getting gang raped daily is a much better option. And to think, dear old Paulie gave us all we needed to take you down. Even from beyond the grave. You know that day he saw me? After he called you and told you that he saw me, he did a little soul-searching, and he figured some things out. Little Paulie put two and two together that I was also the same one who had helped rescue Becky. He had already called you with the good news, but then he realized that I could be his ticket out of this whole freaking mess. He'd already turned CI and had hooked up with the undercover officer. Once he figured out that I was the one who helped the officer get Becky out, he knew that he could use that to his advantage."

"He wasn't a CI, and there was no one undercover in my operation."

"Who do you think gave me the gun, asshole? Anyway, that's what got him killed. The real buyer, not the go-between, figured it out. The other two were just collateral damage. It wasn't hard for them to figure out how he was selling you out to the police. Unfortunate that he lost his life doing what was right."

"The competition didn't kill Paulie. I killed that crooked son of a bitch. I knew that asshole was getting soft on me. I freaking knew it; that's why I ordered the hit on him. The other two weren't collateral damage. They were strategic kills to get my buyer back in line. I knew all along that those idiots were just the go-between. They actually thought they could take over the market later. Idiots."

"Gotta admit, I'm not the least surprised that it was you who took Paulie's life. Thank you, though, for clearing that up. I mean, Paulie did say in his letter that if he ended up dead, it would be by your hand."

"You lying, stupid bitch. There is no letter."

"Of course there is. How do you think the police found this place? Why do you think I was so easily scooped up by your guys? You really should've done better vetting. The guy you sent with your little clean-up guy, what's the name you call him? Oh, that's right, The Fixer. Anyway, the guy with him when they grabbed me is none other than Officer Black. Man, you just can't get it right today, huh?"

"If he's an officer, why did he let my guy kill the guard?"

"He got separated from him and couldn't stop him. Don't worry, your little fixer guy won't be fixing anything for you anytime soon. Pretty sure if he isn't dead, he will be soon."

"The only one dying here is going to be you." He backed to the door and knocked on it twice.

"You just aren't seeing the bigger picture, are you? You killed Paulie, and how did that work out for you? Your buyer seems to have run for the hills on you. Or maybe not. Maybe your buyer decided that we were getting close to them, too. Sure, he's scum, but he knew there was only one way out, and that was to turn state's evidence or maybe not. Maybe your buyer isn't dumb, and neither was Paulie. It seems his mom had taught him not to keep all his eggs in the same basket. At least, that's what he said in the letter he left."

"You keep talking about a letter. It's a nice bluff, but how would Paulie have had time to get a letter to you? He was working all day to get those kids for the order."

"No, he wasn't. He grabbed them all at the last second and then called Officer Black and clued him in on what was going on. That was officially the last straw for him. You pushed him too hard. He'd already left the letter, but it was never intended to be opened unless he died. Then you pushed him to get all those kids, and he was just done with you. It was a surprise, though, when your backup clean-up guy took out Paulie and the other two. The officers certainly weren't expecting that."

She could see when he finally started to accept what she was saying was true. When he realized that the police were set up a little too quickly that night. That was when he finally accepted he'd been had, and it was a glorious moment. Quinn couldn't stop herself from taunting him some more.

"Of course, by the time I got the letter, I already knew you were the one behind it all since you sent Jasmine to me."

"Was that her name?"

Gritting her teeth, she ignored the attempt to get under her skin.

"You couldn't stop yourself from sending Jasmine with that subtle message. He was clever about delivering that letter, though. Got to give him credit where it's due. He walked right into the hospital, strode right into Becky's room, and hid it in her Get Well Soon gift bags. The only unfortunate thing was that it took her so long to look in the bag. It really is a shame you underestimated him, Becky, me. If only you hadn't killed him. If only you didn't think you were infallible. Did you get everything you need? If so, come on in."

The door burst open, and a half dozen of DFPD's finest rushed in, all of them yelling at Vance to get down. But he didn't move to lie down. Instead, he reached for the gun on his waist. The shouts switched over to yelling that he had a gun and to drop it. Quinn was shoved to the ground and pinned there as gunshots rang out, but her eyes were open as she saw the monster, who was only a man, take several shots center mass. She didn't blink, wanting to make sure he was gone, really gone. She watched as his lifeblood spilled out onto the ground and his eyes went vacant. After the last hour of terror, it was all over in one anticlimactic moment. The room became quiet after the ringing from the shots subsided, and then someone called all clear, and the body on top of her eased up.

"Did I hurt you? God, tell me I didn't hurt you!" Ethan said, studying her face closely. "Quinn?"

"No, no, I'm fine. He's really dead?" she asked, still staring at the sightless eyes of the man in the growing puddle of blood. The crimson color of that puddle entranced her as if she was tied to it and unable to tear her eyes away. All she could do was stare. Ethan pulled her to her feet and helped guide her out of the room.

"Come on, let's get you out of here," Ethan said. In the back of her mind, she thought he sounded concerned. But she really wasn't sure she could bring herself to care.

Ethan was standing to the side while Quinn was being examined. Even though she said she was fine, he needed to know it for himself. There was the possibility that her arm had suffered a setback due to how hard he threw her to the ground, but when looking at the big picture, it was small penance to pay to have her otherwise safe and sound. She would need stitches on the wound on her head, but for now, they were going to butterfly it and allow him to take her to the hospital to get it stitched up. There wasn't a chance he was letting her out of his sight for the foreseeable future, or at least until he had to return to work.

Injuries aside, he was more concerned with the distant look that had been on her face since he had helped her out of the room. Caleb was over talking to the captain because Ethan wouldn't stray farther than a four-foot circumference from Quinn. They were securing the crime scene and the recording of what had gone down in the room between Quinn and Vance. Quinn told them that Harrison had been the one to put a recording device in the room. After they had infiltrated the compound, they were able to monitor the scene inside the room. Ethan had thought his heart would stop when he saw Quinn standing with a gun pointed at the chest of the man in the room with her, but even though he had wanted to charge the room, he knew that the information she was getting from Vance Duprey was pertinent to closing the case. Unfortunately, it wasn't going to be able to be used after all because Vance Duprey was as dead as could be, but it wasn't necessarily a bad thing that Vance was dead. As a matter of fact, he was happy that the man was no longer breathing. There was no way he was going to give up his network, and there was always the chance that after a long trial he would still get away with it all. This way saved the taxpayers a lot of money.

His eyes went back to the woman that he loved with every fiber of his being. Logically, he knew he couldn't lock Quinn up and throw away the key, nor would he want to, and realistically, he knew it wouldn't be long before he would have to be back to work to figure out this cluster. But for now, he was fooling himself into believing that she would never be out of his sight again.

While he paced back and forth, lost in thought, he heard gravel crunch under the feet of someone approaching. He knew who it would be without turning around. Harrison Black was a good man and would want to come speak to him himself. When he turned to face him, he saw a man devastated by guilt and full of anguish over how badly this could have gone and the fact that the one man that could have shed some light on important inner workings of the sex trade industry was now a pile of blood and gore. Ethan wanted answers as much as the next man, but he didn't blame Black for killing the man. In a way, it seemed like poetic justice that Black got to be the one to take him out. If it couldn't be Ethan or Quinn that killed the SOB, Black would be the one he wanted to do it, and in his mind, Vance was exactly where he needed to be: lying in his own pool of blood.

"Listen, Ethan, I'm sorry that it went down like this. I didn't know what was all going on behind the scenes and I should have."

"How could you? No one could have seen this coming. You made the best of the hand you were dealt," he said around the lump in his throat as he thought, really thought, about what could have happened.

"Yeah, yeah, they would have. If I had gotten closer to that ass, he would have trusted me enough to tell me why he was really watching Quinn, and he would have told me why the woman he was looking for was so important to him. I knew Paulie had found the woman, but he never told me her name. It was very hush, hush. If I would have known it was Quinn…"

"No one in this operation knew why he was so hell bent on finding her. That was a secret that he kept close to the vest, and Quinn only divulged it to me recently. Also, I'm only going to tell you this once, you aren't responsible for this. You did what you could to make it right."

"I didn't know how important she was to you. Hell, I didn't even know you were seeing someone. All I knew was that he had called in The Fixer to nab this woman. You have to believe me that I didn't know who the woman was until I saw you both standing there. I don't know why he sent me with him to go get her."

"I think that was fate."

"Maybe, but then he killed that guard, and I tried to keep him from the house, but you two walked out, and then all the shit hit the fan…" He trailed off. "I was about to take him out, and then Quinn walked around you and toward me. She knew what I was thinking. I think that's why she risked herself. She didn't want to see me go that route, and I knew there was a way to finally end this."

"Listen, man, I'm telling you, you did your best, and in the end, should it have mattered that she's my girlfriend? No. Because of you and Quinn, this is all finally done. You can come out of hiding and get back to your real life." Ethan placed his hand on Black's slumped shoulders, but he quickly shook off the touch.

"Yeah, my real life. Whatever you say. Anyway, I'm done."

Ethan didn't like the sound of those last two words.

"Sure, I don't think Cap will have a problem if you go home and get reacquainted with your bed for a few hours. He's going to want to debrief you at 0800, though."

Black just shook his head and dug into his pocket, retrieving a tiny flash drive. He handed it to him, his expression somber.

"Everything he needs to know is on this flash drive. All the buyers he's ever sold to. I think this might help take down the network. I don't really know what else is on it. I just know that I managed to get this copy after he scrubbed everything from his system when Paulie died. Paulie's death made him really paranoid. I wasn't able to get ahold of this until tonight."

"This has to be the information Paulie referenced in his letter. Though he didn't know that Duprey had scrubbed the system, he did give us all the passwords to get into his computer files. Thanks, man; I hope this ties it all up for us."

"Me, too. Not that I'm going to be around to see it. Like I said, I'm done." He unclipped his gun, handed it to Ethan, then pulled his badge out from under his shirt. "I've been wearing this all day, I don't know why. With no end in sight, I don't know, maybe I was hoping they would figure out who I was."

Black's monotone voice and expression gave Ethan reason to pause. If the man hadn't handed over his gun, he would have asked for him to do so at that moment.

"Look, Harris—"

"Don't worry, I'm not going to go do something stupid like kill myself. I'm just out." He turned and began to walk away.

"Think about it for a few days. I'm sure Cap would agree."

"I already have."

Ethan watched Harrison Black's retreating back until he couldn't see him anymore.

"There's nothing you can do, Ethan, to change his mind," Quinn said from behind him, wrapping her arms around his waist until he turned in her embrace and held on tight.

"I know, but it doesn't mean I can't worry about him."

"And I know that. It's part of why I love you—your selflessness and the fact that you are such an empath." Reaching up, she placed a kiss on his chin. "Right now, I want you to worry about less, enjoy more. We're here, we're alive." Another kiss at the corner of his mouth. Caleb hollered, jokingly, to get a room. Ethan absently sent a vulgar gesture in the general vicinity of his partner.

If there was anything this group needed it was a good laugh and cops were known to have a sick sense of humor, but right now, even in jest, Ethan wasn't feeling it. Though he was certain Caleb would just brush it off.

"Let's get you stitched up so we can go home, get cleaned up and snuggle in our bed."

"Our bed?"

"Yeah, our bed. Do you have a problem with that?"

"None at all. I, for one, happen to love your gazillion count sheets and mattress made from a cloud."

"And here I thought you loved me."

"That, too; that, too. Let's go home." She liked the sound of that.

EPILOGUE

Today was the day, more important than any day in recent memory. A beautiful April day. Perhaps it was the most important day of her life, meeting Ethan was definitely right up there. Right now, there was so much love coming from the church that she could feel it pulsating through her. The Montgomery family had embraced her as their own, much like they'd embraced Caleb and then Kara. Indeed, she'd been adopted like a stray puppy, and today the whole Montgomery clan, and some extras, including the now very frail Mr. Stanford who had saved Kara and essentially made this day possible, were gathered to christen Caleb and Kara's new son. Throwing tradition to the wind, they had named five godparents: Grayson, Elle, Taylor, Ethan, and Quinn.

Quinn had been honored, and surprised, to be asked. She wasn't part of the family, yet, but she would be in the near future. The ring on her finger still felt heavy, but real and whole and right. The little baby growing in her belly was still a secret that only Ethan and she knew about, and with the wedding only a few weeks away, she might get away with not having to have the dress let out. Even if she had to, it was worth it, and that would be their wedding gift to their hodgepodge family, the announcement of their own bundle of joy warming in her tummy. They had both agreed to not steal the thunder of Caleb and

Kara as well as baby Oliver. Not that they really would have. The family was so cohesive they'd have been thrilled—not angered—by sharing the limelight.

The pastor was announcing for the godparents to approach the baptismal fountain, and they all stepped forward, Ethan holding her hand, to watch the baptismal ceremony take place. Oliver only grunted when the water touched his forehead. It didn't disrupt his sleep for one moment. He had dark hair just like his parents. However, the verdict was still out if he was going to get Kara's green eyes or Caleb's blue eyes—or perhaps he would be unique in that respect. For now, he favored Kara's beauty, with his plump little lips and upturned nose. The perfect addition to fill their family with unending love. Kara had told Quinn that she had been scared through the pregnancy that she would be a terrible mother, incapable of loving her child the right way, but she was no longer frightened, because one look into that little face as he suckled at her breast, and she was a goner. She told her she would do anything for her little boy, and Quinn believed her from the conviction in her voice and the look of love in her eyes when she spoke of her son.

The ceremony flew by, and before they knew it, the church was letting out. There would be a small gathering at the Montgomery house to celebrate the christening. They drove out to the homestead, Quinn staring out her window, worrying the engagement ring on her finger while she thought about Becky Plummer and how it had been so good to see her at the church.

"Nervous?"

"A little." He just looked at her sideways. "Okay, that was kind of an embellishment. I'm terrified."

"What's there to be nervous about? After all, you have this hunk sitting here holding your hand and giving you strength. Stop being a tough girl and lean on me for a change."

"Well, when you put it that way…" She reached out and grabbed his hand, linking her fingers through his. "The ceremony was perfect. Oliver is adorable."

"He looks just like Kara when she was a baby. Perfect in every way. I'm hoping he gets Caleb's blue eyes, though. Poor guy. That baby looks nothing like him." He chuckled.

"Well, I don't think that Caleb seems to care one bit."

"Nope. He loves Kara, and he once told me he could stare at her for hours. Now he has a miniature Kara to look at."

"Those two really are adorable together. Wonder if people think the same about us?"

"Nah. They just think how sexy we are together and how unfair it is." He winked at her, and she pinched him, but she secretly thanked him for trying to take the edge off her nerves.

"I'm so happy that Mr. Stanford was able to come."

"Kara considers him a grandfather. I consider him a grandfather, as well. He isn't just a benevolent stranger that helped Kara one day and then disappeared into the night. He's our family."

"I know, and I think that's beautiful, you and the Montgomerys, you all welcomed him into your family. Like you did me."

"I guess we did, but only because we are family. It isn't just for show, all of us are inexorably linked somehow."

"I know." She blinked back tears. She had learned that pregnancy hormones made her a little more weepy than usual—or at least, that was her story, and she was sticking to it.

"You know that you're now part of that family, right? That you have been for quite some time, that even if you decided not to marry me, you would still be part of this family?"

"I know that, too. But sorry, buddy, nothing could make me change my mind about marrying you."

"That's a relief since I ordered the tux already and have the church all booked and such." She playfully slapped at his arm.

"I was really surprised, but happy, to see Becky at the church."

"Like you said, my mom likes to pull people into her family. As soon as she met Becky, she fell in love with her, and Becky's parents are so great."

"They are. They've done everything in their power to help her transition back into the real world and to do so without smothering her.

Even though I know that their urge to lock her down and never let her out of their sight again is strong."

When they pulled into the Montgomery spread, her mouth dropped as she looked around at the sheer number of cars parked on the road.

"I thought that they were having a small get-together after the christening?"

"Ha! You should know better; the Montgomery family doesn't know how to do small. Like you said, they collect strays."

"Maybe I should have used a better word than stray. I mean, it could be deemed hurtful."

"I kind of like it. If you ask me, it fits the bill."

"Good thing I wasn't asking you." She smiled at him.

It was still hard to believe that this man, the Mr. Panty-Melter himself, was going to be her husband in just a few weeks. Rumor was there were a few bets about if he would settle down and then when they had gone public, the bets had switched to when he would pop the question. Casanova no more, he was now going to be a married man. Caleb said there were women crying all over the city. Of course, he was only partially teasing.

"I have a little surprise for you before we go inside."

"A surprise? I think I've had enough surprises to last me a while."

"You're going to like this one. I promise." They were standing in the driveway, and he covered her eyes with his hands.

"Ethan Vanderbilt, I don't know what you're up to…" He led her forward a few steps and then removed his hands.

Standing in front of Quinn was a young woman, one she recognized well, but hadn't had a chance to meet in person. Megan Ingold. She was as beautiful as all the pictures Quinn had seen of her. The young woman squealed and came flying at Quinn. She only had a moment to brace herself for impact.

"Even after we had talked on the phone, it still seemed almost like a fantasy." Megan hugged her tightly and laughed.

"I'm just sorry it took this long to finally meet you. Our schedules just weren't matching up."

"I know. I got tired of waiting and made my parents promise me that they would let me fly out to see you this weekend. I knew you'd be around; a certain someone told me today is a special day for you, too."

"It is."

"I wanted to get to see you in person before then and tell you how amazing you are."

"You could have just waited until the wedding. You're still coming, right?"

"Wouldn't miss it for the world."

The two women chatted for hours while a chaotic party carried on around them. The weather was gorgeous, which was helpful since the hosts had arranged for outside activities for the little ones, and after a rousing afternoon of yard games and more food than she could ever imagine in her wildest dreams, they said their goodbyes. The party was still going strong, but Megan had a flight to catch, and they had somewhere important to be. Once again, Quinn stared out the window of the car and rotated the ring on her finger. Silent and contemplative. Ethan reached out and grabbed her hand, raising it to his mouth. The hour car ride went by in a flash, and before she knew it, Ethan had pulled to a stop and cut the engine in his car.

"All these years, and only an hour separation..." Tears caught in her throat, cutting the sentence short.

Ethan pulled her into his arms and kissed her forehead.

"How were you supposed to know?"

"I could have known. I could have tried to find them."

"It's all water under the bridge now. Even if you had looked, where would you have started? You didn't know your real identity. You didn't even know that your name wasn't your name or even your age, and those secrets died with him." He gritted his teeth on the last word. He tried not to speak Vance Duprey's name ever, but Quinn made sure that they talked about him, her past. It was cathartic for her in some ways, and she wanted him to know that she was healing and that the monster had no hold on her any longer.

"Vance," she whispered, making him acknowledge the monster's name.

"Yeah, that asshole. Unfortunately, he died before he could help us out. The coward that he is couldn't even do it himself." True, suicide by cop was definitely the coward's way out of dealing with his crimes, but she was just relieved there was no way he could get away to cause more harm. At least the flash drive had all the information to take down dozens of people. "There are so many missing children, it was like looking for the proverbial needle in a haystack. With all my resources, I couldn't manage to find them, and look how long it took for Cole to find them. Port Investigations is the best around, and it still took months."

"Thank goodness for old friends who are geniuses. But I think you would have found them if it weren't for the fact that after the twenty-fifth anniversary, they had given up. It's almost too hard to think how they had given up and moved out of the country, stopped watching the news and going through all the missing person's reports. That even when my sister and brother saw my pleas that I was looking for my parents, that I didn't know who they were, and I wanted to find them desperately, that even then, they refused to look into it. They weren't willing to even hope, and it didn't help that they have such a common name or that when Cole did find them and reached out to them that they refused to look into it. My poor parents thought he was just a charlatan, trying to take their money like all the others."

"Understandable. They'd searched for so long, what are the chances right when they stopped searching someone would come to them?"

"Thank God that he reached out to Hannah and Zach and that they were willing to do a DNA test. I understood them doing it without telling their parents. They'd tried so long to find me, and they wanted to make sure I was the real deal."

"They did the right thing."

"Yes, they did, and the fact that they love our parents that much is a testament to how good they are. Hannah told me that no matter what, they never felt like they were living in my shadow. I just can't believe I have this whole family out there that I never knew about and that I lost so much time with them because I was too stupid to look sooner. I hope they can forgive me."

"There is nothing to forgive you for. They know you can't change the past. You can only move forward, and they have their beautiful twenty-nine-year-old daughter back."

"When did you get so prophetic?" She sniffed and leaned back, looking into his eyes.

"About the same day I fell for you."

"I can't believe I thought I was thirty."

"Look at it this way. There are women all over the world who'd love to get to legitimately do twenty-nine over."

"It's so weird, though, to be two years younger than I thought."

"You can always just go with the age you thought you were."

"Are you kidding? It's almost like a fresh start, and this time I get to do it with you by my side. Think they'll be excited about the baby? I mean, I don't want to spring it on them right away, but I want them to be the first people we tell, and I can't hide it much longer."

"I think they're going to be thrilled to be grandparents. It's like getting two for the price of one."

"Three for the price of one. You're part of the deal."

He leaned forward and kissed her tenderly.

"You better believe it. I think it's time. You have people waiting for you." He motioned with his head behind her, but she didn't turn around.

"Do you think they're upset I don't want them to call me Ashley? I mean, I don't remember being Ashley Smith." Which made her sad.

"I don't think they're going to care one bit what they call you. What I think is that they're going to be so grateful to have you back that you could tell them to call you Cleopatra and they would happily oblige. They love you and just want you back, you've talked to them on the phone several times." He was right. She had talked to them several times, trying to get used to the idea of having parents who really loved her. They had insisted on allowing it to sink in before they rushed her. As her mother had told her, *we can be a bit overwhelming.* "You know all this. Now get that cute tush out of my car, woman." She wrinkled her nose at him. He laughed and then got out of the car, walking around to open the door for her.

Rubbing her belly, she spoke to the baby in her tummy. "Well, it's time to meet your family. They're going to love you as much as your daddy and I do. You will know what love is because you're so loved by us all." Grabbing Ethan's hand, she climbed out of the car and stood next to him, shaking like a leaf, her knees so wobbly she didn't know if they would support her weight, but he was there holding her up, his hand continuing to tether her to the world and to him as he linked their fingers. Always her beacon of light. She took a step forward, and he shut the car door. The sound startled her just a bit, because her gaze was fixed in front of her. Quinn didn't have everything figured out. All she knew was her past was behind her, her present was beside her, and her future was in front of her. With that thought, she took that first step toward her parents and the siblings who looked so much like her—a step toward the family who had never stopped looking for her.

AFTERWORD

Statistics used in this book were obtained from the Cook County Report—provided by Sergeant Wilson and www.unluckythirteen.org.

If you or someone you know need help there are resources available. The following information was obtained from www.humantraffickinghotline.org:

If you believe you have information about a potential trafficking situation:

Call the National Human Trafficking Hotline toll-free hotline at 1-888-373-7888: Anti-Trafficking Hotline Advocates are available 24/7 to take reports of potential human trafficking. All reports are confidential and you may remain anonymous. Interpreters are available.

To report missing children or child pornography, submit a report to the National Center for Missing and Exploited Children (NCMEC) at 1-800-THE-LOST (843-5678) or through their Cybertipline.

www.ingramcontent.com/pod-product-compliance
Lightning Source LLC
Chambersburg PA
CBHW060850250626
47159CB00008B/2681